Dear Reader:

The thinking behind the *Tony Hillerman's Frontier* series which this Ken Englade novel introduces is that truth is not only stranger than fiction but also often more exciting. The traditional "western" gave us gripping tales of gunslingers, cattle barons, clean-cut heroes, fierce Indian horsemen collecting scalps, and the U.S. cavalry racing to the rescue. But, with some notable exceptions, it concerned a frontier as mythic and romantic as Camelot.

Thanks to the work of historians, we now know that what was happening on the western frontier was far more complex than the myths, and far more interesting to today's reader. In the middle years of the 19th century the rules determining who owned that "sea of grass" and the mountains which surround it were being formed. The horse was revolutionizing Indian cultures. Tribes were jostling with tribes over hunting grounds, the Spanish frontier was collapsing, and the new Americans were trickling westward looking for their fortune, their freedom, or simply for adventure.

Ken Englade is best known for books focused on notable criminal trials. In this series he taps a lifelong fascination with the history of the American frontier to give us novels of this era as it really was. I hope you will enjoy this as I have and look for future titles in the series, coming soon from HarperPaperbacks.

Sincerely,

Tony Hillerman

BOOKS BY KEN ENGLADE

Hoffa

TONY HILLERMAN'S FRONTIER
People of the Plains
The Tribes
*The Soldiers**

NONFICTION
To Hatred Turned
Blood Sister
Beyond Reason
Murder in Boston
Cellar of Horror
Deadly Lessons
A Family Business

*coming soon

TONY HILLERMAN'S
~ FRONTIER ~
PEOPLE OF THE PLAINS

THE
TRIBES

Ken Englade

HarperPaperbacks
A Division of HarperCollinsPublishers

HarperPaperbacks *A Division of* HarperCollins*Publishers*
10 East 53rd Street, New York, N.Y. 10022

Cover illustration by Steven Assel

First printing: June 1996

Printed in the United States of America

HarperPaperbacks and colophon are trademarks of HarperCollins*Publishers*

❖ 10 9 8 7 6 5 4 3 2 1

For HJH

Author's Note

This is a work of fiction. Although the story parallels history, especially regarding customs of the various tribes as related by experts such as Robert H. Lowie (writing about the Crow), Virginia Cole Trenholm (Arapaho), George Bird Grinnel and Donald J. Berthrong (Cheyenne), Gene Weltfish (Pawnee), and Stan Hoig (the Plains tribes), some of the dates and locations of intertribal fights have been altered to conform to the overall narrative. The Pawnee regularly sacrificed a captive to their god, Morning Star. Although the last recorded sacrifice took place in 1838, experts such as Grinnel feel that sacrifices were carried out later and were simply unrecorded by Caucasian historians. Actual names—Brigadier General William S. Harney, for example—have been used in some places. Information about the soldiers has been drawn from a variety of sources, but the majority of the Caucasian characters are totally fictional. Any resemblance to actual persons is purely coincidental.

ACKNOWLEDGEMENTS

This book could not have been written without help from a number of people, excluding the published works of experts. I owe special thanks for help on medical details to Dr. Larry Podolsky, retired physician and medical historian, who never failed to respond cheerfully and quickly to my innumerable queries. Details on the Cheyenne language came from Dr. Henrietta Mann, professor of Native American Studies at the University of Montana. And both in this book and others in the series, I was fortunate to have advice from my daughter-in-law, Marian Scheid Englade, on idiomatic German. For help with French, I had the enthusiastic assistance of Francophile Jan Cawley and Jim Finlay, who had to learn his French the hard way, as a soldier in the French Foreign Legion. Any mistakes in details of custom or language are mine and not of those who gave unstintingly of their time and knowledge.

Jean Benoit shifted uncomfortably in his saddle, trying to ease his aching back. *"Merde,"* he groaned, massaging his lower spine, "life on the frontier may kill me yet."

Jim Ashby smiled. "A wood-gathering detail ain't nothing, lieutenant. Wait 'til you get a reg'lar patrol under your belt before you start complainin' about how tough it is out West."

"I wasn't complaining," Benoit said, his cheeks reddening. "I was just commenting on how soft I'd gotten from six weeks of doing nothing. Sore or not, you don't know how good it's felt to get away from the fort."

"Oh, yes I do," Ashby replied, spitting a stream of tobacco juice into the dust. "I git to feelin' like a b'ar on a chain after 'bout two days. I don' see how you can stan' it much longer 'n that."

Private Leonardo Bianchi, who was driving the first of the three wood wagons in the procession wending its way back to Fort Laramie, nudged the man seated next to him, a fellow private named Cornelius Ryan. "Did you ever see a more unlikely looking pair?" he whispered, pointing with his chin toward Benoit and Ashby.

The officer sat high and erect on his large Army roan, like the trained equestrian he was, thanks to being born into a wealthy New Orleans family that could afford professional instruction for their three children. The scout, on the other hand, was slumped over the neck of the slightly swaybacked piebald pony he'd gotten in trade a year earlier from a Crow named Sad Face in return for a dented muzzleloader with a cracked stock, looking as if he might fall off at the next bend. That impression was incorrect, however; Ashby was an Indian-style rider who could sit a horse as competently as any man on the Plains, red or white.

The twenty-two-year-old Benoit, standing just a shade under six feet, had a deep chest and a short, thick neck that made it look as if his head rested directly on his slightly sloping shoulders. His arms were extraordinarily long, a fact that caused him considerable embarrassment when his West Point classmates teased him about being able to scratch his knees without bending at the waist. His hair, which he kept clipped at just above his collar, was thick and dark, and his skin was a creamy off-white. In contrast to this Southern European countenance — not surprising considering that both his parents came from France — his eyes were a startling blue, evidence of some forgotten interloper into the ancestral pool.

Sixty pounds lighter and five inches shorter, Ashby was all whipcord and sinew. Thin almost to the point of emaciation, his ribs, on the rare occasions when he removed the stained elk-skin shirt he wore summer and winter, protruded like those of the buffalo carcasses that littered the route of travel of the westward-bound emigrants. "Whites," he had pointed out to Benoit on the journey between Missouri and Fort Laramie, "kill buffler for the meat or for sport, but injuns make use of the whole damn animal, right down to the asshole."

Aged somewhere between thirty and fifty — it was impossible to judge his exact age because his skin was creased and cracked from constant exposure to the elements — Ashby wore his dark brown hair wrapped in a tight pigtail that dangled down his back almost to his waist. While other frontiersmen favored beards, Ashby's face was smooth. "I ain't much for bathin'," he explained, "but I don' feel decent if I ain't had a shave."

From head to foot, Ashby was covered with scars and gravings of all shapes and configurations. "This 'un," he told Benoit, pointing to a purplish, crescent-shaped mark on his left cheek, "is a souv'neir from a tassel with a young Crow named One Antler back in '48. Dumb sumbitch thought he could use a knife better'n me. And this," he said, lifting his shirt to expose three purple circular symbols tattooed on his chest, "was put there by my Arapaho wife. The 'ho are big believers in tattoos."

"Wife?" Benoit had asked in surprise. "I didn't know you're married."

"*Was*," Ashby said tersely. "She's dead. Kilt by the choller," he added, changing the subject.

Ryan, who had been considering Bianchi's question about the dissimilarities between Ashby and Benoit, nodded in agreement. "I reckon you're right, Len," he replied in a brogue so thick his barracks-mates often had trouble understanding him. "Never in all me born days have I seen two more unalike. But," he added, grinning broadly, "I'm thinkin' they're not much different than you 'n me, what with you being so dark you could pass for a black man, an' me, a fair and handsome gent only a few years removed from the Ol' Sod."

Bianchi, who had joined the Army to escape from the cramped two-room hovel in Brooklyn that he shared with his immigrant parents and six siblings, glanced sideways at his companion. "If I didn't know you were kidding, I'd whip your ass right here," he said, laughingly cursing him in rapid-fire Italian.

A hundred feet back, from the third wagon, Private Andy Thigpen's voice rose in good-natured song, vocalizing a ballad popular with the frontier troops.

We've reached the land of desert sweet,
Where nothing grows for man to eat . . .

"Amen to that," mumbled Ashby, who, in his years on the Plains, had, more times that he wanted to remember, been forced to dine on snakes and lizards to ward off starvation.

Where the wind blows hot, a blast from hell,
No water to give, no water to sell . . .

"Wait 'til he's had to lick the dew off the grass to quench his thirst," Ashby said in an aside to Benoit.

Where the heat's ferocious, it'll drive you insane
Where the cold's so cruel, it'll freeze your brain . . .

"Snow comes down so hard and thick, you go out to take a piss and you couldn't see the end o' your dick if it was painted red," Ashby chuckled.

Where you gaze in awe across the Plains
And pray to God to send the rains . . .

"Lemme hear him say that next time he tries to cross the Platte in flood," Ashby commented.

* * *

This is the land we want to claim,
This is the land of Greeley fame . . .

"It's good to see the men in high spirits," interjected Benoit. "It's a positive sign that they can laugh again after the Grattan affair."

"A right fucking mess that was," said Ashby.

Benoit glanced sharply at his friend. Although Second Lieutenant John Grattan and the twenty-nine troopers under his command had been killed on August 19, more than a month previously, Benoit had never heard Ashby voice his opinion.

"I'd be careful about who's around when you talk about Lieutenant Grattan that way," Benoit remonstrated. "There're a lot of people who consider him and his men heroes."

"Heroes my ass," Ashby spat. "What Lieutenant Grattan did was just goddamn stupid. He was lookin' for trouble, plain and simple. Ridin' into a' injun camp where he was outnumbered a hun'erd to one and then trying to pick a shootin' fight, jus' ain't too smart. Thought he was mean; thought he could bully his way through 'cause he believed injuns is gutless. He deserved what he got. The only bad thing is some good men had to die with 'im."

"You don't think it had to end that way?"

"Nope!" Ashby replied. "Firs' mistake he made was takin' tha' drunken sumbitch with 'im."

"Auguste?"

"Yep. He was a sorry 'un, he was. Drank too much. Didn't like injuns. Talked real nasty to 'em. Bullied 'em even when he didn't have to. He had no business being the interpreter. Grattan was bully enough in his own right. Didn't need no help from Lucien Auguste. Shiiit," he said, drawing the expletive into three syllables, "I

don' blame them Brulé for attackin'. There ain't nothing
in the Fort Laramie Treaty that says soljers have the
right to go into an injun camp and arrest someone. I
woulda done the same as them Brulé, it been me."

"Well, it sure put us in a pickle," Benoit conceded.
"Washington doesn't take kindly to losing thirty soldiers and a civilian employee. Captain Granger's career
is as good as over. The new C.O. is due any day now."

"You know anything about him?"

Benoit shook his head. "Only that he's a major, a
brevet lieutenant colonel actually, named Kemp. He
fought in the Mexican War and did a tour on the frontier
when he was a shavetail."

"Like you?" Ashby asked, softening the question
with a grin that exposed a set of jagged, tobacco-stained
teeth.

"Like me," Benoit nodded, accepting the evaluation
without rancor. "Actually, more than me. I can't even be
called a shavetail. I'm still a brevet waiting for a slot to
open to get my second lieutenant's stripes. But
Lieutenant Dobbs knows him slightly from the Mexico
City campaign. Says he's a bit of a martinet, but he
knows his business."

"A what?" Ashby asked, frowning.

Benoit glanced at him to see if he was pulling his leg.
"He's strict with the men," he replied, deciding the
scout was serious. "Tends to come down hard on people
who don't follow orders. Dobbs says Kemp ordered a
private shot for sleeping on post during the march from
Vera Cruz."

"That don' sound outta line to me," Ashby said.
"Man goes to sleep on his post out here and ev'rybody
in the fort could lose his hair."

"Uuummm," Benoit grunted. "Well, a lot of people,
including not a few soldiers . . . "

"Would you looka that . . ." Ashby interrupted.

As they came over the final ridge overlooking the Platte River Valley, Fort Laramie stretched out beneath them like a painting. The sky was a sparkling blue, brighter and clearer than Benoit could have imagined before he came West. But it was not just the perfect color of the sky that mesmerized him. The sheer vastness of the Western panorama never failed to take his breath away. The plains went on forever in every direction, completely unbounded by trees or buildings.

The fact that it was a near-perfect late September day added to the majesty. The afternoon was just warm enough to make Benoit sweat lightly in his blue wool shirt. The wind, which usually blew hard enough to keep the post flag standing straight out, was only a mere hint of a breeze. In the short six weeks since he had arrived at Fort Laramie Benoit had seen lightening storms so fierce he thought God was signaling the end of the world. One night shortly after the Grattan incident, it had rained so hard he was sure the fort was going to wash away. And a week ago, a clear and cloudless sky had abruptly turned an ugly, gunmetal gray. Within minutes, the temperature dropped thirty degrees and snowflakes had begun to fly.

"Snow!" exclaimed an astonished Benoit, who had never seen the phenomenon until he left his native New Orleans for West Point. Running into the middle of the parade ground, he spread his arms and danced in a circle.

Ashby had looked at him if as he would at a man who had suddenly lost his mind. "Wait 'til you've been out here for a winter," he said with the air of a man who knows what he's talking about. "You'll see more snow than you ever imagined. Provided you can open your eyes, that is, 'cause its so cold your eyeballs might freeze."

Benoit had chuckled, sure the scout had been exaggerating, trying the old veteran-tries-to-scare-the-greenhorn routine.

"Think I'm joshin' you?" Ashby had asked, seeing the disbelief in the soldier's eyes. Leaning over, he pulled off his moccasins. Two toes were gone from the right foot and one from the left. All that remained were tiny, pale stubs that looked like immature onions. "Frostbite," he said laconically. "Come February, you'd be willing to sell your gold teeth, if you had any, to be back on the bayou."

Both men reined their horses to a stop and Benoit turned, signaling to the soldiers to park the wagons and come see the show that was unfolding at their feet.

The fort's spacious parade ground, which normally was all but deserted during the middle of the day, was throbbing with activity. More than a hundred blue-clad, mounted soldiers were forming orderly ranks on each side of the flagpole that pointed skyward like a slender finger at the south end of the complex, just outside the crumbling walled section of the current installation's predecessor.

The present Fort Laramie, Benoit had quickly been told, had begun as a fur trader's haven, conveniently located in the near right-angle formed where the sluggish North Platte and the clear, fast-running Laramie rivers intersected. The first structure had been called Fort William in honor of the trader who built it, William Sublette. That had been in 1835, when the only white faces on the Plains had been those of the tough, weather-beaten men trying to make a fortune in pelts and hides. A few years later, in 1841, another redoubt, called Fort John for John Sarpy, a major stockholder in a competing fur company, was built nearby. But it, too, fell into general disuse with the collapse of the fur trade.

The military took an interest in the site late in the Forties after emigrants headed for the coast began demanding protection from the increasingly hostile Indians whose hunting grounds they had to traverse as they followed the route popularly known as the Oregon Trail through the Rocky Mountains and over the Continental Divide.

From the government's point of view, the location was ideal. Fresh, clear water was readily available from the Laramie River. A mere dozen miles away were the foothills of the Laramie Mountains, whose abundant trees provided firewood and the raw material for planks. The mountains also served as a source for lime, which was crucial to the production of mortar. In 1849, the government paid the fur companies $4,000 for the site. A few months later, a regiment of mounted riflemen arrived to establish an Army presence.

In 1850, the Army, disdaining the old, rotting structures of both Fort William and Fort John, began its own building program, christening the budding complex Fort Laramie in honor of Jacques LaRamee, a legendary trader killed in the area by the Arapahos many years earlier. One of the first structures to rise was an officers' quarters, a white, two-story frame building that looked like an Eastern farmhouse. Nicknamed Old Bedlam, it was the most prominent structure on the site, standing like a lord over the low, adobe-walled lesser structures: the enlisted men's barracks, the smithy, the sawmill, the stables, the bakery, the sutler's store, and various small workshops.

"Speak of the devil," Benoit said. "Looks like Kemp and the reinforcements have arrived."

For half an hour, Benoit, Ashby, and the soldier members of the wood-cutting detail sat atop the ridge, watching attentively as the newly-arrived troopers drew themselves up into formal lines to be inspected by the new commander. Benoit slid out of the saddle and stood stiffly next to his horse, stretching his back. Ashby crossed a skinny leg across his pommel and pulled a small pipe out of his saddlebag, loading it with *shongsasha*, the mixture of red willow bark and tobacco that he kept in a small, beaded pouch slung around his neck.

They were not the only spectators. Across the parade ground, a good-sized crowd of blanket-wrapped Indians, most of them Oglalas and a scattering of Arapahos, stood enthralled as the new arrivals went through their drill.

"That's impressive, isn't it?" Benoit whispered half-aloud as the reinforcements, some one-hundred and twenty-five strong, wheeled their horses and passed in review.

"Look," Ashby said, pointing. On the western side of the fort, a half-dozen Indian horsemen galloped away from the gathering, headed toward the north and west, creating a spiderweb-like network of dust trails.

"Messengers," Ashby said before Benoit could ask. "They're going to spread the word about the new troops."

Benoit nodded silently and turned his gaze back to the fort. Despite the distance, he could easily see a trooper near the center of the "U" formed by the soldiers as he raised a shining instrument to his lips. What seemed like minutes later, the bugle call wafted to them on the high, clear air.

"Well," he said slowly, as if reluctant to break the spell, "I guess we ought to go on down and see what the new order is going to bring."

Brevet Lieutenant Colonel Aloysius Bradford Kemp tapped his knife smartly against his water tumbler, signaling for quiet.

"Young lady," he said imperiously, gesturing to Inge

Schmidt, "please clear these away so we can get down to business."

As the seventeen-year-old girl loaded the china onto a tray, Kemp turned to his aide-de-camp, a sallow-looking lieutenant. "Get my chest," he ordered.

While waiting for the aide to return, Kemp looked around the table. Pointing a stubby finger at Lieutenant Zachary Adamson, he paused, searching his memory. "You're Ben-oight, right?" he said.

"No," smiled Adamson, a pudgy, happy-go-lucky holdover from the command of the recently departed Captain Samson Granger, who already was on his way back to Washington in disgrace because of the incident the Eastern press had dubbed The Grattan Massacre. "I'm Adamson," Zack said with a smile. "That's Benoit, there," he said, pointing across the table.

"It's pronounced Ben-wah, sir," Benoit said wearily. "Not Ben-oight."

Kemp stared at him, unaccustomed to being corrected. "Oh," he said sharply, "a Frenchie, eh?"

"New Orleanian, sir. My parents are French."

"Can't see where it makes much difference," Kemp replied coldly. "You still talk funny. Frenchies and Messicans, they're all alike. Not bad people, mind you, just misguided. Worship the pope and those little stone statues. But they make proper soldiers with a little discipline and a good dose of Calvinism. Are you going to make a good soldier, Ben-oight? Or am I going to have to be climbing your ass all the time?"

"Colonel Kemp," Benoit began hotly. He was ready to say more when Dobbs kicked him solidly in the shin.

"Yes, lieutenant?" Kemp said invitingly. A large, thick-waisted man with chubby, pink cheeks, a slightly upturned nose, and a thick thatch of unruly, straw-colored hair, Kemp was often underestimated by others until they stared into his eyes. In contrast to his somewhat benign features, Kemp's black eyes burned with an inner light that flashed a single, strong signal warning that he was not a man to be trifled with.

A strong-backed, bull-headed farm boy from downstate Illinois, Kemp ran away from home and joined the Army at fourteen, working his way steadily upward through grit and determination. He compensated for his almost total lack of formal education by being the bravest man in every command in which he ever served. Report after report in his thick personnel file in Washington echoed an identical theme: ". . . Most courageous man I've ever seen . . . Not afraid of anything . . . Would take on Satan hand-to-hand given the opportunity . . . Eats wildcats for breakfast and wolverines for supper . . . "

"Well, lieutenant?" the colonel prompted. "Do you have something to say or were you just clearing your throat?"

Benoit flushed, biting his tongue. "I was just going to say, sir, that I'll try my best to live up to your expectations."

Kemp smiled humorlessly. "That's good, Ben-oight. One thing about you Frenchies is you're right tactful. But you need to be warned right up front that I have exceptionally high expectations. If you can live up to 'em you'll probably be a general one day."

Dismissing Benoit with a flick of his eyes, Kemp's gaze settled on Dobbs. "I know you from Mexico. You're a sawbones. You were with Briggs, weren't you?"

"That's correct, sir."

"Davis? Dole? Something short that starts with a 'd.'"

"That's close. It's Dobbs, sir. Jason. Post surgeon."

"Hope you have a lot of medical supplies, lieutenant, and I hope you're good at treating battle wounds because this is going to be a fighting command. None of this namby-pamby, coddle-the- poor-injun bullshit is going to fly as long as I'm commander. Washington sent me out here to do a job: secure the Oregon Trail. I interpret that to mean I'm to make sure the savages learn to respect us and keep the hell away from our wagon trains. Our country is moving west and these emigrants are in the vanguard. They're brave, they're foresighted, and they're our responsibility."

Leaning back in his chair, Kemp fumbled in his jacket pocket and withdrew a long, black cigar. "Now," he said, biting off the end and spitting the wad on the floor, "let me explain how I feel about our current situation."

As Kemp spoke, the captain who had been seated on the colonel's right, pulled a match from a supply he kept in his tunic for just those purposes. Striking it on his pants leg, he obsequiously offered it to Kemp.

"In case I failed to make a proper introduction before," Kemp said, puffing heartily to get his cigar lit, "this officer who never fails to have a match is Captain Jonathan Harrigan."

A medium-size man in his mid-thirties with heavy jowls and dark circles under his hazel eyes, Harrigan looked around the table and smiled tightly.

"He's my right hand," Kemp added. "If he tells you to do something you can assume it has my approval. If you fuck with him, you're going to have to fuck with me. Am I clear on that?"

Adamson, Benoit, and Dobbs nodded, exchanging nervous glances.

"And this," Kemp said as his aide-de-camp, a skinny, nervous-looking first lieutenant with a handlebar moustache returned lugging a heavy Army-issue footlocker, "is First Lieutenant Harold Grant. "Hoppin' Harry, I call him, but you'd better not try it. His uncle Ulysses is a colonel in personnel. Point made?"

"Yes, sir's" echoed around the table.

"Put it here," Kemp directed Grant, pointing to the empty place on the table in front of him.

Extracting a key from his pocket, Kemp opened the footlocker. Reaching inside, he withdrew a sheaf of envelopes bound together with a red ribbon. "This is for y'all," he said throwing the packet in front of Adamson. "Mail from home. Because of the, uh, recent unrest let's call it, in these parts, the stage hasn't been running regularly. This correspondence had piled up at Leavenworth and General Bowen asked me to bring it along. You can read it later."

Kemp stuck his hand back into the chest and came out with a tightly rolled document. "All right," he said, spreading it out on the table. "Just to make sure those dumb-ass map makers on the Potomac know what they're talking about, let's review what they say."

"Excuse me, sir," Adamson said, a tad too deferential to suit Benoit. "For this, I think you should also talk to Jim Ashby."

"The scout? Is that right?" Kemp said, raising a blond eyebrow.

"Yes, sir."

"Well, go get him then."

As Adamson scurried out the door, Kemp turned to Dobbs. "I haven't met the kitchen help yet," he said. "Why don't you introduce me while we're waiting for Ashby."

Dobbs disappeared through a door behind Kemp's back and returned almost immediately with a teenage girl and a woman limping heavily on her right side.

"This is Frau Hildegard Schmidt," Dobbs said grandly, "and her daughter, Inge."

"What's the matter with her leg?" Kemp asked, exhaling a thick cloud of blue smoke.

"I had to take it off last month," Dobbs explained. "Gangrene. The result of an arrow wound."

Kemp nodded. "I read about that," he said. "In Granger's report. She's one of the survivors of the injun attack."

"That's right," said Dobbs. "Her daughter, too. And her son, Erich. But he isn't here right now. He's out with a couple of men hunting buffalo. We're trying to stock up on some meat for the winter."

"Good idea," said Kemp. Turning to Frau Schmidt, the colonel's expression softened. "My sympathy, madam, on the loss of your husband and your friends."

"*Danke, Herr Oberst*," Frau Schmidt replied, bobbing her head. "You will have to excuse. My English sometimes is not too good. But *meine Tochter*, she speaks it *gut*."

"I'm sure we'll get along famously," Kemp said kindly, his tone prompting a puzzled glance between Benoit and Dobbs. "The dinner was delicious. I've seldom eaten venison prepared better."

Hildegard beamed. "*Das ist sehr nett von Ihnen*," she grinned.

"My mother says that's very kind of you," Inge translated. "She takes much pride in her cooking."

"And well she should. I look forward to many a fine meal at your table," Kemp said graciously. Looking away in polite dismissal, he stared pointedly at the door, impatient for Adamson to return with Ashby.

"*Entschuldigung, Herr Oberst*," Hildegard began, wringing her hands.

Kemp looked up, a trace of annoyance fleeting across his face. "Yes?" he asked amiably, smothering his vexation.

Hildegard turned pleadingly to her daughter, spilling out a stream of German.

"My mother asks your indulgence," Inge said. "She asks that you give your highest consideration to any plan that might be offered that would result in the return of Werner and Wilhem."

"Who?" Kemp asked, puzzled.

"The two Mueller children," Benoit interjected. "Their parents were killed in the attack and they were carried off by the Indians."

"Ah, yes," Kemp said, nodding in comprehension. "It's coming back to me. As long as we're on that subject, why don't you refresh my memory. Let me hear your side of what happened."

Benoit sighed. "How much background do you want? It could be a long story."

"Just the pertinent details, lieutenant," Kemp said tersely. "Enough to help me make a decision but not enough to put me to sleep."

"Yes, sir," Benoit said crisply. Glancing occasionally at Dobbs and Inge to see if there was anything they wanted to add, Benoit explained how he and Dobbs had been assigned to accompany a wagon train west from Missouri to Fort Laramie. About halfway between Fort Kearny and Fort Laramie one of the German emigrants's wagon had broken down. Two other wagonloads of Germans, including the Schmidts, decided to stay with the one whose wagon needed repair to help fix it and get it back on the trail.

Unwilling to hold up the train while repairs were made, Wagonmaster Alf Stuart detailed three men to help guard the group of stragglers and pushed on to Fort Laramie with the other emigrants.

The repairs were mostly completed, Benoit said, and the group — he also had stayed behind to help, he explained — were trying to catch up when they were attacked by a roving band of Indians. Five of the Germans, including an eight-year-old girl, were killed, along with the three guards. Among the dead were Heinrich and Johanna Mueller, the parents of the two kidnapped children. Survivors included the mother of the dead girl and two of her other children. Since she and her husband had friends in Oregon, she decided to continue west with the Stuart train. Frau Schmidt, on the other hand, had taken an arrow in her leg during the attack and the wound festered, requiring an amputation by Dobbs almost as soon as they arrived at the fort. As a result, Hildegard and her two children, Inge and Erich, had remained at Fort Laramie. Hildegard and Inge worked in the kitchen. Erich was assigned to assist Ashby.

"What about the injuns?" Kemp asked. "Are they the ones who caused this whole mess with Grattan?"

"I think I can answer that better'n Lieutenant Benoit," a voice said from across the room.

While Benoit had been filling Kemp in on the background, Ashby and Adamson had returned unnoticed.

"You're Ashby?" Kemp asked, sizing up the scout with a quick glance.

"Tha's right," Ashby replied. "I'm a scout now; at the time I was workin' for Alf Stuart."

Kemp shook his head in confusion. "Start at the beginning," he commanded.

Ashby exhaled deeply. "All right," he said reluctantly. "I was workin' for Stuart and ev'rythang was goin' fine until the German wagon busted down. Stuart decided to leave the others behin' to see if'n they couldn't fix it on their own. I thought he was wrong and tol' him so. It jest weren't right to abandon them in the middle of injun country. But he didn't pay me no nevamind. We didn't get too far down the trail 'fore Stuart had second thoughts and sent me back to check on the stragglers, along with a few soljers from Fort Laramie who'd ridden out to meet us. We got there in the middle of the attack and managed to run the injuns off. But Stuart and I had words. I quit 'fore he could fire me. Then Captain Granger hired me as scout 'n hunter here at the fort."

"The injuns," Kemp said impatiently. "Tell me about the injuns."

Ashby rolled his eyes. "This ain't all fac', you un'erstan' but it's the best I been able to piece together since then, from talkin' to some Brulé an' Oglalas."

"I understand it isn't verifiable," Kemp said. "Go ahead."

"Well," continued Ashby, "to my knowledge the attack was mainly the idea of a Cheyenne named Brown Hawk. Him and some o' his men were headin' home after liftin' a few Crow scalps when they run across a coupla Brulé named Blizzard and Bellowin' Moose. Them two was feelin' kinda mean because of a recent upset with the Crow so they agreed to go along with Brown Hawk's proposal to attack some whites."

"Why did they want to do that?" Kemp asked.

Ashby shrugged. "Who knows? My guess is they was just curious about what would happen. The Cheyenne live pretty far off the Trail and don' normally have much contact with the emigrants. I figur' they jest wanted to test 'em."

"So they attacked?"

"Yep," Ashby said. "The Brulé, Bellowin' Moose, was kilt in the raid, along with three of the Cheyenne. Plus, the leader, Brown Hawk, had mosta his hand blowed away and he bled to death later. At least that's what Blizzard tol' his people when he got back."

"Who's this Blizzard?" Kemp asked.

"He's a mean 'un," Ashby said. "He's the reason all your soljers died."

Kemp's eyebrows shot up. "How's that?"

"Blizzard was wounded in the attack," Ashby said. "Shot in the laig. It was fair-to-middlin' bad but not fatal. He was recuperatin' at the camp along the Platte when Lieutenant Grattan started pressurin' Captain Granger to let him go arrest Blizzard for his part in the raid."

"Slow down a bit," Kemp warned. "You mean this was Grattan's idea, not Granger's?"

"Tha's right, colonel. Grattan bragged abou' how he could lick the whole injun nation with a few good men and a couple artill'ry pieces. Convinced Captain Granger he was right."

"So he wanted to *arrest* Blizzard, not kill him?"

"Well," Ashby said hesitantly, "he said 'arrest,' but in my 'pinion you don' take twenty-nine soljers and two cannon into an injun camp less'en you lookin' for trouble. Point is, he foun' it. Ever' one of them men, as you know, was kilt."

"They absolutely were!" Kemp said, slamming his fist down on the table. And in *my* opinion, I don't think the savages should be allowed to get away with it."

"Are those your orders?" asked Dobbs. "Are we going to be marching against the Brulé and Oglalas?"

Kemp shook his head. "Sadly, no," he said bitterly. "I wish we were. But my orders are to establish a strong military presence along the Trail. We're here to discourage any such future attacks, not exact retribution for what's already happened."

"Does that mean we're going to forget about the Grattan incident?" Benoit asked in surprise.

"Hell, no, it doesn't!" Kemp yelled. "Another force will be coming out from the East, probably early next year, to track down those killers and see that they pay for what they did. We can't just let them get away with murder. In the meantime, I'm here to make sure the injuns don't get uppity and decide to attack the fort as well. That, and make sure they abide by the terms of the Fort Laramie Treaty, which guarantees the emigrant trains uncontested passage West."

Frau Schmidt emitted a stream of German.

"My mother asks what about the children?" Inge said nervously.

"Good question!" Kemp said. "What's your opinion on that?" he asked, turning to Ashby.

The scout rolled his skinny shoulders. "I don' think they been kilt or nothin', if tha's what you mean. Injuns are allatime stealin' each other's kids and wimmin. Usually, they try to bring 'em into the tribe, especially the young 'uns. In this case, I'd guess they're intendin' to bring 'em up as good Cheyenne, turn those boys into decent warriors."

"*Mein Gott*," Hildegard muttered, turning pale.

"Ain't nothin' to be upset about," Ashby said, trying to calm her. "I'm jest sayin' I think they're safe; that they ain't been harmed."

Kemp rubbed his chin thoughtfully. "That's a somewhat comforting speculation," he said after a pause. "Do you think you could confirm it?"

"You mean go make sure them kids is awright?" Ashby asked, surprised.

"Why not?" Kemp said sarcastically. "You got something better to do with your time? You're getting paid to scout, ain't you? Why not do a little scouting that might actually be worth something? I don't have the men or the authority to mount a rescue mission, but we can do a little reconnoitering, can't we?" he asked with a wink.

"Sure," Ashby said agreeably. "Why not?"

"Which brings me to one of the reasons I summoned you," Kemp said, turning his attention to the map he had unrolled on the tabletop. "Show me the lay of the land," he ordered. "Show me which injuns are where."

Ashby moved behind the table and studied the map for several minutes, orienting himself. "Awright," he said, placing an index finger in the lower left hand corner. "We're right here. Now over here, almost to Fort Kearny," he said, moving his finger far to the right, "is the 'Hos."

"Who?" asked Kemp, squinting.

"The 'Rapahos," said Ashby. "We usually jest call 'em the 'Hos."

Kemp nodded. "They friendly?"

Ashby shrugged. "Kinda neutral, I'd say. They're allies with the Cheyenne."

Kemp nodded. "Who else?"

"Up here, by the Loup Rivers," Ashby said, moving his finger to the northeast, "is the Pawnee. The Skidi Pawnee to be exac' since there's some Pawnee livin' way to hell 'n gone down south. Call themselves the Wolf People. One thing that makes 'em differen' from the other Plains tribes is they grow a lot of their food."

"Really?" Kemp asked with interest. "I didn't know that."

"It's a fac'," Ashby grinned. "I seen their fields myself. Like Back East. Corn. Beans. Squash. They like their vegetables. Ain't dependent on findin' 'em wild like the others."

"What else about them do I need to know?"

"They don' live in tipis neither," said Ashby. "They build proper lodges. Big thangs, outta logs, thatch, and dirt. Can hol' up to fifty people. I seen a couple of their villages, maybe a hun'erd of them lodges, so that's a passle o' injuns. They're good fighters, alla time at war with the Cheyenne and the 'Hos."

"An' up here," he said, sliding his finger upward to the left, toward the northwest, "is the Cheyenne. Tha's where I figure the German young 'uns is."

"Can you be more specific?" Kemp asked.

"No," Ashby replied. "They don' have permanent camps like the Pawnee. They live in tipis an' they move around a bit. But I think I can find 'em awright."

"They're enemies with the Pawnee, right?" Kemp asked.

Ashby nodded vigorously. "Tha's for damn sure. They're *bitter* enemies. Hate each other's guts. They've had some right good battles since they're both good fighters. 'Specially the Cheyenne. The Cheyenne and the

Teton Sioux, they're the best warriors on the Plains, no doubt about it."

"Are they allies?"

Ashby shrugged. "Sorta. The Tetons or the Lakotas, depen'in' on what you wanta call 'em, are made up o' seven groups." Raising his hand, palm outward, he ticked them off. "There's the Oglalas, the Brulé, the Miniconjou, the Itazichola, the Ohinupa, the Hunkpapa, and the Sihasapa. An' tha's jest the tribes. Each tribe has two or more bands, jest to make thangs confusin' for us."

He paused. "I got sidetracked. The Sioux and the Cheyenne been friends for quite awhile, ever since the Sioux took the Cheyenne Sacred Arrows from the Pawnees and returned 'em. That made 'em bosom buddies, so to speak."

Kemp rubbed his temples tiredly. "Who else?" he asked.

"Really only one other tribe you got to worry about," Ashby said. "Tha's the Crow. They live up here," he said, pointing to the far northwest corner of the map, "up in the big mountains. The Crow is mean, too. They're good warriors but they're too far off the Trail to be much of a bother to the emigrants. They sure like to fight, though. Always warrin' with the Cheyenne and the Sioux, 'specially the Sioux."

"Does that make them allies of the Pawnee?" Kemp asked logically.

"Not neces'arily," Ashby smiled. "jest 'cause they fight the same tribes don' make 'em *compadres*. Now, while we don' gotta worry about 'em, least not yet, there's some other tribes you oughta jest know about. Over here, jest south o' Crow territory, are the Shoshones. An' up north, near the Cannuck border, are the Gros Ventre, the Blackfoot, an' the Assiniboin. I never been that far north myself, but I know they're up thar from what others have told me."

Kemp stood and stretched. "That's been very informative, Ashby. I'll try to remember it all. But don't you forget about that scouting assignment. I don't expect to see you around the fort after noon tomorrow. Not for a few days anyway."

"I'll be pullin' out pretty quick. But if you don' mind, I'd like to take somebody with me."

"Who's that?" Kemp asked curiously.

"The Schmidt boy, Erich," Ashby said. "He jes' got back a little while ago from a huntin' trip, but he's kinda my assistant. You'd call him an 'aide.' I'm trying to bring him along as a scout. I think he's got a right amount of promise."

"That's fine with me," Kemp said. "Just see that the job gets done. Now, if you gentlemen don't mind, I'm going to bed. It's been a long day. Oh," he said, indicating the packet of letters on the table. "Don't stay up all night reading."

Harrigan and Grant, recognizing Kemp's heavy-handed attempt at humor, guffawed.

Dobbs shot Benoit a glance. "Oh, Sweet Jesus," he mumbled under his breath. "Where's Granger when we need him?"

Knifewielder woke with a start, his heart thumping furiously against his ribs. Springing into a sitting position on the narrow bed he shared with his wife, Bright Calico, he parted the privacy curtain and peered anxiously into the dark, certain he would see the deity Morning Star braced regally in front of the altar on the lodge's western wall. The image had been so vivid, the scene so lifelike, Knifewielder could not believe it had not actually occurred. But the dwelling was dark and serene, the predawn quietness broken only by the customary sounds. Nearby, his four-year-old son, Roaming Child, tossed restlessly on the bed he shared with Bright Calico's mother, Imperial Woman. And across the open space in the center of the lodge, his friend, Angry Buffalo, turned heavily on his side and loudly broke wind.

"What is it, *kurahus*?" Bright Calico whispered, using the affectionate term for husband that translated as "old man." Still more asleep than awake, she tugged on the buffalo-hide blanket, pulling it tightly around her to ward off the sharp, autumn chill. "Does Roaming Child need to go outside?"

"No, *raku*," Knifewielder replied in aggravation, using the formal term for spouse. "I have seen him," he added excitedly, his voice louder than the one he would normally have used out of deference to the others who were still asleep.

"Seen who?" Bright Calico asked, her voice muffled by the robe. "Roaming Child?"

"No," Knifewielder said impatiently, "*not* Roaming Child. Morning Star! He came to me in my sleep."

At the mention of the deity's name, Bright Calico poked her head out of the blanket and looked at her husband closely. "Really?" she asked shrilly, also forgetting to keep her voice down. "*Morning Star?* Are you sure?"

"Of course, I'm sure," Knifewielder said, irritated. "Don't you think I know what Morning Star looks like?"

"Certainly you do," Bright Calico replied, chastised. "It's just that He hasn't appeared to any of the Wolf People for many years. What did He say?"

Knifewielder threw off the robe and pushed back the curtain, reaching for his loincloth and deerskin leggings, which were lying on the hard-packed earth at the foot of the bed. "I have to go see Red Calf," he said. "You should know that Morning Star has only one message."

Balancing first on one foot and then the other, Knifewielder pulled on his moccasins and grabbed the buffalo-hide robe that kept him warm in winter. Although only slightly taller than his wife, Knifewielder was solidly built with broad, muscled shoulders, beefy forearms, and thighs as thick and solid as Ponderosa logs. "I'll tell you about it when I get back," he told his wife abruptly. Spinning on his heels, he hurried through the tunnel-like entryway on the eastern side of the lodge.

"What's going on?" Angry Buffalo's deep voice bellowed from the darkness across the lodge. "Are those cursed Cheyenne raiding our horses again?"

"No," Bright Calico replied. "This is much more serious. Morning Star has appeared to my husband."

"*Morning Star*!" Angry Buffalo boomed in amazement, his deep bass reverberating off the lodge's thick mud and log walls. At thirty, Angry Buffalo was older by two years than Knifewielder, but the two were fast friends, so close that they had agreed to share a lodge, each moving his family into the domed dwelling that stood near the western perimeter of Pahukstatu, or Pumpkin- Vine, one of four Skidi Pawnee villages on the eastern edge of the Great Plains.

By Pawnee standards, the Knifewielder/Angry Buffalo lodge was under-occupied. When the two friends built the lodge five years earlier there had been, in addition to the two men and their wives, only their respective mothers-in-law — Imperial Woman and Old-Lady-Plants-the-Corn — and Beautiful Calf, Angry Buffalo's daughter by Left-handed Woman. Since then, Roaming Child had been born and Angry Buffalo, after he had become an assistant to the village chief, Battle Cry, had taken a second wife, Cloudy Sky. Together, they had a daughter, Girl-Chases-the-Enemy, who then, at age three, was one year younger than Roaming Child.

"Knifewielder, old friend," Angry Buffalo called, struggling into his leggings, "tell me about Morning Star."

"You're too late," Bright Calico laughed, slipping on her deerskin skirt and overblouse. "He's gone to see Red Calf. We'll have to wait until he returns. I'm so happy." She added joyfully, "This will bring much prestige to my husband and our lodge."

In the distance, they could hear Knifewielder hollering as he ran through the still-sleeping village. "Red Calf!" he yelled. "Priest of the Morning Star, wake up. I have to tell you about my vision. I've seen the deity."

Red Calf's wife, Tall Corn, heard Knifewielder before her husband. Digging an elbow into his side, she rudely nudged him awake. "Someone's coming," she said urgently. "A man claiming he has had a vision."

Red Calf was instantly alert. As the Morning Star priest in Pumpkin-Vine Village, his sole duty was to deal with matters pertaining to the deity. When someone was rushing to tell him about a vision, it was his responsibility to be ready to receive him.

"Hurry, *tsustit*," he told his wife as he rolled out of bed, showing amazing agility for a man of his advanced age. "I'll go greet him. You build the fire and prepare something to eat. This may take awhile."

Wrapping himself in a hairy buffalo-skin robe, Red Calf ran outdoors. When the yelling man got close enough for Red Calf to recognize him, the priest sighed in relief. Knifewielder was one of the more respected younger men in the village. Although only twenty-eight, he had built a reputation as a fearless warrior and a steady, level-headed thinker. If Knifewielder believes he has had a vision, Red Calf told himself happily, I am very inclined to believe him.

Rushing forward, he threw his arms around the young brave and hugged him tightly as the tears began flowing down his cheeks. "An appearance from Morning Star is always wonderful news," Red Calf said, "and it is especially welcome when it comes from a man of your statute."

"You are too kind," Knifewielder replied, struggling to contain his own emotion. Despite his attempts at self-control, the tears began flowing from his eyes as well. For the moment he said no more, afraid to trust his voice.

"Come inside," Red Calf said after a long pause. "We have much to discuss."

Tall Corn looked up anxiously when the two men entered, holding her breath until they walked into the cone of illumination from the fire that she had hurriedly poked to life. Recognizing Knifewielder when he walked into the light, she exhaled softly, relieved as her husband that the man claiming the vision was an honored villager and not one of the neophyte warriors who might only be interested in gaining a quick reputation and, therefore, somewhat loose with the truth about his dream.

"Sit!" Red Calf commanded, pointing to the place of honor by the fire. "Let me get my pipe."

"First," he said, stuffing the bowl with tobacco from a small, beaded elk-skin pouch Tall Corn handed him, "I will smoke. Then you will tell me of your vision. If I judge it was indeed a communication from Morning Star, then I'll instruct you about your responsibility." Without waiting for a reply, Red Calf took the pipe and walked outside.

Carefully, he lit it and, raising his arms, he thrust it to the east, which was the deity's realm. "Thank you, oh Morning Star," he said softly. "Your absence has been heartfelt and it is encouraging to know that you have decided it is time to return. You have picked a very worthy representative and I ask you, as your most humble servant, to bless him and his mission."

Puffing heartily, he blew the smoke to the east. Then, tapping the bowl against his palm, he emptied the ashes and returned to his fireside, where Knifewielder was waiting impatiently.

"Tell me about your vision," he said, assuming the

role of interrogator. As priest, it was his duty to make sure that the vision was authentic.

"It all happened very quickly," Knifewielder said nervously. "I was dreaming about Bright Calico and Roaming Child . . . they were romping happily in a stream, splashing each other with shining water . . . "

"Yes," Red Calf interjected. "Go on."

"Then suddenly they disappeared," Knifewielder said. "Not so much disappeared, actually, as dissolved. One minute they were there, the next they were gone."

"And then what happened?" Red Calf inquired encouragingly.

"The stream was still there, but it was empty. And in place of my wife and son in the water, there was a man on the bank."

"What did he look like?"

Knifewielder paused, organizing his reply, anxious to make sure he described the vision as accurately as he could.

"He was a stern-looking man," Knifewielder said. "About my age but more majestic-looking. His face was painted a bright red. His hair was adorned with fluffy goose down and he wore a single eagle father in his scalplock."

"And how was he dressed?" Red Calf prompted.

"He had a buffalo robe over his shoulders," Knifewielder replied, screwing up his face in concentration, "and he had it wrapped tightly about him. But below the hem, I could see his leggings, which were decorated with scalps and eagle feathers."

"Did he talk?"

"Yes," Knifewielder nodded eagerly. "But he spoke somewhat harshly. He said," Knifewielder repeated, lowering his voice to imitate that of the speaker in his dream, "'I am *Upirikutsu*, the Powerful Great Star from the East.' Then he seemed to admonish me. He said,

'Your people have forgotten about me; you have ignored me for too many years. It is time for that to be corrected.'"

Red Calf's eyes grew large and took on an inner glow. The more he listened, the more convinced he became that Knifewielder had indeed been visited by Morning Star. "Was that all?" he asked.

"No," Knifewielder said. "I managed to find my voice. I asked him what I needed to do."

"And what did he tell you?"

Knifewielder looked earnestly at Red Calf. "He told me to come to you. He said you knew what to do and you would be my teacher."

Red Calf dipped his head in assent. "Take this," he said, handing Knifewielder the pipe. "Take it outside and offer it to Morning Star. Thank him for appearing to you and beg his guidance. Then return and I will give you further instructions."

Three minutes later, when Knifewielder came back to the fire, Red Calf was returning from his altar with a large package in his hands. "This is the sacred Morning Star bundle," he explained. "It contains the equipment you will need to carry through on Upirikutsu's command. I'll tell you about that shortly. In the meantime, let me tell you about Morning Star."

Knifewielder opened his mouth, ready to say that he already knew all about Morning Star. But Red Calf raised his hand, shushing the warrior before he could talk.

"I know you're familiar with the legend," he said. "But I must tell you anyway. It is my duty."

Knifewielder nodded and leaned forward, warming his hands and waiting for Red Calf to explain.

"In the beginning," said Red Calf, "there was Evening Star, a beautiful woman who lived in the West. She is our goddess of night and fertility and she rules over a paradise where the crops are always successful and the buffalo are plentiful. In her house, she kept a magical bundle containing a sacred buffalo skull and holy ears of corn."

Knifewielder's eyes grew heavy as he listened to the tale he had heard all his life, a story his grandmother used to tell him every winter night before he went to sleep. The temptation to dose was great, but he roused himself, aware that this time the story had special meaning.

"Evening Star's counterpart," Red Calf intoned, completely lost in his recitation, "was Morning Star, who lived in the East. Evening Star was totally feminine, but Morning Star was all male. Evening Star was the epitome of fertility and gentleness; Morning Star the paragon of war and aggressiveness.

"Every morning when Upirikutsu awoke he directed his sunbeam into Evening Star's lodge and lit her fire. Evening Star's cohorts, the guardians of night, were not happy with this and urged her to repel him. But since He was a determined man, He kept at it. Eventually, He had to fight the spirits with which Evening Star surrounded Herself and after a long, difficult battle, Morning Star emerged the victor.

"To consecrate His conquest, He took Evening Star to bed. But She had one more weapon at Her disposal. As a last defense, She had two rows of very sharp teeth in her vagina. If Morning Star attempted to penetrate Her, His penis would have been severed. Knowing this, Morning Star came prepared. Before mounting her, He used a heavy sacred meteor stone He had the foresight to bring with him to break all the teeth.

"After that, He mated with Her and, as a result of Their union, Evening Star became impregnated. The child resulting from that union was a girl. They were so proud of Their daughter that They summoned a whirlwind to carry her to Earth. She became the first human created by the stars.

"Seeing what Evening Star and Morning Star had accomplished, the Sun and Moon mated and produced a boy, who also was carried to Earth and became the mate of the girl. From them, we are all descended.

"But it is not a happy story," Red Calf added, lowering his voice. "Because those two children were human, they died. Morning Star took the death of his daughter very badly; He was terribly saddened. Upirikutsu can take the loneliness only so long. After a period of time He appears to one of our warriors telling him that He is lonely and has a need for the company of a young girl to take the place of His dead daughter. You have been selected to carry out His wishes, to find a companion for Him to help Him while away the days and years. It is a high honor," Red Calf said solemnly, "and you should be very proud."

"What happens if his plea is ignored?" Knifewielder asked.

Red Calf shuddered. "All sorts of misfortune will befall the Pawnee. Our crops will die and the fields will not produce. We will not be able to find the buffalo. Our women will miscarry and our warriors will suffer bad defeats to the Cheyenne and their allies, the Arapahos and the Sioux. It will be a time of much misery." Looking steadily at Knifewielder, he added: "You do not want to be responsible for such calamities, do you?"

Knifewielder was shocked. "Of course not," he said. "I would rather die first."

"I figured as much," Red Calf replied. "Your reputation is that of a competent, responsible man."

Knifewielder, not sure how to reply, ducked his head modestly. "Tell me what I must do," he said softly.

* * *

An hour later, when Knifewielder entered his lodge, he was only mildly surprised to find everyone still gathered around the fire. So anxious were they to hear his story they had postponed the everyday tasks they normally would have undertaken, waiting patiently for him to return.

"Come in, *kurahus*," Bright Calico enthused, rising quickly to greet him. "Come sit by the fire and tell us about your vision while I prepare a bowl of food for you. You haven't eaten, have you?" she asked anxiously.

"Only a bite, *tsustit*," Knifewielder smiled. "Tall Corn offered me food but I was too nervous to eat."

"By all means, sit," Angry Buffalo said in his gravely voice. "We were about to go mad with curiosity. Tell us everything."

As Knifewielder spoke, he dipped into the wooden bowl Bright Calico had pushed into his hand, hungrily shoveling buffalo intestine and corn soup into his mouth with a buffalo-horn spoon. For the sake of everyone in the lodge, he repeated what he had seen in his vision, tactfully adding how beautiful Bright Calico and Roaming Child had been in his dream before they were supplanted by the austere deity.

As his wife beamed with pride, Knifewielder added that he had a new job for her. "I will need new moccasins," he said firmly. "Several pair."

"For what?" she asked, looking puzzled.

"For the long trip to the Cheyenne camp," he replied. "That's where we will capture the girl for Morning Star."

"How many men are you taking with you?" Angry Buffalo interjected. A valiant warrior with the scalps and coups to prove it, Angry Buffalo was too proud to ask Knifewielder to include him among the raiding party. But by inquiring indirectly about his plans, he could give his friend the opportunity to include him in the group without telling him that directly.

Knifewielder grinned tightly, his long, thin face breaking into dozens of small wrinkles. Bright Calico watched him intently. She loved to see him smile. When he laughed his eyes always shined with a special light that belied the stern warrior visage he liked to portray.

"I've been thinking about that," he said with mock solemnity, rattling off the names of men he would ask to accompany him.

"I'd like Dark Eagle, for sure," he said, naming the brawny brave who had the most scars and battle honors of all the warriors in the village. "I think also Young Bull, who is fearless, and Prancing Pony, who is tireless."

He paused. "Walks Fast would be a valuable member because he's the best hunter in the village and we'll have to eat. Then," he said brightly, "just in case, I'll need some good fighters like Rides-the-Bear, Leading Elk, and Little Fox."

Angry Buffalo, struggling to maintain his impassiveness, stared into the fire. "Is that all?" he asked quietly.

Knifewielder laughed heartily. "Of course it isn't all," he said, slapping his friend on the shoulder. "I'd never go off on a mission like that without you. You're the best tracker and scout in all of the four villages. I'd no more leave you behind than I would my knife and bow. You will come, won't you?" he asked softly.

Angry Buffalo beamed. "You couldn't keep me away," he roared. "Just try to get out of the village without me."

Both men began laughing heartily, doubling over and howling until tears streamed down their faces. The women exchanged glances and rolled their eyes while Beautiful Calf stared into her lap in embarrassment, marveling at how grown men could act so childish. The two younger children, Roaming Child and Girl-Chases-the-Enemy, were unsure how to react, but, unwilling to risk their fathers' wrath, chuckled tentatively.

Bright Calico, anxious to demonstrate the new authority her husband's vision had imparted on her, put an end to the merriment.

"You two *boys*," she said, emphasizing the word, "may have nothing better to do than sit around all day making sport, but we *women* have work to do. The food pit needs to be cleaned before winter."

Ignoring his friend's wife, Angry Buffalo wiped his cheeks and turned to Knifewielder. "When do we leave?" he wheezed.

"Not for four days," Knifewielder gasped. "I need to go through a period of instruction with Red Calf. This isn't a horse raid; there's a lot more to this than I was aware."

Knifewielder could hardly contain his excitement as Red Calf shuffled toward him carrying the precious Morning Star bundle as delicately as if were a newborn infant.

"Calm yourself," Red Calf told him with a smile as he settled near the fire, which had been allowed to burn down to coals. The odor of cooked corn still filled the room, adding an earthy touch to a proceeding that Knifewielder felt was almost mystical.

As he watched Red Calf unwrap the bundle, carefully undoing the rawhide bonds one at a time, he felt a chill of anticipation run through his body. Shivering slightly, he pulled his buffalo robe more tightly around his shoulders.

"I know what you're feeling," Red Calf said kindly. "You're wondering why you of all the Pawnee warriors have been chosen to perform this task. Morning Star hasn't appeared to any of our people for almost fifteen years."

"In that case," Knifewielder said in a feeble attempt at humor, "He must have been very happy with the last girl."

"Don't make fun of the deities," Red Calf said harshly. "If you do, your mission may be doomed to failure and your scalplock could wind up on a Cheyenne lance."

"Forgive me," Knifewielder said, abashed. "I was only trying to keep the occasion from being so solemn."

"No," said Red Calf. "It *has* to be solemn. Otherwise, you won't be successful. Morning Star, unlike you, doesn't have much of a sense of humor."

"You're right, priest," Knifewielder said humbly. "I should be much more careful when I'm in the presence of something holy."

Red Calf nodded. "Morning Star understands," he said. "Otherwise he would not have chosen you. Now listen and watch carefully while I explain what you must do beginning today."

Reverently, he threw back the soft elk-skin outer covering of the sacred bundle and, one-by-one, removed the objects that Knifewielder would need to complete his assignment.

Loading the sacred pipe that was enclosed in the bundle, Red Calf rummaged through the remains of the fire until he found a glowing ember, which he used to light the tobacco. Sucking heartily, he drew in a great mouthful of smoke, which he blew in Knifewielder's direction, an official blessing from Morning Star's representative in Pumpkin-Vine Village.

Turning the instrument around so its stem faced Knifewielder, Red Calf waited while the warrior copied what he had done.

"Now," Red Calf said when the tobacco had burned to ashes, "I'll show you what the other objects are."

"This is the otter-skin collar that you will wear

around your neck when you approach the enemy camp," Red Calf said, shaking out the strip of dark brown fur.

"Yes," Knifewielder nodded.

Red Calf reached into the bundle and pulled out another furry object that Knifewielder recognized instantly.

"This is the skin of the wildcat," Red Calf said.

"I know what that is," Knifewielder said. "I have one in my lodge. Bright Calico has made a toy of it for our son, Roaming Child."

"No," said Red Calf, "this is the *sacred* wildcat-skin. See," he said, holding it up to demonstrate, "its legs are filled with tobacco that you will smoke on your mission, and paints that you will use to decorate your body."

"Aaahhhh," sighed Knifewielder.

Reaching again into the container, Red Calf produced a feathered object.

"The sacred hawk-skin," he explained. "It attaches to the otter-skin collar."

Patiently, Red Calf removed the other objects: a buffalo-hair rope to wear around the waist, an ear of corn that symbolized fertility of the crops, and the special Morning Star pipe that Knifewielder would smoke during the journey.

"Is that it?" Knifewielder asked when the bundle was empty.

"What were you expecting? Red Calf laughed. "Maybe a Cheyenne village, too, so you wouldn't have to travel so far?"

Knifewielder blushed. "No," he stammered. "I guess I was expecting something really magical."

Red Calf's face grew rigid. "This *is* magical," he said, "and don't ever doubt it. These may look like everyday objects to you, but they have all been blessed by Morning Star and each has special significance. Now that I've shown you what's in the holy bundle we have to go through a period of instruction so you will know how to *use* each of these objects. Without that instruction, they are meaningless."

Shortly before midnight on the fourth day, Red Calf left his lodge and squatted on the ground before a ceremonial fire in the center of the village, waiting for Venus, the Pawnee's Morning Star, to rise in the east.

Moments before, he had sent a messenger to Knifewielder's lodge, telling him to rise and costume himself in the objects from the sacred bundle. He was then to come to meet him by the ceremonial fire.

When Knifewielder arrived a few minutes later, the priest gave him a final check. The rope was in place around the waist, the otter-skin collar was around his neck, the hawk-skin was fastened correctly over his right shoulder, and the ear of Mother Corn dangled from the left.

Red Calf took the container of red paint and made twin streaks down each of Knifewielder's cheeks, from just below his eyes to his chin. Then he painted three stripes on his forehead in the shape of a bird's foot.

Taking the scared pipe, Red Calf handed it gently to Knifewielder. "Always carry it with the stem pointing upward," he commanded. Then he turned to see if the star had come over the horizon.

As soon as it appeared, Red Calf spread his arms and called to the sky: "Here is your man. He is wearing your clothing. Keep him safe and help him find a girl suitable for you."

Pulling Knifewielder forward, Red Calf turned him until he faced northwest, toward Cheyenne territory.

"Go!" he said authoritatively, summoning his assistants to follow him in the rigidly prescribed order. First came Angry Buffalo and Young Bull, the two principal scouts, their faces painted a bone white. And after them were the warriors who also would take part in the raid: Dark Eagle, Rides-the-Bear, Leading Elk, Prancing Pony, Walks Fast, and Little Fox. Without another word, they marched into the darkness.

Shortly before dawn, Knifewielder called a halt and they lay down along a stream for a few hours' sleep. At noon, they rose and trooped off toward the northwest, marching almost until dark when Knifewielder selected a campsite deep in a stand of towering pines.

This time, they built a fire and ate some of the meat they had brought with them. For the first time since leaving the village, Knifewielder removed the costume and set it carefully at the west side of the fire, where the Morning Star altar would be in Red Calf's lodge.

Ordering the others to try to sleep, Knifewielder himself stretched beside the fire and closed his eyes. Before midnight, he awoke and sat facing the east, smoking the Morning Star pipe and waiting for the planet to come above the horizon. When it did, he woke the others and they again set off on their trek.

Late on the afternoon of the fourth day, Angry Buffalo and Young Bull returned excitedly to the group.

"We've found a Cheyenne village," Angry Buffalo reported enthusiastically. "A half-day away."

Knifewielder grinned broadly. "We'll march a little longer than usual tonight and make our final camp when we're almost there. Did you get a good look at our objective?"

Angry Buffalo shook his head. "We didn't want to chance getting too close yet. We just crept close enough to make sure it was a Cheyenne camp."

"Good work," Knifewielder said happily. "Tomorrow you can take a closer look."

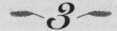

Red Berry Woman lay listening to the sobbing boy, tears trickling out of the corners of her eyes and leaving large dark spots on the deerskin pad she used for a pillow. Over and over, first in German and then in English, the boy repeated the same phrases: "*Ich will zu meine Mutter . . .* I want my mother."

In time, she told her husband, Short Hair, the boy they had named Puma because of his dark blond hair would come to accept them as his parents and the *Tsistsis-tas* way of life as his own.

During the day, as long as the sun was shining and the camp was bustling with activity, the four-year-old Puma presented a strong front, holding his chin high and stubbornly refusing to play the part of the cowering captive. Red Berry Woman watched him carefully, secretly proud of his defiance since she knew in her heart that if the experience of being yanked from his mother's protective arms by a rampaging warrior — in this case, her husband — broke his spirit he would never become the proud brave the Cheyenne code demanded of its males. It was only in the hours just before dawn, when he thought everyone was asleep and he could vent his feelings, that Puma allowed himself to surrender to his emotions.

"How very much like The People he has become already," Red Berry Woman told her husband. In response, Short Hair only grunted. "In time, we will test his bravery," he muttered.

Red Berry Woman was touched, too, by the concern the boy felt for his younger brother, which his foster parents, Large-footed Bull and Lightning Woman, had named Magpie because he was constantly chattering. Undoubtedly, she reasoned, it was because Magpie was only half Puma's age that the adjustment seemed smoother. But the fact that he was protective of his younger brother struck her as totally appropriate. It was not enough, she felt, that a warrior be brave; he must also have a streak of humanity that allowed him to care for others besides himself. The ability to love and empathize was a trait that Red Berry Woman would not allow to be denigrated by her husband or her daughter, a thirteen-year-old named Beaver Woman.

Not that there was any worry on that score. Beaver Woman had immediately taken to Puma, overcoming her initial repugnance at his pale skin, blue eyes, and light-colored hair. She spent hours with the boy, patiently trying to teach him the language and the rudiments of behavior that were expected of Cheyenne children.

That night, after the evening meal, as the fire burned down and Short Hair stared drowsily into the embers, Beaver Woman took Puma into her lap and whispered to him the oft-repeated Cheyenne creation tale. She told him — although she knew he understood little because of the language barrier — about how the Creator had made the first two people, a man from a rib on his right side and a woman from a rib on his left, then perversely put them so far apart, the woman in the north, the man in the south, that they never came together. It was only when the Creator made two more people and put them together in the same place that the tribe grew.

"Enough about the Creator," Short Hair grumbled. "Puma is a boy. Tell him how Rope Earrings killed the *Ooetaneo'o*, the hated Crow, with his magic arrow point, or about the courage of Lone Wolf, the chief of the Kit Fox Society, in which I myself am a member."

"He's too young to hear stories about war and killing, Father," Beaver Woman protested.

"A boy is never too young for that," Short Hair replied tersely.

"Yes, *Ne-ho'e*," Beaver Woman replied respectfully.

"Come here, Puma," Short Hair said gruffly, motioning to the boy.

Puma approached, looking confused.

"Sit here," Short Hair, said, patting the robe by his side, "and I'll tell you about a great Tsis-tsis-tas hero named Alights-on-the-Cloud."

Although he understood little of the language, the boy sat quietly, his eyes riveted on Short Hair as he related the tale. Beaver Woman, who had heard parts of the story many times, also listened attentively, enthralled by her father's recitation of tribal bravery.

"It was ten summers ago," Short Hair began, "and we were on a buffalo hunt when we came across some *Ho'nehe-taneo'o*, who also were hunting. Because we have long been at war with the Pawnee, we decided to attack. Alights-on-the-Cloud, who was much beloved by all the Cheyenne because he was very wise as well as very brave and always kind to others, was wearing the iron shirt he had taken years before from a Comanche he had killed in battle."

He paused, motioning to Red Berry Woman to prepare him a pipe. After he lit it, he continued with the tale.

"For all his bravery and wisdom, Alights-on-the-Cloud had one fault: he thought he was invincible. When the fight started with the Pawnee, Alights-on-the-Cloud told all our warriors that he would ride into the midst of the enemy and force them to empty their guns by firing at him, because as long as he was wearing the iron shirt he could not be hurt."

Short Hair puffed contentedly on his pipe, enjoying himself immensely. "One by one, the Pawnee shot at him but the bullets bounced off his chest. The arrows also were deflected, and it looked as if Alights-on-the-Cloud was going to emerge unscathed.

"But then," he said, his face turning solemn, "one of the Pawnee bowmen got lucky. His arrow hit Alights-on-the-Cloud in the eye, and he was killed instantly. Our warriors were so angered by this that they attacked. The charge was so vicious, that the Pawnee ran away."

"Then what happened, Father?" Beaver Woman asked breathlessly.

Short Hair smiled. "Our warriors were almost to the Pawnee hunting camp when a group of Pawnee from another camp arrived. They outnumbered us two to one, and we were falling back when some more Tsistsis-tas arrived. It was not enough and all of us surely would have been killed if still more of our people had not come to our rescue. Our combined force was too great for the Pawnee and we ran them off, killing many of them as they fled."

Beaver Woman clapped her hands together excitedly, "What a wonderful story, *Ne-ho'e*," she said happily.

"Wait," Short Hair said, raising his hand. "That's not all."

"Well, then what happened, Father?"

"We recovered Alights-on-the-Cloud's body and discovered that the Pawnee had stolen his iron shirt and had taken it with them when they escaped."

"How sad," interjected Red Berry Woman.

"No," Short Hair said, "what is really lamentable is when we discovered what the Pawnee had done to the Tsis-tsis-tas they had killed in battle."

"What had they done?" Beaver Woman asked, wide-eyed.

"They had cut up their bodies," Short Hair said, making a face. "They had cut off their arms and their legs and their manhood, and they had sliced open their chests and removed their hearts. They put the organs in medicine bags, which they took away with them so they could use them later to dip their bullets in and make powerful magic."

"That's terrible," Beaver Woman said. "It makes me want to cry."

"We got our revenge," Short Hair said grimly.

"How?" Red Berry Woman asked, also caught up in the tale.

"We did the same thing to their dead warriors that they had done to ours. We cut their bodies apart and spread the pieces across the prairie. We also broke open their chests and took their hearts, rubbing their blood on our faces to make us powerful. There," he said, pointing with his pipe toward his medicine bundle which hung from a pole across the tipi, "I have one of the Pawnee hearts which I will use one day to make my own medicine against the Ho'nehe-taneo'o." When he voiced the Cheyenne name for the Pawnee, he coughed deeply and spit into the fire, watching fixedly as it sizzled and smoked.

"It took us a long time to collect all the parts of our warriors bodies," he said slowly, continuing the tale. "But eventually we got them all together and respect-

fully placed them in a nearby ravine. It was a sad time,"
he said, tears forming in his eyes at the recollection. "All
the Tsis-tsis-tas cried and cut themselves with knives.
The warriors cut off their hair and the tails of their
horses."

"Did you do that, too?" asked Beaver Woman.

"Of course," Short Hair said with a tight smile.
"That's when I began calling myself by my present
name."

"Is that the same time you got hurt?" said Beaver
Woman, pointing at her father's remarkably misshapen
nose.

"Oh, no," Short Hair laughed. "That was much earlier, in a fight with an *Ooetane*. The Crow tried to knock
my head off with his war club, but his aim was not so
good."

"Tell us about that!" Beaver Woman said delightedly.

Short Hair shook his head. "Not tonight," he said.
"That's a story that will have to wait. Maybe when
Puma understands our language better and can appreciate my tales I'll tell you some stories about what a
brave man your father really is. Now, it's late and I'm
getting sleepy. Take Puma and the two of you go to
bed."

"Yes, Father," Beaver Woman said with a slight bow.

"Do you think we did the right thing?" Red Berry
Woman asked Short Hair after Beaver Woman and
Puma were tucked under their robes. "Splitting the boys
up, I mean."

"Of course we did the right thing," Short Hair said.
"If they were together they would form a bond and hold
on to their Whiteness. But separated, growing up in different tipis, they will learn to think of themselves as
Tsis-tsis-tas, not *Ve'ho'e*."

"I hope so," Red Berry Woman replied uncertainly, dipping her head respectfully as she had been taught since childhood. "Beaver Woman has become very attached to the boy. If he would later decide that he wants to go back and live with the Whites rather than stay with us, it would break her heart."

"You worry about the wrong things," Short Hair said.

"Well, what should I be worry about?"

Short Hair grinned, twisting his disfigured nose still farther out of shape. "You should worry about keeping your husband happy."

Red Berry Woman looked at him and smiled. "That should not be hard to do," she said, chuckling. "You're nothing but an old horse that has little stamina left. In a race, you can't go the distance."

Short Hair laughed. "No stamina, eh? Come here, woman," he said, grabbing her gently by the arm. "I'll show you who's an old horse."

Giggling like a schoolgirl, Red Berry Woman landed on top of her husband and began to snuggle her head into his shoulder. "Are you sure Puma's asleep?" she whispered, breathing heavily.

"What difference does it make?" Short Hair panted. "Don't the Ve'ho'e do this, too?"

Short Hair squatted so his face would be on a level with Puma's. His dark eyes softened somewhat as they locked onto the boy's blue ones. Reaching out, he gently placed his hand on Puma's thin shoulder and squeezed gently.

"I know you can't yet understand everything I say," he said softly, "but I want to tell you what you need to do while I'm away on the hunt. I want you to obey Red Berry Woman and do your chores. And I want you to listen to Beaver Woman, too. Even though she's just a girl, she's older than you and can teach you much. But most of all, I want you to practice hard while I'm gone with the bow I've made for you. You're already far behind the other boys in martial skills so you have to work extra hard to catch up. I know you can do it, though. You're smart and strong and capable of being a great warrior one day. I've watched you playing with the others and I've been impressed with how you've stood up to their bullying. To me, that indicates that you have a brave heart, but it is still too soon to tell for certain. With hard work, you can learn the skills of the warrior but a warrior's real strength comes from inside. That's something you need to remember all your life."

"That's quite a speech," Red Berry Woman said in admiration. "I've never heard you go on like that."

Short Hair, embarrassed, reacted sternly. "That's because I've always been stuck in a tipi with nothing but women," he said in mock severity. "Trying to explain the warrior code to a woman is as fruitless as trying to tell the tell the wind not to blow."

Red Berry Woman smiled, happy with how readily her husband had accepted the white boy. He needed a son, she thought, to fill the gap left by the deaths of their two male children, one of whom succumbed during childbirth and the other who died of the white man's sickness before he could walk. He was proud of Beaver Woman and he loved her deeply, but she was not a son.

Short Hair bounced impatiently on his toes, anxious to leave. "The others are waiting for me," he said, his tone more severe than he intended. "I need to go."

Red Berry Woman nodded. "I'll see you in a few days," she said. "And," she added with a grin, "don't come home empty-handed. The fur on the caterpillars indicate this is going to be a long, cold winter."

She and Beaver Woman watched silently as the men

trooped off in single file toward the south end of the lake, where they would strike Blue Creek, which they would follow for two or three days until they came to the area where each fall the elk began gathering for the winter. With luck, they would be back in a week, heavily burdened with fresh elk meat and a good supply of skins that the women could work on during the winter and fashion into clothing. Before the garments were finished, the women would apply the beadwork for which they were famous throughout the Plains and which made Cheyenne products prime trade goods. In the spring, they would meet with their allies, the *Hetane-vo'eo'o* and the *Ho'ohomo'o'eo'o*, the Arapahoes and the Sioux, and swap clothing for other necessities, such as gunpowder and metal for arrow points.

"Come," said Beaver Woman, "and I'll tell you a nice Tsis-tsis-tas story." Taking Puma by the hand, she led him into the tipi and set him by the fire. Pulling him into her lap, she began:

"One day," she said, "a boy named Wihio was walking along the creek when he looked in the water and saw the stream bed covered with wild plums, for which he had special affection. Shedding his leggings, he dived into the creek, but no matter how much he groped along the bottom, he could not feel any plums.

"Climbing back up on the bank, he looked again at the plums. Scolding himself for not diving deep enough, he tied a heavy stone around his neck and again he plunged into the water. But again, he could not find any plums. Besides, with the stone around his neck, he almost drowned.

"Finally, freeing himself of the heavy weight, he swam to the surface with barely any air left in his body. Exhausted, he managed to crawl out on the creek bank, where he lay gasping for breath. Gradually, his strength came back to him and he opened his eyes. Looking upward, he saw over his head a plum tree whose limbs were so burdened with fruit they were about to break."

Pausing for effect, she added: "Wihio, the foolish boy, had seen the reflection of the plums in the water and thought the plums were under the surface."

When Beaver Woman finished the story she broke into a fit of giggling, impressed with her own wit and storytelling ability. Puma, who had sat quietly in almost total incomprehension, stared at her with a blank face. The incongruity of the situation made her laugh still harder until she was doubled over and tears were streaming down her cheeks.

Red Berry Woman poked her head through the flap. "Are you going to sit there all day laughing at your own humor," she said crossly, "or are you going to help me fetch some water?"

Angry Buffalo shifted slightly under the dun-colored hide he had pulled over his head to cover his black hair that would stand out against the fall landscape like a piece of coal in a snow bank.

"Do you believe how lucky we are?" he whispered to Young Bull, who was lying on his stomach next to him, his head also covered. "Morning Star is really working his magic to send most of the Cheyenne warriors on a hunt on the very day we arrive."

Finding the Cheyenne camp had been relatively easy. Knifewielder knew that one of the tribe's band's liked to winter near Beaver Lake so it was simply a matter of traversing the area until they found the village. Their task was made easier because the Cheyenne were not expecting them and had not posted lookouts to warn them of approaching strangers, which, among the Plains tribes, was almost the universal word for "enemy" as well.

Long Chin, the chief of the Cheyenne village, felt completely justified in this since the autumn was not the usual time when villages worried about being attacked. In the fall, the Plains tribes mainly occupied themselves with making sure they had enough food set aside to last them through the winter and that left little time for horse raids or war parties. What the Cheyenne did not know was that this was a special circumstance, that Morning Star only appeared at unpredictable intervals to make his demands on their enemies, the Pawnee. It was the Cheyenne's ill fortune that this was one of those times.

Carefully, the two Pawnee scouts watched the Cheyenne disappear into the forest, heading south. When the last hunter disappeared into the trees, Angry Buffalo turned and counted the number of tipis in the village below.

"That must be most of the village's warriors," he said quietly to Young Bull, quickly computing the number of hunters with the number of tipis. "Anyone left behind will be too old or too young to put up much resistance. This should be as easy as plucking a louse out of your wife's hair."

"Look," Young Bull said excitedly, pointing toward the center of the village.

Angry Buffalo inched forward slightly to see where Young Bull was pointing. As he watched, a woman carrying a water container emerged from one of the tipis. Following her, also carrying a container, was a girl of about fourteen and a boy. Both Young Bull and Angry Buffalo reacted in surprise when they saw the boy's blond hair.

"A captive!" Young Bull exclaimed. "Maybe we should take him, too."

Angry Buffalo glanced at his companion. "No," he said sternly. "Don't talk like that. We're here to find a girl for Morning Star and we mustn't get distracted."

"That's true," agreed Young Bull, "but that's the

same tipi the girl came out of. We could get both of them at once."

"Uuuumm," Angry Buffalo replied. "That's a thought. Let's see what Knifewielder says. Did you mark the tipi in your memory?"

"Yes," Young Bull nodded.

"So did I. I'm sure I can find it in the dark."

Slowly wiggling backward until they were below the level of the boulder on which they had been lying, the two warriors tossed off their skins and, grinning broadly, happily slapped each other on the shoulder. "Knifewielder is going to be very happy with this information," Angry Buffalo predicted.

"What do you think about the boy?" Young Bull asked eagerly.

Knifewielder rubbed his chin. "It is tempting, isn't it?" he replied.

"It would be easy enough to accomplish," Angry Buffalo interjected. "The warrior is gone; there's no one in the lodge except the woman and the two children."

"I could take him," said Young Bull. "I could make sure he offers no trouble."

"As long as we're taking one, we could just as easily take two," Angry Buffalo added.

Knifewielder paced slowly in front of the smoldering fire that they had built in the center of the temporary camp. "No," he said finally. "We leave the boy."

"Why?" Young Bull asked in surprise. "It would be so simple."

"That isn't the point," Knifewielder said. "We're here on a mission for Morning Star. He has blessed our journey because he knows we're here to find a girl for Him. If we let ourselves be diverted, He may withdraw His blessing. Why take the chance?"

"Morning Star doesn't care if we grab the boy, too," Young Bull argued. "As long as we get the girl, He'll be happy."

"No," Knifewielder said sternly. "We've come a long way to accomplish a single objective. Let's not confuse the issue. Impetuosity doesn't pay. Remember, that's how our people got the Cheyenne Medicine Arrows. Their warriors were too impatient to wait for the blessing ceremonies to be completed before they attacked. As a result Shattered Lance captured the holy weapons. Now is not the time to waiver in our duty," Knifewielder said with finality. "Now all of you, go get some sleep. We'll make the raid before dawn tomorrow. In the meantime, I have many preparations to make."

As the men dispersed, Knifewielder walked slowly to the place in the rocks where he had stored the precious Morning Star bundle. Delicately untying the brittle cords, he opened the package and gently removed the items he would need. Then he, too, went to his blanket for a few hours' sleep.

Shortly before midnight, he awoke, alert and well-rested. Making his way among the men, he shook them all awake and told them to form in the middle of their temporary camp. Once they were there, he ordered them to build a large fire while he donned the Morning Star costume. Tradition demanded that he wear the deity's sacred garments so he could appear as much like Morning Star as possible.

Gingerly, Knifewielder dressed himself, garment by garment. Finally, he took the sacred pipe from its protective covering and filled it with tobacco from its place in the leg of the sacred wildcat skin. "You," he said, pointing to Angry Buffalo and handing him the pipe, "will do the ceremonial smoking."

When the pipe was finished he urged the men to

dance around it, commanding them to stab the flames with their lances as if they were the enemy.

Shortly after midnight, as Venus peeked over the eastern horizon, Knifewielder joined the dance. Throwing his arms open wide to the east, Knifewielder said: "Here is the man you have chosen to represent you on this mission. He is wearing the sacred clothing and he is ready to perform your orders. Protect him and make the mission successful."

Ordering the warriors to throw dirt on the fire, he turned in the direction of the Cheyenne village. "Let's go," he said quietly.

At the perimeter of the village, Knifewielder issued the final orders.

"You," he said, designating Dark Eagle, "go to the north side and keep watch there. You," he said, pointing at Rides-the-Bear, "go to the south and make sure the Cheyenne warriors are not returning. When you are certain that all is clear, make a wolf call so we will know there is no problem. Wait a short interval to make sure we are all in place and give a second call, which will signal the start of the raid."

Turning to Walks Fast and Little Fox, he ordered them to infiltrate the area where the Cheyenne kept their horses and, since they arrived on foot, to capture enough for them to use in their escape.

Leading Elk and Prancing Pony would be ready to protect their rear in the unlikely possibility that the Cheyenne tried to pursue them.

That left Angry Buffalo and Young Bull, both of whom had donned their white face paint in accordance with the tradition explained by Red Calf. "You two," he said, "will go to the tipi that you selected earlier and capture the girl."

"Aren't you going with them?" Leading Elk asked, puzzled.

"No," Knifewielder said, shaking his head. "It is my duty to station myself on the east side of the camp so I can be the closest to Morning Star."

As the men were turning to go to their positions, Knifewielder stopped them with a final instruction. "Remember," he said, speaking slowly and distinctly, "this is not a scalp raid. *No one*," he said emphasizing the words, "is to be killed unless it absolutely cannot be prevented. Our task is only to find a girl for Morning Star. We will have plenty of opportunities later to go to war with the Cheyenne."

Red Berry Woman was not sure what disturbed her sleep. Later she would tell Short Hair that it must have been a signal from *Heammawihio*, the Wise One Above. If she had acted immediately, she moaned, she may have been able to avoid what happened. Instead, puzzled by being jerked suddenly from a sound sleep, Red Berry Woman lay wide-eyed in the darkness wondering what had caused her to awaken.

Throwing off her blanket, she padded across the open space in the center of the dwelling and bent over the sleeping Puma. Red Berry Woman frowned, the boy was sleeping soundly and obviously had not cried out. She turned, planning to return to her bed, when Beaver Woman spoke.

"What is it, *Na-hko'e*?" she asked sleepily. "Is it time to make the fire?"

Red Berry Woman smiled. "No," she said. "Go back to sleep. I was awakened by a bad dream and imagined it was Puma calling out."

"Should I climb under the blanket with him?"

"Not unless you want to. You know your father would object. He feels the boy shouldn't be coddled."

"I won't tell."

"I won't either," Red Berry Woman chuckled.

"Just this once," Beaver Woman said, throwing back her sleeping robe.

Red Berry Woman turned, intending to return to her own bed, when the tipi flap flew open. Before she could move, a large man with his face painted as white as snow quickly slipped inside. He was followed by another man, not as large but equally fearful looking.

"What do you want?" Red Berry Woman stammered, knowing the men would not be able to understand her, and could care less if they could.

The men ignored her but looked quickly around the interior. Without speaking, the larger of the two gestured to his companion, pointing toward Beaver Woman.

Instantly, Red Berry Woman realized what was happening. "Oh, no," she exclaimed, sucking in her breath. She had been only a child the last time the Pawnee had raided the village seeking a young girl for their god, Morning Star, but the details of what had happened then came back to her in a flash. The girl's name had been Little Swift Otter, she remembered with amazing clarity, the daughter of Coyote Ear and Big Heart. She was carried away to the Pawnee village and the following spring she was killed in a sacrifice. Coyote Ear, who had a long list of war honors, did not try to fight the Pawnee who barged into their lodge. "It was the will of the gods," he explained. "For me to have resisted would have been unthinkable."

Months later, though, he extracted his revenge. As the leader of a war party, Coyote Ear attacked the Pawnee camp and personally killed two warriors, one of whom was the one who had captured his daughter. Their scalps still flew from his lance.

Coyote Ear may have had his code, Red Berry Woman told herself, but I'm not a warrior, I'm not bound by their silly standards that dictate when to fight and when to be passive. Bunching her legs under her, she sprang at the closest Pawnee, Young Bull. Using her nails like a bear climbing a tree, she dug in with as much force as possible. Grunting with the effort, she pulled her hands downward as hard as she could, raking Young Bull's cheeks.

"*Iieee!*" she exclaimed in satisfaction when twin streams of blood bubbled to the surface, staining the bone white paint he had so carefully applied.

Young Bull, who had not expected opposition, reeled backward in surprise, cursing and struggling to maintain his balance.

Red Berry Woman did not plan to give him time to recover. Following up on her advantage, she jumped on his chest, locking her legs around his waist. As he tumbled to the ground, Red Berry Woman sank her teeth into his shoulder and bit as hard as she could. With jaw and neck muscles made strong by years of tearing tough meat, she twisted her head and tore free a fist-sized chunk of flesh and muscle. Spitting out the loathsome hunk of Pawnee deltoid tissue, she focused her eyes on the pulsating vein in his neck, determined to try to rip his throat with her teeth.

Angry Buffalo, reacting quickly, swung his lance, catching Red Berry Woman on the side of her head with the butt of the weapon. The force of the blow caused her to loosen her hold on Young Bull, who pushed her off his chest with such force that she went reeling across the lodge, landing on her back. "Ooooff,' she exclaimed as her breath went out of her.

Young Bull pounced. Drawing his knife, he was ready to slit Red Berry Woman's throat when Angry Buffalo threw his arm around his companion's neck and pulled him off.

"Remember what Knifewielder said," he whispered

harshly in Young Bull's ear. "No killing unless its absolutely necessary."

For a second, Angry Buffalo feared he was going to have to fight Young Bull as well. Then the rage in the warrior's eyes subsided. Using the handle of his knife like a club, Young Bull hit Red Berry Woman just above her left temple, knocking her unconscious. Then he turned to the cowering Beaver Woman.

He was reaching for her, intending to grab her by her shoulder, when Puma attacked. Lowering his head, the boy charged like a ram, his head aimed precisely at Young Bull's groin. With a soft thud, he contacted solidly. The result was instantaneous. With a roar of pain, Young Bull doubled over and vomited on his moccasins.

Angry Buffalo could no longer contain his merriment. To him, the spectacle of a Pawnee warrior being bloodied first by a Cheyenne squaw and then by a small, blond-haired boy sent him into peels of raucous laughter. If it had not been necessary for them to grab the girl and make their escape before the whole camp was aroused, Angry Buffalo would have enjoyed standing back and watching to see what Young Bull would do. But his sense of duty overcame his curiosity.

Casually swinging his arm, Angry Buffalo backhanded Puma, hitting the boy squarely in the face. With an audible crunch, the boy's nose flattened and a shower of blood flew upward. The force of the blow sent him staggering against one of the uprights that supported the tipi. When he hit, his head jerked back and bounced resoundingly against the pine log. As Angry Buffalo watched in amusement, the boy's eyes went out of focus and he slid to the ground, blood from his broken nose streaming down his chin.

"Come on," Angry Buffalo said, as if reluctant to end the entertainment. With one fluid motion he scooped up

Beaver Woman and tucked her under his arm. With his other hand, he grabbed Young Bull. Forcing him erect, he pushed him out the opening and toward the east, where Knifewielder and the horses would be waiting.

Slowly, Red Berry Woman regained consciousness. The kaleidoscope that had been flashing behind her eyes began to dim. In its place was a horrendous, dull ache in her head. An even deeper pain stabbed through her heart when she looked at Beaver Woman's empty bed. As she crouched in a ball, unsure what to do next, she was only vaguely aware of Puma's sobbing.

Still slumped against the sturdy pole, Puma, tears mingling with the blood from his broken nose, stared into the near distance. *"Ich will zu meine Mutter,"* he mumbled.

As soon as he saw Angry Buffalo and Young Bull approaching, Knifewielder hurried to meet them, scurrying through the frost-encrusted grass. When he saw Young Bull bleeding copiously from the wound on his shoulder, vomit still dribbling from his chin, Knifewielder stopped and stared. "What happened?" he asked, turning to Angry Buffalo.

His friend chuckled. "It's too long a story to go into right now. I'll tell you later," he said.

As they spoke, Walks Fast and Little Fox appeared with a string of horses, enough so there would be one for each man. Still clad in his Morning Star costume, Knifewielder swung atop one, and lifted Beaver Woman up to ride with him.

"Were there any problems?" Knifewielder asked Angry Buffalo.

"No. Other than Young Bull had his hands full."

"Good," Knifewielder replied. Looking around, he counted heads to make sure everyone was present. "We have a long ride," he said, digging his heels into his horse's ribs.

They traveled all that day and most of the night, pausing only for a three-hour sleep period just before dawn. By late the next afternoon they were almost back to Pumpkin-Vine Village.

While they were still a few miles out, Knifewielder reined his horse to a sudden halt and leaped to the ground. Quickly making a fire, he collected and lit several branches and instructed his men to spread out, setting fire to the dried grass.

"When Red Calf sees the smoke, he will know we are returning with a captive girl," Knifewielder explained to Angry Buffalo. "Then he can prepare the village to celebrate our return."

After the grass had burned for several minutes, Knifewielder walked into the ashes and scooped up a handful. Happily, he smeared his face with soot since blackened countenances on members of a returning raiding party was a sign that they had attained their goal.

The dancing and chanting that followed the raiding party's return went on for two days before Battle Cry, the village chief, called a reluctant halt. "Winter is fast approaching," he explained. "We need to complete one more buffalo hunt before the snows come to make sure we have enough meat to last until Spring."

The next morning, the hunters set out, preceded by scouts who searched the hills and valleys for signs of the buffalo. Riding alongside Knifewielder during the expedition was Beaver Woman, who was just beginning her unknowing role in a ritual that would not be completed until the following April.

Communicating with the girl through sign language, Knifewielder indicated that she was to select a fat buffalo cow for him to kill. While she let her eyes roam among the buffalo that were moving at a leisurely pace a quarter of a mile away, the other Pawnees remained out of sight, hidden in one of the arroyos that crisscrossed the plain. Before they set out, Red Calf had made it clear: The general hunt was not to commence until Knifewielder has slain the designated cow.

Finally, Beaver Woman focused on a young female that was trotting along near the edge of the herd. That one, she indicated, pointing.

Knifewielder urged his horse forward. As he came racing up, the buffalo spooked and their trot turned into a mad dash. Keeping the cow that Beaver Woman had marked in his view, Knifewielder closed the distance.

Sensing the Indian's presence, the cow swiveled her head and rolled her eyes in fear.

Smiling in anticipation, Knifewielder notched an arrow and raised his bow. Just as he was about to loose the missile, the cow dipped her head and tried to hook Knifewielder's horse.

Specially trained for the hunt, the horse nimbly sidestepped the horns, then plunged in closer. Knifewielder's arrow buried itself up to its feathers in the animal's side, just below the hump.

When the cow's front legs buckled and the animal went nose first into the ground, Knifewielder yelled in triumph. Using his shout as the signal, the other Pawnee raced out of the arroyo and attacked the herd. Their intention was to fell as many animals as possible before the buffalo disappeared over the horizon.

While the others kept after the fleeing animals, not stopping until all their arrows were exhausted, Knifewielder yanked his horse to a halt.

Slipping to the ground, bow in hand, he approached the cow warily. More than one hunter, he knew, had been killed by a buffalo he thought was dead.

When he was certain the cow was finished, he rushed

up to the animal and drew his knife. Before the hunt, Red Calf had instructed him about what he must do. Plunging his instrument into the animal's side, he made a slit large enough to accommodate his hand. Sticking his fist into the wound, he groped for the heart, which he removed with a mighty yank.

Turning his attention to the cow's head, he pried open the jaws and firmly grasped the tongue, pulling it as far forward as it would go. With a quick slice, he severed the organ, putting it and the heart into a special parfleche he had brought along for just that purpose.

"Bring me the heart and the tongue," Red Calf had commanded. "I will dry them and put them in a special place. We'll need them in the ceremony."

Having done his duty, Knifewielder gave himself a reward. Enlarging the wound in the buffalo's side that he had made with his knife, Knifewielder reached again into the cow's steaming body cavity and found the liver. Removing it intact, he set it on the carcass, then plunged his hand back into the hole. Groping, he found the gall bladder, which he dislodged and sliced open, sprinkling the liquid over the liver as a seasoning. Finally, he carved off a large hunk of the organ and popped it into his mouth.

As Beaver Woman rode up to join him, Knifewielder cut off another large piece, which he handed to her. Eagerly, she tore off a bite. For several minutes they remained frozen in place, the girl astride a young pony, the warrior standing by her side, chewing vigorously and grinning at each other, their lips smeared with blood and gall. Eat well, Knifewielder thought, studying Beaver Woman. It is essential that you remain happy and healthy through the long, cold months ahead.

Blizzard slammed his open palms together, causing a clap that reverberated like thunder in Scalptaker's snug tipi. "I still say," he argued hotly, "that we should have attacked the fort while we had the chance. Now that reinforcements have arrived, that opportunity has fled."

"We've been through this a hundred times," Fire-in-the-Hills replied tiredly. "It would have served no useful purpose. We showed our mettle by annihilating those soldiers and that cursed interpreter, whose scalp, by the way, is a proud addition to my collection."

"Don't be a fool," Blizzard replied. "Do you believe the *isan hanska* have learned a lesson from this? If you think they're not at this very moment planning an attack against us, you're living in a dream world."

"Of course they're planning an attack," said Scalptaker, the eldest member of the council of the Wazhazha band of the Brulé Sioux. Formerly composed of eight warriors, only seven were gathered in Scalptaker's lodge. The eighth member, Conquering Bear, who gained distinction by signing for the Sioux on the Treaty of Fort Laramie, the pact the Brulé called the Treaty of the Long Meadows, died of wounds suffered in the fight with Lieutenant Grattan and his men. "That's why they have new men. But when they attack, it will be them who are breaking the treaty, not us."

"As if that makes a difference," Blizzard spat.

"It does to some of us," Fire-in-the-Hills replied, voicing yet again his disagreement with practically everything Blizzard said. An aging but nonetheless brave fighter, Fire-in-the-Hills never tried to keep secret his antagonism toward Blizzard, whom he considered hotheaded and impetuous.

"Can't you two agree on anything?" asked Badger, a bull-like warrior in his late twenties famous for his zest for combat and his skill with a bow. "Can you at least concede," he continued with a smile, "that the sun is shining brightly outside and we could be enjoying it rather than sitting in this musty enclosure listening to arguments we have heard time and time again?"

"I'm glad to see that your humor has returned," Fire-in-the-Hills said with a smile. "Now that Summer Rain is pregnant does life seem livable once again?"

"Indeed it does," nodded Badger. "It is time to consign Broken Antler's death to the past. Summer Rain's growing belly has made me realize that life must go on."

"If you ask me," Blizzard interjected, "I think your wife's pregnancy has addled your brain as well. What has happened to the old Badger that used to take great pride in lifting scalps and counting coup?"

"He still exists," Badger replied, "but now he has learned how to temper his impulses. He has, perhaps, come to realize that the warrior who picks his fights carefully lives to fight another day."

"Are you saying that we would have been defeated if we had attacked the fort when I wanted to?"

"No," Badger said. "That's not what I'm saying. We would have taken many scalps, but we also would have lost too many of our warriors in the process. No one here," he said, sweeping his arm around the circle to acknowledge the presence of the other warriors, "doubts that we could have inflicted serious losses against the White soldiers. But it was a battle we do not yet have to fight. It is better if we use the winter to regroup and build alliances with other bands. That way we can be more prepared to meet the soldiers when they come against us next summer, as surely they will."

"I don't agree with that," said Roaring Thunder, who loomed as the most likely successor to Conquering Bear as the band's leader. Although the Brulé had no single chief there always existed a man whose wisdom and bravery was more valued. "I think the isan hanska realize we are not to be trifled with. They must know that it was a violation of the treaty when they sent their men into our camp, and that they paid the price for their foolishness. I predict it will lead to a stronger understanding between us, not more warfare."

"You sound like an old woman," Blizzard said surlily, leaning forward to massage the large, almost-healed wound on his right thigh, a souvenir of an attack against an emigrant train the previous August. "At least the *Sihiyena* still act like brave men," he added.

"That attack you conducted with the Cheyenne was pointless," said Buffalo Heart, normally one of the least outspoken members of the council. "It has caused us much grief."

"Pointless, eh?" sneered Blizzard, straightening his shoulders. When he moved, the muscles along his back and chest rippled mightily, causing the scars that decorated his upper body to jump and twitch, like a double handful of dark insects. "Tell that to the Cheyenne who went home with the blond scalps and the two White children."

"It was successful in the sense that the Sihiyena captured trophies," said Fire-in-the-Hills, "but it also was the indirect cause of our current problems. If you and Bellowing Moose had not joined up with the Cheyenne to attack the emigrants, those soldiers would not have come into our camp at all. Conquering Bear would still be sitting here telling us yet again about the wonderful pipe he got in trade with the Cheyenne and what a great man he was. Don't forget, it was *you* that the soldiers were looking for."

"Are you suggesting I should have surrendered, like a whipped dog?"

"Of course not!" replied Fire-in-the-Hills. "The soldiers' arrogance could not have been tolerated under any circumstances. They are the ones who fired first, but that is a point that probably will count for nothing in the long run."

"What are you proposing now?" Jagged Blade asked. A large, fearless warrior, Jagged Blade also was the most slow-witted member of the council and often the butt of cruel jokes, all of which he took good-naturedly. "Do you still want to attack the fort?"

"No!" Blizzard said sharply. "Not now. That opportunity has passed. But that doesn't mean we should sit on our rumps while the Whites continue to rape the land, scattering the herds that we depend upon for our very existence. We should explore other ways of exacting revenge against the Whites. We should probe for more weaknesses and find new targets."

"But the emigrant trains have stopped for the season," said Jagged Blade. "It's too close to winter."

"The emigrants and the soldiers aren't the only potential marks," Blizzard said impatiently. "Remember the prizes we got from the *Ikace wasicu*'s store."

"And risked our annuities in the process," Fire-in-the-Hills shot back. "Even if the Frenchman deserved it because of the way he has cheated our people in trades."

"Are we going to talk about the annuities again?" Blizzard asked scornfully. "They are just bribes meant to allow the Whites to control us. They tempt us with trinkets and paltry rewards, while their real purpose is to divert us. They hope that by throwing us a few scraps we won't notice while they take away the thing that is most valuable to us: our freedom."

"There is much truth in what Blizzard says," conceded Badger. "At first, there were only a few Whites and they respectfully asked permission to cross our lands on their journey across the mountains. Now the number is staggering; more come each year. In the process, they strip the land of trees, pollute the rivers and streams, and scatter the buffalo, which are vital to our existence. Each year since the Whites appeared, we have had to search harder for the herds."

"Mark my words," Blizzard said forcefully. "The day is coming when we will have to come to final terms with the Whites. I predict that before Badger's new child is thoroughly weaned, we will be fighting the White soldiers as earnestly as we now fight the *Kangi* and the *Padani*."

"But the Crow and the Pawnee are respected warriors," Jagged Blade said, missing Blizzard's point. "The White soldiers are soft and stupid. If it were not for their rifles, they would not be a threat."

"And their numbers," added Fire-in-the-Hills. "There are now more than a hundred new men at the fort, and I fear that we have just begun to see the full potential."

"Exactly my point," Blizzard said heatedly. "We must obliterate them while we have the chance."

"I disagree!" Fire-in-the-Hills replied. "Instead of

fighting them we have to prove that we are worthy of their respect and *unless* they want to fight us, they are going to have to honor our traditions."

"Huh!" Blizzard grunted. "A buffalo will grow wings and soar like an eagle before that happens."

"That doesn't mean we should not try to negotiate," said Scalptaker, reaching for his pouch of shongsasha. "Let us smoke and discuss the alternatives."

"Well, what did she say?" White Crane asked eagerly, his face aglow.

"Who?" replied Crooked Leg, struggling to keep his face a blank.

"*Who?*" White Crane asked incredulously. "Don't play innocent with me. You know who I'm talking about. Porcupine."

"Oh," Crooked Leg replied, averting his eyes. "Her."

"Of course, *her*," said White Crane. "Did you think I was talking about old Buffalo Woman who doesn't even have enough teeth left to chew her pemmican? Porcupine's the one you're interested in; the one you tried to impress by giving her father that magnificent gelding. Did Red Leaf appreciate it, by the way."

"Oh, yes," Crooked Leg replied, hoping he could change the subject. "He was very grateful. Said he couldn't wait until the winter hunt to give him a good run."

"So you have won her father's attention. I'm impressed. But what about Porcupine?"

"I . . . I . . . I'm not sure," Crooked Leg stammered. "I tried to throw my robe over her, but there were so many people coming and going at her tipi that she got embarrassed and ran inside."

"Well, you know she's fond of you, don't you?" White Crane pressed. "That's what her cousin, White Wolf, told you."

"But he's just a *boy*," Crooked Leg said. "He doesn't *know* anything."

"He may be young but he's not deaf," White Crane persisted. "He hears the girls talking at the stream; they don't guard their conversation around him. Anyway, what do you plan to do about it? You can't just afford to sit back and wait. I know that Otter has been eyeing her, too. You aren't just going to step aside and let him take her away, are you?"

"She's not mine to begin with," Crooked Leg replied logically. "How can he take her away?"

"You're playing word games. You know what I meant," White Crane teased, poking his friend's shoulder.

"If you insist on knowing," Crooked Leg said quietly, "even though it's really none of your business, I've been to see Deer Dreamer."

"The shaman?" White Crane asked, surprised.

"Shhhh," Crooked Leg cautioned, holding a finger to his lips. "Can't you keep anything to yourself? Do you have to tell the whole camp?"

"Sorry," White Crane laughed. "You just surprised me, that's all. What's he going to do?"

"He's making me a magic flute," Crooked Leg whispered. "And he's going to teach me the magic music to go with it, the tune that will put her under my spell."

"No doubt he's going to carve an image of a horse on the flute as well. Am I correct?"

It was Crooked Leg's turn to be surprised. "How did you know that?"

"It just figures," White Crane replied. "Everyone knows the horse is a very determined animal, sexually speaking. And you *did* give a horse to Porcupine's father, didn't you?"

"A gelding," Crooked Leg corrected him. "Not a stallion."

"Well, he was once a stallion," White Crane laughed.

"Like I was once a promising warrior," Crooked Leg said somberly, pointing to his damaged leg which had been shattered by a Crow miniball during a horse raid more than six months earlier.

"Quit talking like that," White Crane said severely. "Your life isn't over just because you were wounded."

"My name used to be Running Antelope," Crooked Leg said bitterly. "But now, thanks to that Crow, I'll never run again. I'll be lucky if it heals well enough for me to walk with no more than a very noticeable limp."

"Does it still hurt?" White Crane asked solicitously, gingerly prodding the jagged red scar.

"Of course it still hurts," Crooked Leg winced. "But not nearly as much as before."

"I have an idea," White Crane said brightly.

"Uh oh," Crooked Leg grimaced. "I've seen your ideas at work before."

"No," White Crane grinned. "This is different. How long before Deer Dreamer finishes making your flute?"

"I don't know," Crooked Leg shrugged. "You can't put a time limit on something like that. Making the flute is the easy part; it's writing the music that's so hard. Deer Dreamer has to fast and pray for the proper tune to come to him in a vision."

"It's going to be several days anyway, isn't it?"

"At least that," Crooked Leg agreed.

"So in the meantime, why don't we go on a hunt? You haven't been away from the camp since you were wounded. It would do you good to get away for a few days. We'll take Bear's Ear with us."

"Bear's Ear?" Crooked Leg asked, amazed. "He's only ten."

White Crane laughed. "That's only a few years younger than us. Have you forgotten what's it's like to be ten? You're too old to play boy's games and not old enough to join the men."

"No," Crooked Leg said, nodding. "I remember all too well what it's like to be ten."

"We'll get a couple of elk and you can bring the hide back and ask Porcupine to make you a pair of leggings to keep you warm in the cold winds of the Moon of the Terrible."

"For once," Crooked Leg beamed, "you've had a fairly decent idea. When do you think we can go?"

White Crane shrugged. "Tomorrow. We'll be back in three or four days and by then Deer Dreamer may have your flute ready. Then all you'll have to do is play your magic tune and Porcupine will come running into your arms."

"Will you stop it?" Crooked Leg said in mock anger. Twisting his hands together nervously, he looked pleadingly at his friend. "Do you think magic flutes really work?" he asked.

"All you want to do is talk," Blizzard said angrily. "Talking isn't going to make the situation any more palatable. The first thing we have to realize is that the Whites are as much our enemies as the Crow. If it had been a group of Kangi that attacked our camp and killed Conquering Bear, we wouldn't be sitting here discussing the propriety of revenge. We'd put together a war party and go looking for Crow scalps."

"But we've already extracted revenge," Scalptaker said. "We killed thirty-one Whites and we only lost one warrior."

"Plus," Fire-in-the-Hills added, "we plundered the Frenchman's trading post and captured half a hundred horses in the raid on the unguarded herd at the fort."

"So now you are content to sit back and wait for the Whites to make the next move?" Blizzard asked sarcastically.

"That's the way it's always been," said Roaring Thunder. "We attack the Crow or Pawnee, then they attack us. And so it shifts back and forth. It's the way our life has always been."

"That's because you recognize the fact that the Crow and Pawnee are our enemies," Blizzard said. "We must now realize that the Whites are just as much our adversaries as the others."

"Blizzard's right," agreed Jagged Blade. "We cannot allow the soldiers' attack to go unrevenged. They came into *our* camp; we didn't go into theirs."

"Wait!" Fire-in-the-Hills said, raising his hands, palms outward. "We have to put this in perspective."

"You mean subjugate ourselves to the Whites," Blizzard sneered.

"No! That's not what I mean," Fire-in-the-Hills replied sharply. "We *know* the Crow and the Pawnee are our enemies because we've been fighting them as long as anyone can remember. But the Whites are newly arrived in our world. We have to consider if we're going to make them our bitter foes or accept them as allies, as we have done with the Cheyenne."

"But the Cheyenne, when they first came among us, indicated a desire for peace," said Badger, entering the discussion. "The Whites have made no such move."

"How about the Treaty of the Long Meadows?" asked Fire-in- the-Hills.

"Yes!" Blizzard said angrily. "What about the treaty? It had no sooner been signed than White soldiers went into the camp of our cousins, the Miniconjou, and opened fire. Have you forgotten that?" he said loudly.

"That's true," agreed Roaring Thunder.

"It is a fact," said Jagged Blade.

"But," interjected Scalptaker, playing the role of devil's advocate, "that was not entirely unprovoked. Remember, one of the Miniconjou fired first."

"That's not an excuse," said Badger.

"I didn't intend it as an excuse," Scalptaker fired back. "I'm merely pointing out the facts."

"And the recent incident," said Fire-in-the-Hills, looking pointedly at Blizzard, "was precipitated by the attack on the wagon train, the one which you helped plan and carry out."

Blizzard shrugged. "You exaggerate my role. The instigator was Brown Hawk. If he were still alive, he'd tell you that himself. Besides him, four other warriors also were killed, including Bellowing Moose. Are you willing to go to Bellowing Moose's widow and tell her we should forgive his death? It is not the *Sichangu* way to forgive. Our code demands revenge."

"Revenge against whom?" Scalptaker asked earnestly. "It was not the soldiers who killed Bellowing Moose and the Cheyenne."

"But they *did* kill Conquering Bear," Blizzard argued.

"This argument is getting us nowhere," Fire-in-the-Hills sighed. "Blizzard wants to attack any White we find in our territory, whether they are soldiers or not."

"Whites are Whites," said Badger. "I agree with Blizzard on that."

"Then you're foolish," shouted Fire-in-the-Hills. "We must exercise discretion in picking our enemies. Whites beyond number — more Whites than we could ever imagine — have passed through our country in the last few years. What if they decided not to continue westward? What if they decided to stay here? We could not possibly fight that many and hope to emerge victorious."

"The treaty prohibits them from staying, except for the soldiers," Roaring Thunder pointed out.

"That's my point exactly!" Fire-in-the-Hills exclaimed. "If we break the treaty by killing every White we see, then the Whites can say we have broken the treaty and they will have an excuse to break it as well."

"No, no, no," Blizzard said hotly. "If we don't prove to the Whites that we're not willing to sit idly by while they come into our camp *in violation of the treaty agreement*," he emphasized, "then they will feel free to treat us without respect. If we don't respond *now* to the violation the Whites will believe they can break the treaty whenever they wish as long as it is to their advantage."

"The Treaty of the Long Meadows is not a perfect agreement," conceded Scalptaker. "Perhaps we should seek another council to modify the terms."

"No!" said Blizzard. "*You* seek another council. I believe stronger action is necessary. I'm weary of all this talk. I plan to seek revenge against the Whites."

"You're pushing a boulder over the edge of the cliff," Fire-in-the-Hills warned. "You may be starting an avalanche."

"Then so be it," replied Blizzard. "I plan to raid the Whites. Who will go with me?"

"Not I," Fire-in-the-Hills replied quickly.

"Nor I," echoed Scalptaker.

"I won't go because I think you're acting too rashly," said Roaring Thunder.

"I'll go," said Jagged Blade. "I'm getting bored sitting around all day. I'd like to see some action."

"How about you?" Blizzard asked, turning to Badger.

"I don't know. I'm as worried as you about the potential threat, but I'm not certain that a raid right now is the right move."

"Well, think about. I plan to leave in three days. I'm sure there will be other warriors in the camp who would welcome the opportunity."

Fire-in-the-Hills shook his head slowly from side to side. "No one is going to try to stop you," he said carefully. "It is not our way. But I hope you know what you're doing; I hope you realize the consequences it could have for all of us."

"It will be on my conscience," Blizzard replied. "At least I know I will be fulfilling my obligation as a Brulé warrior."

White Crane stood impatiently outside Crooked Leg's tipi, shuffling nervously from foot to foot. "Aren't you ready yet?" he called.

"What's taking him so long?" Bear's Ear asked, stroking his pony's neck.

"Who knows," White Crane replied with a shrug. "Maybe it just takes him longer because of his crippled leg."

"Do you wish Blizzard had asked you to go along" Bear's Ear asked in his adolescent squeak. "I would have given anything to go with them."

"No," White Crane said, shaking his head. "I've been on one raid where Blizzard was the *blotahunka* and that was enough to last me for a while."

"That was the one in which Storm Cloud died wasn't it?"

White Crane nodded. "It's hard to fault Blizzard. Storm Cloud broke his back in a fall and as leader of the group Blizzard didn't have any choice. We couldn't carry Storm Cloud with us and there was no point in staying with him. He wasn't going to get any better."

"So Blizzard just suffocated him?"

"It was the right thing to do. It's just that I can't forget the look in Blizzard's eyes. He looked like he enjoyed it."

Bear's Ear shuddered. "I hope I never break *my* back," he said. "Or have any other accident like that. When I die, I want to die as a warrior."

"Why are you talking about dying?" White Crane laughed. "You're only ten. You won't even be going on a horse raid for another six or seven years."

"Well," Bear's Ear blushed, "I'm just thinking ahead. I won't always be ten."

"That's too true," Crooked Leg, emerging from his lodge. "I wish I were ten again. No cares. No problems. No lifetime deformity."

"Will you quit feeling sorry for yourself," White Crane said, annoyed. "If you're going to cry all during this hunt I'd just as soon you stayed home. You're going to have to learn to put the past behind you. Accept your fate and move on."

Crooked Leg nodded, chastised. "You're right, of course. It's just that it's very difficult being eighteen and knowing you're never, ever going to walk right again."

"You could be dead," Bear's Ear ventured. "And you would be if it hadn't been for White Crane."

"The cub speaks," White Crane chuckled. "Before we leave you have to understand your position."

"And what's that?" Bear's Ear asked anxiously.

"We asked you to go because we thought it might be instructional," White Crane said officiously. "You have to learn how to get along in the company of men."

"I thought you were asking me because you wanted someone to do the cooking," Bear's Ear grinned.

"He has you there," Crooked Leg guffawed.

"Well, you're going to have to do that, too. It's part of the lesson. You're also going to have to tend our horses and make sure our knives are sharp."

"If that's all you need you could have brought a girl," Bear's Ear complained.

"No, we couldn't have done that," White Crane insisted. "Those are chores that every potential warrior has to learn how to perform. I had to do them. And so did Crooked Leg. You should be happy that we're allowing you to accompany us. You couldn't ask for two more congenial teachers."

"I have a feeling this is going to be a long trip," said Bear's Ear.

"It's going to be longer if you don't quit talking and get moving. Are you ready?" he asked Crooked Leg.

"Let's go," he replied, pulling himself aboard his horse.

"Did you tell Porcupine good-bye?" White Crane asked with a wink.

"Will you stop that?" Crooked Leg said, irritated. "We're not married."

"Much to your disappointment," White Crane laughed, digging his heels into his horse's sides. "On the other hand, if you were, I'd *never* be able to get you out of the tipi."

Jean Benoit stood patiently over the woodstove in the corner of his second-floor room on the back side of Old Bedlam, slowly spooning hot water from the heavy iron skillet into the mouth of the long-necked French coffeepot.

"Can't you hurry it a bit?" Dobbs asked good-naturedly. "If you don't get a move on," he added, rubbing his stomach, "it'll be time for supper."

"You're incredible," Benoit laughed. "You eat more than I do but you're so skinny you have to keep sand in your pockets so the wind won't blow you away."

"I can't help it if Mother Nature has been especially kind to me," Dobbs grinned, stretching to his full six-feet-two. "I've not only been blessed with an excellent appetite and a superb digestive system, but I didn't get passed over in the good lucks department, either."

Benoit looked closely at his friend, to see if he was joking. He was. With his long chin, pointed nose and close-set blue eyes, Dobbs had no illusions about his physical attractiveness.

"You're right, there," Benoit said, going along with the jest. "If you aren't careful, Frau Schmidt is going to be setting her hooks into you."

"I just wish that would happen," Dobbs said. "I don't care if she's a dozen years older than me. She can make it up in other ways. God, that woman can cook."

"But she can't make coffee like me," Benoit quipped, spooning more water into the pot.

"Why don't you just pour it into the pot like everyone else does?"

Benoit shot him a shocked look. "Pour in the water? For real French coffee?"

"It would be quicker."

"As my mother would say," Benoit replied, "'Do you want it quick, or do you want it good?' If you want it good, this is the only way to do it. A spoonful at a time. Besides, it's almost ready. Hand me your cup."

"You homesick yet?" Dobbs asked, watching Benoit as he poured a couple of ounces of thick, dark liquid into the cup, then topped it off with water from a steaming kettle. Taking the cup from Benoit, he lifted it slowly to his thin, almost colorless lips, blowing gently. "Aaaahhh," he said dreamily, taking a tentative sip.

"Maybe just a little," Benoit shrugged. "Getting homesick that is. But it's going to get worse if the stage doesn't start running again soon so I get a packet from home. Dried red beans, rice, and Cajun coffee," he said, licking his lips. "Essentials the Army, in all its munificence, fails to provide."

"Look at the bright side. You're getting a lot of fresh air and exercise, the best medical care money can provide, and loyal companionship. What else could you ask for?"

"Boiled shrimp!" Benoit chuckled. "Jambalaya! Hot boudin! A plate of . . . "

"Now who's talking about food," Dobbs laughed.

Placing his elbows on the table, he slowly sipped his coffee. "Aren't you going to open your mail?" he asked, pointing with his chin to the three envelopes sitting between them on the table.

"In a bit," said Benoit, sipping delicately from his own cup. "It's like Christmas presents. I like to wait; let the anticipation build. That way, I can form a mental picture of the writer and ponder about what's inside that's worth communicating. Didn't you get anything?"

"Not much," Dobbs shrugged. "A brief report from my former sister-in-law saying that Patrick and Mary Margaret are fine. Growing like weeds."

"You miss 'em much?"

"Oh, hell yes," Dobbs said emphatically. "But they're much better off where they are. After their mother died there was no way I could take care of them. Thank God, for Agnes and Sean."

"It must be tough," Benoit commiserated.

"Its been a bitch," Dobbs said more abruptly than he intended. "But I heard from one of my former patient's, too," he added with forced cheerfulness, trying to change the subject. "A grateful sergeant thanking me for saving his life at Mexico City."

"That should make you feel good."

"Well, I'm glad he's alive," Dobbs nodded. "But I had to take his left arm off just below the shoulder. Grapeshot."

"Like you say, he's alive."

"He trained to be a watchmaker before he joined the Army," Dobbs frowned. "Wonder how he's making a living now? His letter didn't say."

"Did you lose many during the campaign?" Benoit asked soberly.

The surgeon nodded grimly. "Too many," he said. "Disease got a lot of them. Cholera. Fever. Pneumonia. Tetanus. The wounded went to infection. Gangrene is dreadful. You don't ever want it to happen to you. Blood poisoning, too. Also, a lot of 'em simply bled to death on the battlefield. Couldn't get 'em back to my surgery tent fast enough. Smallpox was bad, too," he said, slowly shaking his head. "That's why I was so careful to pack a supply of vaccine. If I could just convince the troops out here — the Indians, too, for that matter — that it works, I could save a lot of lives. The Indians have really been ravaged. That's one of the things that's on the top of my list for Kemp. I want him to order every trooper on the post to get inoculated."

Dobbs paused, looking at Benoit. "Did they inoculate you at the Point?" he asked.

Benoit shook his head. "No. There was some talk about it but the superintendent didn't believe in it. Does it really work?"

"Sure as hell does," Dobbs said emphatically.

"How?" Benoit asked. "How does giving someone one disease prevent another?"

Dobbs smiled. "Sounds crazy, doesn't it? The way it works is the vaccine is made from cowpox, which is similar to the smallpox strain that attacks people. The dose is strong enough to cause a mild case of cowpox, but that provides immunity against the more powerful — and more deadly — smallpox."

"You don't get sick at all?"

"Oh, maybe a little. You might run a low fever for a couple of days. And you get a sore at the point of inoculation, but that heals pretty quickly. When the scab drops off you have a scar, but that's a small price to pay for the immunity. Believe me, you don't want to get smallpox."

"More?" asked Benoit, reaching for the pot.

"Sure," Dobbs replied, proffering his cup. "Looks to me," he said, gesturing again at the letters, "judging from the handwriting, like they're all from women."

"It's going to drive you crazy, isn't it?" Benoit chuckled.

"Just my natural curiosity."

"This one," Benoit said, lifting the top envelope, "is from my sister. She's probably telling me all about her love life: her latest beau and the parties she's been to. She's also probably complaining about our younger brother and the mischief he's been up to. What the hell, he's fifteen. What does she expect?"

"Okay," Dobbs replied, reaching for the second envelope. "What about this one?"

"That's my mother," Benoit replied. "She's going to be bubbling with news about the city, the latest developments in her social set, and what cases my father has taken on. *That* part is going to be pretty dull. I can't imagine anything more boring than being a lawyer, especially one specializing in maritime law."

"And this one?"

"Ah ha," Benoit said, frowning. "That's very interesting. I have no idea what that one is going to say."

Dobbs looked at it closely. "Mlle. Marie Fontenot, eh? Posted in Washington. Your former landlady perhaps? The woman at the library reminding you about an overdue book?" He held it to his nose. "A whiff of lavender. Maybe it's something a little more, uh, personal."

"She's a friend," Benoit said, blushing slightly.

"Oh," said Dobbs, his eyes twinkling. "How good a *friend*?"

"She's the daughter of Emile Fontenot."

"The senior senator from Louisiana?" Dobbs asked, arching his eyebrows. "I'm impressed. I didn't know you traveled in those circles."

"A friend of my sister's."

"And of yours, too, undoubtedly. Although probably not in the same vein," he teased.

"Oh, give it here," Benoit said, snatching it from his

friend's hand. "You aren't going to give me any peace until you know what she's written. I swear, Jace, sometimes you're worse than an old lady."

"The word 'chaperone' might be more appropriate," he said with a grin. "I feel responsible for your moral condition. From what I've seen of your sexual appetites, if I were speaking professionally, I'd say you suffer from satyriasis."

"That's not fair," Benoit protested.

"Not fair!" Dobbs said with a twinkle in his eye. "As a British friend of mine once said to one of our classmates in medical school, 'I swear, 'arold, you put your penis into places where I would not insert the tip of my brolly.'"

Benoit grunted, lifting one of the envelopes. Slitting it with the handle of his spoon, he removed two sheets of fine paper.

"What a beautiful hand," Dobbs commented.

"The nuns teach some things besides catechism," Benoit said distractedly, scanning the letter.

Benoit's eyes widened. "Well, I'll be damned!" he exclaimed. "Just what I need!"

"She's getting married," Dobbs ventured. "Giving you the old heave-ho."

"More serious than that," said Benoit.

"She's pregnant. You're going to be a daddy."

"No," Benoit said, giving Dobbs an annoyed look. "Worse. She's coming here."

"Coming *here*?" Dobbs asked in surprise. "To Fort Laramie? All the way from Washington just to see you? By God, that *does* sound serious."

"No, no," Benoit stammered. "I mean it isn't exactly like that."

"Sounds that way to me."

"Senator Carruthers is resigning because of ill health," Benoit explained, reading quickly, "and her father is being named to replace him as chairman of the Senate committee overseeing the army. To get a feel for the job he's going to be making a tour of the frontier posts. Naturally," he said, making a face, "that includes Fort Laramie."

"Ahhh," Dobbs said sagely, "I see. She's coming with him. And when is this going to occur?"

"Next summer, Benoit said, flipping quickly to the second page. "June or July. Depending on what she calls 'the Indian situation.'"

"Well, you have plenty of time yet. This is only November. By next summer you may have run off with a squaw?"

"Not much chance of that," Benoit said quickly.

"Or married young Inge? You know she's in love with you, don't you."

"That isn't funny," Benoit said hotly. "She's only a child."

"A child! She's eighteen or nineteen, isn't she?"

"Seventeen," Benoit corrected him.

"Almost eighteen, I'll bet. And that would make her plenty old enough."

"I don't want to talk about Inge," Benoit said, reaching for the next letter. "She's not old enough to know what she wants."

"But you are, aren't you?"

"I said I didn't want to discuss it," Benoit said defensively. "I'd rather" he said, slicing open the envelope, "read to you about Mrs. Schexnayder's . . . "

"Wait," Dobbs said, holding up his hand. "Mrs. Check . . . what?"

"Not 'Check,'" Benoit smiled. "Schex. With an 's.' Sssssch."

"What the hell kind of name is that? It doesn't sound French to me."

"It's German," Benoit said. "There are a lot of

Germans in New Orleans who's names have been Frenchized."

"It doesn't sound very German to me either."

"The story," Benoit explained, "is that the first Schexnayder got his name when he went through immigration. The Irish officer on duty asked him his name and he said, 'Jake Schneider.' But being a mick and not knowing how to spell so well, he corrupted it to 'Schexnayder.'"

"Sounds apocryphal to me, not to mention a bit anti-Irish . . ." He stopped, looking at Benoit, whose face had drained of color.

"Oh, Jesus," Benoit mumbled.

"Bad news?"

"The worst," Benoit replied, tears building in his eyes. "My father's dead."

"Dead?" Dobbs asked in surprise. "How? When?"

Benoit shuffled quickly through his mother's letter. "August. Yellow fever. There was an outbreak. My father sent the rest of the family to stay with friends in Thibodaux. He said he had too much work to do to leave. Goddamnit," he said angrily. "He *knows* better than that. When the fever comes, everyone who can leaves town. My father knows what the disease can do . . ."

Dobbs shook his head. "Yellow fever is mean," he said slowly. "I've seen it work."

"I can't believe it," Benoit said, his eyes glowing wetly above his pale cheeks. "He can't be dead."

"I know how you feel," Dobbs commiserated. "It hit me the same way when I got the news about Colleen."

"What's my mother going to do?" Benoit asked, tears running down his cheeks.

"She's going to muddle through, like we all do in situations like this. At least be thankful your sister and brother are there."

"I should be, too," Benoit said. "Goddamn, I never expected this to happen."

"None of us do," said Dobbs. "Death is too frequently unexpected."

Benoit pushed his cup aside. "I need some time to deal with this," he said quietly. "I need some time alone."

Dobbs nodded. "That's a natural reaction. Go saddle your horse. Take a long ride and sort things out in your mind."

"I can't just ride away."

"Sure you can," Dobbs replied, clasping Benoit's shoulder. "Kemp isn't going to object. There's nothing going on right now. Go get your horse saddled; I'll talk to Kemp."

"Thanks, Jace," Benoit said, looking vacant. "I can't believe my father's dead. He can't be dead."

Ten minutes later, Dobbs found Benoit in the stable. He was standing by his horse, leaning with his forehead on the saddle, softly sobbing.

"Like I said," Dobbs said almost in a whisper, "Kemp had no objection. But be back before dark. We're still not sure how the Indians are going to react to the Grattan incident."

Benoit nodded silently, wiping his cheeks.

"When you get back, if you want someone to talk to, knock on my door," Dobbs said.

Benoit swung aboard the large roan and dug his heels into the horse's flanks, heading northwest toward snow-covered Laramie Peak.

"Don't forget," Dobbs called after him. "Be back by sundown."

The sun glistened brightly off the snow, sending daggers of light knifing through the heavy shadows. The

mountain air was so crystalline that Benoit, if he had a
mind to, could have counted the needles on a pine
bough forty or fifty feet distant. But he was all but oblivious
to his surroundings, only barely noticing that as he
climbed higher up the slope the pines gave way to firs
and spruces and the drifts got deeper.

For hours he had been wandering aimlessly around
the hills, unaware of the serenity and beauty that surrounded
him. The only sounds were the shrill cries of
the jays that flitted through the trees and the soft
whoosh of snow falling off a sun- warmed branch. From
time to time, as his roan picked its way carefully along a
barely distinguishable trail, there was the muffled roar
of a tumbling creek that had not yet frozen over.
Overhead, an eagle soared majestically, hoping to find a
rabbit foolish enough to sprint across a clearing. In the
shadows it was cold, but when Benoit drifted into the
sun, his heavy wool jacket grew unconsciously oppressive.
He opened and closed the front flap reflexively,
totally unaware of his actions.

What was happening back in New Orleans? he wondered.
Who was sitting around the parlor of the handsome
Benoit house — almost a mansion, really, thanks
to his father's prosperous law practice — on the
Audubon Park end of St. Charles Avenue? His mother's
letter had been dated in September. It had taken almost
two months to reach him, roughly twice the normal time
because of the Indian unrest. By now, he was certain,
life at home had returned almost to normal. His father,
God rest his soul, had long ago been laid to rest in the
family tomb, shaded by a towering oak dripping gray-
green moss.

As he rode, his mind darted from subject to subject,
from the important to the mundane. Thinking of the
family tomb had led him recall how visitors to the city
were always fascinated by the way New Orleanians

buried their dead above ground. For some reason, the tourists were captivated with the knowledge that such a practice was a necessity in a city that lay below sea level, a place where heavier than normal storms frequently washed up coffins interred below ground and sent them bobbing down the cobblestone streets on small rivers of rainwater which often ran three to four feet deep.

His mother was strong; she would adjust quickly to the loss of her husband, Benoit knew. He was not so sure about his sister. Although she was two years older, she still thought like a girl in many ways, more interested in parties and balls, and the young men that flocked around her. The last time he had seen her, at Christmas the previous year when he took a few days off from his new job in Washington, she was all atwitter with the excitement of the season. "What did you bring me from up North?" she had asked Benoit delightedly, even before he had a chance to unpack his suitcase. "Maybe you have a nice, young New England gentleman packed away as a surprise."

She did not appear disappointed when he assured her that he did not. "It doesn't matter," she had trilled. "The Mardi Gras balls will be starting in less than two weeks and there will be more than enough eligible bachelors to go around."

His brother, seven years younger, had accepted his holiday presence quite differently. Theophile all but drove Benoit crazy, asking him endless questions about the army and life in the military. Although he was interested in West Point, Theophile had told him, he thought instead he would set his sights on the still relatively new naval academy at Annapolis. "It would be good for the family," he had said in all sincerity, "to have sons in both services. It won't hurt me to learn about the sea and ships either," he had added, "so in case I decide later to join Papa in his practice I will already be a maritime expert."

Benoit, trying his best not to laugh, had nodded vigorously and slapped Theophile on the shoulder. "I think that's an excellent plan," he said enthusiastically.

I must have been a great disappointment to Papa, Benoit told himself. I never showed any interest at all in the law or politics, which were the two driving forces in his life. I was obsessed with sport and having a good time. If I were home now, I'd pester Papa until he agreed to go hunting with me. Out of filial obligation, he'd be willing to sit in a duck blind deep in the Atchafalaya, shivering in the humid chill, fighting off the omnipresent dampness of the vast swamp, for no reason other than it gave me pleasure. God, he thought, wiping his cheeks, I'm really going to miss him.

Wandering haphazardly through the evergreens, heading nowhere in particular, Benoit was startled when his horse unexpectedly emerged from the shade of the forest into bright sunlight. Halting to let his vision adjust to the high altitude radiance, Benoit blinked and let his eyes roam around the pristine valley that sprawled Eden-like at his feet. How different from home, he thought as he studied the area with his practiced outdoorsman's eye, noting with pleasure the fast-running, clear stream that cut diagonally across the glen. In Louisiana, that would be a brown bayou chugging turbidly along. And instead of the small copses of bright green firs there would be scrub oak. Because it was open to the sun and it was too early for the heavy storms that would come in January and February, the valley was almost entirely free of snow, exposing winter-browned grass that was almost the exact color of the boulders scattered randomly around the expanse.

Benoit slumped in his saddle, soaking up the beauty like a parched man trying to quench his thirst. As he watched, four dark shapes appeared on the far side of the valley and approached him slowly at an acute angle.

Elk, he realized, his heartbeat quickening in typical hunter's response. Almost afraid to breathe, Benoit studied the animals carefully as they meandered along the near bank of the stream, unhurried and totally unaware of his presence. One was a huge bull and the other three were cows, not as large but more graceful. What a wonderful gift for Frau Schmidt he thought as they approached, in his mind already savoring a juicy roast fresh from the German's oven.

Without taking his eyes off the magnificent animals, Benoit carefully eased his Sharps from the scabbard beneath his left knee. Am I close enough? he wondered. Never having shot an elk before he was uncertain how much fire power would be needed to drop a beast almost as large as his horse. Unconsciously, his hunter's mind took over. They're heading this way, he thought, and if they keep to their present course they'll cut across my path at a forty-five degree angle about a quarter of a mile away, right about where that big boulder is. Calm yourself, he cautioned himself; just sit tight and wait for them to come to you. The wind is in my face so unless I make a sudden move, they will keep coming. Slowly shifting his heavy rifle to his right side, he gently stroked his horse's neck with his left hand. Keep calm, old boy, he whispered. Be patient.

Benoit was so intent on the animals he almost failed to notice another flash of movement on the other side of the valley, a mile and a half away. Ignoring it, figuring it was just a limbful of snow falling to the ground, he kept his gaze on the game. Then it moved again, more insistently. This time the elk noticed it too. All four of them stopped and swiveled their heads to the east, their nostrils quivering, their ears pointed straight up. Frowning, perturbed by the intrusion, Benoit focused his attention across the clearing. The elk recognized trouble long before Benoit. While he was still trying to identify the disturbance, they bolted. With a thud of hooves, they bounded away to the southwest, disappearing into the trees.

"Putain de merde!" Benoit cursed, kissing his dreams of a juicy elk roast good-bye. Angrily, he raised himself in his saddle and squinted into the high-country glare. Straining, he identified three horses which were approaching as fast as their riders could drive them. "Indian ponies," Benoit said aloud, noting the animals' size. His first thought was that the Indians were after him. He was on the verge of wheeling his roan and galloping away when he realized that was ridiculous. He and his horse had been standing motionless and virtually invisible at the edge of the trees. Not even the alert elk had known they were there. It would have been impossible for the three Indians to detect his presence.

Cautiously, he double-checked to make sure his Sharps was ready to fire, then settled back in his saddle, deciding to wait to see what developed.

As the riders dipped into a shallow depression and seconds later reappeared, Benoit could see additional movement behind them. "More Indians," he said, counting another eight horses.

Benoit smiled tightly, suddenly becoming aware that he was witnessing a budding skirmish. The three riders he had seen originally were running from the others, evidently in fear of their lives.

Benoit cocked his head. By listening carefully, he could hear the pursuers whooping in the excitement of the chase. The pursued were too intent on escape to take the time to yell.

This is like having a box at the theater, Benoit told himself.

As the three got closer, Benoit was surprised to see that they were so young. The one in the rear was only a boy. Ten or eleven, Benoit estimated. The others were older, maybe seventeen. Age hardly seemed to matter to the pursuers, however, who seemed determined to ride the three down and slaughter them no matter how old they were.

Despite their efforts to escape, the three youths were losing ground to the more experienced horsemen coming up behind them. As Benoit watched in fascination, the three rode almost directly at him.

One of the pursuers rose slightly on his horse's back and lifted his arms. "He's going to try to get one of them with an arrow," Benoit told his horse. "He thinks he's within range."

The arrow fell thirty yards short of the three youths, who were unaware that one had even been fired. The attempt, however, drew enthusiastic whoops from the pursuers, who urged their horses forward with renewed vigor.

Within minutes, the pursuers had narrowed the gap still farther and several of the pursuers swung their bows up and loosed arrows.

Benoit's mouth dropped open. The rapidity with which they could fire came as a huge shock to the solider. One arrow was barely halfway to the target before another was being loosened. To Benoit, it seemed as if the air was filled with sharp-pointed missiles.

"Unless they find cover those three are doomed," Benoit mumbled.

As he watched, the youngest of the three took an arrow in his thigh. Benoit imagined he could even hear the thud as it struck home. The boy didn't flinch; he simply kicked his horse in the ribs with his uninjured leg and leaned forward as if to whisper something in the animal's ear.

The three were very close now, perhaps three hundred yards from Benoit's perch. The arrows were flying thicker since all eight of the pursuers were within bow range.

Benoit turned his attention to the three youths who

realized that they would not be able to outrun their
attackers. Their only hope was to stand and fight. The
one in the lead swung his head from side to side, looking for a defensible position. He saw it about the same
time Benoit did: the large boulder that Benoit had
marked as the place where he planned to shoot the elk.

With the first youth leading the way, the three veered
slightly and made straight for the rock. Before they
could get there, however, their luck ran out.

The boy who had been shot through the thigh
straightened when another arrow slammed into his
lower back. As he threw his shoulders back and grabbed
in pain at the shaft protruding from just above his kidney, another arrow hit him in the back of the neck and
exited out the front of his throat. He tumbled to the
ground, obviously dead.

The youth in the lead almost made it to the boulder
before an arrow hit his horse in the left eye. The animal
let out a terrible scream and dropped to the ground like
a falling tree, throwing the rider over his head. The
youth landed on his stomach and slid full force, head
first, into the boulder. He did not move.

The third youth, so far untouched, wheeled his horse
to a halt and vaulted to the ground. As he scurried to try
to reach his fallen comrade, undoubtedly intending to
drag him behind the rock, Benoit was surprised to see
that he was lame. Despite the arrows that were flying
his way, the youth, limping heavily, made his way
determinedly toward his companion, pausing momen-
tarily to loose an arrow or two in defense. One of his
missiles — it must have been luck, Benoit thought,
because he had no time to aim — struck one of the pursuer's in the center of his chest. Without a sound, the
Indian flipped backwards off his horse and lay unmoving on the ground, the arrow protruding from just
below his sternum vibrated like a tuning fork.

Turning his attention back to the boulder, Benoit noted with satisfaction that the crippled youth had managed to pull his companion behind the large rock and was returning fire in a less panicky fashion.

The pursuers, Benoit saw, had also reigned to a halt. As if on signal they turned and galloped just out of arrow range, where they gathered in a tight circle to confer on a plan of attack.

It would only be a few minutes, Benoit knew, before they charged the boulder and overran the lone defender.

"All right," he said to his horse, "what do we do now?"

Initially, Benoit planned to take no part in the action. It was not his fight; he was just an accidental spectator. At the same time, he was certain he would have to act. If the sides had been more even, he might have been content to remain an uninvolved witness. But he also knew that he offered the only hope the two youths had. Long before, Benoit's military mind had processed the information that none of the Indians had firearms; they were armed only with bows, tomahawks, and knives. Since he had both his Sharps and his pistol, that gave him a tremendous advantage. The only question was should he intervene?

Without consciously articulating an answer, Benoit snapped his rifle to his shoulder and settled the sights on the Indian who appeared to be the leader of the pursuers. Slowly, he exhaled and squeezed the trigger. There was a loud blast and a cloud of smoke. As Benoit watched, the Indian raised his hands to his face and flew off his horse's back, screaming horribly in pain. He shuddered once and lay still.

Caught completely by surprise, the other aggressors whirled their horses, struggling to see into the shadows where Benoit was hidden.

Benoit did not give them time to evaluate the

unexpected new threat. While they were still confused, he quickly reloaded the Sharps, took quick aim, and fired a second time. An Indian doubled over, grabbing his left forearm. "Sonuvabitch," Benoit laughed, "I am one hell of a marksman."

Letting out a shout that he hoped imitated the whoops he had heard the attackers make, Benoit whipped his pistol out of his holster and charged the group, hoping his brazenness would make them panic. It did. Shocked and disorganized, the Indians fled. As they turned, the lame youth let loose another stream of arrows, one of which hit the closest of the attackers squarely in the temple. He flew off his horse as if catapulted and lay in a heap in the dirt.

Suddenly, the tables had turned. The attackers, who had once numbered eight, were now reduced to five with one of them wounded. Compounding the losses was the realization that they did not know how many opponents they faced, only that they were at a severe disadvantage without firearms. Letting common sense override their lust for blood, they whooped loudly and rode off almost as quickly as they had appeared, abandoning their dead along with their dreams of an easy victory.

Benoit stopped his horse and watched them depart. Turning slowly toward the boulder so as not to give the youth an excuse to starting shooting arrows at *him*, Benoit lifted both his arms in the air and rode slowly in his direction.

Communicating with gestures, Benoit signaled the youth that he was going to approach his unconscious companion. Sighing in relief when he felt a strong pulse, Benoit lifted the injured youth's head and examined the wound. Although there was a long gash across his forehead that was bleeding copiously, Benoit could not see any sign that the skull had been crushed. Grabbing a handful of snow from the shadow of the boulder, Benoit rubbed it across the wound, recoiling somewhat when he felt the huge knot that had already formed. "I'm not a doctor," he told the lame youth, knowing he could not understand him, "but I think your friend is going to be all right."

Slowly lowering the unconscious youth on a sunlit patch of grass, Benoit mounted his roan and rode off to gather the ponies, which were grazing nearby. When he returned, he was only mildly surprised to discover that the lame youth had already collected the scalps of the dead attackers.

By waving his arms and drawing images in the dust, Benoit communicated to the crippled youth that it would be wiser for him to accompany him back to Fort Laramie rather than trying to get back to his village alone with an unconscious companion. The attackers might well be waiting in the trees, waiting to pounce as soon as he left.

Hurriedly, the two of them collected enough branches from a nearby thicket to make a crude travois on which to transport the still unconscious Indian. Rushing to beat the setting sun, Benoit and the crippled youth dug a shallow grave for the dead boy, piling on heavy stones to keep predators away.

"I don't know what your customs are when you bury a friend," Benoit said, "but we don't have time to say a Mass. It's better for both of us to get going."

Understanding the tone if not the words, the youth nodded in agreement. With an effort, he swung onto his pony and motioned to Benoit that he was ready to go.

"Damn wise of you," Benoit mumbled, spurring his roan. "We still have a good ride ahead of us."

6

Jason Dobbs was halfway to bed when Benoit pounded on his door.

"Goddamn, Jean," Dobbs sighed in relief, "you had me worried. I thought for sure the Indians had gotten you."

"It's the other way around," Benoit grinned, his face lined with fatigue. "I got the Indians. Come with me. I brought you a patient."

The two of them lifted the unconscious Indian off the travois and carried him into Dobbs's makeshift hospital, a converted storage room at one end of the enlisted men's barracks. The room was bare except for three cots and a table on which the surgeon kept the tools of his trade, a fearsome looking collection of knives, saws, and fierce-looking equipment that Benoit could not identify.

"Lay him here," Dobbs directed, pointing to one of the beds, "while I get some water and get that wound washed. You," he said gesturing at the crippled Indian, "can make yourself comfortable over there."

"I can't find any sign of a life-threatening injury," Dobbs told Benoit after cleaning the wound and making a quick examination. "Has he regained consciousness at all?"

Benoit shook his head.

"Ummmmm," Dobbs frowned. "That isn't good but it isn't necessarily that bad either. With head wounds, it's often hard to tell for certain how much damage has been done until they regain consciousness, if they do."

"You mean sometimes they don't?"

"Oh, yeah. I've seen 'em stay in a coma for weeks. Months. Sometimes they just quietly die. Other times, they wake up complaining like hell about a headache and demanding food. Speaking of which," he added, "I asked Frau Schmidt to bring a couple of plates. Figured you didn't stop along the trail to fix a five-course dinner."

"Now that you mention it, I'm famished," Benoit said. "Oops, I guess that's our food service now," he said, turning to answer a knock on the door.

Hildegard Schmidt entered the room as regally as she could on her new wooden leg.

"I bring you something to eat," she said in a heavy accent, handing Benoit a tray covered with a napkin. Glancing around the room her eyes widened when she saw the Indian sitting cross-legged in the corner. "Goddamn *rothaut*," she grumbled.

Dobbs smiled. "I'd say Holz's English is improving. 'Goddamn' has become part of her regular vocabulary."

"For the life of me, I can't understand where she picked it up," a feminine voice said from the open doorway.

"Hi, Inge!" Benoit said, grinning broadly, his eyes glowing. "I didn't know you were still up."

"I wasn't exactly," she said, pulling a woolen robe more tightly around her. Beneath the hem, Benoit could see the train of a blue flannel nightdress. "When *Mutter* is up, everyone's up. I'm really sorry about your father," she said, looking at Benoit, tears forming in the corners of her eyes.

"*Ja*, me too," Hildegard added. "It is a sad thing, no?"

"Yes, it is sad," Benoit said, sobering. "But it's something I'm going to have to get used to, just like you had to get used to the death of your husband."

"The difference," Inge interrupted, staring intently at the Indian youth, "is that *Vater* did not have the privilege of dying in his bed."

"You have to let that go," Dobbs said. "It wasn't anything personal on the Indians' part. They've been killing each other ever since the world began, I guess, and as far as they're concerned we're just another tribe. The new kids in the neighborhood, so to speak. The attack in which your father and the others died was just their way of testing us."

"That's easy for you to say," Inge said, her cheeks flaming. "You didn't see *your* world suddenly collapse."

"You sure are pretty when you get excited," Benoit teased, trying to lighten the mood.

"Just a goddamn minute," Inge said angrily. "I'll have you know . . ."

"And you wonder where Holz learns her language," Dobbs laughed.

"Are you sure your mother doesn't resent us calling her 'Holzbein?'" Benoit asked. "Sometimes it doesn't seem very respectful to refer to her as 'Wooden Leg.'"

"Don't try to change the subject," Inge said, still simmering.

"But that's precisely what I *am* trying to do," Benoit said, raising his hands in surrender. "We're not trying to tell you *not* to be mad at the Indians. God knows you have the right. We're just trying to say that you have to learn to live with it. You have to understand and forgive."

"'Forgive' my ass."

"Ahhh," Dobbs sighed. "Out of the mouths of angels."

"And *you* can lay off the 'angel' crap," Inge replied, turning on the surgeon.

"I swear," Dobbs said, shaking his head. "You have the filthiest mouth of any girl . . . "

"And I'm not a *girl*," Inge said hotly. "I'm a full-grown woman."

"Nobody except Jean's questioning that," Dobbs rejoined. "But you *really* ought to try to curb your cursing. People who don't know you like we do might get the wrong idea."

"So?" Inge said, shrugging. "What do I care what others think?"

"What's going on?" Hildegard asked her daughter in German. "You're talking too fast for me."

Inge smiled beatifically. "Don't worry, Mother," she replied in German. "We're just having our usual friendly argument. Jean was just saying that he felt somewhat uncomfortable calling you '*Holzbein.*'"

"Oh!," Hildegard replied, smiling broadly, "Tell him not to worry about that. I know he and Lieutenant Dobbs use it affectionately, like you and Erich. In fact, if it had not been for you two, they never would have known the word."

"That's true, Mother," Inge smiled.

Benoit, not for the first time, noticed how much the two women resembled each other physically. Both had long, blond hair which they wore either in braids or tight buns. Both were sturdy, with fine, full figures. Both had eyes the color of highly polished turquoise. And both were so stubborn Benoit could hardly believe it. "Strong-willed," was the word Dobbs preferred. "Yeah," Benoit had agreed. "'Strong-willed!' And as immovable as that mountain over there," he had said, pointing toward Laramie Peak.

Mother and daughter knew their minds. Inge knew she was in love with Benoit, had been ever since they met on the trip West from Missouri. Hildegard knew it, too, and wholeheartedly accepted, even encouraged, it. Already she treated Benoit like a son.

Benoit, on the other hand, refused to fully acknowledge his affection for Inge. Judging by his sister's example, Benoit figured that Inge, at seventeen, was too young to know what she wanted and her attraction toward him might be nothing more than a passing infatuation. Once, as they were sitting around a campfire a few days before the attack in which Hans Schmidt and the others were killed, Benoit had discussed this with Dobbs.

"You can't judge all young women by your sister," said Dobbs. "She sounds very flighty to me."

"Indeed, she is that," replied Benoit, "but I thought most young women were. Her best friend," Benoit had paused, deciding not to tell Dobbs of his relationship with Marie Fontenot, "is the same way."

"Well, I don't know about *most* young women," Dobbs had said tactfully, "my Mary Margaret is far too young yet. But I'd say 'flighty' would be the last adjective I'd use to describe Inge Schmidt. She's a remarkable young woman; she's going to make *someone*," he said pointedly, staring at Benoit, "a terrific wife."

Benoit had blustered and mumbled something about taking Erich Schmidt antelope hunting the next day.

"Aren't you going to answer?" Inge said loudly, breaking his reverie.

"I'm sorry," Benoit apologized. "I was woolgathering. What did you say?"

"Mother asked you why you felt you had to go off by yourself when you got the news of your father. That's what families are for. She thinks of you as part of the family."

"I know," Benoit stammered. "I'm not sure why I felt I had to be alone. I guess I was just feeling sorry for myself."

"You certainly were," Hildegard said through her daughter. "Grief is something that needs to be shared, not bottled up inside where it can fester. We are part of your life whether you want to admit it or not; we want to share both your good times and your bad times."

Benoit stared at his feet, uncertain how to reply. "Well," he said, blushing, "why don't we share the food you've brought along?"

Lifting the napkin on the heavy tray that Hildegard had brought in, Benoit saw it covered a freshly baked loaf of dark German bread, a cold ham, and the remains of a wheel of sharp cheddar.

"God," he said, licking his lips. "This looks wonderful. Where have you been hiding the cheese?"

Hildegard smiled. "Eat!" she commanded. The *Handkäse*, it will too soon be . . . be . . ." she said, searching for the word.

"Moldy," Inge interjected, smiling at her mother.

"*Ja*," Hildegard said, nodding her head. "Moldy."

"Well," Benoit laughed, "I guess we should finish it up then before it goes bad."

Walking to the corner where the Indian sat motionless, Benoit offered him the platter. The youth, who had been following the conversation with intense interest without comprehending a word, looked at the food, then looked at Benoit.

"It's all right," Benoit assured him.

When the youth continued to sit immobile, Benoit took the knife that was on the plate and cut off a hunk of bread and some cheese. Taking a slice of ham, he put it on the bread with the piece of cheese. "It's good," he said slowly, biting into it. "Here," he said, offering the morsel to the Indian.

The youth took it in his hand and slowly turned it over. Lifting it to his face, he stuck it under his nose and inhaled. "Ugghhh," he said, making a face.

"No," Benoit said patiently. "It's really very good. Look, I'm going to eat some."

The Indian watched Benoit, then took a tentative bite of the bread. "Nnnnhhh," he said, spitting it out.

"If that's the way you feel about it . . . " Benoit said with a shrug. "I guess you'll eat when you get hungry enough." Turning to Hildegard and Inge, who had been watching the performance with a mixture of disgust and fascination, he smiled. "And I thought the Germans were the most mule-headed people I'd ever met," he said with a laugh.

13 November 54
Fort Laramie

Dear Mamman,

It feels so strange not to include Papa in the salutation. I can't begin to tell you how much my heart is breaking, but I imagine it is even worse for you. My greatest hope right now is that you have come to terms with his death and have been able to put your life back in order. Above all, you mustn't allow it to consume you. If I were a religious person — and you know I am not — I think I would be seriously questioning God's wisdom in taking Papa from us too soon. The problem is, I know that you are a good Catholic and I worry that this will rock your faith. As strange as it may sound coming from your heathen son, I sincerely hope that will not happen. Life must go on; you must persevere.

I regret very deeply that I cannot be there when I know you need me. Marion and Theophile will have to be your crutches. You know that I am praying for

Papa's soul and for you. If God is indeed just, he will have found a comfortable place for Papa at His right hand and He will serve as your strength during this ordeal.

I don't want this to sound too maudlin; I know you have enough on your mind without the burden of my grief as well. It is something I must find the strength to deal with and I don't want you to worry about my state of mind. Or about my well-being, for that matter.

Life continues a pace here on the outskirts of civilization. Activity is feverish at the moment to make sure all preparations are complete for the winter, which by all accounts is most grueling. I have to confess that as a Southerner born and bred, I am not in the least looking forward to the rigors of winter on the Plains. Jim Ashby, my friend the scout, has warned me sufficiently that I had better prepare for the worst wind and cold I have ever experienced. Although I know there is much truth to what he says, I also suspect that he is trying to frighten me. It's part of my initiation. My other friend, Jason Dobbs, has tried to calm my anxieties. A native New Englander, he tells me that winter here cannot be more difficult than a winter in Massachusetts, and he has been through many of those. Even young children survive, he says in jest. Right now, I can laugh, but come the first blizzard I may well change my mind.

My duties for the most part are fairly boring. As the post's junior officer I have little say in policy-making and serve mainly as a fetcher. That doesn't bother me particularly since I know I can't remain a mere brevet second lieutenant forever. Can I?

I had a bit of adventure yesterday when I stumbled across a clash between opposing Indian groups. I helped resolve the conflict in a small way. As a result, two of the Indians, they are both only boys really, scarcely older than Theophile, are currently in residence in

Jason's surgery. One of them is still unconscious after suffering a severe fall and the other, his companion, sits loyally in the corner of the room day and night, not even eating the food we offer him, waiting for his friend to recover. For all the talk about what savages the Indians are, I confess that I am much impressed by this boy's demeanor. So far, I know nothing of the incident that resulted in their being here. The boy speaks no English and since the post's interpreter was killed in August we will have to wait until Jim Ashby returns from a special mission to learn more. At this stage, we do not even know the boy's name or to which tribe he belongs, although several of the post old timers say his clothing indicates he is Sioux.

Needless to say, Frau Schmidt and her daughter, Inge, are not taking the Indian presence very well. Understandably, they are still bitter toward the savages because of the attack on the wagon train that . . .

Oh, Mamman, forgive me but I must run. Someone has just knocked on my door to tell me that Jim Ashby and Erich Schmidt are approaching from a distance. They also are dragging a travois, carrying what appears to be yet another potential patient for Jace. I will close this for now, but will give you the latest information at the earliest possible moment. Remember, please, that I love you dearly and miss you terribly. Please give my love as well to Marion and Theophile and tell them to be strong.

Your Loving and Lonely Son,
t-Jean

"This looks as though it's shaping up to be a busy week for you," Benoit said, barging into Dobbs's surgery. "Hi, Jim," he said, waving to the scout who was peering over the surgeon's shoulder. "Hi, Erich," he added, greeting the tow-haired teenager standing on the other side of the bed. Neither Dobbs nor Inge, who had been pressed into emergency service as a nurse, looked up.

"I reckon the lieutenant's too busy to talk," Ashby drawled, not taking his eyes off a man who was stretched out on the bed.

"Jesus!" Benoit gasped, getting a good look at the new patient. "What happened to him?"

"B'ar," said Ashby.

"Grizzly," amplified Erich.

"I'll be damned," Benoit said, bending closer. "He looks like he's been through a thrasher."

Lying deathly still and as white as snowbank was a man Benoit guessed to be in his mid-thirties although it was hard to tell for certain since he was covered top to bottom with dried blood and deep gashes, several of which had re-opened and were leaking red all over the freshly laundered sheets. Well over six feet tall with a heavy chest and shoulders, the man lay semiconscious while Dobbs and Inge worked feverishly to clean the wounds with rags dipped in alcohol. The tip of the man's nose was missing and his left ear was hanging by a flap. When Dobbs lifted the man's left hand to examine it, Benoit could see that the little finger was missing at the knuckle and the ring finger was gone at the first joint.

"It's a good thing you got a tourniquet on this hand," Dobbs said softly to Ashby. "Otherwise he probably would have bled to death."

The man's eyes were half open, just enough of a gap for Benoit to see irises so dark they looked black. His buckskin clothing was in tatters and one of his moccasins was gone, exposing a foot that was missing three toes.

"Old frostbite, not the b'ar," Ashby said, noticing Benoit's glance.

Although the man had wounds over almost all of his

upper body, his arms and shoulders were particularly ravaged.

"Get a fire going in the brazier," Dobbs commanded Ashby. "Look in the cabinet over there and you'll see some pieces of steel with wooden handles. Those are my cauterizing instruments. Put them in the coals and tell me when they get red. Inge," he said, his fingers flying, "go to my bag and get my packet of needles and catgut. While you're there, there's a brown bottle with the initials LAU on the label. Bring that, too. That's Laudanum. We'd better help this poor bastard to dreamland. We've got a lot of sewing and burning to do.

"Jean! Erich!" he said, acknowledging them for the first time. "Stand back and let us work."

"You want us to leave?" Benoit asked.

"Not yet. I may need you to help me hold this guy down."

Benoit looked closely at Erich, noticing that he seemed almost as pale as the man on the table. "What the hell happened?"

Erich shook his head. "Damnedest thing I've ever seen."

"You *saw* the attack?"

Erich nodded. "We were on our way to try to find the Cheyenne camp, like Colonel Kemp ordered us to do," he explained, speaking slowly, "when we heard a god-awful ruckus coming from a cave just above us. Screaming and hollering like you've never heard before," he added, grimacing at the memory. "A woman screaming. A man screaming. A bear roaring. I tell you, I just about shit my pants."

Benoit had been so intent on the man on the table that he had not noticed the other stranger in the room, a small, dark-haired, dark-eyed boy of about eight, who was chattering with the crippled Indian who had been sitting on the floor by the bed of his unconscious companion since Benoit brought them to the fort two days ago.

"Who's that?" Benoit asked in surprise.

"Who?" Erich asked, his eyes glazed.

"The boy over there," Benoit said, pointing.

"Oh," Erich replied, following Benoit's gesture. "That's the man's son."

"We'll get to him later," Benoit mumbled. "Tell me in detail about the bear attack."

Erich shrugged. "Not a lot to tell. That man — Jim says he's a trapper — was fighting a grizzly. Biggest goddamn animal I've ever seen. Huge and evil smelling. Eyes as red as a firepit. Saliva flying out of his mouth and teeth that looked a foot long." Erich gulped, steadied himself, and continued.

"The bear had the man up against him, like this," Erich said, hugging his arms to his chest, "and was trying to get his head in his mouth. The man had a pistol and he managed to get one arm free. Just as we came running up, he shot the bear in the face. Took off part of his jaw, but that just seemed to make him madder. Jim shot the bear in the back with his rifle at twenty feet. That sent him spinning and made him drop the trapper, but he didn't go down. I shot him, too, but that didn't seem to have much effect either. Jim jumped on the bear's back, put his pistol right up against his ear and pulled the trigger. That did the trick. He dropped like a boulder. Jim stabbed him a couple of times in the heart just for good measure. We didn't want that son of a bitch getting up again." Erich paused. "Jesus, that was a mean bastard."

"You said you heard a woman."

"Oh, yeah," Erich said. "There was a rothaut woman, guess it was this guy's wife. But she was dead. The bear got to her first. Just plain ripped her to shreds."

"And the boy? He doesn't look like he's been injured."

"The man boosted him up a pine tree before he took after the bear so he ain't hurt. Just shook up." Erich paused, then added, "Like me. And I ain't ashamed to admit it."

Erich twisted his hands. Remembering the incident, his lower lip began trembling and his body shook, as if with fever.

"Just a second," Benoit said, walking over to the cabinet where he knew Dobbs kept a bottle of medicinal whisky. Returning with the bottle and a glass, he poured an inch of amber liquid into the tumbler and handed it to Erich. "Drink this!" he said.

Erich looked at the proffered glass. "I ain't old enough," he said weakly. "Mutter will whip me good."

Benoit smiled. "After what you've been through I think you qualify as old enough. Come on, bottoms up."

Erich made a terrible face and for a minute Benoit feared he was going to vomit.

"I guess that's better," Erich mumbled.

"You have any idea what happened?" Benoit asked, pouring some more whisky into the glass.

Erich nodded. "Jim talked to the boy some on the way back. He's half Miniconjou, by the way. That's a Sioux."

"I know what a Miniconjou is."

"Oh, sorry. Anyway, the boy said his real mother died of smallpox five years ago and the woman who was killed in the cave was his father's second wife. That would make her the boy's stepmother, I guess."

"All right. Was she a Miniconjou, too?"

"No. She was a Southern Cheyenne. They'd been up with the northern bands and were heading back to spend the winter with her people in the south. As they were coming through the mountains, the man thought he smelled a storm coming. Since the woman was pregnant . . . "

"Wait!" Benoit said in surprise. "You didn't say she was pregnant."

"I was getting to that," Erich said crossly. "She was almost ready to deliver. Big as a wagon. The man didn't want to get caught in the open by an early winter snowstorm so he saw a cave and decided that would be a good place to shelter. He didn't know a grizzly had gotten there first. Real bad luck on his part, Jim said. It was too early in the season for the bear to be sound asleep and when the woman came in the cave, he woke up madder than hell. The man was still outside, maybe looking for a rabbit for them to eat, when the bear jumped the woman. She never had a chance."

"So the man put the boy up the tree and then attacked the bear?"

"That's right. Awful brave of him, you ask me. God, that bear was big. Must've been seven feet tall if he was an inch. Head as big as a pickle barrel. Paws . . ."

"You didn't talk directly to the boy?"

Erich shook his head. "You know I don't speak Indian. Or the other language the boy used either. I think it was French."

"French, eh? That's interesting," Benoit said. Leaving Erich, he walked across the room. As he approached, the boy and the crippled Indian, who had been talking animatedly, grew silent.

Squatting so their eyes were on a level, Benoit put his hand on the boy's shoulder, noticing that it was trembling. "*C'est quoi votre nom?*" he asked gently, speaking slowly and distinctly.

The boy smiled in relief. "David," he replied, pronouncing it Dah-veed, in Gallic fashion. "But," he added in fluent French, "among the Miniconjou I am called Plays-with-His-Toes."

Benoit smiled. "If you don't mind," he said in French,

"I'll call you David. But you do understand me, don't you?"

"*Mais oui,*" said David.

"How did you learn French?"

"My father," he said gesturing with his head toward the injured man. "We talk a lot in the language, especially after my mother died and before I got a new mother."

"What's your father's name?" Benoit asked.

"Etienne. Etienne Legendre. He's Canadian, whatever that is."

"Tell me," Benoit said, pointing at the lame Indian. "You were talking with this other boy. Can you speak his language, too?"

"Oh, yes. His name is Crooked Leg. He's a Brulé. They are cousins to the Miniconjou so we had no trouble with language."

"Did he tell you the other boy's name? The one who is asleep."

David nodded. "His name is White Crane. He is a Brulé, too."

"Did he tell you what happened to them?"

"*Certainement,*" David replied, bobbing his head. "They were hunting elk. They had a third boy with them. His name was Bear's Ear and he was older than me but not as old as the other two. While they were searching for elk they happened upon a group of Crow. When the Crow saw them, they attacked. They ran, but the Crow chased them. Bear's Ear was killed and White Crane's horse was wounded. White Crane was thrown off and he hit his head against a rock. He has been asleep since."

"Did . . . what's his name, Crooked Leg? . . . "

David nodded.

". . . Did he tell you where their village is?"

"They are members of the Wazhazha band. Their people are in their winter camp. Up there," he said, pointing to the northwest. "In a valley in the mountains."

"How far away?"

David shrugged. "I don't know. I didn't ask him that. My mother, White Girl, is dead, isn't she? That's why those men wouldn't let me go into the cave, isn't it?"

Benoit nodded sadly. "Yes, David, your mother is dead."

Tears rolled down the boy's cheeks. "She was good to me," he said. "Almost as good as my real mother. Please tell me about my father. Will he be all right?"

"I don't know," Benoit said. "I'll have to talk to the man who is tending his wounds. But he's a very good and powerful doctor and if anyone can make your father well, it will be Lieutenant Dobbs."

David smiled for the first time. "I am very glad to hear that," he said. "Now do you think I can have some food and a place to sleep. I'm very hungry and very tired."

"Of course," Benoit replied quickly. Resting his hand on the boy's slim shoulder, Benoit started walking him toward the door. "Come with me," he said.

As they were walking down the stairs toward Frau Schmidt's kitchen, Benoit asked the boy if the Indian called Crooked Leg had said anything else.

David frowned, trying to remember. "Oh, yes. He said he hoped his friend would recover soon so they could return to their camp. He, too, is terribly hungry."

"But he's been offered food," Benoit said in surprise. "And he has refused it every time."

"He's not accustomed to the White man's cooking like I am," David said proudly. "He thinks your food is strange. He says if he were in his village, they would feed that to the dogs."

For God's sake, Benoit thought, I hope he doesn't tell that to Frau Schmidt. She'll take a cleaver to him.

* * *

Colonel Kemp waved his empty cup in the air, signaling for more coffee. While Frau Schmidt was hobbling to his place at the head of the table, he drew one of his long, black cigars from his pocket, bit off the end, and waited expectantly for Captain Harrigan to light it. "Thanks," he said absentmindedly when the match was proffered.

"Well," he said expansively, spreading his hands on the tabletop, exposing ten stubby fingers with neatly clipped nails. "Things have been rather hectic for the last day or so, eh?"

When no one volunteered an answer, the colonel turned to Dobbs.

"You first, lieutenant. Bring me up to date on your patients."

"Well, sir . . . ," Dobbs began, his voice heavy with fatigue.

Kemp glared at him. "When delivering a report, lieutenant, I expect you to be on your feet."

"Of course, sir," Dobbs said, rising tiredly and throwing his shoulders back a half inch. "The least serious case first," he said. "That's the Indian boy. He regained consciousness late this afternoon and seems alert enough. No indication that he's suffered any permanent damage, but there's evidence of subdural hematoma . . . "

"What's that?" Harrigan interrupted.

"Intracranial bleeding," Dobbs explained. "Bleeding between the brain and the skull."

"And that's not serious?" asked Kemp.

"No, sir. It's normal with severe concussions."

"Is there any treatment you can offer?"

"I'm giving him a purgative."

Kemp smiled tightly. "And how, pray tell, does that help his brain?"

"Contemporary medical wisdom says the vomiting it induces dehydrates the patient, and this reduces swelling in the brain. Now that he seems on his way to recovery, I'll stop the purgative and begin rehydrating him."

"Good idea," Kemp grunted. "When will he be mobile again?"

Dobbs rolled his shoulders. "A day or two, I expect. But he may have problems for a while yet: Vertigo, loss of memory, impaired hearing, that sort of thing. I'll be surprised if he doesn't walk like a drunken sailor for a few days, but I think he's going to be fine."

"And the Frenchman. What's his name? Legendre."

"That's pronounced Lay-zhan," Benoit broke in.

"Damn it, Ben-oight, how many of these blasted frog names do I have to learn? This is America, isn't it?"

"To be technical, no, sir. We're in Indian Territory, which isn't part of the United States."

"Don't crack wise with me, lieutenant. You *do* want that bar don't you?"

"Yes, sir," Benoit said as contritely as he could manage. "Sorry, sir."

Kemp turned to the surgeon. "And what about your other patient, lieutenant?"

"That's a little harder to predict, sir," Dobbs replied, struggling to squelch a laugh at Benoit's predicament. "That bear really tore him up. I think I have all the bleeding stanched . . . his missing digits don't appear to be a problem since I have the wounds cauterized. But . . . "

"But what?"

"Well, sir, there's still the danger of tetanus. If lock-jaw sets in, that can be real trouble. It's very rare when someone survives that."

Kemp waved him to his chair. "Very well, lieutenant. It seems as if you have done everything you can. I'll expect reports daily from now on. In my office, though, and not at the supper table. Ben-oight," he said, swiveling his gaze. "What's the latest on the kidnapped children?"

Benoit almost turned his chair over popping to attention. "Not much, sir. As you know, Ashby was on his way to the Cheyenne camp when he came upon the Legendres."

"So we don't know squat?"

"No, sir, that's not necessarily true. The injured trapper has some knowledge of the children through his Cheyenne wife . . . excuse me, his late Cheyenne wife . . . and he communicated this to Mr. Ashby."

"Well, get Mr. Ashby in here then," Kemp said impatiently.

In a succinct summation, Ashby told what little he knew from Legendre: that the children were alive and were being well cared for, that they had been split up — sent to different families — but there was every indication they would not be harmed, that they would, instead, be raised as members of the tribe.

"Damned awkward situation," Kemp said, chewing his lower lip. "But in any case there's nothing we can do about it before spring at the earliest. Are you fairly confident that they'll be safe during the winter?"

"Oh, yes, sir," Ashby replied. "Since they're young, healthy boys you don' have much to worry abou'."

"If tha's all you need from me, colonel, I reckon I'll be goin'." The scout was walking out the door when Lieutenant Grant called out to him.

"Mr. Ashby," he said. "If you have half a minute there's a question I'd like to ask you."

Ashby turned, studying Grant through half-closed eyes. "Yep," he muttered. "What is it?"

Grant's cheeks turned pink and he stared at the table in front of him. "W . . . w . . . well," he stuttered, "it's about the indigenous fauna?"

Ashby stared at him. "Huh?"

"The wildlife," Grant said, blushing even more. "The local animals."

"Yeah," Ashby said carefully. What about 'em?"

"It just seems," Grant said, "that everything in this environment is malevolent."

Ashby's eyebrows went up.

"Antagonistic," explained Grant. "Hostile. Un - friendly to people."

"I'm not sure what you mean . . ." Ashby began.

"Well, for example, there are spiders as big as my fist . . . "

"Tarantulas," said Ashby. "They're ugly, but they ain't mean. You just about have to beg 'em to bite you."

"And there are lions . . . "

"Pumas. They're right shy. More'n likely, you'll never even see one."

"Wolves . . . "

Ashby shook his head. "Nothin' for you to worry about. They're interested in buffler, not soljers."

"Well, how about bears?" Grant said in exasperation. "Don't tell me they aren't dangerous to people. We have an example in Lieutenant Dobbs's surgery."

"Oh, yes, sir," Ashby said, nodding vigorously. "B'ars can be a real problem, specially if you catch 'em unawares, as Mr. Legendre did. They don't much like surprises and they partic'ly don't like nobody messin' with their cubs."

"My point exactly," Grant said in satisfaction.

"There's two kinds o' b'ars out here," Ashby said. "Brown and grizzly. Both of 'em can be mean, but grizzlies is by far the worst. They're big, evil-tempered, and have no fear since they don't have no natural enemies. Bes' thing to do is cut a wide path aroun' any b'ar you see."

"Well," continued Grant, "how can you tell the difference? Between a brown bear and a grizzly, I mean, should you encounter one on a path sometime?"

Ashby pursed his lips and looked reflective. "In that case, I reckon the best thing to do is climb a tree."

Grant looked puzzled. "How will that help you tell them apart?"

"Well," Ashby said slowly. "If you go up a tree an' the b'ar comes up after you, you know it ain't no grizzly 'cause grizzlies don't climb trees."

"What do you mean, *gone*?" Kemp asked angrily.

"Vanished," Dobbs said sheepishly. "Disappeared. Absent. I mean I went in this morning to check on him and the room was empty. Both of them were missing. Headed back home, I guess. Afraid they might be stuck here all winter."

"That's goddamn negligent on your part," Kemp added. "You should have kept a closer watch on 'em."

"Sir," Dobbs said earnestly, "if I'd known it was that important to you, I would have. You never indicated to me that they were to be considered as prisoners. If you had, I would have put a guard on the door."

"They weren't *prisoners*," the colonel said in a calmer voice. "It's just that they had some information that may have been important to us. That half-breed boy told us they were Brulé, didn't he?"

"Yes, sir," Dobbs nodded. "So?"

Kemp's face reddened. "Well, *lieutenant*," he said emphasizing the word, "it doesn't take a goddamn genius, does it, to figure out they may have known something about the murders of Lieutenant Grattan and his men? The murderers were Brulé, weren't they?"

"That and Minniconjou," Dobbs conceded. "But these were just boys."

"Boys, my ass," said Kemp, his voice rising. "They were injuns. Injun *boys* are warriors. I guarandamntee you either one of 'em would have cut your throat in a flash if they thought it was necessary."

"Begging your pardon, colonel," Dobbs said blanching, "I don't think they were the violent type."

"Sweet Jesus," Kemp mumbled in exasperation. "As far as I'm concerned every fucking injun's a *violent type*. I don't care if he's six or sixty. We're fighting a war out here, Dobbs. Or we will be pretty soon. And when we do, every redskin within a thousand miles is going to be considered an enemy until they prove otherwise."

"Sir, I think you're exaggerating . . . "

"Exaggerating, am I?" Kemp asked, thumping his hand on the desk. "Do you know what this is?" he asked, lifting a sheaf of papers.

"No, sir, but I don't . . . "

"This is a recommendation to the Secretary of War," Kemp said. "I'm explaining to Jefferson Davis that we're in a very precarious position out here. We have too few troops and too many miles to cover. There's way too many fucking injuns no matter which way we turn. They have us outnumbered a thousand to one. Two thousand to one. Who in hell knows for sure how many thousand to one? The point is, we can't control 'em by sheer force. They're going to have to fear us. Respect us. And the only way they're going to get to that position is prove to 'em we're strong. Do you see where I'm going, lieutenant?"

"Yes, sir."

"Well, I'm glad that you understand that much. The Injuns live by the code of revenge. If the Crow attack the

Brulé and kill a couple of warriors, the Brulé don't sit around discussing whether they should attack the Crow to avenge themselves. It's a given; they strike back. The Crow *know* they can expect a Brulé attack. And vice versa if its a Brulé attack against the Crow. What I'm saying is, the Injuns don't respect anyone who doesn't fight back. So unless I want my men in danger every time they go on a woodcutting detail or leave the post on a patrol, I'm going to have to kill me a few Brulé just to show 'em we mean business. You follow me?"

"Yes, sir," Dobbs said. "I follow you. But respectfully, sir . . . "

"I don't want to hear any of this 'respectfully' shit, lieutenant. Assume that I consider an attack against the Brulé to be the top priority. And that's what I'm telling Secretary Davis. We need to attack the Brulé as soon as possible."

"But we don't have the men . . . "

"I know *that*, lieutenant. Sending our couple of hundred troopers against the Brulé and Minniconjou might put us in a worse position that we already are. I didn't mean we in the literal sense of the detachment at Fort Laramie. I meant the U.S. Army we. I'm recommending that Washington send a force from Back East to move against the injuns at the earliest feasible time, probably next summer."

"Sir," Dobbs persisted, "I didn't think revenge was part of the Army strategy."

"Don't be so fucking naive, lieutenant. You don't have to call it revenge. Call it a preemptive strike. Call it insurance. Call it whatever the hell fits your moral sensibilities. What I'm saying is, the U.S. Army is going to have to attack the Brulé and the Minniconjou or we may as well pack up and go home. If they don't bury us here first. That became a certainty as soon as those savages murdered Lieutenant Grattan and his men. Tell me honestly, can you see the Department of the Army telling all those thousands of people who are just waiting to go to California and Oregon that they can't do it because of a few fucking redskins?"

"No, sir, I can't see that," Dobbs admitted. "I just think we ought to try to negotiate first."

"Negotiate my ass," Kemp sneered. "That's what we did three years ago in the Treaty of Fort Laramie. All the tribes came together and they met with us and we agreed that the emigrants would be unmolested on their way west and that there would be no fighting between the injuns and the soldiers. The treaty is a joke. The tribes are fighting among themselves, as they promised they would not do, and they are fighting with us. Just in the last six months you yourself have seen an emigrant group attacked and a number of people killed. You've seen a thirty-man detachment wiped out on a peaceful mission. Do you think Frau Schmidt would like the thought of *negotiating* with those bastards? She'd like to see them all castrated and shot, if you ask me. And how about the families of Lieutenant Grattan and his men? You think they want to *negotiate*? I tell you, lieutenant, no matter how much you disagree with it, the mood in this country is not to negotiate. The mood is to *kill* the murdering bastards."

"Sir . . . "

"That's enough, lieutenant. I'm not in any mood to argue with you. You're a sawbones, not a military strategist. Your job is to patch up our wounded and try to heal our sick. You stick to that and I'll stick to running this post and dealing with the Injuns. Is that clear?"

"Perfectly, sir," Dobbs said, coming to attention.

"I'm not going to try to say this gently to you, lieutenant. You fucked up by allowing those *boys* to skedaddle before we had a chance to talk to 'em, to see what they could tell us about the mood in the Brulé camp and pump them for other important pieces of information. Thanks, captain," he said, leaning forward to accept a light from the ever-present Harrigan. "That's done with. I don't believe in holding a man's mistakes against him. But I don't suffer a man who makes the same mistake twice. You understand me?"

"Yes, sir," Dobbs said smartly. "Is that all, sir."

"For now," Kemp said, exhaling a stream of blue smoke. "You're dismissed. Captain," he said, turning to Harrigan, "go get Mr. Ashby. I want to ask him if it's feasible to try to go after those boys and bring 'em back for a little chat."

"By God, he really reamed me out," Dobbs said with a nervous laugh.

"It isn't fair," Inge said indignantly. "You didn't know those boys were to be considered prisoners."

"Nobody says a colonel has to be fair," Benoit added. "It isn't a factor the promotion board considers."

"Still," Inge persisted, "you'd think he would want to treat his men justly. He expects them to obey his commands, doesn't he?"

"More coffee?" Benoit offered.

"Yes," said Dobbs. "Thanks."

"Just a little," said Inge. "You make it awfully strong."

"But," Dobbs said, addressing Inge's question, "you're talking in contradictory terms. Justice and obedience have nothing to do with each other. We *have* to obey orders. There's nothing that says we have to obtain justice."

"Even bad ones?" Inge asked in surprise.

"It's not for us to judge what a bad order is," said Benoit. "We're only junior officers. We do what anyone with a higher rank tells us to do, regardless of whether we agree with it or not."

"That's goddamn stupid," Inge said.

"*Goddamn!*" interjected David, who had been silently following the discussion. Looking at Benoit he asked in French. "What does 'goddamn' mean?"

"Jesus," Benoit sighed. "How does this kid manage to pick out the very words he's not supposed to learn? Inge, you really have to remember not to curse so much around him."

"Well, hells bells, Jean," Inge replied with a mischievous grin, "it's the only way he's going to learn the language. Now if you *really* want me to teach him . . . "

"No!" Benoit grinned. "I do *not* really want you to teach him anything. He's quite capable of learning all by himself. By the way," he asked, speaking to Dobbs, "how's his father?"

"So-so," Dobbs shrugged. "He's running a fever, but that's to be expected. No sign of any infection so far. His wounds, even the damaged hand, seem to be healing."

"Tetanus?"

Dobbs shook his head. "Too early to tell. I pray not, because once it develops its almost always a sure killer."

"Have you talked to him at all?" Inge asked.

"A little," Dobbs replied, "when he's awake. The laudanum makes him sleep a lot."

"Can he speak English?" Inge wanted to know.

"A little," said Dobbs. "Mostly the kinds of things he needed to know to trade. But he speaks French and several Indian languages."

"When he's well enough, I wish you'd ask him about the missing children," said Inge. "That really troubles my mother."

"He talked a little about that last night, as a matter of fact," Dobbs said.

"Well, why in hell didn't you tell us?" Inge asked, irritated.

"I meant to," Dobbs said. "It's just that the matter of the missing Indians came up and that sidetracked me."

"Well, what did he say?"

"He hasn't seen them himself, you understand. He made that very clear to me. But he said he had heard about them from someone who had been in the camp where they are being held. He said they are fine. In good health and adjusting to the change. Of course, some of that may have been colored by the bearer of the news. But Legendre doesn't believe they have been harmed. Indians love children and they are always anxious to adopt them into their tribe. He doesn't think they're in any danger."

"David here," Benoit said, nodding at the boy, "told me something else interesting."

"Oh?" said Dobbs raising his eyebrows.

"He was there when his father was talking to the man from the village where the two children are being held. He says the man claimed that one of the children from that village was recently kidnapped by the Pawnee?"

"Not Werner or Wilhem?" Inge asked in alarm.

"No," Benoit assured her. "This was an Indian. A girl."

"A girl, eh?" said Dobbs. "That's curious. Was there a raid on the village? What happened?"

"David isn't real clear on it. But from what I can gather there's wasn't a raid or an attack or anything. The Pawnee just swept into the camp, grabbed this girl, and left. Apparently, that was the only reason for their appearance."

"Really!" Dobbs said excitedly. "Did he say why they wanted the girl?"

"That's something David wasn't very clear on. He said he understood it had something to do with some kind of star or something."

"Morning Star!" Dobbs said, slamming his hand on the table. "By God, that *is* interesting."

"What's morning star?" Inge asked.

"Not 'what,' *who*," Dobbs explained. "Morning Star is a Pawnee deity. Actually, it's a planet, Venus. But the Pawnee attach mystical attributes to it. They believe that every few years they have to sacrifice a virgin to the god to maintain their good fortune."

"How barbaric!" Inge blurted.

"It all depends on whose standards you're going by," said Dobbs. "I remember reading about it. It interested me because the Pawnee is the only Plains tribe that actually performs live sacrifices. In fact, the only other North American tribe having a similar rite is the Natchez, Back East. Of course, the Aztec in Mexico did, too, but for some reason it never became part of the North American Indian culture. I thought the practice had died out. As far as I know, no one has reported an incident for more than a dozen years. The anthropologists just assumed it had been abandoned."

"Do they really kill her?" Inge asked, making a face.

"Absolutely," Dobbs said. "It's a *very* elaborate ceremony. Stretches over several days, as a matter of fact. Damn, I'd love to know more about this kidnapping."

"Maybe Etienne can tell you some more when — and if — he's able to carry on a natural conversation," suggested Benoit.

"He probably doesn't know any more about it than what David has already related. What I'd really like to do is talk to a Pawnee. But they're way to hell and gone off to the east. Almost as far away as Fort Kearny."

"You think we ought to tell Kemp?" Benoit asked thoughtfully. "I wouldn't have thought so until he got so upset about those two boys leaving."

"Ummmmm," said Dobbs. "That's a good point."

"Why would he possibly be interested in the

Pawnee?" asked Inge. "We don't have anything to do with the Pawnee."

"Not directly," agreed Dobbs. "But the Pawnee and the Cheyenne are bitter enemies. And it's the Cheyenne who are holding Werner and Wilhem captive."

"I think we'd better tell him," Benoit said. "Nothing's lost if we do and I don't want to see you get your ass chewed all over again."

"Let's wait a day or so," said Dobbs. "I'd like to see if I can talk to Legendre in the meantime. It would probably be better if you asked him in French since his English is limited. Also, I want a chance to look at my reference books, see what I can dig up about the Morning Star ceremony."

"Just curious," Inge said nervously. "Do they ever use white girls in those sacrifices?"

Pahukstatu Village

"Everything to do with the maiden's sacrifice is prescribed," Red Calf explained to Knifewielder as they sat in his lodge, smoking Red Calf's everyday pipe. The priest had returned the sacred pipe to the Morning Star bundle and it would not be brought out again until the spring, when final preparations began for Beaver Woman's sacrifice.

"For the next few months, she will live with Old Dog and Happy Lady, who will treat her as a granddaughter."

"Why them?" Knifewielder asked curiously. "I would have thought she would be living here with you and Tall Corn."

Red Calf shook his head. "No. Tradition dictates that she will have to stay with the Keeper of the Wolf Bundle."

"Why?" Knifewielder persisted. "What does the wolf have to do with Morning Star?"

"Remember what I told you right after you experienced the vision?"

"No," Knifewielder frowned. "Tell me again."

"It is because of the wolf that all people must die," Red Calf explained patiently. "Back when the world was still being created all the gods met in council to try to decide how to go about it. But they forgot to invite the wolf and he was very annoyed. As a result, he tried to impersonate the great god *Paruksti,* who had been designated by the council to inspect their handiwork once the earth had been created. When the people — our ancestors — discovered the wolf had tried to trick them, they killed him, making him the first creature to suffer death. Although they thought they were doing Paruksti a favor, he was unhappy with their action. He commanded them to preserve the wolf's skin and keep it in a sacred bundle so they would always remember how they had acted precipitously. To this day, that is why we are known as the Wolf People and why Wolf is our god of death and war."

"But what does that have to do with Morning Star?" Knifewielder asked.

"Because," Red Calf said, "it is Wolf Star that occasionally rises in the southeast just before Morning Star. When the wolves see Wolf Star they think it is Morning Star and they prematurely begin their howling to greet him. The Keeper of the Wolf Bundle has to watch over the girl because he is associated with death. During the winter," Red Calf continued, "the girl will wear the special clothing that is part of the Morning Star Bundle: a calfskin skirt and overblouse, a warm buffalo robe, black moccasins, and a fluffy down feather in her hair. Although she will eat her meals with you and your wife, she will have her own special bowl and buffalo horn spoon. You must," he said, tapping Knifewielder on the knee to make sure he had his attention, "be sure that no one in your family uses her utensils."

"Why is that?" Knifewielder asked, puzzled.

"Because those implements belong to Morning Star. If you or anyone else uses them, Morning Star might think they too are part of the sacrifice and that could be very dangerous."

While they talked, the wind had picked up until it was howling across the prairie.

Red Calf cocked his head, listening to the gale. "This storm signals the beginning of the most cruel time of the year for us," he intoned. "From now until spring we will have to roam the Plains like the other wandering tribes, trying to find enough buffalo to keep us alive. Before we return to our village, we will lose many horses to the winter, and usually a number of people, too. But it will be worth it this year," he added, "because Morning Star has blessed us with a visit and He will be watching over us until the time He takes the girl into his house."

"How will we know when it is time for the sacrifice?"

Red Calf smiled. "*I* will know," he said with a wink. "Morning Star will tell me. When He rises ringed in red, I will know He is ready to welcome the girl."

"Will she be made aware of the fate that awaits her?" Knifewielder asked, taking the pipe from Red Calf.

"No," Red Calf said, shaking his head. "But undoubtedly she will suspect something is amiss. In the Cheyenne camp, she is bound to have heard of what happened to previous captives."

"There is one thing I do not understand," Knifewielder said. "Why won't the Cheyenne try to rescue her? If Roaming Child were to be kidnapped I would make every effort to steal him back."

"The answer is simple," replied Red Calf. "Even though the Cheyenne are our enemies they respect our religious beliefs, just as we respect theirs. To be sure, you can expect a war party of Cheyenne, but they will be looking for revenge, not freedom for the girl. They won't try to interfere with the ceremony. In their minds, it was the will of the gods that she be taken; to them she is already dead."

Cheyenne Winter Camp

Red Berry Woman wailed and thrashed about on the ground, tears streaming down her cheeks. Grabbing the knife she used to butcher buffalo, she whacked at her hair until it was ragged and uneven. Then, with a scream that expressed grief rather than pain, she made four long gashes in each calf, watching expressionless as the blood streamed down over her ankles and stained her moccasins.

Short Hair undid his braids and removed his leggings, promising not to don them again for at least a month. Then, feeling the need to purify his body and soul, he disappeared into his sweat lodge. When he emerged two days later, he went straight to Long Chin's tipi.

"What is it that you wish to do?" the village chief asked Short Hair, passing him a pipe.

"Organize a war party to move against the Pawnee," Short Hair replied.

"That goes without question," Long Chin said solemnly. "But to do so now would be foolish. The Ho'nehe-taneo'o won't be back in their village until spring. It would be sheer luck to find them while they are roaming around the Plains."

"That's true," said Short Hair. "I didn't mean to sound impatient."

"Your grief is understandable, but let me give you a few words of caution. It is better to wait until the

Thunderbird returns and chases the Winter Spirit back into his lair. That will give you time to plan carefully since I'm sure you want the raid to be a resounding victory."

"I want to kill as many Pawnee as possible," Short Hair replied vehemently. "I plan to carry only my war club when we move against them."

Long Chin sucked in his breath. "That is indeed a brave decision. Only a truly courageous Tsis-tsis-tas would go into a fight without a lance or bow, not to mention a rifle."

"It is what came to me while I was in the sweat lodge. I had a vision in which a wolf appeared. Speaking to me like a man, the animal said he was very displeased with the behavior of those who called themselves Wolf People and he was calling on me to try to remove the stain from his reputation. He said if I did as he instructed I would be successful. "

"And what did he tell you to do?"

"He said I must invoke his spirit when the time came to attack, that I should add some wolf hair to my medicine bundle and gird myself with a belt made from wolf skin."

Long Chin nodded knowingly. "I would add one more suggestion."

"And what is that?" Short Hair asked respectfully.

"I think you should carry the pipe to our Arapaho allies. Take advantage of the time you have before spring. Go to the Hetane-vo'eo'o and enlist their aid in this venture. A combined war party would teach the Pawnee a lesson they would not soon forget. If our warriors collect enough scalps, it may be many, many years before the Wolf People return looking for another Tsis-tsis-tas girl."

* * *

"Why are you so sullen?" White Crane asked. "I'm the one who took the crack on the head. By all rights, I should be the one whose chin is dragging the ground, not you. Will you please cheer up and offer me some comfort?"

Crooked Leg forced a weak grin. "My apologies, old friend. You're right. You should be morose and I should be cheerful."

"Then what is it?" White Crane asked, gingerly touching his head, which felt as it were as large as a full moon and filled with constantly shifting boulders.

"Does it still throb?" White Crane asked solicitously. "Would you like me to fix another snowpack for you?"

"It isn't so much the pain that bothers me, it's the periodic spells of dizziness that make me feel unsettled. One minute, everything is normal and the next, the whole world is spinning."

"Maybe we left too soon," Crooked Leg ventured. "The White doctor seemed to be treating you well."

"That's because I was unconscious, you fool. Once he realized that I was recovering he would have thrown us both into a room and locked the door."

"Why would he have wanted to do that? The White soldier saved us from the Crow and then the White doctor treated you. If they had wanted, they could have killed us at any time."

"They treated us well because they did not know we were Brulé and that our band took part in the battle along the Platte. But that young boy, Plays-with-His-Toes, took care of that. It's a good thing I regained my senses when I did or we would have been in for a rough time."

"Maybe, but I don't think so. I think their help was offered sincerely. But it seems that you are always the one who's right and I'm always the one who's wrong."

"That's not the way to look at it," White Crane said. "I just seem to have more of an understanding of human nature than you do. You're a thinker."

"Well, I'm certainly not a warrior."

"That's not true!" White Crane said, turning so suddenly that pain stabbed through his brain and made him grimace in agony. "Ooohhhh," he said, grabbing his head. "I have to learn to restrict my movements for a few days. But you *are* a warrior," he insisted. "You saved my life. If it had not been for you, my scalp would be hanging from a Crow lance."

"It wasn't I that saved your life," said Crooked Leg. "It was the White soldier. He saved both of us. But," he added sadly, "he did not arrive soon enough to save Bear's Ear. Now I have to go to his parents and explain how their oldest son died while he was my responsibility."

"You take too much upon yourself," said White Crane. "Bear's Ear was the responsibility of *both* of us. Besides, that's the fortunes of war. Bear's Ear died very bravely; his parents, despite their grief, will be very proud to learn that he conducted himself like a man."

"I'm a jinx," Crooked Leg said gloomily. "Every time I go on an expedition, someone close dies. On our first raid it was Storm Cloud. Now, Bear's Ear."

"You're just feeling sorry for yourself. Three days of not eating has made you surly. By tomorrow we'll be back in our camp and we'll have a feast. Pale Otter has a fat white puppy I think I can persuade her to part with."

"No," said Crooked Leg. "It's more than that. I think I may not be cut out to be a warrior. I should have realized that after Storm Cloud fell and broke his back and I got wounded. When we get back, I'm going to seek a vision. I feel in strong need of spiritual guidance."

White Crane looked closely at his friend. He opened his mouth to reply, then clamped it shut. Crooked Leg knows better than I what is good for him, he thought.

He has been troubled ever since that fight in the Crow camp. It is better now for me to say nothing. Let him take his time to work it out in his own mind. After all, he has nothing else to do all winter.

Fort Laramie

"Would you look at that snow?" Benoit said in awe, staring into the storm that arrived at the fort on a wind strong enough to bend the flagpole almost to the breaking point.

"Close the door, Jean," Dobbs urged, "or we'll all freeze. You're going to have five months of looking at blizzards. By the time April gets here, you'll be so sick of seeing white that you won't even want to get into bed until the sheets have been dyed purple."

"I've never *seen* it snow like that before," added Inge. "And I'm not a Southerner either."

"A mere preliminary," Dobbs added. "From what Ashby has told me, it's going to get a lot worse before it gets better."

"If you ask me," said Inge, "they should just let the Indians keep this goddamn country. No civilized person wants to live in conditions as extreme as they have out here."

"I'm just glad I'm not out in it," said Benoit.

"I hope," added Dobbs, "those two Indian boys got back to their camp before the storm hit. The one with the concussion shouldn't be trying to fight this, too."

"To hell with the Indians," said Inge, "I just hope the wagon train made it to Oregon in time."

"Oh, God," said Benoit, "I'd almost forgotten about the train. That seems like a thousand years ago. Wasn't there a group that got caught in the California Mountains a few years ago?"

"That was in '47," Dobbs added. "The Donner party. They tried to take a shortcut over the Sierras and got caught in a blizzard. Only about half of the group survived and they had to turn to cannibalism to stay alive."

"How do you remember all that stuff?" Inge asked in amazement.

Dobbs grinned. "Just my exceptionally keen, incisive mind, I guess."

"Then how come you can't remember to ask Mutter to mend your socks?"

Dobbs shrugged. "There *are* limits to genius."

"Genius!" Benoit exclaimed. "By God if you're . . ." he stopped. "*What* was that?"

"I think," Dobbs said, springing to his feet, "that Mr. Legendre just fell out of bed."

"I'll . . ." Inge began, rising.

"No," Dobbs said, waving her back. "I'll check. If he did fall out of bed you're not strong enough to lift him anyway."

"How is he doing?" Benoit asked Inge as Dobbs left the room.

"Not very well," she said, shaking her head. "He's suffering from a terrible fever. Jace thinks if it doesn't break soon, he's not going to make it."

"That would make David an orphan."

"I know. I've thought of that, too. Mutter has really taken him under her wing. I'm afraid she's going to get too attached to him."

"How are you going to stop her from being a mother? That's the reason she was born."

"What she really needs," Inge said, looking pointedly at Benoit, "is a grandchild or two."

"Waaait a minute," Benoit said, holding up his hands. "I know what you're getting at and it isn't going to work. I'm too young to be a father."

"But I'm not too young to be a mother," Inge shot

back. "When are you going to surrender to the inevitable?"

"Surrender is the right word," Benoit said. "As some famous general once said, 'I have not yet begun to fight.'"

"Fight all you want," Inge smiled placidly. "Just make sure that you understand that you're eventually going to lose the war."

14 March 55
Fort Laramie

Dear Mamman,

What a relief it is for me to learn that you are well and in good spirits. I received three of your letters at once yesterday, as well as the most welcome packet of delicacies, thanks to the unexpected arrival of a stage from Fort Kearny. For weeks, all traffic has been halted by a seemingly never-ending series of blizzards, but for the last week we have been experiencing a thaw. I got excited, figuring this signaled an end to winter. But Jim Ashby warns me not to get my expectations up. He says there is plenty of snow to come. I discovered, among other things, that Jim was not exaggerating the fierceness of the Plains winters. The snow began falling in earnest early in December and continued until the recent warm spell, a phenomenon referred to locally as a Chinook. In one storm, the wind blew down the flagpole *and took the roof off the new sutler's store, that had been opened only two weeks before by Bertrand Sevier, one of the numerous Canadians still hanging on in the West. Personally, I am glad for their presence; it gives me a chance to speak French.*

That poor Canadian who was wounded so severely by the bear last fall, Etienne Legendre, has finally recovered. His return to good health was no forgone conclusion. If I did not have the utmost confidence in Dr. Dobbs, and absolute respect in his healing ability, I would say that Mr. Legendre is alive today only because of a miracle and excellent care by Jace and Inge. How he escaped contracting tetanus is still a great mystery.

Even after Jace repaired his wounds as best he could, Mr. Legendre was ravaged by a fever so severe I felt sure his brain was going to be cooked. For days, he alternated between chills so violent that Jace had to keep a piece of wood lodged in his mouth for fear he would bite his tongue in two, and hot spells so intense that I could feel the heat radiating from his body several feet away. During the worst of the storms, it was so bad that Jace, Inge, Erich, and I had to maintain four-hour shifts in order to keep a fire going in the woodstove to try to make sure that Mr. Legendre did not come down with pneumonia. His fever finally broke around Christmas, but his body has not yet fully recovered. He has lost a considerable amount of weight, perhaps forty pounds, but he has hung on and the prognosis for his recovery seems greater with the coming of spring.

As I was saying about the season, even Jace had to concede that it made a New England winter seem like a carriage ride down St. Charles Avenue. He had erected a thermometer in a sheltered position on the back of our living quarters, checking it with fanatical regularity and recording its extremes in a little journal he has been keeping. During one spell in January, the thermometer dipped to fifty below zero and probably would have gone lower still but that was as low as the instrument would record. During that week, it never rose above zero. In his colorful way, Jim Ashby explained that it was so cold that if one expectorated, it would freeze before it hit the ground.

Despite how awful it sounds, winter had its pleasant days as well, days when the sun would shine and the sky would take on a hue of blue as beautiful as any you can imagine. One of the troopers harked back to his Norwegian ancestry and began spending the days working on several pairs of skis of the style used by his ancestors in the Old Country. I tried out his creations one day and, after a little amount of practice, I managed to propel myself for several miles into the countryside. The only word I can find to describe the experience is magical. It was completely silent except for the occasional snapping limb or the cry of ravens searching for food. Surrounded by the cathedral-like silence, I stood on a slight rise and watched a coyote trying to find a meal. What a marvelous sight. Although the snow was well above his belly, the coyote used his unbelievably keen sense of hearing to listen for the sounds of small animals burrowing underground. When he detected activity, he bounded like a cat, covering several yards in each leap, until he landed precisely at a spot where an unfortunate groundhog had poked up its head. Needless to say, the coyote devoured the hapless rodent in one quick gulp. On my tour, I also found the remains of several buffalo and one elk that either froze to death or starved during the successive blizzards. Their carcasses had been picked clean and the bones gnawed to stubs.

Thank goodness officers have private rooms because life in the barracks has been dreadful for the enlisted men. Stuck in their quarters with no outlet for their

*energy, the men have turned to two time-honored tradi-
tions: gambling and fighting, one practice feeding on
the other. I've lost count of how many times I, as junior
officer, have been summoned to the barracks to break up
violent disagreements. Although one of the troopers, a
private from New York, once pulled a knife on a fellow
solider I always arrived in time to make sure that the
altercation did not result in serious injury. Only occasionally do the fisticuffs proceed to the stage where medical treatment is necessary.*

*I, too, have been exceedingly bored but so far I have
not resorted to violent action, although I came close just
after Christmas when Jace and I got into a rather heated
discussion about President Pierce's signing of the
Kansas-Nebraska Act. We agreed this was good because
it created two new territories. But we fiercely disagreed
on the underlying factor, the clause that permits settlers
in each of the territories to decide if the expected new
states shall be free or slave. This is an argument we
have had before: Jace is an ardent supporter of a strong
federal government, one which has the authority to dictate to all the member states precisely what they can do.
I, naturally, take the opposite point of view. I believe
our founders did not intend for this country to be
rigidly governed from Washington, that each state
should have the right to reserve unto itself decisions
concerning its own inhabitants. Our argument precisely mirrors the debate now going on in Washington:
States Rights versus Federal Dictatorship. Of course,
we were not able to resolve the disagreement and it
ended only when we simultaneously admitted it would
be better to call a truce. By mutual agreement, at least
for the duration of the winter, we have vowed not to
discuss national politics. Instead, bridge has taken the
place of political debate. A group of us have taught Inge
the game and now she is a consistent winner, much to*

Lieutenant Grant's frustration. He cannot seem to understand how a girl who is not yet eighteen, therefore a mere child, can defeat him at a game at which he has been excelling for years. It is really quite comical. Every time Inge beats him, Grant's face turns a bright red and he begins to stammer uncontrollably. Jace and I, out of sheer perversity, have vowed that Inge's next instruction shall be in chess so she can challenge Captain Harrigan, the undisputed post champion.

I also spend a lot of my spare time reading and many hours in conversation with Mr. Legendre, who is remarkably knowledgeable about the Sioux and Cheyenne. No doubt Jim Ashby carries at least an equivalent amount of material in his head, but he is more taciturn and, by choice, speaks very little. Mr. Legendre, on the other hand, is quite voluble and jovial. Besides, except for his young son, and Mr. Sevier, I am the only one on the post with whom he can converse without inhibition since his ability with English is limited. He has brightened my days, however, by enlightening me about Indian legends and by imparting little tidbits of information about the people. For example, he has told me that the Indians have no concept of time as we know it, not even of years. Their "year" begins in April and lasts for roughly thirteen months since it is lunar based. From December to late March, they too, are virtual captives in their lodges and they spend the time telling and retelling stories from their history and reliving events in the recent past. They also use this period to compile what they refer to as a "winter count." In reality, it is a recorded history of what happened during the previous year. While we number our years, the Indians name theirs, alluding to each period from April to April by a significant event that occurred during that period, keeping a record of it with detailed pictographs painted on finely tanned elk hide. For *instance, the Miniconjou (a division of the Teton Sioux; see how much I am already learning?) recall the year that we designate 1852 as "Heavy Snow," because that winter the snow was so deep in their camp that only the tips of the tipis were visible. The year before that was called "Big Issue" because that was the time when the Treaty of Fort Laramie was signed. And so forth. They also have very colorful names for their months and connect them to events that have significance in their lives. March, for example, is "The Moon When the Eyes Are Sore from The Bright Snow." January, when the blizzards are at their worst, is "The Moon of the Terrible." In contrast, May is "The Moon to Plant" and August is "The Moon When All Things Ripen."*

Mr. Legendre also confirmed what his son, David, had told us soon after they were brought to the post: that the Pawnee had indeed captured a Cheyenne girl named Beaver Woman, who they plan to sacrifice to a god called Morning Star in the spring, probably in April although the exact time will be determined by a tribal priest. He says all of the Plains tribes consider this a most barbaric practice and regard the Pawnee as outcasts for continuing to perform the ceremony. That is quite a surprise to me, considering their common sanguinary nature. How is it that, on one hand, they kill and mutilate each other and think nothing of it, yet, on the other hand, they condemn their Pawnee brethren for making death part of a religious rite? Although I am most obligated to Mr. Legendre and others for my education on Indian matters, I am fast becoming convinced that I shall never fully understand these people, even though I have a great deal of sympathy for their plight. Even as they struggle to maintain the equilibrium that has governed their existence since before the Whites came to this country, their way of life is unquestionably threatened. They sense this and resent it, even though they do not yet rec-

ognize the totality of the changes our presence is going to make in their lives. These feelings, however, will not keep me from doing my duty. Of that I am certain.

On to more pleasant subjects, like post gossip. I mentioned earlier that just before winter a man named Sevier had been commissioned post sutler and had opened a store. Sadly, the goods are regulated mainly to whisky, items necessary for survival, and a few frills. That is why I am so grateful for the packages that you and Marion so thoughtfully assemble.

I don't think I wrote you previously about our other new arrival, the Reverend W. Cleveland Longstreet. Perhaps this will eventually mean time in purgatory for me, but I find it very difficult to have anything but contempt for this preacher, who I consider an extremely bigoted and self-righteous person. Even his physical appearance grates on my normal good humor. He is short with a huge, round belly that makes me suspect he has little regard for the prohibition against gluttony. Although he smiles a lot and would have everyone believe he is cheerful, his eyes belie his intent. They themselves are most unusual, one is brown and the other blue, but they never show amusement, even when he is trying to portray bonhomie.

The good reverend, and I use that term rather guardedly, showed up just before the first blizzard and announced his intention to stay, using the post as a headquarters while he ventures forth "to convert the savages." I dare say, he will not get far with that attitude. He also has made more than a few enemies among the men because of constant harping at Colonel Kemp to close down the Hog Ranen, a sporting house that operates just west of here. Colonel Kemp's position, and I agree with it, is that the establishment is beneficial to us since it gives the troopers an outlet for energies that otherwise would be directed toward fighting each other.

*The reverend would like the colonel to send the women
packing to San Francisco and burn the facility to the
ground, but so far his entreaties have not been heeded.*

   *Reverend Longstreet also has earned my animosity,
and that of several other Catholics on the post as well,
by constant criticism of the "Papists" and bitter attacks
against other denominations. Jace and I have a friendly
bet about who will be the first to attack the unwelcome
preacher: the women from the sporting house, the
Indians, or the unhappy troopers. I believe the odds are
tipped in favor of the Indians.*

   *I must close this because I want to send it back East
by return stage. Also, Jace has just knocked at my door
to tell me that Colonel Kemp has called a meeting of the
officers in thirty minutes in the dining room.
Something unusual must be afoot. Please give my love
to Marion and Theophile. I miss you all more than I can
possibly say.*

   Your Loving Son,
   t-Jean

"All right, gentlemen," Colonel Kemp intoned, tapping
his spoon against his coffee cup. "Since we have a lot to
discuss, let's get down to business. If you want some
more coffee, go get it now."

"First," he said, when no one left the table, "let's talk
about the news that came in the mail packet. As some of
you may know," he said, picking a sheet off one of the
stacks of papers that lay before him, "the renowned and
much respected Tom Fitzpatrick, the man most responsible for negotiating the Treaty that we are here to
uphold, recently died of pneumonia during a visit to
Washington. That left the job of Indian Agent in our
area open. Well, it isn't open any longer. President
Pierce has appointed George Teasley to take his place."

"*Major* Teasley?" Captain Harrigan asked in surprise.

"The very same," Kemp nodded. "For those of you who don't know him or about him, George Teasley was a career officer who resigned his commission after the war. Now it looks like he's gone political."

"What will this mean for us?" Benoit asked.

"As far as I'm concerned, it's good news," Kemp replied. "Teasley has extensive service on the frontier. He knows the injuns. He's not going to put up with a lot of bullshit. I suspect he's going to be a strong supporter of the Army in bringing the injuns under control. Teasley was my adjutant when I commanded a company at Leavenworth in '45. He was a good soldier and he has my confidence. Now that you all know that, I expect you to act accordingly. Is that clear?"

"When does he arrive, sir?" asked Grant.

Kemp studied the paper in his hand. "This dispatch is dated a month ago. It said he was leaving Washington immediately, so I assume he's going to show up very soon. He may be staying here, which means a couple of you are going to have to double up your quarters. Do I have any volunteers?"

Benoit fidgeted. Under the normal scheme of things, assuming no one offered to share, he expected Kemp would order him and Zack Adamson, since they were the two junior officers, to move in together.

Dobbs spoke up quickly. "If you need a room, I'll move in with Lieutenant Benoit," he said. "I spend a lot of time in the hospital anyway."

"Done," Kemp mumbled, his mind already on the next item on his schedule.

"Thanks," Benoit whispered to Dobbs in gratitude.

"Don't thank me," the surgeon whispered back. "Thank your mother. If she didn't send you such good coffee you'd be out in the cold."

"Next," Kemp said, shooting Dobbs and Benoit a

look that commanded silence. "Washington agrees with me about the injun problem."

"What Indian problem?" Benoit blurted.

"Maybe you've forgotten about the Grattan massacre, lieutenant," Kemp said sternly, causing Harrigan to smirk and Grant to stifle a laugh.

"No, sir," Benoit replied, red-faced. "I just didn't think it was a continuing problem."

"Of course, it's a 'continuing problem,'" Kemp replied brusquely. "I've made it clear how I feel about that. It was murder, pure and simple, and we can't let the injuns get away with it. We have to demonstrate that we mean business when we say that attacks against Army personnel will not be tolerated; that if they kill a solider they can expect instant and appropriate retaliation. Seems like Jeff Davis himself agrees. This is a note from him. He says he thinks the murder of Grattan and his men was, and I quote, 'a result of a deliberately formed plan,' unquote, by the Brulé."

"Why would they do that?" asked Benoit. "What motive could they have had?"

Kemp shrugged. "The Secretary of War seems to believe it was so they could clean out the warehouses and Boudreaux's trading post."

"That doesn't make much sense," argued Benoit. "They were going to get the annuity goods anyway."

"Tell that to the Secretary," Kemp shot back. "What is it, captain?"

"Are we going to move against the savages, sir?" Harrigan asked.

"Unfortunately, no," said Kemp. "We don't have the manpower. Washington is sending six hundred men out of Leavenworth."

"Six hundred!" Dobbs said in surprise. "Isn't that rather a lot to deal with a handful of Indians?"

"Washington doesn't think so," Kemp said harshly.

"Apparently the War Department feels strong action is called for."

"Who are they sending?" Harrigan asked.

"Good question," said Kemp, flipping through the papers in his hand. "Ah, here it is. Hmmmmm, mostly infantry it looks like. Company E of the Tenth under Lieutenant Colonel P. St. George Cooke, Companies A, E, H, I, and K of the Sixth under Major Cady . . . "

"Infantry!" interjected Harrigan. "They need dragoons, not foot-soldiers. The Indians don't have any respect for infantry. They think any soldier who doesn't have at least one horse is a joke."

"Well, I guess they'll find out differently," said Kemp. "But I was getting to that. The expedition also is going to include Companies E and K of the Second Dragoons and Company G of the Fourth Artillery. That ought to fix 'em."

"Who's the commander?" asked Adamson.

"I thought you'd never ask," Kemp grinned. "Bill Harney. Old Mad Bear himself!"

"Isn't he just a colonel!" Grant exclaimed, then quickly recovered. "No offense, sir."

"He's not a colonel now," Kemp said, smiling tightly. "He's been breveted a brigadier."

"Do you know him, sir?" Benoit asked.

Kemp shook his head. "Only by reputation. I know he fought in the Black Hawk War and against the Seminoles, as well as in the Mexican War. I understand he's first rate."

"Excuse me, sir," Grant broke in. "What's the Black Hawk War?"

"Jesus, Harry, I keep forgetting what a kid you are," Kemp frowned. "Or maybe its just that I'm getting old. It was a brief rebellion in Wisconsin and Illinois. Back in, let me think, '32, I reckon. Only lasted a few months. Wasn't really a war despite what the history books say.

You were probably still on the teat. I was a baby-faced lieutenant. My captain was Jeff Davis."

"And the Seminoles?" Adamson asked tentatively.

"That was in '35," Kemp said gruffly. "What is this? A goddamn history lesson?"

Dobbs coughed. "What's Colonel, er, General Harney's schedule, sir? When is he due to arrive?"

"Soon," said Kemp, fumbling for a cigar. Biting off the end, he leaned toward Harrigan for the expected light. "When this was written," he said, puffing vigorously, "Harney was in St. Louis. From there, he's going to Leavenworth, then Kearny. He's due to start marching up the Platte in our direction in late April, early May."

"Are we going to play any role in this?" asked Adamson.

"I'm going to send a detachment to join him at Kearny," Kemp said. "Mainly just a few men to let him know he has our support."

"Who's that going to be?" asked Dobbs.

"I don't know yet," Kemp said, scratching his chin. "I haven't made up my mind."

"Does that dispatch say what Harney's orders are?" asked Harrigan. "Any details?"

"No," said Kemp. "Just that his mission is to teach the Brulé a lesson. I expect we'll get some more details in the next packet. In the meantime, let's take care of other business. Now that winter is loosening its hold we might be able to get back to being soldiers rather than captives. Do any of you have any reports?"

"Not good news, I'm afraid," said Harrigan, staring at his knuckles.

"Well, what is it captain? Don't make me play guessing games."

"Looks like the expected rash of springtime deserters has started. Three privates were missing at roll call this morning."

"Oh!" Kemp said, slamming his hand on the table. "Goddamn, I hate deserters. Fucking cowards is what they are. Back stabbers. Who are the scum?"

"A couple of malcontents named Breedlove and Henderson," Harrigan said softly, "and a kid named Ryan. I'm not surprised about Henderson and Breedlove. They were troublemakers anyway. But Ryan had some promise. I thought he was going to make a good solider."

"Any idea which way they went?"

"No, sir. Some of their barracks mates said they seemed awfully interested in the news we got just before that first big blizzard. You know, about that stage that was ambushed by the Indians. Rumor is the savages, after killing all three men on the stage, made off with a strongbox containing twenty thousand dollars in gold."

"That's a strange case," mused Kemp. "Injuns don't have any use for gold, so they must have attacked the stage just to kill the White men. I'm surprised they took it."

"You're right," agreed Harrigan. "It is a strange case. Ashby said the rumor he heard was that the leader of the raiding party was that troublemaking Brulé named Blizzard."

"Blizzard!" Kemp said. "Is that the same one . . . "

"That's the one, sir," said Adamson. "He also is believed to have been in the group that attacked the Germans last summer. In fact, he was the one that Lieutenant Grattan planned to arrest when he went to the Indian camp."

"Sounds like a real bad apple to me," said Kemp.

"Getting back to the deserters, sir," said Harrigan. "Apparently "Unicorn" and "Notch" — those are Breedlove's and Henderson's nicknames, sir — told some of their friends they planned to get that gold."

"'Unicorn' and 'Notch,'" Kemp smiled. "Where in hell do the men come up with these names?"

"In this case, sir," added Harrigan, "they're deserved. It's like the Indians that assign names to people because of their physical characteristics. Unicorn gets his name because he's got a large knot in the middle of his forehead . . . "

"It's a bone cyst," Dobbs threw in. "This one's considerably larger and more prominent than most, but they're not at all uncommon."

". . . Whatever," said Harrigan, glaring at the surgeon, "there's this, shall I say, *projection* just above the bridge of his nose that looks like a small horn."

"And 'Notch?'"

"Much easier to explain, sir. He's missing a large part of the lobe of his left ear. Rumor is it was bitten off during a barroom brawl. He's big and he's mean. Unicorn's smaller but he has the look of a sneak. Several men have complained about him cheating at cards but no one was ever able to catch him at it. To be honest, I think we're better off without 'em."

"That's beside the point, goddamnit," Kemp said, annoyed. "I want all of you," he said, looking around the table, "to talk to the troopers. Make it plain that I'm not going to tolerate desertions. Violators will be tracked down and if they're caught, they're going to be punished severely. First offenders will get thirty days on bread and water. Second timers get fifty lashes. And if they're stupid enough to try it a third time and they get caught, they get branded. In the meantime, let's get a patrol out after 'em. Get a group together, lieutenant," he said, turning to Adamson. "Six men. Make sure you include an NCO. And take Ashby with you, too."

"Yes, sir!" Adamson said eagerly, jumping to his feet. "Right away, sir."

Kemp sighed. "Sit down, lieutenant. It'll wait until the meeting is over."

"You think the strongbox story is valid, captain? About the deserters going after it, that is?"

Harrigan shook his head. "Frankly, sir, I don't put a lot of faith in it. Henderson and Breedlove are dumb, but I can't imagine they're *that* dumb. Trying to get into an Indian camp to steal a strongbox would be suicide. My guess is they're headed for California."

"All right," Kemp nodded. "Adamson keep that in mind." He picked up another paper. "Next item. Lieutenant Dobbs," he said, turning to the surgeon. "Have you been down to the Hog Ranch this week? I'm getting a lot of pressure from Reverend Longstreet. He keeps leaving messages with Harrigan. Wants me to shut it down."

"I know," Dobbs replied. "He's been after me, too. I swear, I'll be glad when spring gets here and he takes his Holy Roller show into the mountains or wherever the hell he wants to go. Anyway, I checked out the girls and they're all healthy. Ellen — that's Miss O'Reilly, the madam . . . "

"I know who Miss O'Reilly is," Kemp said impatiently.

". . . she's as anxious as we are to make sure they stay clean. Nothing ruins business faster, she says, that an outbreak of clap. Longstreet has been haranguing her, too. Even worse, he's been trying to talk to the girls and convince them to give up their so-called 'sinful ways.' But so far, he hasn't made much progress. One of the girls told me that the good reverend massaged her bottom during one of his impromptu gospel sings."

"I hope she slapped his chops," Kemp chuckled.

"Hardly," smiled Dobbs. "That's not conducive to good business. She told him he could have more than a rub but it was going to cost him three dollars."

"Good for her," Harrigan said with a smile.

"All right," Kemp said briskly. "Enough chatter. You men sound like a sewing circle. Anything else we need to take care of?"

"One thing," said Benoit. "I'd like to suggest we hire Mr. Legendre."

"Hire him? To do what?" asked Grant.

"Interpret."

"Isn't that why we have Ashby?" asked Kemp.

"Not exactly," said Benoit. "Ashby's a scout, which isn't the same as an interpreter. He speaks some Sioux and can't be beat communicating with the Cheyenne, but he knows very little Pawnee and almost no Crow. Besides, when we need him he's usually off hunting or with a patrol. We need someone who pretty much stays around the post and is available full-time."

"But Legendre's English is atrocious," argued Harrigan.

"True," agreed Benoit, "but it's getting better. He's proved to be a quick learner. Besides, I can help with French when he can't express himself in English. If I'm not here, Mr. Sevier can fill in."

"Sounds complicated to me," said Kemp. "Injun to French to English."

"Only until Legendre's English improves," said Benoit. "He not only knows the Indian languages, but he's up on the culture as well. He's lived with 'em longer than Ashby and knows more about tribal politics."

"You have a point," said Kemp. "We could use a full-time interpreter to take Auguste's place. How much does he want?"

Benoit shrugged. "I haven't asked him. I believe he'd be happy with twenty dollars a month and a place to stay."

"Twenty!" Harrigan exclaimed. "There are a lot of

men on this post that would be more than happy with twenty. The privates only get thirteen."

"But a private gets his food, too. And uniforms. Legendre would provide his own food or pay for his meals with the troopers. And he has a son to support as well."

"Offer him fifteen," suggested Harrigan. "See if he jumps at it."

"You're right," said Kemp, turning to Benoit. "We could certainly use him. Tell him we'll pay him seventeen starting in April."

"While we're speaking of Legendre," said Harrigan, "has he had any more to say about that Pawnee plan to sacrifice the Cheyenne girl?"

"No," Benoit said, shaking his head. "He really doesn't know about it directly. Only what he's been told. Only that the Pawnee kidnapped a girl of about thirteen whose name is Beaver Woman."

"It's disgusting," spat Harrigan. "Human sacrifice! Noble Indians my ass. I'd like to suggest, colonel, that we conduct our own little raid while General Harney is moving against the Brulé."

"What kind of raid, captain?" Kemp asked, raising his eyebrows.

"Just a little party to go into the Pawnee camp and grab that girl back. It would help in our negotiations with the Cheyenne if we could return, what's her name?"

"Beaver Woman," said Benoit.

"Right. If we could get Beaver Woman from the Pawnee the Cheyenne might be willing to return the Mueller children. You know, trade. Child for child. Or in this case, children."

"That's an interesting concept," said Kemp, knocking the ash from his cigar. "That shows imagination."

"I disagree," said Benoit.

"How's that?" Kemp asked.

"If we lead a raid against the Pawnee that's a direct violation of the Treaty. We don't have any authority to involve ourselves in affairs between the tribes. Besides, the issue of the Mueller children is something between us and the Cheyenne, not the Pawnee. So far, we've never had a problem with the Pawnee but if we raid their camp you can bet they're not going to be too happy about it. Do we really want to make another enemy at this point?"

Kemp nodded. "That's also true. I guess if we're going to raid the injuns we might as well raid the Cheyenne and try to snatch the Mueller kids ourselves."

"But that won't stop the sacrifice," Harrigan argued. "That's purely uncivilized. It's our *duty* to keep that from taking place."

"That sounds like something Longstreet would say," Benoit shot back. "Who are we to interfere with tribal customs? Next thing you'll be saying have to stop the Indian from killing the buffalo."

"Just a minute . . ." Harrigan began hotly.

"Gentlemen. Gentlemen," Kemp interrupted. "You've both made sound arguments. Let me think about it for a bit. I want to get the Mueller children back as much as anyone on this post except possibly Frau Schmidt. I'm just not convinced we have to fight with the Cheyenne — or, if Captain Harrigan has his way, with the Pawnee — to do it. My inclination right now is to wait until Teasley gets here and turn the problem over to him. That's what he's getting paid for. As I see it, there's no big hurry. It's still too early in the year to send men against either the Cheyenne or the Pawnee. And from everything we've heard the children are in no immediate danger. In fact, they're probably being treated quite well. Anything else?"

"One minor issue," said Dobbs.

"Let's hear it," Kemp said brusquely.

"It's about Frau Schmidt," said Dobbs. "She's getting fifteen dollars a month. That isn't very much."

"We can't afford to give her a raise," Kemp said hurriedly. "Certainly not if we're going to hire Legendre too."

"That isn't what I was going to suggest," said Dobbs.

"Sorry, lieutenant. What is it you propose?"

"That she and her daughter be allowed to solicit work from the enlisted men. Right now the troopers are responsible for washing their own clothes. Let the Schmidts offer to do their laundry for them at a dollar per soldier per month."

"That's pretty steep," said Grant.

"Not really," said Dobbs. "If the troops can afford to gamble and spend their money on girls and drink at the Hog Ranch, they can probably come up with an extra dollar for their laundry."

"All right," Kemp nodded. "Let's give it a try. I know the women work hard and if we can help them, I'm in favor of it. They deserve it. Now let's get back to work."

"Are you not going to do anything but sit around and brood?" asked White Crane, his voice pregnant with concern. "It's been four months since Bear's Ear was killed. You have to forget about it."

"I can't help it," Crooked Leg replied sorrowfully. "My spirit is sad. He was just a boy."

"No, that's where you're wrong. He was a 'young warrior.' He died the way I want to die, the way all young warriors want to die — in battle. I don't want to grow old and feeble. Do you?"

"I'm already feeble."

White Crane shook his head. "Sometimes I don't know why I try so hard to remain your *kola*. You can be very difficult to get along with."

"That's what best friends are for," said Crooked Leg. "To help each other get through the rough times."

"But you have more rough times than most," White Crane said, smiling to take some of the sting out of his words. "And you bring it all on yourself. You accept too much responsibility for things that are beyond your control. Recognize that you can't bend the gods to your will. If they want something bad to happen, there's nothing you can do about it. Your real responsibility is to those around you; a true warrior has to be of good cheer, it isn't all in fighting the enemy. Winter is almost over. Don't you want to let your spring sap flow? Maybe formally court Porcupine?"

Crooked Leg was silent for so long that White Crane thought he had not heard him. "Are you getting deaf?" he asked, leaning closer. "I said 'Porcupine,' the love of your life. When are you going to try to ask her to marry you?"

"Marry?" Crooked Leg said shrilly. "I can't think of marriage. My life is too disrupted. Before we went on that horse raid against the Crow last spring I thought I was normal, that I would follow the natural progression into a warrior society and win much honor as a brave and compassionate man. But that Kangi musket ball changed my whole future. None of the warrior societies are interested in an initiate who is lame."

"You may not be able to walk as long and as fast as I can, but your horsemanship is much superior to mine. Once you get aboard a pony, it doesn't matter if one of your legs is bent. And your skill with the bow is considerable. Almost," he grinned, "as good as mine."

"Don't make jokes with me right now," Crooked Leg said tensely. "My mind is too crowded with questions. I can't give my full attention to what you're saying."

"What can I do to improve your disposition?" said White Crane, putting another small log on the fire. Despite the frigid temperature outside, the tipi was snug and comfortable. A few feet away, just beyond the thin hide wall, it was cold enough to freeze a chunk of buffalo meat solid in a matter of minutes. But inside the well-sealed tipi, the two youths were comfortable wearing only leggings with buffalo robes thrown lightly over their naked shoulders.

"You're a loyal friend," Crooked Leg said, clasping White Crane's forearm. "But there are things I must work out on my own. I've decided to perform a *han-belachia*, to 'go on the hill' and seek a vision."

"Have you talked to the *Wicasa* about this?" White Crane asked.

"Yes. Deer Dreamer has agreed to be my sponsor. But I need other help as well. Will you go with me?"

"Of course," White Crane said eagerly. "When?"

"Soon!" Crooked Leg said quickly. "This is troubling me greatly. I'd like to find peace with my spirit."

Along the Platte

Jim Ashby leaned over his pony's neck and studied the ground, picking out the tracks in the newly-thawed ground and translating that into practical detail, such as who made the tracks and when. With his practiced eye, Ashby could deduce other things as well, like how heavily the travelers had been loaded down, the condition of their horses, where they stopped to eat or rest, and whether they had been in a hurry.

"It's all a matter of knowin' what to look for," Ashby explained to his alert young companion, "things an injun boy begins learning about the time he can walk. Me and you got started late, so we have a lot of catchin' up to do."

"Like what?" Erich asked.

Ashby looked around. "See them droppin's yonder. What made 'em?"

Erich rode a little closer. "That's easy," he said. "Deer."

"That's right," Ashby nodded. "But what kind o' deer an' how big was it? Was it buck or a doe? Was it young or old? When was the last time it et, and what?"

"You can tell all that from the tracks and droppings?" Erich asked in surprise. "You a seer?"

No," Ashby chuckled. "You don' have to be a seer. You jest got to learn to keep your eyes open. Can't never slack off, not if you intend to be a good tracker. You got to see and remember ev'rythang."

"Everything?"

"Pret' near. Look at them trees. What do ya see?"

Erich shrugged. "Cottonwoods. Indicates water nearby. And over there are some evergreens, fir and spruce, and a few lodgepole pine."

"Look carefully. Which side of the trees have lighter colored bark? Which side has the most reg'lar branches?"

"Is that important?"

"It's all important," Ashby said, "if your life depends on it. What birds do you see or hear? More to the point, what birds *don't* you see and hear, and why not? You need to larn what spooks what kinds of birds. You gotta larn your birds, larn to recognize 'em not only by their colors but their songs, by the shape of their bills, the color o' their eggs. Where do they build their nests? What do they feed on? All tha's important. Even more so for the big animals. You watch the wolf, for instance. Even when he's running for his life, he'll pause and take a gander over his shoulder at whatever skeered 'im 'fore he *really* puts on the speed. Tha's sumthin' you need to know 'cause you have to know what skeered him yourself. When you get a chance, sit an' watch a frog. He'll be watchin' you jest as close 'cause they be one of the watchingest critters I ever seed. The b'ar'll show you which berries you can eat; the deer'll lead you to water. An' I ain't even touched on humans yet, how to tell one kind o' injun from another by his tracks. Where was he goin'? Was he huntin'? Off to cut a few horses? Or was he jest out for a quiet stroll? Boy, there's a whole mess of thangs you don't know yet, but you got to larn enough to keep you alive 'til you do."

"I guess you're right, Jim. When you put it that way, there's no end to what I don't know."

"Well, tha's why you got me," Ashby smiled. "You lissen to me and maybe I can larn you. Now I wan' you do sumthin'."

"What's that?"

"I wan' you to spend the rest of the day jest lookin'. I want you to watch *ev'rythang*, and tonight when we make camp I'm goin' to ask you some questions about what you seed. You un'erstan'?"

"Yes. But what if I miss something?"

"You can count on it," Ashby laughed. "If you see even a fraction what you shuda seen, I'll be right pleased. But don' be discouraged. It takes a lot of practice and a lot of concentration. It's one hell of a lot harder than readin' words in a book or figurin' your sums, I g'arantee you that."

March was a transitional month on the Plains. Sometimes it was as cold as January; sometimes it was as warm as May. More often, though, it was winter one day, spring the next, swinging back and forth between seasons like the bat-wing doors of a popular saloon. When Ashby and Erich set out from Fort Laramie with Zack Adamson and his small detachment looking for the three deserters, it had been warm enough for them to shed their jackets. So far, they had been on the trail for two days and the weather was holding.

Adamson was in a good mood, excited about the possibility of overtaking the three since there were no obvious signs that they were hurrying along.

"Guess they figured we wouldn't be chasing them," Adamson told Ashby. "They're so dumb they probably reckoned Colonel Kemp would just sit back and let them go without making an effort to find them."

Ashby grunted but did not reply.

"What do *you* think, Jim? You think they're stupid enough to figure that?"

"That's a bit hard to answer, lieutenant," Ashby said, reaching for his chewing tobacco. "I don't rightly know the men we're lookin' for 'cept by sight. I got no idee if they be stupid or pret' damn smart."

"Smart!" Anderson said, looking up in surprise. "How do you come to that conclusion? You certainly haven't had any trouble tracking them."

"You're right about that," Ashby said. "Easier 'n readin' a newspaper."

Although it had been one of the most brutal winters in recent memory, the recent thaw had been of sufficient duration for the ground to thaw considerably, especially where it was exposed to the bright Wyoming sun. Along the trail, while snow was still deep in the Laramie Mountains that loomed just ahead and to their left, it had melted in their direct path, leaving large expanses of bare ground dappled with mud puddles. "Looka this here," Ashby said, pointing out a clear hoofprint in the soft ground, a mark so evident that even the inexperienced Adamson had no trouble spotting it.

"My point exactly," said Adamson. "They're leaving a trail even I could follow. So how does that make them smart?"

"Maybe," Ashby said, biting off a chew of the rock-hard tobacco, "they want us to see their trail."

"Want us to?" Adamson chuckled. "Now why would they want that?"

"Jes' to argue a little," Ashby said, "might be they want us to think they're headin' one way when they really plan to go another. I tracked men like that afore. I'll be followin' along on a nice, clear trial an' all of a sudden, it might vanish. Poof! Jes' like that. Like they suddenly grew wings and flowed away. Another possibility," he said carefully, "is they may be leadin' us into an ambush."

"Ambush!" Adamson said loudly, reigning his horse to a stop. "By God, I never thought of that. Maybe I ought to send some men out on the flanks."

Ashby laughed softly. "Jes' testin' your reflexes, lieutenant. I ain't of the 'pinion that an ambush's likely."

"Why not?" Adamson asked, glancing quickly from one side of the trail to the other.

"'Cause *that* would be stupid," Ashby said. "Them boys know they might get away from us if they be real clever. But if they was to lay an ambuscade an' some or all of us was to get kilt, Colonel Kemp would empty the fort sendin' men out to find 'em. And that ain't what they want."

"Good point, Ashby," Adamson said, smiling tightly. "I have to admit you had me going for awhile there. My sphincter almost cut a notch out of my saddle."

Ashby roared. "Save that for real trouble, lieutenant. Like if we was to run into a passel of angry Sioux."

"I've been thinking about that," Adamson said. "I mean, I know the redskins wiped out Lieutenant Grattan and his men without hardly breaking a sweat. But does that make them real warriors? Seeing as how they had our men outnumbered a hundred to one, I mean."

Ashby paused before answering, shifting his wad of tobacco from one side of his jaw to the next. "Don't make any mistake about it, lieutenant," he said in little more than a whisper. "Man for man, the Sioux could whip the Army's ass quicker 'n you can say 'dagnabit.' If they had the equipment y'all have, there wouldn't be no Fort Laramie 'cause all you soljers would still be runnin' into the sunrise." "

"Oh, come on, Ashby. Don't you think you're exaggerating just a tad. After all, they're just ignorant savages."

Ashby spit a long stream of juice, then carefully wiped his mouth with the back of his hand, leaving a large brown streak across the winter-whitened skin.

"Tell me sumthin', Lieutenant, just out of curiosity?"

"Yes," Adamson said carefully. "What's that?"

"You went to West Point, didn' ya?"

"Yes. Class of '52. Why?"

"Where you from?"

"Baltimore, Maryland."

"Baltimore. That's a right proper city. What did yore daddy do?"

"He's a bookkeeper at the Atlantic Tobacco Company. Why? What's that have to do with what we were discussing?"

"Well, it's kinda like I was tellin' young Erich a li'l earlier. An injun's different. You had four years o' military trainin', right?"

"That's correct."

"Well, an injun's military training begins as soon as he's born. His first toys are little bows and lances. All his games are military oriented. He knows more about fightin' 'n tactics 'n strategy by the time he's twelve than most Dandy Jacks larn in a lifetime."

"Should I be insulted by that, Ashby?" Adamson asked sharply.

"No, lieutenant," the scout chuckled. "Weren't nothin' personal. I'm jest tryin' to 'splain to you the difference between white soljers and red soljers. With injuns, being a warrior ain't a career, it's *life*. Injuns have only two reasons for livin' — huntin' and fightin'. Their whole society is set up with them two thoughts in mind. Nothin' else matters. They grow up believin' it's better to die young in a good fight than get old 'n gray."

"But they don't all die young. Some of them get quite old."

"'Course they do, but it ain't sumthin' they look forward to."

"That helps explain why they're so bloodthirsty," Adamson said.

"Naw, you don' un'erstan' what I'm sayin', lieutenant. They ain't bloodthirsty. It's jest the way they *live*. They been fightin' each other for so long that they don't know nothin' else. If those dunderheads in Washington are able to get 'em on res'vations, it's gonna be the end of the injun. Coop 'em up, don' let 'em hunt, don' let 'em kill each other, they'll jest dry up and blow away."

Adamson rode silently for several minutes, digesting what Ashby had told him. "Answer something for me?" he said at length. "Why do they hate us?"

"Agin, it ain't nuthin' personal, lieutenant. Hate ain't got nuthin' to do with it. Far as they're concerned, we're just another tribe that they have to fight because *everybody* is an enemy until proven differen'. They make alliances, like the Sioux an' the Cheyenne an' the 'Hos, they's always fightin' the Crow and the Pawnee. But tha's jest connections of convenience. Like they say back in 'Tucky, 'The big dawg always eats first.' It's the same out here. The strongest tribe gets the best huntin' grounds and the best warrior gets the most honors."

"They say we're decimating their forests, ruining the best grazing land, chewing up the prairie. Worst of all, we're killing all the buffalo, depriving them of the animal that is absolutely vital to their existence."

"You gotta take tha' with a grain o' salt, lieutenant. It's true, the emigrants been killin' a few buffalo, but that ain't nothin' like I seen the injuns themselves do."

"What do you mean?"

"Once I hired on as a guide to an artist fellow named Catlin. I was with him once in Brulé country when we

seed the Sioux kill an entire herd of buffler jest to get
their tongues so they could take 'em to the tradin' post
and get liquor and gunpowder. Left all them carcasses
jest rottin' on the ground. Woulda fed a whole band all
winter, easy. I heard tales o' the Oglalas doin' the same
thing up on Laramie Fork. Wiped out a hun'erd or so
buffler just to get the tongues, livers, and hump ribs.
Left ev'rythang else for the wolves and coyotes. An' as
far as forests go, I seen 'em kill many a cottonwood
stand while strippin' the bark to feed to their horses
during the winter."

"Jim! Jim!" Erich called excitedly, galloping to meet
Ashby and Adamson. "You've got to come up here. This
is crazy."

Ashby looked at him calmly. "Don't get so excited,
boy. This trail's so plain even a blind man could follow
it."

"That's just it, Jim. Just over that rise," he said, pointing to a small hill five hundred yards to the west, "the
tracks just disappear. They just vanish into thin air."

Ashby smiled grimly at Adamson. "I hate to say I tol'
you so," he said quietly, digging his heels into his
pony's flanks, chasing after Erich.

The Brulé Camp

Deer Dreamer, White Crane, and Crooked Leg worked
until midafternoon constructing a purification lodge in a
sheltered cove a two-hour walk from the main camp. First
they dug a shallow pit which would be the receptacle for
the heated stones. Around the pit, they erected a framework of supple willow, bending the branches until they
formed an igloo-like structure less than five feet tall at
its highest point, its entrance pointing due east.

After the framework was up, they covered the

branches with overlapping buffalo robes layered carefully to make sure the lodge was tightly sealed. On the
ground inside they spread a thick coating of sage.

When they dug the pit, they carefully piled the dirt in
one spot two paces in front of the entrance. This tiny
mound was called the hanbelachia, or vision hill, and
was the origin of the name commonly applied to the
ceremony. The space between the hanbelachia and
the entrance was painstakingly leveled, with all pebbles
and stems of grass conscientiously removed. This was
called the "smoothed trail" and was important to the
ceremony because it, along with the pit and the mound,
were symbolic of the entire vision quest.

Around the perimeter of the lodge, the three plunged
into the ground sticks to which were attached small
pouches of tobacco. These were meant as offerings to
the gods, supplicatory inducements to draw them
closer. On the smoothed trail, with its stem pointing
directly to the east, was placed a special pipe that
Crooked Leg and Deer Dreamer would smoke while
they were in the lodge.

White Crane's job was to stay outside and pass them
heated stones on a forked stick and refill the pipe when
Deer Dreamer commanded.

After all was ready, Deer Dreamer and Crooked Leg
stripped off their clothing and crawled into the lodge,
carrying with them sprays of sage to cover their genitals. Once they were comfortable, White Crane passed
them four red-hot stones, which Deer Dreamer placed
delicately inside the pit. Using a consecrated sheep-horn
spoon, he dipped water from a container that he had
brought with him and sprinkled it on the rocks, sending
clouds of steam billowing into the air. Four times he did
this, until the lodge was filled with thick steam.

As they sweated and baked, Deer Dreamer lit the
sacred pipe and he and Crooked Leg smoked energeti-

cally. When one of them felt as if he was about to suffocate, he excused himself and stuck his head out the entrance to take a few breaths of fresh air.

"Look at this," Crooked Leg said in amazement when they had been in the lodge quite some time, pointing to a spot on his forearm that appeared to be a serious burn.

Deer Dreamer smiled. "Here's how you make it go away," he said, popping a pinch of sage into his mouth. After chewing it for several seconds, he spit on the burned spot and the lesion vanished, the skin becoming cool. "Those spots," he explained, "are where the impurities in your body are trying to escape.

Crooked Leg and Deer Dreamer remained in the lodge for most of the night. A few hours before dawn, after they had repeated the heated-stone process precisely four times, they emerged into the cold air, sweating heavily and gasping for breath. "Look," Deer Dreamer panted, pointing excitedly at the mound of earth they had created earlier at the end of the smoothed trail. In the soft earth were the distinct impressions of small deer hooves. "That's my supernatural animal helper leaving his mark," Deer Dreamer said happily. "He approves of what we're trying to do."

"Did you have a dream?" he asked Crooked Leg anxiously.

Crooked Leg shook his head.

"Then we will continue," said Deer Dreamer, reaching for a parfleche he had brought along. Removing a chunk of pemmican, he instructed Crooked Leg to take no more than a bite because it was important that he fast if he hoped to have a vision. "And take only a swallow of water," he added.

After Crooked Leg had eaten and drunk, White Crane and Deer Dreamer led him to the top of a small hill about a mile away from where they had built the purification lodge. There they dug a pit about four feet deep and three feet long, barely large enough for Crooked Leg to squeeze into. They lined the pit with fresh sage, then covered it with a platform of branches, leaving a small entranceway through which Crooked Leg could wiggle.

Finally, before leaving Crooked Leg alone, White Crane poked more sticks into the ground. This time, to the tobacco that was in the pouches, Deer Dreamer added bits of skin trimmed from Crooked Leg's forearms and thighs, the better to entice the spirits.

Without farewell, White Crane and Deer Dreamer turned and plodded down the hill, leaving Crooked Leg standing alone with only the sacred pipe. As the sun rose brightly over the wooded hills to the east, Crooked Leg aimed the stem of the pipe directly at the fiery ball and chanted a song asking the gods to come to him and give him directions.

All day he stood, singing his song until he was hoarse, turning so he always faced the sun. For several hours after sunset, oblivious to the cold, he stood, still whispering his plea. Shortly after midnight, near the point of exhaustion, he climbed into the pit and collapsed onto the bed of sage.

For three more days, he repeated this routine, standing naked in the sun, arrow straight, from before dawn until well after dark, then scurrying into the pit for a few hours of fitful sleep.

Shortly before noon on the fifth day, weak from hunger and thirst, he was standing on the verge of collapse when he heard a deep voice calling him by his old name, the one he had before he changed it to Crooked Leg following the fight in the Crow camp.

"Running Antelope," the voice said, "do you hear me?"

Crooked Leg looked all around but the hill to was

barren. Looking up, he shielded his eyes from the glare but could see nothing but the huge, white sun.

"Don't you know that what you are doing is very dangerous?" the voice continued.

"Yes," Crooked Leg replied weakly. "I know it could kill me, but I think that would be preferable to living as a man without purpose."

"The very fact that you are trying to find your way speaks strongly of your courage," the voice replied. "Do you think you are brave enough to follow the path that might be prescribed?"

"I don't know," Crooked Leg answered, his voice barely audible.

"It will be very difficult," the voice persisted. "You will wish many times that you had never ventured upon this quest."

"It was not of my choosing," Crooked Leg replied. "I knew in my heart that I could not continue to live until I found my destiny. If I had not chosen to perform the hanbelachia I would have tossed myself off a cliff or jammed an arrow down my throat. Without purpose, my life was unbearable."

"Well," said the voice, "why do you think it will be bearable once you know what the gods have planned for you?"

"Because just knowing that it is the will of the gods would be reason for me to persevere, just as I have persevered in the hanbelachia," Crooked Leg squeaked. "Point me down the right path and I shall prevail, no matter how many difficulties may lie ahead."

"You have shown an extraordinary proclivity for accepting responsibility," the voice said. "Can you continue to do that if it is the will of the gods? Can you put aside the desires that would entice most men and do what you know has to be done?"

"I will, or I will die in the attempt."

"Very well," said the voice. "We shall see. You have demonstrated phenomenal stamina in a demanding ceremony that is not intended for the weak or meek. Climb back into your pit and sleep soundly until your body tells you to awaken. While you are asleep, the gods will speak to you and give you further directions. Have courage, my son. Your destiny will not be an easy one but if you fulfill it, your name will be remembered as long as Our People inhabit the earth."

Gratefully, Crooked Leg sank to his knees. Reaching with shaking hands for the flask of water that sat nearby —water he had ignored throughout his ordeal despite his overwhelming thirst — he tipped it and drank deeply. Instantly, his stomach rebelled and he vomited the water back out almost as quickly as it went down. Chastising himself for his greed, Crooked Leg again tipped the vessel to his lips, this time taking only two small swallows. When that stayed down, he took two more, then two more.

With his thirst partially appeased, he dug into the parfleche of pemmican. Lifting one of the bars to his lips, he took a small bite, careful this time to indulge with moderation. He washed that down with two more small swallows of water, then took another bite. Finally, feeling sleepier than he ever had before, he fell to his stomach and crawled like a snake into the pit. Within seconds, he was sound asleep.

Crooked Leg slept for almost eighteen hours. When he awakened it was late in the afternoon of the sixth day. Feeling rested, but incredibly hungry he exited the pit and stood staring at the setting sun, marveling at the inner peace that had come over him. On shaky legs, he staggered down the hill and into the small temporary camp where Deer Dreamer and White Crane were waiting.

"Behold," White Crane cried heartily when Crooked

Leg approached. "My kola lives. I feared that we would have to bury you in the vision pit."

"Don't make light of a man who has been on the hill," Deer Dreamer said sharply. "Until you yourself have done it you have no right to speak so lightly of the experience."

"It's all right," Crooked Leg said, his voice still hoarse from so much singing. "He means no harm. It is the custom we have always observed between us."

"You're right," White Crane said sheepishly to Deer Dreamer. "I should have been more respectful."

"That is not the important issue," Deer Dreamer said, waving away White Crane's apology. "Sit here, Crooked Leg," he said, pointing to the spot of honor at the fire. "Tell us what happened. Did you find your vision?" he asked, removing his robe and throwing it over Crooked Leg's shoulders.

"Yes," he replied, "but I'm not sure it wasn't a creation of my fevered brain, considering the state of near physical exhaustion I was in."

The wicasa smiled. "That's the way it always is, my son. Let us smoke a pipe, thanking the gods, and then you can tell us about your vision."

"It was more a dream than a vision," Crooked Leg said once the pipe was finished and the ashes had been emptied. "But before I tell you, may I please have some water?"

"Of course," Deer Dreamer said, signaling to White Crane to fetch his friend a drink.

"Ahhhhh," said Crooked Leg after he had drunk. "I never thought water would taste so good."

"Your vision," Deer Dreamer prompted. "Tell us."

Speaking slowly at first, as if uncertain of his memory, Crooked Leg explained how he had been on the point of collapse when a voice had called to him.

"Can you describe the voice?" asked Deer Dreamer.

"No," said Crooked Leg. "There was nothing unusual about it except that I found it very comforting. I wasn't at all threatened."

"Continue," Deer Dreamer nodded.

Crooked Leg told how he was instructed to go into the pit, where he immediately subsided into a deep, coma-like sleep. While he was unconscious, he said, he dreamed that he saw himself riding among the Brulés on a large, dark chestnut horse that was totally strange to him. As he wended his way through the tipis, he noticed that many of the people were crying. A number of women were wailing and slashing their legs as they do when they are in mourning. But as he went among them they all turned to look at him and they began begging him to do something about their troubles.

Without knowing exactly how or why because dreams are often so disorganized, he was suddenly transported from the village to a vast plain. It was late summer or early autumn, he recalled, because there was a crispness in the air that made him feel vibrant. He was still mounted on the horse, and when he turned to look behind him he saw hundreds of Brulé warriors painted for war, waiting for his signal. Although he was not sure exactly why, he urged his horse forward and began galloping across the plain. Although he was all by himself in front of the group, he felt no fear, not even when the arrows began flying at him thicker than raindrops in a summer storm. He could hear guns exploding as well, so many than it sounded like children shaking a thousand gourd rattles. He continued his charge, still unafraid, as the arrows flew straight at his breast. He could even clearly see the small round balls that came from the guns. But when the missiles got within arms length they simply disappeared, melted faster than a piece of ice thrown into a blazing fire. There were so many, he said excitedly, that he should have been killed a hundred times over, but he remained untouched.

"Was that when you awoke?" asked Deer Dreamer.

"Oh, no," said Crooked Leg. "That was only the first dream battle."

"There were others?"

"Yes," Crooked Leg nodded. "Many. Variations of the same theme repeated themselves time and again," he said. "Always, at the beginning of each sequence, the people are sad and they call upon me to go to war for them, to seek revenge for some unspecified wrong. But no matter what I do, no matter how many times I ride into the face of almost certain death, I always emerge unscathed. Despite this, the plight of the people never changes. They are always sad. Tell me," he said to Deer Dreamer, "does this mean that our people will henceforth suffer hardship and privation?"

Deer Dreamer waited a long time before answering. Sitting silently in the campfire glow, he chewed his lip until it bled. Since he had given his robe to Crooked Leg, his body began to show the effects of the cold night air. Goose pimples rose on his arms and back, and he began to shiver. But he was oblivious to the reactions of his body, concentrating with all his might on what Crooked Leg had told him.

"Yes," he said sorrowfully, "I think your vision foretells that our people are in for much anguish. But you hold the key to their possible salvation, or at least their relief. They will accept you as their leader. It will be your responsibility to try to find them peace. It will not be an easy road to follow, but you undertake the journey knowing that you will be invincible to the weapons of your enemies."

Crooked Leg slumped forward, extending his hands

over the fire, where he slowly twisted them, absorbing the warmth like the soil absorbs rain after a drought. "That is what I thought the dream meant, too," he said tiredly. "It was not a happy conclusion."

"No one promised you your vision was going to be an optimistic one," Deer Dreamer said sharply. "You have to accept what the gods give you."

"You're right," Crooked Leg replied. "I was just hoping that it might be more uplifting."

"You are still exhausted," Deer Dreamer said. "Right now you need to sleep some more. Then when you awaken we will talk some more and you will tell me in more detail about your vision."

"But what if I dream again?" Crooked Leg asked in alarm. "What if my new dream contradicts or nullifies what I dreamed on the hill?"

"Don't worry about that," Deer Dreamer said. "Any dreams you have now will be normal man dreams. What you had on the hill was a supernatural dream and you will never forget it."

"I am relieved to hear that," Crooked Leg sighed. "I would not want to go through that experience again. At least," he added hurriedly, "not right away."

He paused, obviously recalling his vision. "There was one thing," he said slowly, "that I did not mention earlier but was rather strange."

"And what was that?" Deer Dreamer asked.

"When I was moving among the people and they were talking to me, they did not call me 'Crooked Leg.'"

"Oh," said Deer Dreamer, raising an eyebrow. "What did they call you?"

"Red Horse," Crooked Leg replied. "Like my steed. They called me Red Horse."

"Oh, no," interjected White Crane, speaking for the first time since Crooked Leg began telling them about his dream. "Just when I was getting used to calling you

'Crooked Leg.' I wish the gods, while they are deciding your fate, would please quit changing your name."

Along the Platte

"Jes' what I was afeared of," Ashby said, halting his pony where Erich was pointing at the ground. "You're right," he said, staring at a surface of solid rock. Nearby, Ashby could see deep grooves cut into the granite by steel-rimmed wagon wheels.

"I know they wouldn't normally leave tracks over the rock but I can't find where they resume," said Erich. "It's like the three just disappeared."

"Disappeared by intention," said Ashby. They *wanted* us to follow them this far, now they don't *want* us to follow them any further."

"Does this mean we've lost them for good?" Adamson asked uneasily. "I don't want to go back and tell Colonel Kemp that we've failed."

"We ain't failed yet," Ashby said emphatically. "These sumbitches didn't count on Jim Ashby being on their tails. Give me a while. The rest of you may as well relax. Build a fire and fix some coffee while I have a looksee. I'll find their trail agin, I promise ya."

While Adamson and the other troopers slipped to the ground and began collecting firewood, Ashby, with Erich following closely behind him, began riding slowly in ever-widening circles, his eyes glued to the ground.

Two hours later, Erich came galloping back to where the troopers had stopped. "Jim says mount up," Erich said happily. "He's found their trail again. It's off this way," he said, pointing over his shoulder.

"Ya know," Ashby said when Adamson trotted to his side, "there may have been something to that barracks gossip after all."

"What do you mean?"

"Those there wanted us to believe they were headin' to Californy. Maybe they figured we'd only stick with the trail long enough to see which way they was goin', then we'd turn back to the fort and tell the colonel they was headin' for the gold fields."

"But you don't think they are?"

"If they are," Ashby said with a straight face, "they're going through Inja 'cause they're headed east by north. And that sure as hell ain't the right direction to San Francisco."

"Would you care to guess where they might be headed?" Adamson asked.

"If I was a bettin' man, I'd say they're goin' to where they think there's gold, except it ain't in no Californy river. I think they's headed for the Brulé camp. They jes' might be plannin' on trying to get that strongbox after all. And if tha's the case, I might change my mind about them agin."

"How's that?" asked Adamson.

"If they plan on trying to take property from the Brulés, I reckon they're pretty goddamn dumb after all. The best thing that could happen to them now is that we catch up with 'em first. Spending some time in chains with a bread and water diet is definitely better for their future health that what the Brulé would do if they catch 'em sniffin' around."

"Then I guess we'd better get cracking," Adamson said, ready to urge his horse forward.

"Hol' on jes' a second, lieutenant. I ain't finished yet."

"Oh no? I thought you'd just about summed it up pretty well. You *can* follow this trail can't you?"

"Oh, yes, tha's no problem. But I don't advise it right away. Ya see, there's a big storm comin' and the best thing we can do is find us a nice, warm place to ride it out."

"Storm?" Adamson asked, puzzled. Looking up, the sky was as blue as a colleen's eyes, not a cloud to be seen in any direction. "How can you say there's a storm coming? How could you possibly know that?"

"The same way the injuns would," Ashby said, tapping his nose. "I can *smell* it."

≈ 10 ≈

Just as a new storm was forming over Laramie Peak and a northwest wind came whipping through the Platte River Valley, the new Indian Agent, George Teasley, slogged into Fort Laramie, both horse and rider on the verge of collapse.

"Jesus," Kemp said, hurrying to meet his old adjutant, "you look like death warmed over."

"Hi, Brad," Teasley said, his voice a bare whisper. "It's been a long ride from Kearny."

"What the hell? Did you try to make it all in one go?"

"Two, actually," said Teasley, slipping to the ground, where he tottered and would have fallen if Kemp had not supported him. "Camped one night on the way. Other than that, I've been in the saddle for forty-eight hours straight. I have to admit," he grinned ruefully, "that I ain't as young as I once was."

"Private!" Kemp yelled to Bianchi, who happened to be passing by. "Take Major Teasley's horse. Come on, George," he said, grabbing Teasley's elbow, "we've got

a room all ready for you. Frau Schmidt will draw you a
hot bath. Stay awake long enough to wash off the crud
before you climb into your bunk. We can talk in the
morning."

"Appreciate it, Brad. I don't think I'd be a very good
conversationalist this evening."

"Well, George," Kemp said, watching Teasley use a bis-
cuit to mop up the last of the yolk from the four eggs
Hildegard had basted for him. "Looks like you arrived
just in time. A new storm came in last night. Another
goddamn twenty-six inches of snow. Doesn't look like
we're going to be doing anything for the next few days
anyway. Thought this might be a good opportunity for
you to meet the staff and brief us on what you have in
mind. This is Jon Harrigan," he said, pointing to the captain who was sitting, as usual, on his right. One by one,
he introduced the officers, then Legendre who had been
asked to join the group.

"Two men are missing," Kemp explained.
"Lieutenant Adamson and Jim Ashby, my scout.
They're out looking for deserters."

"I hope they had enough sense to find some good
shelter," Teasley said.

"I'm not worried about 'em," Kemp replied. "Ashby
knows what he's doing. My fondest hope is they found
the deserters frozen stiffer than boards. Save everybody a
lot of trouble. There's someone else you need to know,"
Kemp said with a smile. "Frau Schmidt," he called
loudly. "Would you please come in?" Turning to Teasley,
he winked. "Be nice to her and she'll see that you eat like
a king." Reaching in his pocket, he produced two cigars.
"Smoke?" he asked offering one to Teasley.

"Don't mind if I do," the new Indian Agent replied,
stretching. "By God, I slept well last night. Who's room

did I appropriate?" he asked with a smile, revealing a set of even, white teeth.

"Mine," Dobbs replied, returning the smile. "But don't lose any sleep over it. Bad pun intended."

"I won't," Teasley chuckled, nodding at the surgeon. "You can be sure of that. Fifteen years in the Army taught me not to lose sleep over *anything*."

As Teasley joshed with Dobbs, Benoit studied him, trying to take his measure. He was tall and slim, with a thick, well-trimmed dark red beard which was a shade or two deeper than his hair, although both were flecked with a few strands of premature gray. His voice was deep and even, a parade ground voice, Benoit perceived, and its tone suggested someone who was accustomed to having his commands obeyed. He smiles too readily, Benoit thought. He's too clever by half, and he's way too full of himself. He's a politician masquerading as a soldier. Benoit felt his jaws clench involuntarily. I think, he said to himself, that I don't like him worth a damn.

"By the way, Brad," Teasley continued, oblivious to Benoit's stare, "before I forget. Jeff Davis sent you a box of cigars. They're in my kit. Said he was sure you could put 'em to good use."

"Well, that was right kind of him," Kemp replied, beaming. "'Course, he could have sent me another couple hundred men and that would have been even kinder."

"You won't need 'em, Brad," Teasley said confidently. "You aren't going to *have* any Indian problem now that I'm here."

"That's very encouraging," Kemp said, sobering. "And just how," he asked, eyeing the agent carefully, "do you plan to see to that?"

"Simple," Teasley said facilely, smiling a thanks to Harrigan for lighting his cigar. "Remember what you

used to try to pound into our heads back at
Leavenworth? 'The secret to success on the battlefield,'"
he said, lowering his voice to imitate Kemp, "'is divide
and conquer . . . divide and conquer . . . divide and conquer.' Remember how you used to harp on that? Jesus,
you were a real fanatic about it."

"And what does that have to do with our current situation?" Kemp asked, irritated by Teasley's inadvertent
lampooning of him in front of his men.

"Look," Teasley replied, "I've been giving this a lot of
thought. In fact it's all I've thought about since I knew I
was going to get the appointment. The solution came to
me in flash, about a quarter of the way between
Leavenworth and Kearny."

"Just like that!" Kemp said, snapping his fingers.
"Divine inspiration."

"Sort of," Teasley admitted, ignoring the sarcasm.
"But it's really not difficult. Listen to me. There are a lot
of Sioux out there, right?"

Kemp nodded.

"You can't possibly go against all their warriors and
hope for a victory. Not even with the men Harney is
bringing."

"Go ahead," Kemp muttered.

"So what I plan to do is this. I'm of the belief that
not all of them want to fight the U.S. Army despite the
fact that they're encouraged by what happened to
Grattan. That wasn't the Army's finest hour. I'm convinced," he continued, "that there are a large number
of them, particularly those other Teton Sioux who are
not Brulé, and even some of the Brulé, who want to
abide by the terms of Fitzpatrick's treaty, and who
don't believe there's anything to be gained by fighting
the White soldiers."

"I'm listening to you," said Kemp, "but I'm not sure I
agree with you."

"Well, there's one way to find out," Teasley said, knocking cigar ash into the dregs of his coffee.

"What's that?" asked Harrigan.

"I plan to send word immediately to all the Teton bands — the Oglala, the Hunkpapa, the Sans Arc, the Miniconjou, the Two Kettles, the Blackfeet Sioux, and, naturally, the Brulés. I have to act quickly, before Harney gets here. I want them all to know that the Great Father in Washington is very upset by what happened, and that he plans to seek revenge. At the same time, he doesn't want to kill a lot of innocent people. By innocent, I mean those who didn't participate in the massacre, and that eliminates all but the Brulé and the Miniconjou."

"What is he saying?" Legendre whispered urgently to Benoit.

Covering his mouth with his hand, Benoit half turned to the interpreter and began explaining to him, in French, what Teasley was proposing.

"I'm going to send runners to all the camps, today, tomorrow at the latest. To hell with the snow. I want to tell them that troops are coming and they've got revenge on their minds. Revenge is a word the Indians understand, you can bet your ass on that."

"You mean tip our hand?" Harrigan asked, horrified. "Just come right out and warn them of an impending attack?"

"As if it's going to be a big surprise to them," Teasley said sharply. "You think they don't *know* what we're planning."

"Go on," said Kemp, disregarding Harrigan.

"Well, here's the kicker," said Teasley. "I'm also going to tell them that the North Platte is going to be the dead line, that all of the bands and divisions — all those who want to maintain peace with us — must move south of the river."

"And what if they don't?"

"Then," Teasley said frostily, "they will be considered hostile. Then you guys will go in and kill as many of them as you can."

"Are you going to put a time limit on this?" Kemp asked.

Teasley nodded. "Mid-April."

"God," said Harrigan, "that's not very much time. Only a month."

"That's all the time I want to give them," Teasley replied. "I don't want to let them talk this to death as they are prone to do. Indians are notorious procrastinators. They'll drive you goddamn crazy, given half the chance. If we allow them to dither, we lose the initiative. I want to make it understood that the time limit is firm; any of them who haven't moved south of the Platte by mid April will be considered enemies and they will be subject to attack."

"*Putain de merde!*" Legendre cursed when Benoit translated Teasley's plan. "Is he crazy? Does he want to start a full scale war?"

Kemp glared at the Canadian. "Go on," he said to Teasley.

"That's about it. By getting those friendly to us south of the river, we've divided the enemy at least in half. Then we have to fight only those who ignore the warning."

"You mean *ultimatum*, don't you?" asked Dobbs.

Teasley shrugged. "Warning. Ultimatum. I don't want to argue semantics."

"But won't those south of the river join their fellow tribesmen once we start attacking?" Grant asked.

Teasley shook his head slowly. "Probably not. Not once they see the huge amount of firepower we can bring to bear."

"It won't work," whispered Legendre. "He doesn't know the Teton Sioux. He doesn't know how proud they are. What fearless warriors they are. What good fighters they are."

"What about the ones who took part in the Grattan massacre?" Harrigan asked. "Are we going to let them come south so we can slap their wrists? Just smile and say everything's forgiven?"

"Absolutely not!" said Teasley. "When I instruct the runners I'm going to make sure they explain that we know who the murderers are, that we have them identified, and they are going to have to be punished. That's a given."

Kemp rubbed his chin. "It just may work," he said slowly.

"Of course it will work, Brad. What we're doing, really, is buying time until we're strong enough to meet them on an equal footing, warrior for warrior. No one back in Washington doubts for a moment that a showdown with the Indians is coming. It's just a matter of when and how."

"God, that's callous," said Dobbs, shaking his head.

"Callous or not, it's true," Teasley snapped. "The East is all fired up with this Manifest Destiny crap. The people hear about all this empty land out here and they want it. Do you know what they're saying in the Congressional cloakrooms and the Georgetown bars? Of course you don't, you haven't been there. But I have. What they're saying is, 'Why should all those half-naked savages be allowed to control all of that prime land? They can't read and write. They don't even believe in God . . .'"

"That's not true!" Benoit interrupted.

"Hey," Teasley said, raising his hands in mock surrender. "*I'm* not saying that. The Senators and Representatives are. I'm just repeating it."

"It looks to me as though you're awful cheerful about 'repeating' it?" Benoit replied hotly.

Teasley stared at him, acknowledging the young officer for the first time. "What's your point, Mr. Brevet Second Lieutenant? What are you? An Indian lover? Maybe I'm mistaken, but it looks to me like you're wearing a blue uniform."

"And what are you?" Benoit said, his face redder than Teasley's hair. "You're an *Indian Agent*, aren't you? You're supposed to be looking after their welfare."

"I'm a *presidential appointee*," Teasley answered smoothly. "My obligation — my duty — is to my President and Congress. If they want to make war with the Indians, if they want to drive them off the land and force them to live on barren stretches of wasteland, that's not *my* decision. My job is to try to make it easier for the Indians, not take up arms on their behalf. I'll treat them fairly; I won't steal from them. But I'm not going to be their standard bearer. If I believe it's to their benefit if I can convince them not to go to war with the Army — even if I know what's in store for them if they listen to me — that's what I have to do. And I don't care," he said, looking coldly at Benoit, "whether you like it or not."

"You can't do that!" Benoit said angrily.

"What do you mean, 'I can't do that?' Of course I can. I'm the Indian Agent; you're the lowest ranking officer on this post."

"Maybe," Benoit said, jumping to his feet, "you'd like to step outside and we'll see if we can *debate* this in a different forum."

Teasley laughed, but his eyes remained as cold as two blocks of blue ice. "You're out of line, lieutenant!"

"*Goddamn* it!" Kemp roared. "Ben-oight, I will not stand for that in my command! You are about *this* far," he said, putting his thumb and forefinger a quarter of an inch apart, "from being thrown into chains for insubordination. Apologize to Mr. Teasley right this goddamn minute!"

"It's all right, Brad," Teasley said calmly. "The lieutenant is just venting some of the energy he's been storing all winter. Isn't that right, Ben-oight?"

"I'm waiting," Kemp said loudly. "Lieutenant, either you apologize right now or I summon the men with the leg irons."

Benoit looked at his hands, studying his clenched fists and his white knuckles. "Yes, sir," he said softly, keeping his eyes down. "My apologies. Both to you and Mr. Teasley. I spoke out of turn. I let my temper run away with me. Please forgive me."

"Apology accepted," Teasley said glacially. "Maybe we can continue this debate at another, more suitable time."

"Very prudent, Ben-oight," Kemp said. "Very prudent indeed."

"*Kaffee?*" Hildegard said loudly, bustling into the room with a fresh pot of hot coffee. "Who wants more?"

"What a capital idea," Teasley said. "But I'm afraid I've dirtied my cup. May I please have another?" he asked, showing her how he had used it for an ash tray.

"*Ja,*" Hildegard nodded. "Inge," she said loudly, calling into the next room. "*Bring mir eine saubere Tasse.*"

"Yes, Mutter," Inge replied, bustling through the door with the cup and a tray of freshly baked *Topfenstrudel.*

"Where the hell did she get cream?" Benoit whispered to Dobbs, hungrily eyeing the pastry. "She hasn't served us anything like that for weeks."

Dobbs chuckled. "Never underestimate the resources of a woman trying to make an impression."

"How wonderful," Teasley said, helping himself. "And *who,*" he said, staring at Inge, "is *this*? I don't think we've been introduced."

Kemp coughed. "My oversight. This is Inge Schmidt, the daughter of your resourceful cook."

"What a pleasure," Teasley said, taking Inge's hand in both of his. "It was," he added, letting his eyes slip to her bosom, "worth the arduous trip just to make your acquaintance."

Inge's cheeks turned a flaming red. "You're too gracious, Major Teasley."

"*Espécé d'enculè*," Benoit muttered under his breath.

"*Bitte, Herr Oberst*," Hildegard said in aside to Kemp. "I talk to you quick, no?"

"Certainly, Frau Schmidt," Kemp replied. "What is it."

"Here," Frau Schmidt said, motioning him to one side. "*Privat*."

"Yes, Frau Schmidt?" Kemp asked curiously, excusing himself from the group.

"That *Prediger*," she said angrily. "Longstreet."

Uh oh, Kemp thought. "What about him?"

"He try," Hildegard said, "how you say? Put his hand *unter Inges Kleid*."

"What?" asked Kemp, puzzled.

"*Kleid*," Hildegard said, grabbing her skirt and shaking it. "*Rock. Kleid. Verstehen Sie?*"

"That rascal," Kemp muttered angrily, comprehending. "Don't worry, Frau Schmidt," he said soothingly, patting her on the shoulder. "I'll take care of it."

"*Nein! Nein!*" Hildegard said. "Inge will do."

Kemp frowned. "Inge will do *what*?" he asked uncertainly.

"Inge!" Hildegard, said motioning to her daughter. "I told him what Longstreet did," she said in German. "Now you tell him what will happen if he tries it again."

Inge nodded and smiled innocently at Kemp. "You see what happened to my mother?" she asked dulcetly, pointing to Hildegard's prosthesis. "Well, if that son of a bitch tries one more time to put his hand where it doesn't belong, he's going to have to get a wooden tallywacker because I'm going to do to him what Jace did to my mother's leg. Whaaaack!" she said, making a brief chopping motion, "Off it comes."

"*Ja, Ja,*" Hildegard echoed cheerfully. "*Sie wird seinen Penis amputieren.*"

Kemp had to bite his lip to keep from laughing. "I'm sure you can handle it, Inge. But I think I'd better have a talk with the reverend anyway." Turning, he sobered when he saw Benoit chatting with Legendre.

"Ben-oight!" he said loudly, "In my office. Right now!"

"All right," he said sternly, slipping behind his desk. "What in *hell* was that all about with Major Teasley?"

Benoit reddened. "I don't know, sir. That is, I'm not sure. I just sort of took an immediate dislike to him . . . "

"Dislike to him, huh?" Kemp barked. "And you think that justifies the way you acted? You think you can insult a man I just told you two days ago I had total confidence in?"

"No, sir. But . . . "

"No buts, lieutenant. I don't want excuses. I want to see your behavior change. Do you understand me?"

"Clearly, sir," Benoit replied, bracing.

"Let me look at your file," Kemp said, rising and walking to a nearby cabinet where he held his personnel records. "All right," he said, returning with a sheaf of papers bound together with red ribbon. "West Point," he said, skimming through the documents. "Not bad grades. Athlete. Expert fencer. Expert marksman it says here, too. Is that right?"

"Yes, sir."

"Hmmmm," he said. "What's this? Cited for disciplinary misconduct. Not once but twice. Fighting with upper classmen. Do you have a problem with authority, Ben-oight?"

"No, sir."

"Well, that's not the way I read these files. One cadet you beat pretty badly. Broke his jaw. Knocked out three teeth . . . "

"He asked for it, sir."

"Goddamnit, soldier!" Kemp yelled. "I told you no excuses."

"Yes, sir. Sorry, sir."

"What's this?" Kemp asked, scanning one of the sheets. "After graduation you were posted to Washington. The Pentagon. But it looks like that didn't last long did it?"

"No, sir."

"Hmmmm, this is really interesting. Your orders to Fort Laramie were signed by Jeff Davis himself. What is that all about, Ben-oight?"

"It's a long story, sir."

"You think we're going somewhere?"

"It's a personal matter, sir."

"Personal, eh. Do you know the Secretary?"

"No, sir."

"Well, if you don't, you must know someone who does."

"Secretary Davis is a close friend of Senator Fontenot, sir. The Senator was my father's best friend."

"Ahhh, now it's starting to come clear," Kemp said, digging for a cigar. "Senator has a daughter, doesn't he?"

Benoit's face turned even redder than it had before.

"Well! I'm waiting for an answer."

"Yes, sir," Benoit said. "Her name is Marie. She's the best friend of my sister, Marion."

"Is that right?"

"Yes, sir."

"And maybe your best friend, too?"

"Something like that, sir."

"All right, Ben-oight," Kemp said, slamming the papers down on his desk. "That's none of my business. But what *is* my business is what you do on this post. You understand me?"

"Yes, sir."

"I'll *tell* you what you're going to do, lieutenant. You're going to get that temper of yours under control. One more incident like that and you're in *real* trouble. Clear?"

"Yes, sir."

"According to these papers, my predecessor had some question about your judgment. Seems you went off and left the German group virtually undefended."

"May I speak, sir?"

Kemp nodded. "Speak."

"I didn't exactly go off and leave them, sir. I just went down the road a way at the insistence of Inge, er, Miss Schmidt. And they weren't undefended, sir. There were armed men there detailed as guards by the wagonmaster, Alf Stuart."

"Is that it? You through?"

"Yes, sir."

"Ben-oight," Kemp said, not unkindly. "You have guts. You stood your ground against a berserk trooper at Kearny even though you were injured. At least that's what it says here. Is that summation accurate?"

"Yes, sir."

"Also, you single-handedly attacked the Indians. And you rescued those two Brulé boys from the Crow, endangering yourself in the process. You seem to get along well with the men here at Laramie. I'm not questioning your courage or your leadership ability, you understand. It's just that you don't seem to have shit for sense."

Benoit rolled his eyes. "Yes, sir."

"I tell you what I'm going to do, Ben-oight. I'm going to see if I can help you grow up a little. I want you and a half dozen men to go to Kearny and wait for General Harney. I'll write you some orders temporarily assigning you to his command. You do what he says, you understand? *Exactly* what he says."

"Yes, sir," Benoit sighed in relief. "Thank you, sir."

"Don't thank me, Ben-oight. I'm not doing you any favors. You're probably going to get mixed up in your first real battle. You could get your scalp lifted. But," he said, wagging his finger, "being scalped will be mild compared to what I'm going to do to you if you screw up one more time. Understood?"

"Yes, sir," Benoit said meekly. "May I say one more thing, sir? Make a small request?"

Kemp sighed. "What is it, lieutenant?"

"Will you please call me Ben-wah, sir?"

Kemp exhaled a long stream of blue smoke and stared without speaking. "Ben-oight," he said after a long pause, "get the fuck out of here."

"You were damn lucky," Dobbs said shaking his head. "I've seen men shot for less insulting comments."

"I know, Jace," Benoit said, shaking his head. "I know."

"And it isn't as if Teasley couldn't do it. Thanks to his good nature or his self-control I don't have you stretched out on my operating table right now. Or overseeing you being measured for a wooden box. What the hell got into you?"

"Kemp just asked me the same thing."

"And what did you tell him? That you were struck by a sudden attack of incredible stupidity?"

Benoit smiled. "Something like that."

"Well, tell me. What the hell *did* inspire you?"

"I don't *know*, Jace. It's just that everything about Teasley rubs me the wrong way. He's nothing but an oily politician. An opportunist."

"And that's from a man who used to work and live in Washington?"

"But this is different. Don't you see, Jace? He's nothing but a hypocrite. He's supposed to be protecting the Indians, but he's really just setting them up to make it easier for the Army — for us — to massacre them."

"It's a cruel world, Jean. I don't like it any better than you. But it's reality. It's what he has been told to do. He's a soldier in civilian clothes. He's following orders."

"Some orders! It makes me sick. I want . . . ," he paused. "Who could that be knocking?"

"You won't know until you open it."

"All right, all right," Benoit said, walking across the room. "I'm coming."

"Hello, boys," Inge said lightheartedly, sticking her head in before Benoit could get to the door. "I hope you're not dressed."

"Awwww Christ, Inge," Benoit said sulkily. "Did you come here to give me a hard time, too?"

"Of course, not," she said breezily. "I just came over to chat with Jace about the new developments. Why don't you go groom your horse or something?"

"Please, I'm in no mood."

"No mood for what?" she asked innocently. "Does it bother you that I might have a little conversation with the surgeon? That I might want to speak to an *adult male* once in a while. Tell me, Jace," she said beaming, "don't you think he's absolutely the most charming person you've ever met?"

"Well . . ." Dobbs began.

"Goddamn, Inge . . . "

"Shame, shame, Lieutenant Benoit," she said, shaking

her finger under his nose. "Is it because Major Teasley has come up with a viable plan on how to deal with the Indians? Is it because he has the respect of Colonel Kemp? Is it because he had everyone in the room except you eating out of his hand? Or is it because he had the good sense to treat me like a woman?"

"That's not fair, Inge . . . "

"Of course it isn't fair, Mr. Hot-blooded Frenchman. Love and war are never fair."

"Love? Who said anything . . . "

"Oh, it's just a matter of time," she said lightly. "I can tell he's smitten with me."

"Lusting for you is more like it."

"Whichever," she said, waving a handkerchief that she pulled out of her sleeve. "At least he's paying attention to me, which is more than you normally do. You think I'm just a child."

"I do not!"

"You do, too! I've heard you say it to Jace."

"She's right, my friend," Dobbs interjected. "You've said it more than once: 'but she's *only* seventeen.'"

"See," Inge said, making a face at Benoit. "*And* I'll be eighteen in three months. How old was your mother when she married?"

"Eighteen," he whispered.

"And how old was your father?"

"Twenty-eight," Benoit said triumphantly. "And I just turned twenty-three."

"But there was ten years difference in age between your mother and father, only five between us. And you call *me* a child."

"Well, I certainly didn't mean it that way," Benoit stammered. "Besides, Teasley's old enough to be your father."

"Hmmmmph," she grunted. "A fat lot you know. He's probably no more than thirty-three or thirty-four."

"Inge, for God's sake, He was in the Army for fifteen years."

"Oh, all right. Maybe thirty-seven. But that certainly isn't ancient."

"It is according to *my* math."

"Then I guess you'd better go back to school. What did they teach you at the Academy anyway?"

"They taught me how to recognize a phony!"

"Oh, a phony is he? I'll have you know that my mother is an excellent judge of character and *she* thinks he's quite charming, too."

"Well," said Benoit, slumping on his bunk. "I guess that makes it unanimous. Don't you want to hear about my assignment?"

"Assignment?" she said archly. "Oh, dear. How boring. I want to hear what's happening in the East. What the latest books are. What new songs are popular. What the fashion is for spring . . . "

Benoit sunk his head in his hands. "It must be because I haven't been saying my prayers . . . "

"Maybe you need to have a nice long talk with the good reverend," Inge said with a smirk. "See if he tries to get into *your* knickers."

"Now what does *that* mean?" Benoit said sharply.

"It doesn't mean a thing," she said, smiling sweetly. "But I don't have time to chit-chat. I just stopped in to tell you two not to worry about our bridge tournament this evening. I know you thought with Zack gone there wouldn't be enough for two tables. But you see, Reverend Longstreet may be right after all, about how God works in mysterious ways. In just happens that Major Teasley is an *avid* bridge player. He told me so himself. And he said he would be *honored* to join our group. He can take Zack's place tonight and yours while you're busy with your *assignment*."

"Inge . . ." Benoit began.

"*Guten tag*," she said brightly, waving good-bye. "I'll see you after supper."

"Sit down," Kemp said amiably. "Cigar? A drab of Tennessee whisky?"

"Thank you, colonel, but no. When I heeded the call to be God's servant I forsook alcohol and tobacco. Lucifer's tools, I say."

"Ummmmm," Kemp mumbled, studying Longstreet.

Short and as solid as a block of granite with a thick thatch of dark brown hair that hung far down on his forehead, the preacher gazed quizzically at Kemp with large eyes that tilted slightly upwards at the corners, all the more dioconcerning because of their colors. His thick, rubbery lips parted slightly in a smile that exposed double rows of small, pointed teeth coated with green just abovethe gum line, like the ring in a bathtub. "You had a reason for summoning me?" Longstreet asked in a high, squeaky voice, folding thick fingers over his ham-hock fists.

"I just wanted us to get to know each other a little better," Kemp said. "We haven't really had time to chat since you arrived last December."

"I figured you were probably avoiding me," Longstreet replied. "Figured you didn't want me to remind you about your pact with Satan."

"My *what*?"

"Your contract with Old Scratch. You and Ellen O'Reilly. Allowing that house of assignation to continue to function. It is an abomination, a slap on the cheek of Our Blessed Lord."

"Hold on a second, Mr. . . . ."

"'Reverend,' if you please, colonel. I address you by your proper title and I am due the same respect."

"Very well, *Reverend* Longstreet. First, let me make

sure you understand. I have no *pact* or *contract* with Miss O'Reilly. I've never met the lady . . . "

"She's no lady. She's a harlot. A scarlet woman."

"As I was saying," Kemp said, annoyed at the interruption, "I have no jurisdiction whatsoever over Miss O'Reilly's establishment since it is considerably removed from Fort Laramie."

"Not far enough to prevent your men from patronizing it every chance they get."

"My men are entitled to time away from their duties. What they do with that time is their business as long as it isn't illegal and they cause no trouble. If they are producing problems for Miss O'Reilly, I'm not aware of it. She has never complained to me."

"Hah!" Longstreet replied explosively. "Why would she complain? Fort Laramie is making her a rich woman."

"Tell me, Longstreet, er, *Reverend*, what is your purpose here? Why did you come to Fort Laramie?"

"I didn't come to *Fort Laramie*," Longstreet said, leaning forward. "I was on my way to California to spread the word of the Lord among the miners, when He appeared to me in a vision . . . "

"A vision, eh?"

"Verily. He came to me in my sleep. His long, black hair flowing . . . his coppery skin shining . . . "

"His *coppery* skin?" Kemp asked in surprise. "You think that God is an Indian?"

"Oh, most definitely," Longstreet replied smugly. "A Cheyenne I believe, although I have never met any representatives of the tribe . . . "

"How does he talk to you? What language does he speak?"

"Oh, He doesn't *speak*. He uses sign language, the lingua franca of the Plains."

"I see. And what does he say, er, communicate to you?"

"He has instructed me to forget about the miners. They are worthless Whites. He has ordered me to stay here. To work with His people, who regretfully have drifted away from His teachings. It has been so long since they have recognized Him that they no longer even know His name or about His divine plan. He wants me to bring them back to Him, to make them once more His servants in this vast Garden of Eden."

"Well, if he wants you to take the message to the Indians why are you hanging around here, harassing Miss O'Reilly's girls and giving my men a hard time?"

"Colonel," Longstreet smiled, "Maybe you haven't looked outside lately. That white material that covers the ground is snow. In the mountains, it is piled in tree-high drifts. I *cannot* take His message to the tribes until the spring thaw. Be assured, though, in another few weeks I will be out of your hair."

"Is that a promise, Reverend Longstreet? Will you give me your word that as soon as the snow begins to melt you'll get the hell out of Fort Laramie?"

"I swear, colonel. On everything that is holy."

"That's the best news I've heard all day. In the meantime, do you think you could do me a favor?"

"I'll try, colonel," Longstreet grinned, causing Kemp to avert his eyes in disgust. "I will try to be agreeable to you because He would have it that way. Not that you have tried to cooperate with me."

"Do you *think*, Reverend Longstreet, that you might be able to keep away from the Hog Ranch until you head off into the hills?"

"Oh, my heavens, no! As long as I'm here, the Lord expects me to be busy. Idle hands are the devil's workshop, you know."

"I can't order you to stay out of there, Longstreet, but I'll tell you this. If Miss O'Reilly or any of her girls complain to me about you harassing them, or worse, like maybe trying to massage their bodies, I'll have you on the carpet. And while I'm on the subject, let me add something. This is *not* a request. You may consider it a threat. If you try anything untoward with Miss Schmidt again, I'll throw your ass in the stockade. Am I clear on that?"

"I'm afraid you and Miss Schmidt are gravely mistaken, colonel. I wasn't being unseemly; I was demonstrating a common religious practice known as the laying on of hands . . . "

"Well, if you *lay your hands* on Miss Schmidt one more time you'd better hope I get to you first because if she has a knife handy you'll be squatting to pee and your voice will be rising another three octaves. Now please leave. Go say a novena or something."

Longstreet rose. "Papists say novenas," he said disdainfully. "True Christians, true *red* Christians, have nothing but contempt for those primitive rituals. Talking to you has been an enlightening experience, colonel. I can see why He and His people would like to expel you from the Garden."

Kemp watched him go, slowly shaking his head. "God help the Indians," he mumbled. "With friends like Longstreet they certainly don't need enemies like me and Harney."

For three days, the eleven chiefs of the band that included the people of Short Hair's camp had been meeting to endorse the proposal to send a major war party against the Pawnee in retaliation for the kidnapping of Beaver Woman.

"Why is this meeting of the chiefs necessary?" Red Berry Woman had asked angrily. "We don't need their permission to kill our enemies."

"It's because this goes beyond us," Short Hair said, trying to soothe her. "We took the pipe to the Arapaho and they have agreed to send some warriors to accompany us. For that reason, the chiefs thought it would be better to formalize the decision."

"And what if they don't?"

Short Hair shrugged. "Then we will go anyway. My brothers in the Kit Fox Society will go with me whether the chiefs approve or not."

"I've been thinking about it," Red Berry Woman said, carefully watching her husband for his reaction, "and I've decided I'm going, too."

"What?" Short Hair asked in surprise. "*You* go on a war party? That's impossible."

"Oh, no, it isn't," Red Berry Woman replied determinedly. "Don't you remember how Yellow Haired Woman, the wife of Many Shields, fought against the Shoshones two years ago? She knocked a young warrior from his horse and split his skull with his own tomahawk."

"But that was different. She was a very big woman, as strong as a man."

"And you think size makes a difference? Didn't I fight well against the attackers when they came into the lodge to seize Beaver Woman? If I had had a weapon then, they would not have taken her away. There would have been two more dead Pawnee," she said bitterly.

"Indeed, woman, you were very brave. But that was not the same thing as joining a war party. You were obeying your instincts, fighting in self defense. On a war party, it is much more deliberate. Then, you are actually seeking blood, not just responding to a threat. Besides, I will be carrying only my war club, it is all I will need against those cowardly dogs."

"So I will carry only a war club as well. And I'll stand by your side and fight until either we are killed or we are victorious."

"It's impossible," Short Hair repeated gruffly. "I have spoken."

"Oh, no, you haven't," Red Berry Woman insisted. "Beaver Woman was my daughter, too. You alone should not be allowed to avenge her death. If this were a normal war party, I would have no interest in it. But this is a raid of revenge against the men who came into our lodge and took our daughter away. I am going along with or without your permission."

Short Hair studied her carefully, knowing what she said was true: that there was nothing he could do to stop her from joining the group. Although it was rare for women to take part in scalp raids, it was not unheard of. If he made a fuss about it and she went anyway it would only make him a laughingstock among the other warriors. If she were really determined, he decided, it would be far better for him to acquiesce.

"Very well, woman," he said, "but you will have to carry a tomahawk and a shield. The war club is too heavy; you are not strong enough."

Red Berry Woman grinned. "I knew you would see it my way," she said softly. "When do we leave?"

"Don't be so anxious," Short Hair said, still far from happy with her decision. "We have many preparations to make. Right now, concentrate on your tasks and fix me something to eat."

Puma, who had been listening intently to the discussion, grabbed Red Berry Woman's skirt. "Mother, did you just say you were going with the war party?" he asked apprehensively.

"See how quickly he is learning the language?" Red Berry Woman said proudly. "In another six months he will have forgotten he is White."

"Yes," she said, answering the boy, "but you are not to be worried. We will not be gone long. You can stay with your brother and Lightning Woman."

"What if you die?" he asked, tears starting to form in the corners of his eyes. "Like my first mother."

"Neither of us will die," Red Berry Woman assured him. "Your father is a very brave and very skilled warrior, very capable of fighting the craven Pawnee."

"But you are not," the boy said, his voice beginning to crack.

"But I will watch your father very carefully and do everything that he does. That way we will both be safe, and we will have an advantage because there will be two of us. Besides . . ." she began when she was interrupted by a crier riding through the camp yelling that the chiefs had decided to immediately begin forming a group to attack the Pawnee village.

"That makes it official," she said.

"Please stop chattering," Short Hair said brusquely, angry with himself because he felt he may have given in too quickly. "I'm starving."

Pahukstatu Village

"I don't know about you," Knifewielder said, "but this sitting around doing nothing is making me very restless."

"I know how you feel," replied Angry Buffalo. "I was thinking the same thing myself. But there's not much we can do. We can't leave the village until the planting ceremony is complete."

"That won't be long," said Knifewielder. "Since Spotted Doe had the vision telling her that she would preside at this year's rite, the preliminaries have been completed. Her husband, He-Kills-by-Stealth, slew the special buffalo and the meat is packed in her storage pit. The boys have gathered the willow sprouts and delivered them to the ceremonial lodge. Tomorrow night is the rehearsal, then the ceremony. After that, we have no obligations until Red Calf tells us it is time for the Morning Star sacrifice."

"Are you getting anxious about that?" Angry Buffalo asked. "I think that you've become quite attached to the Cheyenne girl."

"She has a very good nature," admitted Knifewielder. "I'm going to miss her. But her role is very important to the Wolf People. If it were not for her, we might not survive. When she goes to Morning Star, he will be so happy that he will give us good fortune for several years to come. I wonder what her people are thinking," he mused. "I wonder if her parents have reconciled themselves to her loss."

"Don't get soft-hearted," Angry Buffalo chided. "It is the way things are meant to be. Tomorrow Roaming Child could be killed by a grizzly, or Girl-Chases-the-Enemy could fall into a stream and drown. It is the way things are; no one lives forever. Besides, I know what her people are thinking."

"You do?" Knifewielder asked in surprise.

"I'd be willing to wager my best war horse that even while we're sitting her, the Cheyenne are planning a revenge raid. We're going to have to warn the lookouts to be especially alert because it's only a matter of time until they attack."

"In that case, why are we just waiting for them to come to us? Why don't we attack them first?"

Angry Buffalo smiled. "My thoughts exactly. I'd like to put together a war party and move on the Cheyenne as soon as the planting ceremony is complete. Would you be willing to go?"

Knifewielder grinned. "Do buffalo graze? Do eagles soar?"

The Cheyenne Camp

"I think," Short Hair told Red Berry Woman as she prepared breakfast, "that is it time for me to be a war party leader. It is especially true on this expedition, where the purpose is to avenge our daughter's kidnapping."

Red Berry Woman nodded. "I will send Puma to summon Long Chin, our oldest and most decorated warrior."

Several hours later, Long Chin settled comfortably on the small stack of robes that Red Berry Woman had spread before the fire.

"Great warrior," Short Hair said, lifting his pipe. "I offer you my pipe and ask your advice on leading a war party against the Ho'nehe-taneo'o."

Long Chin studied him carefully, weighing in his own mind if he thought Short Hair was capable of being the pipe carrier on such an important expedition, one which would not only include many of the camp's best warriors but also a group of their allies, the Hetane-vo'eo'o. Short Hair, he knew, was a veteran of many raids, both horse cuttings and revenge raids, and he had proved himself a brave and able warrior. He had, the old man recollected, even killed a Pawnee in hand-to-hand combat. It was time, he decided, to give his blessing to Short Hair's quest. Taking the pipe, thereby symbolizing his consent, Long Chin nodded solemnly. "Before you begin gathering your men," he said softly, "it would be wise for you to make an offering to the medicine arrows."

"Thank you, Long Chin," Short Hair said in relief. "I have been saving some eagle feathers which I will take to the arrow keeper, Rock Forehead." Grabbing his buffalo robe, which he was careful to don hair-side out as was the custom under such circumstances, he burrowed in his parfleche until he found the feathers he had been saving for just such an event. Filling his pipe, he left his tipi and set out for Rock Forehead's tipi. Long Chin and Red Berry Woman could hear him moving through the village, wailing loudly so that everyone would know his mission.

Once he got to Rock Forehead's tipi, he paused and wailed some more to make sure the arrow keeper knew he was there, then he entered and placed his pipe on the ground. Stepping back, he reached under his robe and produced the eagle feathers which he handed to Rock Forehead.

Obeying tradition, the arrow keeper took the feathers

in his left hand, touched the palm of his right hand to the ground, then ran it down the feathers. Twice he did this, then repeated the procedure with his left hand before handing them back to Short Hair. "Tie them to the arrow bundle," he said, pointing to the four arrows gathered in a bundle that hung at the head of his bed.

As he followed the arrow keeper's instructions, Short Hair began to pray, speaking the words loudly and clearly because it was believed that the arrows could hear whatever was said to them. "I ask your assistance," he said fervently, "because I am going against the Pawnee to seek vengeance for my daughter, who they have kidnapped to sacrifice to the Morning Star. I beg you to protect all the warriors who go with me, allowing them to return safely with blackened faces and many horses."

Rock Forehead smiled sadly. Lifting the pipe, he lit it with a coal from the fire and motioned for Short Hair to sit next to him while they smoked.

"I am fortunate," Short Hair said to Red Berry Woman when he had returned to his lodge, "that Long Chin and Rock Forehead so quickly accepted my pleas. Now I have to choose the men who will go with us. But first, I need to make my own sacrifice."

Early the next morning, he took up his robe and told Red Berry Woman and Puma that he was going into the hills for a few days to prepare for the ordeal ahead. Climbing through the pines until he was on a ledge that looked down on the village and Beaver Lake, Short Hair gathered several armfuls of sage that he spread on the ground for a bed. During the day he stood, slowly turning on the axis of his body so that his face always faced the sun. And after dark, he stretched out on the sage and tried to sleep. He did this for four days, neither eating nor drinking, praying the whole time for success on the forthcoming raid.

When he felt he was sufficiently purified, he returned to the camp and sent out word that he was seeking men to accompany him and Red Berry Woman on the expedition against the Pawnee. One of the first to show up at his lodge was Frightened Rabbit, the twelve-year-old son of Red Deer and Proud Pine Woman.

"You're too young," Short Hair told him when the boy pleaded earnestly to go. "Come back next year or the year after and I'll be more receptive to your request," he said.

"Please, Short Hair," Frightened Rabbit said deferentially, being careful not to raise his ire. "This raid is very important to me. Beaver Woman was a friend of mine and I would very much like to revenge myself against the Pawnee."

"No," Short Hair said gently, shaking his head. "You are only twelve. You're not yet ready. War is for men, not children."

"But Red Berry Woman is going," Frightened Rabbit said quietly. "She's not a man. I am good with the bow and I ride as well as any sixteen-year-old."

At the mention of his wife, Short Hair clenched his jaw. *I was afraid this was going to happen,* he told himself. *We haven't even started and already my decision is coming back to haunt me.* "I said no," he told the boy in harsher tones than he intended. "Perhaps next year."

Pahukstatu Village

Angry Buffalo watched drowsily as the four young girls rose from where they had been sitting in the ceremonial lodge and walked forward, toward where another group of young women with hoes in their hands completed the dance that emulated the planting process. Each of the girls, selected because she was a virgin, held in her hand a filled pipe, which she presented to one of the four young warriors who had come forward to join them.

"What is the significance of the girls meeting the warriors?" Beaver Woman whispered to Knifewielder, who was impressed with her fluency. Over the winter, she had learned much Pawnee and now could converse fairly easily in the language.

"The girls represent fertility," Knifewielder replied, "and the young men, of course, represent war. It is a theme that is repeated in many of our ceremonies. It is designed to show a balance between the opposing forces in our culture."

"I wish they would get on with it," interjected Angry Buffalo. "This has been going on for too long. It's all I can do to stay awake."

"Shush!" warned his younger wife, Cloudy Sky, poking him in the ribs. "You're ruining a beautiful ceremony."

"Huh!" he grunted. "The only beautiful thing about it is that second girl from the end. I wouldn't mind taking her into my bed."

The remark drew stern looks both from Cloudy Sky and his older wife, Left-handed Woman.

"Oh, ho," whispered Knifewielder. "Are you going to be in trouble. I think you'll actually be lucky to get out on the war path. There's nothing the Cheyenne could do to you that's going to be worse than what you get from your wives."

"I don't now if I can wait until all the planting is done," Angry Buffalo answered. "Six more days of this is going to drive me crazy."

The Cheyenne Camp

For the next several days, preparations grew to a feverish pitch. The twenty-three men Short Hair had selected to go with him and Red Berry Woman had been told to get their equipment ready: sharpen their knives, make new arrows, and put new staffs on their lances.

On the afternoon before they planned to leave Short Hair and his two top lieutenants, Crippled Wolf and Sliced Nose, went into the sweat lodge with the village's most-respected shaman, White Wolf.

While the two young men who would be making the trip as part of their initiation into warriorhood — Carries-the-Otter and One-Eyed Bear — carried hot stones to the lodge, the leaders sat inside and prayed.

"I ask you," said Short Hair, handing his war club to White Wolf, "to consecrate this instrument. May it draw much Pawnee blood. At the same time, pray that we may be fortunate, that none of the warriors will be killed or wounded. I ask particularly that the gods protect Red Berry Woman, who is suffering deeply from the loss of her only daughter."

Pulling his knife from the scabbard at his waist, Short Hair sliced off a half dozen thumb-sized strips of flesh from his arms and thighs, offering them to White Wolf, who was the human representative of the gods of war. "These," he said, blinking away tears of pain, "are offerings to show my sincerity."

That night, only hours away from the scheduled departure, the men who would accompany Short Hair on the raid marched through the camp, stopping occasionally to sing war songs in front of tipis picked at random. Although Red Berry Woman was not a warrior, she accompanied the men as they made their rounds, her soprano voice sounding strangely out of place among the deeper voices of the men.

Pahukstatu Village

"Why do I have to get up before the sun?" Angry Buffalo grumbled. "You can't see to plant in the dark anyway."

"Before the planting can start there are ceremonies to be performed," Cloudy Sky said. "You know that. You've been through this often enough."

"It doesn't mean I have to enjoy it. Why don't you go to the ceremonies and I'll join you in the fields after I've had breakfast."

"No!" Cloudy Sky whispered harshly. "The ceremonies are to benefit *all* the Wolf People and anyone who is not ill or disabled is required to participate."

"Tell them I'm ill," Angry Buffalo pleaded. "Say I have a terrible stomachache."

"Then," his wife said, grinning, "Old-Man-High-Water will show up with some of that potion you like so well?"

"That did it," Angry Buffalo said, springing to his feet. "The last time I took that I was sure I was going to die. If the illness didn't kill me the medicine surely would."

When they got to the fields, Angry Buffalo grumbled some more when Young Bull, who was directing activities, pointed to a section of land and directed him to go there to help pull up weeds in preparation for the sowing.

"This is women's work," he complained as he hefted a bundle of weeds. "Warriors shouldn't be required to do this," he mumbled, carrying the brush to a cleared spot in the center of the section where Happy Lady, wife of Old Dog, the Keeper of the Wolf Bundle, was putting them into a pile so they could be burned.

"Look at this," the old woman said angrily, pointing to the greenery in Angry Buffalo's arms.

"What's the matter?" he asked. "Didn't I bring enough?"

"It isn't how much you brought but what you brought," she said in exasperation. "You *know* you're supposed to separate the sunflower heads so we can use them for fuel this summer when we begin roasting the corn."

"How thoughtless of me," Angry Buffalo muttered in mock remorse. "Perhaps I should just carry them all back to your lodge and you can store them there."

"Don't be impertinent!" Happy Lady hissed.

Angry Buffalo glared at her. "The thing I keep wondering about," he said sullenly, "is how you ever got the name *Happy* Lady."

The Cheyenne Camp

By custom, Short Hair, as leader of the party, rode in front of the group, carrying his pipe in one hand, his war club in the other. Immediately behind him, trotting proudly, was his war horse, the animal he would not mount until just before joining the Pawnee in battle. Since Red Berry Woman had no horses of her own, she rode one of Short Hair's, leading one of his young war horses by a rope. The other twenty-three men followed in single file, each also riding one horse and leading another.

They continued all day without stopping, heading steadily southward, keeping the fast-running Blue Creek on their right. Short Hair's plan was to follow the creek for three days, then turn abruptly eastward toward the Loup Valley where the Pawnee villages were located.

That night, as they sat around the fire waiting for the meat to roast, Short Hair addressed the men briefly. "I know it is tradition for the pipe carrier not to help himself to food and drink, that he should wait for the amenities to be offered to him. But on this raid, I'm ignoring that convention as well as several others."

"Why are you doing that, Short Hair?" asked Sliced Nose. "Don't you have any respect for the customs?"

"Of course I do," Short Hair answered tartly. "But if we try to observe too many of the old ways there are too many things that could go wrong and provide excuses for calling off the expedition. I'm not going to let that happen. We're not going back until we are burdened with Pawnee scalps. Now let's eat, I'm famished." Without waiting for the others, he walked to the fire and carefully eyed the sizzling chunks of meat. Although he had made it plain he was not going to observe many of the usual customs, there was one he intended to keep: the prohibition against the leader eating any of the choice parts of the buffalo. Until after the expected battle with the Pawnee, Short Hair would not indulge in hump meat or any delicacy that came from the buffalo's head, including the tongue, of which he was particularly fond.

The next day, since old habits die hard, two of the men killed a badger, which they brought into the camp and ritually slaughtered. Carefully, they lay the dead animal on its back and slit it down the middle, removing the internal organs and tossing them into the bushes. But the carcass was left on the edge of the fire on a bed of white sage with its head pointed toward the east.

"What is the purpose of that?" Red Berry Woman whispered to her husband.

Short Hair shook his head in disgust. "Some men believe that tomorrow morning when they look into the badger's body cavity they can see their future in the reflection that appears in the animal's congealed blood."

"Their future?" Red Berry Woman asked in astonishment. "How can that be?"

"It's a silly belief," Short Hair replied, "but one that refuses to die. They think if they see themselves with gray hair they will live a long time and therefore they will return alive from the raid. If his reflected image has closed eyes, a man might believe he is soon to die. And if his reflection has its scalp missing, that is really bad news. I've seen more than a few men abandon the war party after viewing their images in the badger's gut."

"Does everyone have to do it?"

"No," Short Hair said. "It is strictly voluntary. I think you'll see that only the older warriors follow the practice."

As they were speaking, there was a clatter of hooves and a rider burst suddenly into the circle. As the men dived for their arms, a high-pitched youth's voice called out. "Don't be alarmed," he said. "I am one of you. Don't attack me."

"Oh," Red Berry Woman said in surprise, recognizing the voice, "it's Frightened Rabbit."

"Him!" Short Hair said furiously. "I told him he couldn't come."

"Don't be angry," the youth said, jumping to the ground at Short Hair's feet. "Because I was so fond of Beaver Woman, I could not obey your orders. Please don't send me back."

Red Berry Woman put her hand on Short Hair's shoulder. "Do as he asks, husband. Please. He was indeed a good friend of our daughter's. It would be wrong not to let him help avenge her fate."

Swallowing the wrath that threatened to overcome him, Short Hair nodded abruptly. "All right," he said. "You're here, you may as well stay. But it isn't going to be easy. I expect you to do more than your share helping the two other youths."

"Willingly," Frightened Rabbit grinned. "And thank you." Turning to Red Berry Woman, he winked. "And thank you, too," he whispered.

Pahukstatu Village

It took two and a half days to clear the fields, even with

all the villagers, men and women alike, working from dawn to dusk. Once that was done, the planting began.

Before going to bed the previous night, Bright Calico had taken a basket of dried corn kernels and put them to soak in a large pot of water. Before going to the fields the next morning, she divided the kernels and placed them in smaller vessels, one each for her and Beaver Woman.

When they got to the fields, Beaver Woman watched Bright Calico carefully so she could imitate her action. First, she took her hoe made from the shoulder blade of a buffalo and loosened the earth to a depth of about two inches. Then she piled the loose dirt into a small hill, about eighteen inches in diameter. Using her fist, she made a depression in the center of the hill, creating a miniature volcano. Meticulously, she sprinkled four to six kernels around the sides of the hill, then placed one kernel exactly in the middle before rounding off the earth into a small mound. Three feet away, she repeated the process.

It was exacting, but monotonous work, leaving the women ample time to chatter.

"My people knew about this at one time," Beaver Woman said, kneeling to help. "Long ago when we lived far to the east. Before we moved to where we are now, my ancestors lived in permanent houses, as you do, and we planted crops along the river banks."

"I didn't know that," Bright Calico said, surprised. "Why did you give it up?"

Beaver Woman rolled her shoulders. "It was long before my time," she said, "so I don't really know. I just remember listening to the tales the Storytellers told during the long winter nights about life in the days before we chased the buffalo. I love stories. Telling tales is my favorite activity."

"Isn't that strange," said Bright Calico. "I thought the

Cheyenne had always been here. Our tribes have been at war for many generations."

"I wonder why there has to be war," Beaver Woman sighed. "If our tribes were not enemies I would be in our tipi with my family."

"Uuummmm," Bright Calico said noncommittally.

"I have a new little brother," Beaver Woman said brightly, "a White boy my father captured in a raid last year at the time when the cherries are ripe. I don't remember what he said his White name was, but we call him Puma because his hair is the color of a mountain lion's fur. I wonder," she said sadly, "how he is doing. I imagine he's grown. I wonder if he has learned to speak Cheyenne as well as I speak Pawnee."

"You do speak it very well," Bright Calico said. "Do you think you mother and father will return Puma to his people?"

"I doubt it. My parents, Red Berry Woman and Short Hair, have begun to feel about him like a son. Do you and Knifewielder," she asked, turning to Bright Calico, "consider me your daughter?"

"Yes," Bright Calico said hesitantly. "You've become part of the family."

"That's good," Beaver Woman smiled, "because I feel very well cared for. I've grown to love Roaming Child very much. He reminds me of Puma in so many ways. But," she added quickly, "that doesn't mean I don't miss my own family. Do you," she asked earnestly, "think I'll ever be allowed to go home again?"

"I'm just a woman," Bright Calico stammered. "I don't have any part in such decisions. Those determinations are made by Battle Cry and his sub chiefs. And who," she added, forcing a smile, "can tell what men are going to do?"

For several minutes the two concentrated on their work.

"Did you," Bright Calico asked, breaking the silence, "ever think of trying to escape?" Bright Calico said this as nonchalantly as she could, studying Beaver Woman out of the corner of her eye.

"Oh, yes," Beaver Woman replied. "All the time at first. But then I calmed down a little and begin considering it more carefully."

"What do you mean?"

"Well, it would be easy enough to get away. There are no guards watching over me and I have much freedom of movement. But then I wondered where I would go and how I would survive. My camp is somewhere over that way, I think," she said pointing vaguely to the northwest, "but it is a long way away. It took us four days to get here on horseback. What would I eat? How would I know I was going in the right direction? Who would protect me from the wild animals and the monsters that roam the forests at night? Although I miss my family very much, it could be a lot worse."

Bright Calico grunted and pretended to be concentrating on her planting.

"When Young Bull and Angry Buffalo took me out of my home I was sure I was going to be raped and killed. But they brought me here unmolested and since then everyone has been very kind. I'm treated almost like an honored guest."

Bright Calico sighed and rose to her feet. "I think we are done," she said. "And it is still early," she added, glancing at the sun. "It is such a nice warm day, why don't we take our implements to the creek and wash them. Then, if the water's warm enough, we can have a quick swim."

"That sounds wonderful," said Beaver Woman.

"I'll show you a game the Pawnee women play," Bright Calico said later, after they had cleaned their hoes and were drying on the bank. "Do like this," she said, slapping her foot against the water. "Whoever can make the loudest noise is the winner."

"Such fun," Beaver Woman giggled. "I'll be glad when summer truly arrives."

Along Blue Creek

Shortly after dawn, just as they were preparing to break camp, Short Hair called the warriors together. "Today, we enter Pawnee territory so we must start being especially vigilant. Also, you will have to eat cold meals and depend on your robes for warmth at night since there will be no more fires."

"You have an advantage," a warrior named Hollow Hip commented.

Short Hair frowned. "What do you mean?"

"You have your wife to keep you warm," he giggled, covering his mouth with his hand. "Maybe we should all have brought our wives."

Short Hair bit back a sharp response, remembering his responsibilities as war party leader. "Yes," he said, forcing a grin, "but in my case it isn't much of a blessing because Red Berry Woman is so small. If you're so worried about getting cold in the middle of the night, maybe you should try to find a grizzly for companionship."

"Very good!" Sliced Nose roared. "That should silence him."

"Perhaps," Short Hair said quietly, "but it won't be the last time one of them mentions Red Berry Woman. I just hope I can hold my temper." Turning back to the gathered warriors, he loudly called for two men, Fat Bear and Kills-in-Their-Sleep.

"Fat Bear is not here," said another warrior, Trembling Leaf.

"What do you mean he isn't here? Where is he?"

Trembling Leaf scuffled his moccasins in the dust. "He left after gazing at his reflection in the badger this morning. He said when he looked into the blood he saw a figure that had no head, there was just empty air above the shoulders. To him, that was a sign that if he continued he would be decapitated by the Pawnee."

"I was afraid of that," Short Hair sighed. "Did anyone else turn back?"

"Ledge Walker went, too," said another warrior. "He said his image had no nose."

"If that's all the men we lose, we'll be lucky," Short Hair mumbled. "You," he said pointing to Kills-in-Their-Sleep, "take Hollow Hip with you and be the scouts for the day. Remember to be cautious of the ridge tops because we don't want any Pawnee to see you. Travel in the arroyos and otherwise remain in the trees."

"We've done this before," said Kills-in-Their-Sleep. "We know how to do it."

Short Hair smiled. "Of course you do," he said. "I'm just being cautious. We're going to try to make it to the creek called Cherry Bush by tonight. Meet us there unless you have something more important to tell me first. Understood?"

"May I go with them?" Frightened Rabbit asked.

Short Hair glanced at him sharply. "No!" he said. "What they are doing is dangerous. They won't have time to watch over you as well."

"Let him come," said Kills-in-Their-Sleep. "I know his father well and he says the boy has potential to be a good warrior. He may as well start learning some of the finer points. Besides, we could always use him as a messenger if the need arises."

"Go," said Short Hair, waving them off. "I'll see you at sundown."

Near the headwaters of the South Loup River

"I thought we were never going to get out of the village," Angry Buffalo said as they waded across one of the many streams that fed into the still-narrow river. "It seemed to take forever to get the corn kernels into the ground, then there were the beans, the pumpkins, the squashes, and the melons. Six days lost because of women's work! We could have been to the Cheyenne camp by now."

"We'll be there soon enough," the pipe carrier, Dark Eagle, replied. "If we travel every day from before dawn until after sunset, we can be at the Cheyenne camp on Beaver Lake in three days."

"I hope they didn't loose too many horses during the winter," said Young Bull, "I could use a couple of fast ponies. And this time," he added, "I want to make that woman pay for what she did to me last autumn."

"That was a sight to see," Angry Buffalo chuckled. "I still laugh thinking about how you got beaten by a woman and a young boy, a *White* boy at that. If they would have had knives, you'd be dead."

"I'm glad you think it's funny," Young Bull said angrily. "But I can promise you those two won't. I'm going to eviscerate that boy in front of the woman, then make sure she dies a long, slow death."

"We have to get there first," Dark Eagle cautioned. "Right now, there's probably a Cheyenne war party moving this way."

"I hope there is," Young Bull growled, "and I hope I get to them first."

Along Cherry Bush Creek

"Welcome," Short Hair said, clasping Frozen Eye's outstretched hand. "Your timing is perfect."

"That's because your warrior draws good maps," the Arapaho said, pointing to White Moon.

After it was decided when the war party would leave, Short Hair had taken White Moon into his tipi and spent most of the afternoon coaching him on his planned route of march, scratching the various landmarks into the dirt floor. "Go to the Arapaho and guide their warriors to the rendezvous. Meet us here, on Cherry Bush Creek where it runs below the peak that looks like a woman's breast," he had instructed him. And that was precisely what he had done.

"How many men did you bring?" Short Hair asked.

"Eighteen," Frozen Eye replied.

"That's wonderful," said Short Hair. "That gives us a combined force of forty-one, including me and my wife."

"Your wife?" Frozen Eye exclaimed.

"It is too long a story to go into right now," said Short Hair. "Let your men eat — but no fires," he cautioned, "and then we will move away from the creek up to the base of that hill, into the timber. If the Pawnee have lookouts this far away from the village, they will be searching along the creek, thinking we'll be stupid enough to bed down where they can find us. We have about an hour's worth of light left. Let's eat and be out of here before sundown."

"That sounds like . . ." Frozen Eye began. "What's that," he said, reaching for his war club.

Short Hair cocked his head. Not far away he could hear what sounded like dogs barking.

"Do you think the Pawnee village is closer than we thought?" Frozen Eye asked, his face furrowed with concern. "That sounds like dogs."

Short Hair smiled. "It's my scouts," he said. "They have instructions to imitate dogs if the enemy is close and they suspect it might arouse suspicions if they give their usual wolf calls. Look," he said, "there's Kills-in-Their-Sleep."

The Indian was on the edge of the trees, sitting on his horse with his profile to the group. While they watched, he lowered his head and barked sharply, four times. Then, he urged his horse forward and galloped up to Short Hair, a grin creasing his broad face.

Short Hair hastily filled his pipe and motioned for the scouts to be seated in front of him. Lighting it, he passed it first to Kills-in-Their-Sleep. "Is what you are about to tell me true?" Short Hair asked earnestly.

"I swear it," Kills-in-Their-Sleep grinned.

"Then tell me."

"We came across two Pawnee," he said. "They were watering their horses at a stream, looking as relaxed as if they were back in their village."

"They didn't see you?"

"No. We slipped up on them totally unawares."

"Well, what happened?"

"We killed them both," Kills-in-Their-Sleep said proudly. "I got one of them with an arrow straight through his heart. He just gurgled and fell over dead."

"And the other?"

"The other," said Kills-in-Their-Sleep, "ran straight to the bushes where our young warrior, there, was hiding." As he said this, he pointed at Frightened Rabbit, who looked pale and shaken.

"Well, what did you *do*?" Short Hair asked, turning to the boy.

"I p . . . p . . . p . . . pulled out my knife and held it in front of me to p . . . p . . . protect myself," he stuttered. "He didn't see me b . . . b . . . because I was b. . . . b . . . behind a b . . . b . . . bush. He ran straight into it. The knife went into his s . . . s . . . stomach and he fell to the g . . . g . . . ground."

"He began writhing and crying out," Hollow Hip interrupted impatiently, "so I ran over and cut his throat."

"What about their horses?" Short Hair asked anxiously. "Did you capture them?"

"Of course," said Kills-in-Their-Sleep, gesturing over his shoulder. "They're tied in the trees over there."

"Hmmmmm," Short Hair pondered. "That's good and bad. I'm glad we were able to kill two Pawnee so quickly, but when they fail to return, the enemy will be alerted. Were they lookouts? Were they out hunting?" he asked the scouts. "Or do you think they were scouts for a war party?"

"Scouts," Kills-in-Their-Sleep answered quickly. "They were carrying war garments and paint in their parfleches."

"That means the Pawnee are moving this way," Short Hair mused. "I wonder how many."

"I don't know," Kills-in-Their-Sleep shrugged. "After we killed the scouts we came back here to tell you instead of following their trail."

"You did the right thing," said Short Hair. "We can find them easily enough."

—— *12* ——

Short Hair called his warriors together, gathering them in a tight circle around a bare spot of earth among the trees at the base of the breast-shaped hill. It was growing dark and a light rain was falling, further chilling the men, many of whom were grumbling about the pipe carrier's order prohibiting fires.

"Here's the situation," Short Hair said, squatting. "We're here," he indicated, marking in the damp earth with a branch he had broken off a nearby bush. "Here is Cherry Bush Creek, and over here," he said, making another mark, "is where I believe the Pawnee war party to be."

"Why do you think they're there?" asked Crippled Wolf, a short, incredibly thin man who almost died when a musket exploded in his hand. As a result, his face was scarred so badly that Cheyenne mothers tried to frighten their children into obeying by telling them if they did not behave Crippled Wolf would carry them away.

"Deduction," said Short Hair. "Since they are not yet

in our territory, their scouts probably did not roam very far from their main body. And, if they're moving toward Beaver Lake, they probably left their village, which is about here," he said, punching another dot into the ground. "I assume they followed the river north from their village since that would be the most sensible route. Therefore, they must be in this area here."

"And what if you're wrong?" asked Crippled Wolf, his grin looking more like a leer.

"Then we have to look harder for them. They aren't far away, I know. I can smell them."

"That isn't the Pawnee you smell," giggled Hobbled Horse, an overweight young warrior known for his joviality. "It's Hollow Hip. He's been particularly flatulent all day, which I know because I've been riding behind him."

Short Hair was in no mood for humor. "Are we through making jokes?" he asked brusquely. "This is not a laughing matter."

"I apologize," mumbled Hobbled Horse. "I was just trying to loosen every one up a little."

"What is the plan?" asked Sliced Nose, who had been studying Short Hair's quickly sketched map.

"We have to spread out," Short Hair replied. "I don't want the Pawnee to slip through our grasp. I want to entrap them like this," he said, scratching a hoof-shaped impression into the ground.

"Crippled Wolf, you take eight warriors and move this way. Head due east until you reach the river, then turn south. Since you have the farthest to go, pick your men and leave now. At the signal, three wolf howls, sweep back to the west. But it's very important that you wait for the signal. If you move too soon you will alert the Pawnee, and it would be better if we could catch them by surprise.

"Sliced Nose," he said, turning to his other lieutenant,

"take eight men and follow Crippled Wolf, but don't go south along the river. When you get to the stream, stay there and wait for the signal, then move southwesterly."

"And my Arapahos?" asked Frozen Eye. "Where do you want us to go?"

"I want you to seal off the Western flank. Move due south from here, spreading your men in a long line for a mile or so."

"Then attack to the east on the signal?"

"Exactly," said Short Hair.

"And where will you be?" asked White Moon.

"Here," said Short Hair, making a mark at the top part of the crudely-drawn hoof. "I will take Red Berry Woman and the rest of our warriors and make a line along here. Then we will move straight to the south."

"If they panic and retreat to their village, should we pursue?" asked Crippled Wolf. "I say we follow them in and ravage the place."

Short Hair paused. The temptation was great. With more than forty warriors under his command he was sure he could wreak much havoc among the Pawnee, perhaps even rescue his daughter, Beaver Woman. But the shaman, White Wolf, had been very explicit about that. He had worked his magic and carefully explained to Short Hair the limitations of his action. His words still rang in Short Hair's ears. "Do *not* go into the village," he said. "Do *not* try to liberate Beaver Woman. It is the gods' wish that she be there and if you try to interfere you will bring much misfortune upon our people." Although he had argued vigorously, trying to get the shaman to revise his prediction, the old man had remained firm. "It is not *my* orders you are following," White Wolf had said. "If it were up to me, I'd say try to rescue Beaver Woman. I, too, have daughters, and I dislike the Pawnee practice of sacrifice as much as any man. But I have prayed long on it and the gods have told me what must be done." Reluctantly, Short Hair had agreed. "If we can't bring Beaver Woman back," he had told his wife, "at least we can avenge her by killing as many Pawnee as we can." Red Berry Woman had nodded understandingly. "I hope I see the two who came into our lodge," she had replied, her eyes flashing. "I would like to kill them with my own hands."

Turning to his lieutenant, Short Hair slowly shook his head. "White Wolf has cautioned us against going into the village," he said softly. "It would be contrary to the will of the gods. But," he added vehemently, "kill as many of them of them as you can before they run away."

Because surprise was vital to the success of the plan, Short Hair began moving his warriors into position in the dark, even without being fully certain of the Pawnee position. As it turned out, he need not have worried. An hour after breaking up the gathering, Kills-in-Their-Sleep and Hollow Hip, who Short Hair had immediately sent back out to do some additional scouting, this time on foot, came running back. After giving the agreed upon recognition signal, Short Hair welcomed their return.

Ignoring the pipe-smoking ritual normally used when interrogating returning scouts, Short Hair got right to the point.

"Did you find the enemy camp?" he asked anxiously.

"Yes," Kills-in-Their-Sleep said, bobbing his head rapidly in confirmation. "They are exactly where you predicted they would be."

"Camped along the river," Hollow Hip added. "Lying there as if they didn't have a care in the world. Sitting around a small fire, smoking and joking."

Short Hair nodded. "Apparently the two scouts have not yet been missed. Maybe since the Pawnee were still deep in their own territory the scouts had orders to return only if they found something unusual. That way, if they did not come in at dusk, the Pawnee pipe carrier would assume that all was well."

"That sounds reasonable," Kills-in-Their-Sleep said.

"How many are there?" Short Hair asked.

"I counted twenty-six."

"As did I," echoed Hollow Hip, "but there may have been a couple off in the bushes that we did not see."

"How far away?"

"Two hours running," Hollow Hip replied. "Not far at all."

A look of relief washed over Short Hair's face. "The hardest part is over with," he said softly to Red Berry Woman. "Now all we have to do is fight. Are you sure you want to continue? No one will think ill of you if you have second thoughts."

Anger sparked in Red Berry Woman's eyes. "I haven't come this far to change my mind now," she said. "My soul still burns with hate. The fire can be extinguished only with Pawnee blood."

"Very well," Short Hair replied. "We will continue as planned. Let's get a few hours sleep, if we can, then be ready to move out an hour before dawn. That will give us time to get into position around the Pawnee camp. Tend your horses well; your lives may depend upon it."

Long after the others had stretched out to sleep, Short Hair and Red Berry Woman sat propped against a large boulder, whispering about what they would do the next morning. "Hollow Hip says they are camped at the far side of a narrow meadow," Short Hair explained, "with the river out of sight to their west. He thinks it is about a mile distant although he did not go there to make sure."

"Does it matter?" asked Red Berry Woman.

"No. It is only important because I don't want Crippled Wolf stumbling into their camp in the dark on his way down the river. But he's too experienced for that. He will certainly have scouts out as well."

For several minutes, neither spoke, each lost in thought. "Husband," Red Berry Woman said so softly that Short Hair barely heard her.

"Yes," he said, almost as softly. "What is it you wish?"

"Will . . ." she said, then stopped.

"Yes," Short Hair prompted.

"I want . . ."

"You want what?"

"I want very much," she said, her voice strong with determination, "to find the men who kidnapped our daughter and kill them."

"As do I," Short Hair replied. "As do I."

With daylight only a half hour away, the Cheyenne were poised for attack. All night long the rain had continued, but it had not been heavy enough to make footing difficult for their horses when they rushed the Pawnee. Short Hair's warriors had risen an hour earlier and calmly went about preparing for the battle: donning their war garments, painting their faces and their horses, and softly singing their war songs. While others checked the primer in their muskets and strung their bows, Short Hair stood by patiently, slowly swinging his heavy-headed war club.

"Is that all you're going to arm yourself with?" Frightened Rabbit asked nervously.

Short Hair nodded. "It is my vow. Since I was not present when they came into our camp and kidnapped Beaver Woman I need to demonstrate my bravery, to show the Pawnee that had I been in my lodge the outcome would have been decidedly different."

"And Red Berry Woman," the boy asked, noticing she carried neither bow nor musket. "Did she also take a vow?"

"No," Short Hair smiled. "But she has never practiced with weapons that require skill so they would be useless in her hands. Instead, she will carry a tomahawk and a knife I sharpened for her especially for this moment."

"I . . . I . . . I'm very much a . . . a . . . afraid," Frightened Rabbit confessed, his stammer returning.

Short Hair turned to him and smiled. Placing his hand on his shoulder, he squatted until he could look directly in the boy's eyes. "You may not believe it by looking at me, but so am I," the pipe carrier said gently. "So is every warrior here. It is a natural reaction. Anyone who says he isn't is a liar. In the Kit Fox Society we have a saying that applies to warriors going into battle."

"And wha . . . what is that?" the boy asked, his eyes wide.

"We say, 'It is a bad thing to live to be an old man. A man can die but once, and it should be while he is young.'"

Frightened Rabbit stared at Short Hair, digesting what he had said. "I d . . . d . . . don't want to be old," he mumbled, "but it would be nice to see th . . . th . . . thirteen."

Short Hair opened his mouth to reply but before he could speak Red Berry Woman nudged him. "They are stirring," she said. "One of them just went into the bushes."

Short Hair looked at the sky. Because it was cloudy, it was not as light as it would have been on a clear day but it was still bright enough to clearly see movement across

the meadow. Under normal circumstances, Short Hair
would have ordered his men to make a mounted charge
on the Pawnee camp at first light, hoping to catch them
while they were still asleep. But this was a special situation; Short Hair wanted light to carry through his plan.
He wanted to make sure the Pawnee could see who they
were fighting.

"Are you ready," he said, turning to Red Berry
Woman.

Nodding, she hefted the tomahawk and swung it in a
gentle arc across her body. "I like the feel of this," she
said. "It isn't heavy at all. I think the gods have given
me extra strength today."

Short Hair turned to Hobbled Horse. "Red Berry
Woman and I are going to walk into the meadow and
call to the Pawnee. I want you to give the wolf call signaling the attack, but not until the Pawnee have
mounted their horses and are coming at us. Is that
clear?"

"Yes," said Hobbled Horse, patting his pony to calm
him. "Are you two going out there alone?"

"Yes," said Short Hair, grinning humorlessly. "Let's
go," he said to his wife. "Stay behind me and guard my
back."

Short Hair walked ten paces into the meadow, then
stopped and cupped his hands over his mouth. "Wake
up!" he yelled. "Wake up you cowardly Pawnee dogs.
Open your eyes so you see who it is who kills you."

Knifewielder threw off his robe and jumped to his
feet. "It's the Cheyenne," he said, shaking Angry
Buffalo's shoulder. "They have come sooner than we
expected."

"All the better," said Angry Buffalo, also jumping to
his feet. "My lance is thirsty for Cheyenne blood."

"Do you see who that is?" added Young Bull, rubbing his eyes. "That's the woman from the lodge. Beaver

Woman's mother. And that must be her spineless husband with her. I'm going to get both their scalps."

"Wait!" Angry Buffalo cautioned. "It must be a trap. They would not come alone."

"Alone or not, it is an answer to my prayers," Young Bull said, swinging aboard his pony which he had tethered nearby while he slept. Without looking back, he charged across the meadow, yelling loudly as he went.

Short Hair turned and yelled to Hobbled Horse. "Not yet!" he cautioned. "Not yet! Wait until the whole camp is astir."

"This is for making a fool of me," Young Bull screamed as he leveled his lance, aiming directly at Red Berry Woman. Short Hair stepped in his path and grabbed the weapon just behind the point, twisting is with all his strength.

Young Bull's momentum was such that it actually aided Short Hair. When the Cheyenne pulled and twisted, Young Bull flew forward, over his horse's neck, landing with a thud on the ground at Red Berry Woman's feet.

"This is for Beaver Woman," she yelled, swinging her tomahawk.

Young Bull raised his arm to protect himself and the tomahawk struck him across the forearm, just below the elbow. He grunted loudly in pain as his forearm snapped with a loud crack.

"Ah hah," Red Berry Woman mumbled in satisfaction. "This is not as easy as you thought it would be, is it?"

"You she devil," Young Bull cursed, gathering his feet under him and reaching for his knife. "This time without doubt I will cut your throat."

So intent was he on Red Berry Woman that he had forgotten about Short Hair. As he bunched his legs to spring at her, Short Hair stepped forward and swung his war club with both hands, catching Young Bull across the back of the right shoulder.

Screaming in agony, he dropped his knife. For several seconds he stared at the two of them, standing helpless with both arms immobilized. "I will stomp you to death with my feet," he yelled, spittle flying from his lips. When he lifted his leg to kick Red Berry Woman, Short Hair hit him behind the knee with his war club, sending him crashing to the ground.

Red Berry Woman was on him in an instant. "You despicable Pawnee," she hissed at him between clenched teeth. "I hope your soul wanders the earth forever and never finds peace." Lifting the tomahawk, she brought it down cleanly between his eyes, watching spellbound as his head split like a melon.

"Good work, wife," Short Hair said, lifting her off the dead Pawnee. "Was he one of the men who took Beaver Woman?"

"Yes," she nodded. "My only regret is he died too quickly."

"Don't worry," he reassured her, "the battle is just beginning."

Red Berry Woman was wiping her tomahawk in the grass as Short Hair spoke. Looking up, she saw a line of Pawnee warriors, mounted on their horses, forming for an attack.

"Now!" Short Hair yelled to Hobbled Horse. "Give the signal."

As the last wolf call echoed around the valley, Cheyenne and Arapaho warriors poured out of the woods, converging on the Pawnee force. The air seemed to fill with arrows zinging their way in both directions across the meadow. Since many more warriors carried bows rather than guns, there was only the occasional musket shot, but it was impossible to tell who was firing once the men were intermingled. One Pawnee broke away from the main fight and galloped toward Short Hair and Red Berry Woman, waving a war club menacingly as he charged. Short Hair was braced to withstand the attack when an arrow thudded into the back of the man's head, its point coming out just below his left eye. Short Hair went running to the fallen man to touch him and gain honor by counting coup. As he did, he noticed the markings on the missile that killed him. "Pawnee," he said in mild surprise. "He took an arrow that was meant for us."

When Red Berry Woman did not respond, Short Hair turned and saw that she was locked in combat with another Pawnee who had vaulted from his horse and attacked her on foot. As he watched in fascination, Red Berry Woman dodged the Pawnee's knife, then swung her tomahawk in a powerful undercut, catching the Pawnee — a warrior named Little Fox who had participated in Beaver Woman's abduction — squarely between the legs. With a horrible scream, he dropped his knife and grabbed his genitals. He had no sooner hit the ground than Red Berry Woman pulled her knife and plunged it into his throat.

Short Hair turned just in time to dodge another Pawnee who was trying to impale him with his lance. Deftly sidestepping the jab, he swung up on the back of the horse behind the surprised Pawnee. Grabbing him in a headlock, Short Hair forced his head back, then sliced at this exposed torso, inflicting a deep gash that ran from the man's sternum to his waist. With a shocked look, the Pawnee tried to stuff his entrails back into his body cavity before his eyes rolled back in his head and he fell heavily to the ground.

"They have us greatly outnumbered," Knifewielder yelled to Angry Buffalo, ducking under a swinging

Cheyenne war club. "We'd better make a break for it while we still have some men left."

"That's a wise decision," Angry Buffalo replied, feeling his hand go numb as Crippled Wolf's club thudded against his shield. "By the gods," Angry Buffalo screamed, driving his knife into Crippled Wolf's thigh, "I think you're the ugliest man I've ever seen."

Throwing down his club, Crippled Wolf lunged at Angry Buffalo, clasping his hands tightly around his throat. Shaking off the blackness that threatened to engulf him, Angry Buffalo slashed blindly with his knife, gasping in relief when he felt the blade strike home and the hands slipped from his neck.

Angry Buffalo lifted his tomahawk above his head, ready to finish off Crippled Wolf, when an arrow buried itself in the inside of his right biceps, nicking a nerve that caused him to lose all control. "You're right," he panted, turning to Knifewielder, his arm dangling loose, "I think it's time we retreated."

"First, let me deal with this Cheyenne," Knifewielder replied. Lifting his club, which consisted of a heavy oval stone fixed to the end of a supple wooden handle no bigger around than his index finger, he whipped it in a furious arc. The pointed end of the stone caught Crippled Wolf on his left temple, gouging a deep hole in the side of his head, killing him instantly.

As quickly as it began the battle was over. The Pawnee disappeared into the forest, abandoning everything at the camp site. Sliced Nose and several of his men started to follow them, but Short hair called them back. "Let them go!" he yelled. "Do not give chase! Remember White Wolf's prohibition!"

The Arapahos, however, who were not under the same restraints, charged after the fleeing Pawnee. A warrior named Huge Belly was only a few feet behind the wounded Angry Buffalo when Dark Eagle, the

Pawnee pipe carrier, stopped and drew his bow. His arrow slammed into Huge Belly's chest, knocking him from his horse.

Another Arapaho, Fast Colt, was closing on the Pawnee Prancing Pony when his horse tripped on a small boulder, throwing him crashing to the ground.

Unable to resist the opportunity, Prancing Pony wheeled his horse in a tight turn and was about to run down the dazed Arapaho when another pursuer named Shattered Hand leveled his bow. Thrown off his horse by the impact of the arrow, Prancing Pony stared in amazement at his stomach. Only the feathered end of Shattered Hand's missile was visible in the front; the main part of the arrow went cleanly through Prancing Pony's body, exiting just above his left kidney. The Pawnee died with a puzzled look on his face.

The Arapaho might have followed the Pawnee all the way to Pahukstatu Village had not their leader, Frozen Eye, called them back. Realizing that the Cheyenne were not in the chase, the Arapaho prudently commanded his men to halt as well.

"Let them go," Frozen Eye hollered again. "They are defeated. They're heading for their village."

His heart no longer pumping wildly, Short Hair sagged tiredly, letting his arms dangle at his sides. It had started raining again, harder this time, and the water poured down his face. Looking around, he was surprised at the destruction in the once-peaceful meadow. The turf was pounded into a quagmire and bodies littered the area, their contorted forms scattered from one tree line to the other. A Pawnee horse, a sleek bay gelding, lay on its side, kicking feebly, three arrows protruding from its side. A Cheyenne roan, the pride of White Moon's string, galloped riderless around the open space, screaming loudly, a long gash on its neck. His owner lay face down in the mud, a Pawnee knife buried deep into the back of his neck.

As Short Hair watched, Cheyenne and Arapaho moved swiftly among the fallen, calling out loudly when they touched the casualties and counted coup. To his surprise, Red Berry Woman was among those jumping from one body to the next. She was not interested in battle honors, however Short Hair quickly discerned. Her attention was focused on seeing if Angry Buffalo was among the casualties.

"This one's still alive," she said, lifting the head of a badly wounded Pawnee who could not have been older than sixteen. The Pawnee, whose name was Rides-the-Bear and who had been on his first war party, looked at her hatefully, cursing her inarticulately. Dispassionately, Red Berry Woman lifted his arm and plunged her knife as deep as it would go into the pit. The boy's eyes opened wide and blood gushed from his nose and lips as he slumped in death.

"He is not here," Red Berry Woman said in disgust. "The devil escaped. I saw him take an arrow in his arm and I was hoping he had fallen, but he must have been able to get away."

Short Hair walked up to her and put his arm around her shoulders. "Be satisfied," he said, exhaustion evident in his voice. "We killed one of them and we know the other is wounded. We have our revenge. We can rest easier."

"Never!" Red Berry Woman said angrily, her eyes blazing. "I will not feel real peace until I know the other Pawnee is no longer among us. I hope his wound festers and he dies a slow, lingering death."

With exhaustion pulling at him like a heavy weight, Short Hair made a tour of the battlefield. There were three Cheyenne dead: Crippled Wolf, White Moon, and Hobbled Horse. Hollow Hip was seriously wounded with an arrow in his stomach. "Rest easy, young warrior," Short Hair said, trying to make him comfortable. Looking up at Kills-in-Their-Sleep, who was gazing anxiously over his shoulder, Short Hair slowly shook his head. Five others, including the boy Frightened Rabbit, suffered minor wounds.

"I've lost three men," Frozen Eye reported, "including one of my best scouts, a warrior named Huge Belly. In addition, I have four wounded."

"Any seriously?"

"No," said Frozen Eye. "One, Elk Ear, may lose a finger but he will survive."

"Have you counted the Pawnee?" he asked Sliced Nose.

His lieutenant grinned. "Six dead here. We know at least seven others were wounded, several of them seriously. A couple of them probably will die as well."

Looking uncomfortable, he leaned closer to Short Hair. "Have you thought of asking Red Berry Woman to come along on every war party?" he whispered. "She alone killed three Pawnee, if you count the boy she put out of his misery."

Despite his weariness, Short Hair could not help but laugh. "I think she's made something of a legend of herself today. I've never heard of another woman who's so distinguished herself in battle."

"Look at that," Sliced Nose said proudly, pointing at Red Berry Woman. "Just like a warrior."

Short Hair turned to see what Sliced Nose meant. Thirty yards away, his wife was struggling to remove Young Bull's scalp. "Maybe you'd better go help her," Sliced Nose said.

"Well, wife," Short Hair said as he approached.

"You've acquitted yourself well. But I didn't think you were interested in battle trophies."

"Only this one," she said, pointing at the dead Pawnee. "He is special. I plan to hang his hair proudly."

"In that case, let me inform you of the proper procedure," Short Hair said.

Nearby, several of the warriors had built a small fire and gathered material necessary for the consecration of the scalps they had taken during the day's fighting.

"Let me get my pipe," Short Hair said. "Come, sit by the fire. And bring the scalp with you.

"Sliced Nose says you should be a member of every war party," he said as he filled the pipe. "You're something of a terror with a weapon in your hands."

"Only when I'm interested in who gets killed," she replied, watching him dig for a coal with which to light the pipe.

Clearing his throat, Short Hair chanted a short prayer asking for further good fortune in battle. Then, lighting the pipe, he pointed the stem toward the sky, the ground, and finally toward the hunk of hair that Red Berry Woman had cut from Young Bull's head.

In anticipation of Pawnee deaths, Sliced Nose had collected and brought with him several buffalo chips. Short Hair took one and placed it on the ground between him and the fire, being careful to see that it remained intact. Reaching into Sliced Nose's proffered parfleche, he took out a small piece of bitterroot and a few leaves of white sage, which he put into his mouth.

While he was chewing this mixture, he directed Red Berry Woman to stand before him and hold out her hands, palms up, edges touching. Leaning forward, he spat into each palm. Then he rose and instructed Red Berry Woman to sit in his place. Taking the scalp, he laid it flesh side up on the buffalo chip.

"Take a piece of charcoal from the fire," he told his wife, "then rub it on each side of the blade."

When she had done that, she looked up at him.

"Now hold the knife over the scalp and say these words: 'May we meet the Pawnee again and when we do, may I again be so successful.'"

When she had repeated his words, he told her to take the knife and perform four incisions into the flesh, making one cut north to south, the other east to west.

"Now scrape as much flesh as you can from each of those sections and put it on the buffalo chip."

When she had done as he instructed, he summoned Frightened Rabbit. "Take this," he said, handing him the chip, "to the far end of the meadow and leave it there." Frightened Rabbit looked at the object and swallowed hard. Short Hair was afraid he was going to vomit, but he did as he was told.

Again, reaching into Sliced Nose's parfleche, Short Hair removed a willow twig, which he bent into a crude hoop. "Use this," he said, producing sinew and an awl, "and sew the scalp to the hoop, stretching it as much as you can."

When she had done that, he went into the trees and returned with a thin branch, which he quickly trimmed and peeled. Using his knife, he sharpened one end of the branch and cut a notch in the other. Measuring off some more sinew, he tied one end to the hoop and the other to the pole, over the notch, so the scalp could dangle freely. He then pushed the sharpened butt firmly into the ground.

"Leave it here until we're ready to go," he told his wife, "then bring it with you. But be careful to hold it only in your left hand. You have to do this all the way back to Beaver Lake. You can't relinquish it until after the scalp dance."

Red Berry Woman smiled for the first time since

before the battle. "Curse this Pawnee warrior," she said. "He caused us trouble and grief in his lifetime and now his scalp is going to be an additional burden for days to come."

Pahukstatu Village

"You have to be very careful," Red Calf warned, "that word does not get to the girl about who you fought. She mustn't be alarmed."

"That will be very difficult," Knifewielder said. "How can you possibly keep a secret like that, when you have nine men dead and eight wounded, including Angry Buffalo, who shares my lodge, where Beaver Woman takes her meals?"

"You raise a good point," Red Calf mused. "I guess it would be impossible for her not to be aware of something. But try, at all costs, to keep her from knowing that her parents were involved in the battle, especially that her mother killed Young Bull."

"I will try," Knifewielder promised. "But I can't guarantee it. How much longer do you think it is going to be before the ceremony?"

"Who knows. If it were up to me, it would be immediately. But I have to wait until Morning Star notifies me it is time. Usually, it is not long after the planting ceremony, so I suspect it will not be much longer."

"I hope not. It will be very difficult to keep the information from Beaver Woman."

"Have you become fond of her?" Red Calf asked, looking carefully at the warrior.

"Who could help it?" Knifewielder said, spreading his hands. "She is obedient and very bright. I have become to think of her as a sister."

"Then her sacrifice will be difficult for you?"

"No," Knifewielder said, shaking his head. "I realize that it will be a great honor for her to go to Morning Star. I must put the deity's needs before my own. He will welcome her to the heavens with open arms while I could offer her no more than a continuation of life with Bright Calico and Roaming Child."

"That is a very wise way of looking at it. I am proud of you."

Knifewielder snorted. "There's nothing to be proud about. I am responsible for many men being killed and wounded."

"That's the way of war, my son. It is a warrior's life. It could not be any other way. Tell me again, who were those who were killed."

Knifewielder lifted his hands and ticked off the names: "Walks Fast, Young Bull, Little Fox, Leading Elk, Prancing Pony, and Rides-the-Bear died on the battlefield. Kills-by-Stealth bled to death before we could get back. And Wolf Chief and Good Badger died the next day of wounds."

"Young Bull was one of those who kidnapped Beaver Woman?"

Knifewielder nodded. "Along with Angry Buffalo. It is ironic that one was killed and one seriously wounded in the battle with her parents."

"How bad is Angry Buffalo hurt?"

"Superficially, the wound does not look serious. The wounds made by the arrow will heal. Unfortunately, he still has no use of his arm. Eagle Spirit, the shaman, is trying to effect a cure."

"And how is Angry Buffalo reacting?"

"Very badly," Knifewielder said. "He is finding it very difficult to be a cripple. I'm afraid he is going to say something in front of Beaver Woman since he already is agitating to form another war party for a revenge raid against the Cheyenne."

"The time for the ceremony is getting too close now. You mustn't leave the village before then, not even for a war party. Your role is too important."

"I know," Knifewielder said unhappily. "But if things don't improve in the lodge, I may have to ask you to fix a bed for me here."

"I hope," Red Calf smiled, "it doesn't come to that."

13

"I say we kill him before he causes any more trouble," Blizzard contended.

"Giant Crane isn't causing the trouble," Badger replied. "He's only a messenger."

"He's fomenting treason, therefore he must die," Blizzard insisted. "We can't allow him to continue past this camp."

"Wait!" said Fire-in-the-Hills, raising his hand, palm outward. "Badger's right. Killing the Arapaho isn't going to stop the others from hearing about the new agent's plan. We can't make decisions for the Miniconjou, the Oglala, the Hunkpapa, or any of them. You can't be foolish enough to believe that Giant Crane is the only messenger sent from Fort Laramie?"

"We shouldn't be arguing about Giant Crane," said Badger. "We should be discussing what we are going to do. Do we take the camp south of the Platte River, as the *isan hanska* suggest? Or do we ignore the demand and wait for them to attack?"

"We *know* they're going to attack regardless of what we do," argued Blizzard. "What we should be doing is formulating plans to attack them first. Haven't I proved over the last few months that they are not invincible? My men and I have killed a half dozen of them without suffering a single casualty. And we've stolen a hundred or so horses in the process. They haven't offered more than token resistance."

"But you haven't been fighting the soldiers," Badger volleyed back. "You've only been attacking their trading posts and their wagons."

"Whites are Whites," Blizzard snapped. "They are no match for Brulé warriors."

"Their soldiers all have good rifles," Scalptaker pointed out propitiatorily. "And there are many of them, many more than the few you have seen at the fort."

"That's my point!" Blizzard responded in exasperation. "We have to establish our superiority. We have to make them respect us, and we can't do that until we show them that we are not weak."

"Just what *are* you proposing?" Badger cut in. "It was your ill-judgment that caused this crisis to begin with. It was the attack on the wagon train — the one carried out by you and Bellowing Moose in conjunction with the misguided Cheyenne — that prompted the soldiers to come into our camp. Therefore, it was *your* action that led ultimately to the death of Conquering Bear. Now you want to compound that and see that even more of our people are killed. Is that it?"

"This has nothing to do with having our people killed," Blizzard said fervidly. "It has to do with our people being intimidated. The Whites are the intruders here. This is our country, not theirs. We signed a pact with them to live in peace, yet they are the ones who repeatedly have violated it."

"This is true," nodded Fire-in-the-Hills. "I don't agree with Blizzard very often, but he is right on that score."

"The way I see it," said Roaring Thunder, "is we have two choices. We can comply with the agent's request to move our people south of the Platte, thereby escaping, at least temporarily, the threat of hostilities. Or, we can ignore the demand and risk attack."

"No!" Blizzard added forcefully. "There is another factor you haven't mentioned."

"And what is that?" asked Fire-in-the-Hills.

"That we still have to comply with the other part of the demand; that we surrender all of those among us who participated in the battle against the soldiers."

"Would you, by chance, be worried about your own safety?" asked Badger. "You were the one they came to arrest; you were the one who initiated the fighting."

"I resent that!" Blizzard said loudly. "Are you calling me a coward?"

"If the appellation fits, then you must wear it," Badger replied stubbornly. "Would you have countless others killed because of your thirst for blood? Would you like to see women and children die because you don't have the heart to face the consequences for what you did?"

Blizzard half rose, his hand on his knife. "I will not be insulted in that manner," he said.

"Enough!" Scalptaker said loudly, pulling Blizzard down. "There will be no fighting in the council. You are acting like boys and now is the time when we have to be men. Restrain yourselves. We need to discuss this sensibly, not in anger."

"Wisely spoken," said Fire-in-the-Hills, reaching for his pipe.

"I will have no part of any discussions with *him*," Blizzard said, pointing at Badger. "Besides, as far as I'm concerned, there is nothing to debate. I do not intend to comply with the White agent's command. To do so would require that I surrender, which means I would be taken into the fort and executed. I would die without honor."

"That isn't what was said," Fire-in-the-Hills asserted.

"It may not have been said, but it is what was meant," countered Blizzard. "I will die like a warrior, with my weapons in my hands, not shackled like an animal. Debate the issue all you want, but for me there is no choice. By the time you talk this to death, I'll be halfway to the Black Hills. Let the White soldiers try to find me *there*."

"Sit close to the fire, *Ata*," Summer Rain urged, "while I fix you some food. You look exhausted."

"It has been a very tiring day, *Ina*," Badger said. "Talk, talk, talk from early this morning until now."

Summer Rain scooped boiled buffalo meat from a kettle simmering on the back of the fire into a bowl and handed it to her husband. "And what was the result? Was anything decided?"

"Yes and no," he said, spearing a large hunk of meat with his fingers and popping it into his mouth. "Scalptaker and Fire-in-the-Hills are going to comply. Roaring Thunder is being stubborn. He says the next few weeks are very important to him because he needs to replenish his food and hide supply. And since the herd normally is north of the Platte River, he intends to follow the herd regardless of the unreasonable demands from the White agent. Jagged Blade and Buffalo Heart probably will go with him although they have not totally made up their minds. Blizzard, naturally, absolutely refuses to even consider the idea. He is getting more unreasonable by the day. I don't know what fire burns in his belly, but it is getting impossible to talk to him without him going into a rage. I fear that he is on the verge of doing something very foolhardy for which we are all going to have to pay."

"And what about us, Ata," she asked softly. "What are we going to do?"

"How is the baby?" he asked, reaching over to pat her stomach.

"The baby is fine," she said, "but I'll be glad when the birthing time is here."

"When do you figure it will be?" he asked.

Summer Rain shrugged. "Another moon, I think. No longer. But why are you ignoring my question?"

"I wasn't ignoring it. I wanted to hear about the baby before I made a final decision."

"And have you?" she asked anxiously.

"Yes," he said. "Just now. I think it's best if we go south with Scalptaker and Fire-in-the-Hills. I disagree strongly with Blizzard's decision to confront the isan hanska at this time. I don't like the Whites much better than he does, but I think this is not the time to go to battle. When the time comes — and I'm convinced it will — it should be at a moment and place of our choosing, not theirs."

"But we wouldn't have to go with Blizzard; we could go with Roaring Thunder."

Badger shook his head. "I think what he's doing is very dangerous, too."

"Since when were you one to skirt danger?" Summer Rain laughed.

"That's not the point," Badger smiled. "I don't mind taking risks but I want to be sure that the odds are not stacked totally against me. A good warrior needs to know not only when to fight but when to retreat so he can live to fight another day. We know the Whites are in a nasty mood because of what happened last summer. They are going to be looking for trouble and I believe Roaring Thunder is going to be unnecessarily putting himself in their path. I don't want to endanger you and the child. Our supplies are sufficient to last us awhile yet so I don't have to make a hunt right now. I have all summer to kill buffalo."

Summer Rain beamed. "You know that I would do whatever you want, but I am glad you have come to this conclusion. Would you like some more meat?"

Summer Rain rose awkwardly and walked to the fire. "This may not interest you," she said, refilling his bowl, "but I talked to your brother today."

"Crooked Leg?"

"No," she grinned. "Red Horse. That's what he calls himself now."

"He changes names more often than I change my moccasins."

"He is pining over Porcupine," Summer Rain said. "He wanted my advice."

"And what did you tell him?"

"I told him to take his new flute and go play for her. If he has learned his music well, she will not be able to resist."

"Well, he'd better hurry."

"Why is that?" Summer Rain asked, puzzled.

"Because Porcupine's father, Red Leaf, is probably going to go with Roaring Thunder and I imagine Croo . . . Red Horse . . . will want to go south."

"I hadn't thought of that," she said pensively. "Why is everything always so complicated?"

"There's nothing complicated about us," he said, reaching out and grabbing her arm. "And there's certainly nothing complicated about making love to a pregnant woman."

"Oh, no," Badger groaned, his light slumber disturbed by a bright flash of light and a huge clap of thunder. "*Wakinyan* is announcing his arrival."

"It is that time of year, what else would you expect?" Summer Rain said sleepily. "Do you . . ." she began but her voice was drowned out by another thunderclap.

"It sounds like a big storm," Badger said. "I'd better go see to the horses."

"Don't be long," Summer Rain replied, trying to roll onto her stomach until she realized it was an impossible task.

Badger arrived at the pasture at the same time as the rain. While he moved quickly among his animals to make sure they had not loosed their hobbles, the rain began coming down in force, huge, fat drops that thudded when they hit, bounding off the still-bare limbs like pebbles thrown by small boys. "Steady! Steady!" he cautioned his horses, stroking their necks and haunches to calm them.

In a matter of minutes, the ground was soaked and puddles were beginning to form.

Once he had quieted his own animals, he moved through the herd to see if any others needed attention. Moving from one horse to another, he soon found himself at the far side of the pasture, on the edge of the woods. He was adjusting the hobble on one of Jagged Blade's horses when he noticed a movement out of the corner of his eye. Squinting to see through the rain, which was coming down harder than ever, he thought he saw the figure of a man.

His heartbeat quickened. "Crow!" he thought. "Come to steal our horses, and I'm caught without a weapon other than my knife." He cupped his hands and raised them to his lips, prepared to sound the alarm, when he realized there was something familiar about the shape. To his surprise, he realized the figure was not that of a Crow but Blizzard. "What is he doing off in the trees?" he asked himself. He has no horses there.

Stealthily, he moved through the underbrush at the

edge of the forest, coming up short when he got close enough to see clearly the drama unfolding in the trees.

Blizzard was crouched in a small clearing, bent over the form of a man lying on the ground. Behind them was a horse, saddled for travel. Looking closely, Badger saw that the man on the ground was the Arapaho, Giant Crane, and that he was lying in a large pool of blood. Badger could see him kicking weakly, so he knew he was still alive. As he watched, appalled, Blizzard expertly ran the edge of his knife completely around Giant Crane's head, from the base of his neck to the top of his forehead. Planting his knee firmly in the middle of Giant Crane's back, he gave a mighty yank. When he did, Badger could hear Giant Crane's backbone snap and his scalp, ears and all, came off in one piece in Blizzard's hand. Giant Crane uttered a final yelp and lay still.

"Have you lost your mind?" Badger yelled, jumping into the clearing. "This is not an act of war. This is murder!"

Blizzard looked up, startled. Then recognition dawned. Like a wolf disturbed at a kill, Blizzard's eyes blazed and his lips curled back over his teeth. A growl emerged from deep in his throat. "The gods are being very good to me today," he snarled, leaping like a mountain lion at the unprepared Badger.

"What . . ." Badger began but he never finished the sentence. It ended in a gurgle as Blizzard plunged his knife into the cavity at the base of his throat. Badger died instantly with a questioning look in eyes.

"You have had that coming for a long time," Blizzard said, his voice as steady as if he were discussing the weather. "Too many times you have let your woman's heart overrule your warrior instincts. Now you will no longer be a problem to me or anyone else."

Removing his knife from the wound in Badger's throat which gaped like a third eye, Blizzard lifted the dead warrior's head by his hair and made a long, thin incision across the top of his forehead.

Summer Rain moaned and wailed, not so much in physical pain as a consequence from the slashes she had made across her thighs and calves, but in mental anguish resulting from the loss of her husband.

"To die in battle is one thing," she sobbed to Short Woman, the wife of Fire-in-the-Hills, "but to have your husband murdered by a member of his own band is a truly terrible thing indeed."

"Do not worry," said Red Horse, struggling to conceal his own agony, "I promise you that he will be avenged."

As was the custom, Red Horse, the brother of the murdered warrior, and some members of the warrior society to which Badger had belonged, the *Sotka Yuhas*, had inserted thin, sharp pegs carved from willow branches through the skin on their thighs, calves, biceps, and forearms. But, as with Summer Rain, the agony that Red Horse was suffering was inconsequential compared to the anger that burned within him.

Although the Brulé code mandated that murder was a crime punishable by death, there was no provision for carrying out the penalty. Traditionally, execution was the responsibility of the victim's family, in this case Red Horse since Badger's father, Stomping Bull, had died years before in a hunting accident. Blizzard's father, Spotted Wolf, had tried to appease Red Horse by offering the young warrior several horses, but Red Horse refused to smoke Spotted Wolf's proffered pipe, indicating that he planned to seek revenge.

"Do you plan to kill him yourself?" White Crane solemnly asked.

"Of course," Red Horse nodded abruptly. "But before

we can discuss that, we need to complete the mourning ceremony."

Willing the thoughts of revenge and the distress caused by the willow pegs from his consciousness, Red Horse concentrated on his duties.

A rack had been set up in front of Badger's tipi, upon which the majority of the dead man's robes and leggings had been placed on display. As Red Horse sat immobile in the place of respect, White Crane brought forward three of Badger's horses and two donated by Red Horse from his own small herd.

Once the horses were gathered, Fire-in-the-Hills, who was acting as Red Horse's herald, announced that Red Horse was giving away the horses and the clothing in his brother's memory. The recipients, who were summoned one at a time to take their gifts, were members of the Sotka Yuhas.

Once that was done, Fire-in-the-Hills summoned Lazy Bear, the least well-to-do member of the band, and commanded him to remove the pegs from Red Horse's arms and legs. As a reward, Red Horse gave him the next to last of Badger's horses. He kept one horse, Badger's favorite, since it would play a role later in the burial.

As Lazy Bear led his pony away, Jagged Blade, a fellow member of the Sotka Yuhas, walked to the center of the group. Handing his knife to Red Horse, he raised the skin of his forearm and asked that Red Horse thrust the point through the skin so he too could suffer to show his grief. In turn, members of the society who had not pierced their skin with pegs came forward and repeated the ritual.

After the fraternal brothers had reseated themselves, Red Horse nodded to two young girls who had been appointed servers. As the Sotka Yuhas sang about Badger's bravery, the girls went among them passing out bowls of meat provided by Red Horse and Summer Rain.

After all had eaten, Red Horse went into the tipi to help Summer Rain dress Badger for burial.

"You know," he said, slipping on the special burial moccasins with beaded soles that Summer Rain handed him, "that I plan to follow the custom of our people and take you for my wife. It is my obligation as Badger's only brother."

"But your heart belongs to Porcupine," Summer Rain said, slipping an eagle feather into the lock of hair that had not been removed by Blizzard when he scalped his victim.

"My heart has nothing to do with it," said Red Horse, smearing red paint, the symbol of bravery, across Badger's face. "It is my duty and, unless you have strong objections, I intend to carry it out."

Summer Rain did not answer immediately, buying time to prepare an answer by fiddling with Badger's war club and his bow, which she placed gently at his side.

"Perhaps it would be a good idea," she conceded, stealing a sidelong glance at Red Horse. "Our child is due in less than a month and I will need someone to hunt for us."

"Then it is decided," Red Horse sighed "I think your decision is a wise one."

Without further conversation, they wrapped Badger in his best remaining robe and then, over that, they placed a tanned elk hide, which they secured with strips of buffalo hide.

While they had been dressing the body, members of the Sotka Yuhas had been erecting a burial platform on a small hill a short distance outside the camp. As they worked, their wives peeled bark from the supports and daubed black paint onto the newly exposed wood to show that Badger had been a brave warrior who had accumulated many battle honors during his life.

As Red Horse and Summer Rain stood by, the Sotka Yuhas wives carried Badger's body out of the tipi and placed it on a waiting travois so it could be transported to the scaffold.

Once the body was secure, Red Horse took the rein of Badger's favorite mount, which had been decorated with red splotches and covered with a robe, and led the procession to the hill.

After the women had lifted the body onto the platform, Fire-in-the-Hills, who had been Badger's closest friend, came forward. Taking the reins of the dead warrior's horse, he made a short speech about how Badger would need the animal in the afterlife, culminating the oration by taking his knife and severing the horse's jugular. Bending forward, he cut off the horse's tail and fastened it to the burial scaffold.

That completed the ceremony. As Red Horse and Summer Rain returned to the tipi, the Sotka Yuhas wives spread thorn bushes around the base of the scaffold to keep predators away, then they too returned to the main camp.

As the mourners trudged away, the boy White Wolf came running to meet them. "Two riders are coming," he said excitedly. "The White man, Buffalo Shoulders, and his son, Plays-with-His-Toes.

"Is this a social visit or are you here on behalf of the new agent?" Scalptaker asked Legendre once they had eaten and smoked.

"Purely social," Legendre replied. "I am taking my son to spend some time with the Cheyenne. My second wife, White Woman, was killed by a bear last autumn and the responsibility of raising him has fallen on me."

"You don't have much luck with wives, do you?" said Fire-in-the-Hills, grinning to show he meant no malice. "I am sorry for your loss."

"Thank you," Legendre said, nodding. "She was good to the boy and to me."

"But your son is Miniconjou," Jagged Blade pointed out.

"That's true," said Legendre, "but his mother died when he was very young and he knows the Cheyenne better because White Woman was from that tribe. It will just be for the season. I plan to bring him back with me next autumn."

"Are you taking him to the Cheyenne because you think he should get to know his people or because you fear for his life if you keep him in the fort?" Scalptaker asked shrewdly.

"You are very perceptive," Legendre replied, picking his words carefully. "Let me explain my position. The Army doctor, Dobbs, saved my life after I was mauled by the grizzly. When the Army chief said he needed an interpreter and offered me the position, I thought it was wise to take it."

"Have you given up trapping?" Roaring Thunder asked in surprise.

"Regretfully, yes. Times are changing; the era of the White trapper has ended."

"What do you mean?" asked Jagged Blade, slow-witted as usual.

"More and more Whites are coming here," Legendre said. "Right now they are just passing through. But I have been listening carefully to the talk around the fort and it is the belief among the White soldiers that it will be only a matter of time before they decide to stay."

"You mean permanently?" Jagged Blade exclaimed, shocked. "To live as we do?"

"Not exactly," Legendre smiled. "They probably will build cabins and plant crops."

"You mean try to cultivate the grazing land?" said Jagged Blade, shaking his head in disbelief. "They can't do that! That would drive the buffalo away for good."

"Sadly, it's true," said Legendre. "The Whites far to the east, in the large cities they call Washington and New York, care nothing about the buffalo or about you or any of the tribes. They feel they have become crowded in the territory they control now and they are looking voraciously at this land."

"Blizzard was right!" Jagged Blade swore. "We should have listened to him. We should be preparing for war against the Whites."

"Don't be hasty," said Legendre. "All of this may not begin to happen for many years yet. The Whites at the fort also talk of deep divisions among their own people. There are strong differences between those who live in the north and those who live in the south. There is talk even of coming war."

"Divisions? War?" Scalptaker asked, puzzled. "What could possibly elicit such strong feelings?"

"It is very complicated," said Legendre, "Something — and I say this with no disrespect — that you could never understand without a thorough knowledge of how the White man thinks and lives. Believe me, you don't want that knowledge."

"Tell us about this new agent, the man called Teasley," urged Fire-in-the-Hills.

"Ahhh," Legendre spat. "That *fils de pute*, that son of a whore. He is not your friend no matter what he tries to tell you. He wants this land and if it means your ruination, that is something that will not keep him awake at night."

"And what of his demand that those of us who do not want war must demonstrate our desire for peace by moving south of the Platte River?"

"It is a clever scheme to divide you," Legendre said. "I argued vociferously against it but that *cochon* Teasley, he told me to close my mouth and tend to my own business."

"More evidence that Blizzard was right!" Jagged Blade interjected. "We should prepare for war."

"Hold on," said Legendre, raising his hands and pushing the palms downward. "Calm down. Teasley is very crafty. Just because he is detestable does not mean he is not very intelligent. He knows the Indians because of his previous service as an Army officer on the frontier. Or at least he thinks he does. He figures that he can stall a major confrontation by convincing some of you to move south. If you remain together and fight the Whites, you may be able to win the battle but you surely would lose the war."

"Explain that!" said Fire-in-the-Hills. "How could we win *and* lose?"

"Because you possibly could defeat the soldiers that are here now. But if you do, it will only fire the anger of their leaders in Washington and they will send more soldiers than you could imagine. Eventually, they would overpower you, all of your people would be killed or driven onto expanses of undesirable land where they could control you and keep you from being a threat.

"You see," he continued, "Teasley's evil genius becomes apparent only if you study his plan minutely. Either way, he wins. If you comply with his demands and move south of the Platte you will be giving in to him and putting yourself in a bad position for the future. If you don't, you will be sealing your own fate because still more soldiers will be sent to destroy you.

Make no mistake, I think blood is going to be shed in the near future. Indian blood, mainly."

"Why is that?" asked Fire-in-the-Hills. "If we comply with the demand to move our people, the troops will have no reason to attack us."

"The leaders of the troops are in a very foul mood," said Legendre. "They want revenge for those soldiers killed in your camp last summer. They will find an excuse, no matter how weak, to attack."

"What about the treaty?" asked Scalptaker. "The one we signed with Broken Hand, the previous agent, four winters ago."

"For the Whites, it was a pact of convenience," said Legendre. "Nothing more. They wanted to buy time until they could build up their forces."

"How do you feel about this demand?" asked Scalptaker.

Legendre rolled his massive shoulders. "Unfortunately, that is your decision and it is a tough one. My natural inclination would be to fight . . . "

"See! See!" Jagged Blade said excitedly. "He thinks like Blizzard!"

"You didn't let me finish," Legendre said, annoyed. "But it might be wiser to pretend to go along. Then, if the troops attack you, and I believe it is all but a foregone conclusion that they will no matter what, you will at least be morally right. You can appeal to the more sympathetic ears in Washington that you have been wronged, that the treaty has been shattered by the Army. What compliance does for you is what the treaty did for the White man. It buys you time. If war comes between the Whites they will be too occupied with their own troubles to worry about fighting you. Then you will be able to better assess your situation, decide if indeed you want a major war or if you can negotiate a more advantageous peace."

"To be honest," said Scalptaker, "you surprise me. You have much more wisdom than I ever gave you credit for."

Legendre laughed. "I should take the compliment and be grateful. But I have to confess I have not been smart enough to figure this all out by myself. I may not be too intelligent but I *am* honest. Most of what I have been telling you, I did not figure out on my own. It is what I learned from eavesdropping on conversations between sympathetic soldiers."

"Then all the Army men are not our enemies?" asked Fire-in-the-Hills.

"Absolutely not," said Legendre. "Two of them to whom I am the closest, the doctor, Dobbs, and his friend, a lieutenant named Benoit, are very understanding about your plight. They, too, argued against Teasley's plan but, since they are junior officers, were also ordered to keep quiet. There is a scout named Ashby, who once was married to an Arapaho, who also commiserates with you and your people. But the Whites also have some troublemakers other than Teasley. Which reminds me, you must be on the lookout for three deserters . . . "

"What are deserters?" Roaring Thunder asked innocently.

"Men who turn against their leaders," Legendre explained. "Men who have no scruples and decide to no longer be a part of their group."

"Like Blizzard," exclaimed Jagged Blade.

"What about them?" asked Roaring Thunder.

"They ran away from the fort. There is reason to believe that they are headed your way with intentions of stealing back that large box that Brulé warriors stole from the mail wagon last fall."

Fire-in-the-Hills doubled over, roaring with laughter.

"What is so funny?" Legendre asked, baffled.

"The thief was Blizzard," Fire-in-the-Hills wheezed when he could catch his breath. "And he, too, is now what you would call a deserter. He killed Teasley's messenger, the Arapaho Giant Crane, and a Brulé warrior named Badger. Then he ran, presumably far to the north. Whatever it was he stole from the Whites, he apparently took with him because he left nothing behind except a tipi in bad need of repair. If your deserters want it back, they are going to have to find our deserter first."

"You see," Legendre chuckled, "there *is* justice in this world after all."

"What did you think?" White Crane asked Red Horse later, after the meeting had dissolved and they were sitting in White Crane's lodge, eating boiled buffalo and warming themselves around a small fire.

"It was very enlightening to be allowed to attend the council discussions even if we are still too young to participate in the debate," Red Horse said tactfully.

"That is *not* what I mean," White Crane said testily.

"I know what you meant," Red Horse grinned. "I could not resist having a little sport with you."

"But you still haven't answered my question."

"I know," Red Horse said soberly. "Several thoughts are running through my mind."

"Such as?"

"Well, for one thing I was very impressed to hear Buffalo Shoulders's statements about the two soldiers at the fort, the one who rescued us and the doctor who treated you. I, too, thought they were good men and it was encouraging to hear my judgment upheld."

"You're still being evasive," White Crane replied. "Why can't you give me a straight answer."

"If you insist," Red Horse said. "I think much of what

Buffalo Shoulders said, even if the words were not his, is true. That it is to our advantage to bide our time, to escape a fight with the soldiers for the present."

"That is why Blizzard killed your brother," White Crane pointed out.

"I know. But that doesn't mean I am going to change my mind. I think it is best for our people right now to go along with the demands from the new agent."

"Does that mean you still plan to go south?"

"Yes, but not for long."

"Now what does *that* mean?" White Crane said, giving his friend an exasperated look.

"It means my plans have not changed. That I still plan to marry Summer Rain, as I promised her I would — as is my duty — and take her south to await the birth of Badger's child."

"And then?" White Crane asked expectantly. "I know you too well. I know there is more."

"Yes, there is," Red Horse smiled. "Once she is settled and has given birth, I plan to go north, to find Blizzard and kill him."

"Just like that?"

"Just like that."

"What makes you think you're a match for Blizzard? You know how strong and cunning he is. I'm certain he's not trembling over the thought you are coming to seek your revenge."

"That doesn't matter," Red Horse said determinedly. "I must do it. It is my responsibility."

"You know," White Crane sighed, "you can carry this responsibility excuse only so far."

"I can't help it if I have an overdeveloped sense of duty. I *know* what is right; I know what I have to do."

"And that itself is sometimes frightening."

For several minutes neither of them spoke; each stared into the fire, lost in his own thoughts.

"You are my best friend," White Crane said at length.

"So," Red Horse grunted.

"So, it is the duty of best friends to help each other in times of need."

Red Horse looked at him carefully. "What are you saying?"

"I'm saying that I'm going with you when you go looking for Blizzard. He may be mean, but he's no match for the two of us."

"You know," Red Horse said with a smile, "I am very lucky to have you for a kola."

Dobbs slowly lifted the cup to his lips, savoring the aroma of the freshly brewed coffee pilfered from Benoit's private stock. Grinning in anticipation, he bent his head and took a tentative sip. It was all he could do to keep from spitting the liquid across the table. "This is awful!" he gasped, making a face. "What could I have done wrong?"

Inge shrugged. "I thought you were doing it right, too. Maybe we should have watched Jean more carefully."

"Who would have suspected that there's such an art to making Cajun coffee. Coffee is coffee, isn't it? Just because he uses a funny-looking pot doesn't make the process any different. You have ground beans, you have water, and supposedly you have coffee."

"Maybe if you added more water," Inge suggested. "Jean always adds more water to the coffee from the pot."

"Could be," said Dobbs, reaching for the kettle. "That's pretty inconsiderate of him to go gallivanting off to Fort Kearny without giving us detailed instruction on how to make decent coffee."

"You think he's going to be all right?" Inge asked anxiously. "What if they get into a battle?"

"He can take care of himself," Dobbs said. "I don't think you ought to worry. Besides, I thought you were interested in George Teasley."

"Don't be silly," Inge said, making a waving motion with her hand. "I've just been pretending so I could get Jean jealous. George is way too old for me. Anyway, he's not interested in me."

"Oh," Dobbs said, raising an eyebrow. "It looked to me as if he were."

"It's just George's way," Inge laughed. "He's interested in *every* woman. If I weren't here, he'd be chasing after Mutter. The last thing I'd want would be to get involved with him. But," she added hurriedly, frowning, "don't tell Jean!"

Dobbs shook his head. "Women!" he said with exasperation. "Always scheming. Why can't . . . "

A hard, loud rap on the door interrupted him.

"Doctor Dobbs!" a female voice called anxiously. "Doctor Dobbs, please open the door."

Glancing curiously at Inge, Dobbs leaped to his feet and crossed the room in three quick steps. "Kathy!" he said in surprise. "What are you doing here? What's the matter?"

"It's Miss Ellen," the girl replied, nervously wringing her hands. "You have to come back to the Hog Ranch with me. She needs a doctor right bad."

"What happened?" Dobbs asked, reaching under the bed for his emergency kit. Opening the small leather bag, he quickly checked the contents: knives, saw, needles and catgut, bandages, a block of wood to bite down on, pliers, a bottle of laudanum, and several containers of salves and liniments. "Did she fall? Get kicked by a horse? Burned?"

"No," Kathy replied. "She got beaten. It was the reverend. He worked her over real good."

"Longstreet!" Inge said in surprise. "That fat little man?"

"Fat little man, my ass," Kathy replied. "He tried to get in Miss Ellen's knickers. She laughed and told him he'd have better luck with Rastus. That's the mule. He didn't take too kindly to that. Went right off his rocker, he did. Beat her something fierce and then raped her. And that son of a bitch calls himself a man of God. More like a man of the Devil, you ask me."

"I've got everything," Dobbs said. "Let's go. Inge," he said, "would you come along and give me a hand? Wounded soldiers I can treat all day by myself but when it comes to women I'm sometimes all thumbs."

"Let me get a shawl," she said, hurrying out the door.

"How is she?" Colonel Kemp asked later.

"Not bad, considering," Dobbs said. "Three cracked ribs, two chipped teeth, and a broken thumb."

"Did she give you any details?"

Dobbs nodded. "Seems Longstreet had been in to see the girls earlier, sniffing around as usual, trying to get something for nothing. When he refused to pay, none of the girls would go in the back room with him. Ellen, that's Miss O'Reilly . . . "

"I know who Ellen is."

"Sorry. Ellen didn't pay him any attention; he was always coming and going anyway. She went out to the shed to saddle a horse, telling Kathy she planned to come to the post to get some supplies from Mr. Sevier."

"What time was this?"

"About mid-morning, why?"

"Just wondering."

"Seems Longstreet was waiting for her in the shed.

She said he had a strange look in his eye and was ranting about God's vengeance on whores. Told her it wasn't too late to save her soul if she would just kneel down with him and pray for forgiveness."

"I'm sure she was happy to hear that," Kemp said, smiling tightly.

"About as thrilled as a trapper with a toothache. She told him he must have been out on the Plains too long because his brain was frozen, not to mention certain other parts of his anatomy."

"God," Kemp sighed. "I thought a woman with her experience would have known better than that."

"Me, too," agreed Dobbs. "I guess he wasn't in a very good mood or something. Anyway, the next thing she knew, she was flat on her back and bells were ringing in her ears. She looked up and Longstreet was standing over her. Had his pants unbuttoned and his pecker in his hand. Since she had been preparing to come to the fort, she had her quirt with her. She found it on the ground where she had dropped it, spun around and lashed him a good one across the, uh, exposed organ."

"Did she now!" Kemp roared. "Good for her, by God."

"I think that set him off. She must have hit him a good one because there was blood on her that wasn't hers, at least as far as I could tell in my professional opinion. That's about the size of it. He beat her, raped her, and then took off."

"I feel responsible for this to a large degree," Kemp said, rising to go to the door.

"How's that, sir?" Dobbs asked, perplexed.

"I knew weeks ago, when I first met the man, that he was trouble. I should have put him in irons as soon as Miss Schmidt said he made advances toward her. At least tossed him off the post."

"You can't blame yourself. Even Inge thought he was harmless."

"I should have followed my instincts," Kemp said. "That's what I getting paid for." Sticking his head out the door, he bellowed for Adamson.

"Lieutenant," he said when Adamson came running. "Take a couple of men and go to the preacher's quarters. Put him under arrest and bring him back here. Right now!"

"What are you going to do to him?" Dobbs asked after Adamson left.

"I should hang him, but that probably will depend on Miss O'Reilly's condition. Is she going to get better?"

"Oh, yes. Her injuries are not life threatening, barring an unexpected development."

"How's she taking it psychologically? She about to have a nervous collapse?"

"Oh, no," Dobbs said. "She's tough. Said she reckoned it was just an occupational hazard. But next time she sure as hell won't turn her back on any man who wears his collar backwards."

"In that case, I have to think about the punishment. In the meantime," he said, reaching into his desk drawer, "this came for you in the latest packet from Kearny. It's from Ben-wah."

Dobbs smiled, sticking the letter in his pocket. "You mean, Ben-oight?"

"Shit, no. I mean Ben-wah. I can talk Cajun as well as the next man. I just call him that to piss him off. Keeps him on his toes."

"It probably . . ." Dobbs began, only to be interrupted by a loud rap on the door.

"It's Reverend Longstreet, sir," Adamson said, sticking his head in without waiting to be told. "He's gone," he panted. "His room is cleaned out, his horse is not in the stable. One of the men said he heard him mumbling something about going to see God. You think that means he's contemplating suicide?"

"We should be so lucky," Kemp laughed. "I think it means he's run off to join the Cheyenne."

"The Cheyenne?" Adamson said, furrowing his brow.

"It's a long story, lieutenant. Reverend Longstreet is operating under the impression that God is a Cheyenne warrior."

"Oh, I see, sir," Adamson said uncertainly. "Should I roust Mr. Ashby? Get a search party out?" he asked hopefully.

Kemp hesitated. "No," he said firmly. "I don't want to waste the manpower. I don't think the Cheyenne are going to like him any better than we did. I'd be willing to bet you he's back here in two weeks, begging forgiveness. Not that it will do him any good. Anyway, he'll be back. He's running out of places to go."

"I asked Mutter if she knew how to make French coffee," Inge said, pouring Dobbs a cup. "See if this tastes any better."

Dobbs blew on the dark liquid, then took a small taste. "*Much* better," he smiled. "Still not as good as Jean's but better than my miserable effort. Oh," he added, "speaking of Jean, I got a letter from him. Shall I read it?"

"By all means," said Inge. "But if it's . . . "

"It isn't private," Dobbs interrupted. "We all know each other's business. Or most of it anyway." He dug into his bag and drew a knife, which he used to slice open the envelope.

"It's dated last Tuesday," he said, glancing at the paper. "Hey look at this. It's addressed to both of us. Guess he knows us pretty well."

"Forget the address," Inge said impatiently. "What does he have to say?"

Dobbs cleared his throat.

Dear Jace and Inge,

I know you are sharing this, so this will save me writing two letters.

I arrived on schedule three days ago and have been assigned to E Co. of the 2nd Dragoons. I don't really have any duties since Kemp specified in his letter to Cooke — that's Colonel P. St. George Cooke, in case you've forgotten — that I was here as an observer. He seems like a nice enough fellow and a competent officer. Of course, that last judgment is based almost solely on the fact that he knew right away how to pronounce my name. Seems he had a cousin who married a New Orleans debutante several years ago and he spent some time visiting in the city.

I know you will be delighted to learn that Kearny is exactly the same since we last saw it except for the new commanding officer, one who actually sits at his desk and obviously is not troubled by hemorrhoids . . . "

"What is that all about?" asked Inge.

"I'll explain later. Let me read on."

. . . It goes to show how much I was impressed by him because I've temporarily forgotten his name. But that bothers me not a bit; he probably doesn't remember mine either.

Cooke has a captain and two lieutenants in his command, all of them new to the West, so I feel like a veritable veteran. All the troops, too, are fresh out of the East and still spend most of the day gawking at the blue skies and marveling about the lack of trees. Have we been out here so long that now seems commonplace?

If enthusiasm could be converted into money, all the men would be millionaires because every last one of them, from General Harney on down, is incredibly anxious to get on the march and "teach those savages a lesson they'll never forget."

This attitude causes me no little amount of concern. Obviously they have been drilled about the need for revenge: give and take no quarter. A few of the NCOs and some of the older officers fought in Mexico so they are a little more blasé about the exercise, but General Harney evidently has issued orders to his officers to keep the men enthused about the prospect of a bloodletting because this is manifest in everything they do. At night, they spend their time making sure their rifles are clean— they all are equipped with the new Sharps, which are very impressive and have a much longer range — and their knives are sharp. Most of them seem to think it is going to be a regular picnic.

I haven't yet met the general, only seen him from the far — let me amend that, the very far — end of the table at supper. He's a much taller man than I expected, probably about six feet two or three, with broad shoulders, full lips, a bushy white beard, and a hairline that has receded almost as much as yours. I'm speaking to you, Jace, not Inge. From what little I have heard, he is a man of remarkable contrasts. On the one hand, he is a dedicated, driving soldier: loud, profane and very demanding. During a discussion after the table was cleared the other evening, he ended debate by slamming his hand down and screaming, "By God, I'm for battle, not peace." No doubt he was talking about the expected encounter with the Teton Sioux. I don't know what prompted the outburst since my chair is too distant to hear all that is said, but there was no doubt what I heard him yell.

On the other hand, he is supposedly a very compas-

sionate man whose hobbies, when he has the time, are growing vegetables and flowers. Cooke told me that he heard on good authority about how Harney once threw a private into irons for unnecessarily beating a mule. However, I fail to detect this vein of compassion, if indeed it does exist, in his expressed feelings toward the Sioux. Perhaps he thinks a mule is more deserving of his sympathy. And perhaps I am judging him too harshly. I can confirm that his nickname, spoken in whispers by the junior officers, is indeed "Mad Bear," but no one seems to be able to offer an explanation of its origin.

As to Cooke, I've found myself growing quite fond of him. He, too, is tall and slim with a beard even bushier than Harney's. A native of Leesburg, Virginia — you see, Jace, we Southerners are everywhere — he graduated from the Academy in '27. Originally an infantryman, he went with the 1st Dragoons when they were organized in '33 and to the 2nd Dragoons as a major in '47. Lately, he has been at Fort Union, in New Mexico, where he has been protecting the Santa Fe Trail, until ordered to link up with Harney. I am developing quite a bit of respect for him, especially when I look at the men with which he has been saddled. Many are recent immigrants — no offense, Inge — mainly Italians and Irishmen, and give him quite a few discipline problems. Also, they have been greatly troubled by cholera. Two of them died just yesterday. It's too bad Kemp didn't send you along, too, Jace; your services would have been most welcome.

The officer with whom I have become the most friendly, however, is a fellow lieutenant named Kemble Warren. I knew him slightly at the Academy but since he graduated the year I was a plebe, it was not a close relationship. He is now a topographical engineer and a member of Harney's staff on loan from Fort Pierre. Although he is staff and I am a lowly errand boy, he is seated next to me at meals and we seem to get along quite well.

That brings you up to date on what is happening Back East. Present plans call for us to depart sometime late next week for the 350-mile march to Laramie, following the same trail we took in the wagon train, that is, along the North Platte River. As you recall, that is not exactly a scenic route, but is the best the area has to offer.

I hope that Teasley has not replaced me permanently in the bridge game and other sensitive positions as well. Although this assignment has not proved as dull as I had feared, I still sorely miss your smiling faces. Most of all I miss my coffee. I give you fair warning: If you have drunk it all before I get back there will be hell to pay.

"That's it," said Dobbs, placing the letter carefully on the table. "He signs it 'Your friend, Jean' and . . . wait, there's a small postscript here."

"Oh," said Inge, leaning forward, "what does it say?"

Dobbs laughed. "It says, and I quote: *I hope I will be able to return before too many Sundays have passed because I don't want to think that Inge has suddenly,* and he underlines this, *gotten religion.*"

Inge giggled. "Well, he will be happy to know that I did not have to follow through on my threat against the Reverend Longstreet. Miss O'Reilly seems to have made a valiant attempt in her own right. But I wish she had been armed with a sabre rather than a quirt. And you can tell him that, too."

Along the Laramie River
Southwest of Fort Laramie

"He looks just like his father, doesn't he?" Summer Rain gushed.

Red Horse leaned forward and stared at the infant. "I know what you want me to say, Summer Rain, but to me all babies look alike. They're all ugly."

"That's just what Badger would have said. In the last few weeks I've discovered how much alike you two really are. And why don't you call me 'Ina' since I'm now your wife?"

Red Horse tried to smile. "I know, it's just that I'm not yet accustomed to being married."

"But you don't mind if I call you 'Ata'?"

"Of course not, if it makes you comfortable."

"You have made every effort to make me comfortable in every way, Ata. You show a remarkable degree of maturity for being so young."

"I'm not *that* young," he said, annoyed. "You're only six years older."

"I know," Summer Rain smiled, "but sometimes I feel vastly older."

"I want to make sure that you have everything you need," Red Horse said solemnly, "because in two days White Crane and I are leaving."

"You persist in going after Blizzard? Why don't you be patient? Wait and he will come back here eventually."

"Why postpone the inevitable? Sooner or later, I will kill him and I would just as soon go looking for him rather than leaving it to him to choose the time and place."

Summer Rain sighed. "I will mend your robe, Ata. It may be cold when you go into the northern mountains."

"White Crane and I will go first to Roaring Thunder's camp. Perhaps someone there will have more recent information about where we can find him."

Ash Hollow
Along the Platte River Southeast of Fort Laramie

"We just missed them, general," Honoré Bordelon

drawled. "Couldn't have been more than a day. Look," he said, pointing to a stained spot on the ground, "this is where they butchered a buffalo. It's still fresh."

"Which way did they go?" Harney asked.

"That way," the scout replied, pointing to a valley that opened to the north. "They're probably camped up there on a creek they call *Meenatowahpah*. Means 'Blue Water.' My guess is they're not going anywhere anytime soon. They'll need to finish trimming their meat, get it at least partly dried, and work the hides before they can move their camp. I'd say they're stuck right where they are for at least three days."

"Very well, Bordelon," Harney nodded. "Good job. We'll camp here. This seems to be a favorite spot for the emigrants so I guess it's good enough for us. Lots of grass, water, and firewood. You take a couple of men and go up the valley. See what you can find and come back as soon as you can." Turning, he signaled his executive officer. "Colonel, prepare the camp, then notify the officers of a staff meeting at twenty-three hundred hours. By then, with any luck, I'll have a report from Bordelon on the disposition of the hostiles."

"I'm going with Bordelon," Lieutenant Warren said, turning to Benoit. "If he finds the Indian camp, Harney will want a quick map of the area. Want to come along?"

"Would you look at that," whispered Benoit, pointing to the valley that spread before them. Both men were lying on their stomachs, leaning over the edge of a bluff. Five hundred feet below them and a half mile away, Indian tipis were arranged in an orderly fashion along a meandering stream that ran swift and clear, tumbling toward the Platte.

"Quite impressive, isn't it?" agreed Warren, studying

the terrain with a professional eye. "They picked their campsite well, tucked in among the Sand Hills with only one good entryway. Under normal circumstances, if they were fighting other Indians, it would be damn near impregnable. But they don't know about our new rifles. Harney can set up sharpshooters on this bluff and the one over there," he said, pointing to his right, "and they can blast them all to hell and gone without worrying about return fire because it's well out of the range of any weapons the Indians might have."

"How many tipis do you count?" Benoit asked.

"Thirty, but I think there's more around the bend. Bordelon is scouting over there and he can give us a better idea when he gets back."

"Jesus," said Benoit, "I can't help but feel sorry for these poor bastards."

"How's that?" Warren asked, looking at him sharply.

"It's going to be like shooting ducks sitting on a pond. Only worse, because the ducks can fly away. The Indians have no place to go."

"Be careful how you say that around Harney," Warren warned. "He's right bent on revenge."

"Here's the situation, gentlemen,"" Harney said, laying Warren's freshly drawn map on the campaign table in front of him. Benoit looked around, noting the hungry look on the faces of the assembled officers. The lantern light cast deep shadows in the tent, giving the scene a surreal appearance. "Bordelon tells me there are forty-one lodges of Brulé, six Miniconjou, and five Oglalas. The Miniconjou and the Oglalas are off here, up in the north, with the Brulé in the front. From our point of view, that couldn't be better. It's the Brulé we're really after since they're the ones who murdered Lieutenant Grattan and his men.

"Now here's the plan," he continued, using a small dagger he wore on his waist, an affectation common to high-ranking officers, to point to specific spots on the map. "Cooke," he said, looking up at the colonel, "I want you to take your men and circle around behind the camp. Get them on these hills here to cut off possible retreat. According to Warren, that's pretty rough ground so you can count on any movement being disorganized."

"When do you want me to move out, general?" Cooke asked.

"Zero two hundred," Harney said briskly.

"Two hours from now?" Cooke asked in surprise.

"You have a problem with that, colonel?" Harney asked sharply. "Did you come here to fight or spend the day in your tent sipping tea?"

"Y . . . y . . . yes, sir," Cooke stammered. "I'll have my men ready to go."

"And you, Howe," he said, turning to the captain of artillery, "I want your men here, on the right flank. Understood?"

"Clear as day, sir," Howe said vigorously.

"Cady!" Harney called loudly.

"Here, sir," came a voice from the shadows almost behind the general.

"Ah, there you are, major. I want you to march your troops to these positions: here, here, and here," he said making small holes in the map with the point of his dagger. "Make sure they all have plenty of ammunition."

"What time will the attack commence, sir?" asked Cady, a plump, pink-cheeked Irishman from the Hell's Kitchen section of Manhattan.

"I was getting to that, major, if you would have given me a goddamn minute. I want the operation to get underway," Harney said, staring at Cady, whose face had turned a brilliant scarlet, "as soon after dawn as practicable. Oh seven hundred at the latest."

"Sir," said Cady timidly, "we'll need some light for the riflemen. If that camp is surrounded by bluffs the sun might not be high enough at that time to illuminate the target area."

Harney rocked back on his heels. "Good point, major. Let's say oh eight hundred then. No later. I want this all wrapped up by mid-afternoon. Questions?"

"How about the enemy, sir?" asked Howe. "What's their strength?"

"It's hard to tell, but I'm figuring four hundred or more."

"How are they armed?" asked a captain named Todd, the commander of one of the infantry companies.

"That's the good part," Harney grinned. "Hardly at all. They have a few old muskets but far and away all most of them have are bows and lances. I figure it's going to be a real turkey shoot."

Benoit shyly raised his hand. "Where do you want me to go, general?" he asked.

Harney stared at him. "Who the hell are you?"

Benoit smothered a laugh. "Jean Benoit, sir, from Fort Laramie. Detached to your expedition as an observer. I've been with Colonel Cooke for the last couple of weeks."

"Then *stay* with him, lieutenant. That doesn't take a lot of brainpower does it?"

Without waiting for a response, Harney let his eyes rove around the room. "There are few things I want you to remember, gentlemen. First, we're making history here. The six hundred men in this command represent the largest single force ever to move against hostile Indians in the West. I'm depending on you to see that we do ourselves proud. There are some things I want you to remember as you go into battle tomorrow. First," he said, his eyes blazing, "these are the same scheming, sneaky, no-good little pricks who shot down Lieutenant Grattan and his men. Murdered them in cold blood and left their mutilated bodies rotting on the plain. Lifted their scalps and, not content with that, cut off their heads, their arms, and their manhood. Think of *that* when you have one of those red bastards in your sights. Second, recall, too, these are the same fucking savages who have repeatedly — and I emphasize 'repeatedly' — raided our wagon trains, killed a lot of emigrants heading westward with nothing on their minds except a better life. They have *butchered* these people, helpless civilians. Raped the women and girls, smashed the heads of young babies. They aren't deserving of any mercy and I don't want you to think that they are. Our mission here is to make the Oregon Trail safe for the emigrants, and the only way we're going to be able to do that is to keep the savages under control. Our task is to make it very clear to them that *we* are the ones in power and unless they want to be wiped out to the last man, woman, and child they're going to do as we say. What they're going to get tomorrow is an object lesson in humility, a taste of what's in store for them if they persist in their lawless ways. Now go get 'em. And good hunting."

Benoit turned to Warren. "By God," he said, in disgust, "I've never heard a general officer talk like that to his men. He's advocating murder, plain and simple."

"I think you've been isolated too long, Jean," Warren said gently. "He's echoing the sentiments of the Secretary of War and the Congress. Maybe he's using a little stronger language, but the underlying message is the same: Teach the Indians a lesson; show them we mean business."

Benoit shook his head slowly. "God help us," he said.

The Brulé Camp
Along Blue Water Creek

It was near midnight by the time Red Horse and White Crane dragged themselves exhausted into Roaring Thunder's camp. After asking for directions, they presented themselves at Red Leaf's tipi, asking if they might spread their robes by his fire. Red Horse's face lit up when he saw Porcupine, who smiled brightly in greeting.

"Remember, you're married," White Crane whispered, nudging him in the ribs. "When you have many horses you can take a second wife but now your duty is to Summer Rain."

"Thanks for reminding me," Red Horse whispered back angrily. "I don't need you to be my conscience."

"Why are you here?" Red Leaf asked, filling a pipe. "I thought you were living in the camp far to the south."

"We are," Red Horse replied, "but I am on a mission. I'm searching for Blizzard. I plan to kill him in revenge for the murder of my brother. My friend, White Crane, is here to help me."

"But he's here!" Porcupine blurted, quickly covering her mouth.

Red Horse turned to her, shocked. "Here!" he exclaimed. "Blizzard is *here*? I thought he was in the north."

"No," Red Leaf interrupted. "He showed up two days ago. He didn't stay in this camp. There is still much resentment toward him for what he did to Badger and Giant Crane. Roaring Thunder ordered him to leave."

"Then where did he go?" Red Horse asked anxiously. "It is imperative that I find him."

"Not far," Red Leaf said, smiling grimly. "I heard that he is staying with the Miniconjou, whose tipisare pitched just to the north."

"Then that is where I must go," said Red Horse, making to rise.

"Sit, young warrior," Red Leaf said authoritatively. "You can't accomplish anything at this time of night. Eat with us. Smoke a pipe. Then tomorrow at first light you can go to the Miniconjou camp."

"What you say makes sense," Red Horse replied, resuming his cross-legged position in front of the fire. "I wanted to talk to Roaring Thunder, too, but perhaps you can give him a message."

"What is that?" Red Leaf asked, passing the pipe.

"Tell him that on our way here we skirted a White soldier's camp. They are stopped along the Platte, about six miles south of here. More soldiers than I have ever seen. Hundreds of them, armed with a large number of wagon-guns. The camp was quiet and the men we could see looked very solemn, like warriors on the eve of a battle. This is obviously the group sent to avenge the death of the soldiers last summer. Warn Roaring Thunder; impress upon him that this may be his last chance to make peace with the isan hanska."

"I will tell him, but I doubt if it will do any good."

"Why is that?" White Crane asked, speaking for the first time. "Is his head filled with rocks? Does he need a mountain to come crashing down on him before he recognizes the danger of an avalanche?"

"He is convinced that the Whites are not going to attack," Red Leaf said. "He says we are all camped peacefully here doing nothing but hunting buffalo. We are not attacking any emigrant trains or raiding trading posts. He feels the soldiers will realize this and leave us alone."

"I think he is wrong," Red Horse said earnestly. "I think the soldiers are at this moment planning an attack. Otherwise why would they be camped on the Platte when Fort Laramie is only a few hours away? It would make me happy if you and Porcupine would leave the camp when I do in the morning. Go west, then swing to the south and join our group along the Laramie River. You must hurry because I fear for the worst."

"I will think about it," Red Leaf said, knocking the pipe ashes into the fire. "Maybe you have let your imagination run away with you."

"I would consider it a personal favor if you would do as I ask," Red Horse pleaded. "Please take Porcupine and flee while you can."

Red Leaf stared at him, exasperated. "I told you I will think about it," he said firmly, his tone indicating the discussion was over. "Would you like something to eat before you sleep?"

~ *15* ~

Despite his exhaustion, Red Horse had been unable to sleep. Excited by the prospect of confronting Blizzard and troubled by the unexpected and unexplained appearance of the White troops, Red Horse had tossed restlessly during the short night, reviewing the events of the previous day and trying to divine the future. The more he thought about it, the more convinced he became that an attack on the camp was imminent; there could be no other explanation for the sudden appearance of such a large body of soldiers. If their purpose had been to intimidate, they would have made their presence known earlier so Roaring Thunder and his people could be properly awed by their show of force. Instead they had crept quietly into place, hovering threateningly just outside the camp's perimeter. In his opinion, it was not a good omen.

It was barely light enough to see the trail when he and White Crane rolled up their robes and unhobbled their horses. Standing under a large cottonwood in the weak

light of a fingernail moon, his breath coming as white puffs
in the cold night air, Red Horse made one last attempt to
persuade Red Leaf and Porcupine to listen to reason.

"Roaring Thunder is not exercising good judgment,"
Red Horse maintained. "For some reason he refuses to
recognize the danger all of you are in. I urge you to
leave. Don't even pack your tipi. All my instincts tell me
an attack will come at dawn."

Red Leaf shook his head. "I have faith in Roaring
Thunder," he said stubbornly. "He is a skilled negotia-
tor; he can convince the soldiers that we are a peaceful
group. They will not attack."

"Then at least let Porcupine leave," he begged.
"Porcupine," he said, turning to the girl, "will you come
with us?"

"No," she said, shaking her head. "My place is with
my father. If he wants me to stay, I will stay."

"Come on," White Crane said impatiently to Red
Horse. "You have a better chance of enticing the sun not
to rise. If you want to catch Blizzard before he slips
away, we need to go."

Reluctantly, Red Horse hopped aboard his pony. "Be
very watchful," he told Red Leaf. "If there is any indication that fighting is about to begin, run into the hills and
hide. Don't try to outrun the soldiers because you'll
never make it."

"Red Horse, we *have* to go," White Crane urged,
pulling at his friend's arm. "We must get to the
Miniconjou camp before sunrise."

"Remember," Red Horse said in parting, "don't try to
be brave. Find a good place to hide and stay there."

The sun popped over the horizon, bathing the top of the
bluff in bright, flat light. Down in the valley, along the
creek bank, it was still almost as black as night, but

Benoit could see the Brulé were already beginning to stir. Peeping through the branches of a juniper tree, he could see vague shapes beginning to emerge from the tipis and wander off into the bushes.

"Wouldn't it be a be a rude awakening to get kilt while you was taking your morning crap?" a teenage enlisted man cracked to his friend, who giggled in response. "Quiet!" Cooke hissed, restraining himself from running down the incline and knocking the two boys' heads together.

Gradually, as the light grew stronger, the camp came into clearer view. Women walked down to the creek and filled containers which they carried back to their tipis. Here and there a warrior came out, stretched and walked over to his horses to make sure the hobbles had not slipped during the night.

As Benoit watched, a woman with two children started climbing the path leading up the hill below him, apparently heading toward the Miniconjou and Oglala tipis which were farther up stream. One of the children, chasing a grasshopper, ran into the scrub and almost tripped over one of Cooke's dragoons, who had wormed himself down the incline to have a better shot. The woman let out a scream, grabbed the children, and ran back down the hill, yelling loudly. Within minutes, the camp was in a frenzy.

"Goddamnit," Cooke muttered, "there goes the surprise."

"Should we open fire, colonel?" a corporal called from Cooke's left.

"No!" Cooke said harshly. "Don't give away your positions. Stick to the plan. Wait for the infantry to fire first."

Benoit looked to the south, where the ground troops were supposed to be, and was surprised to see General Harney gallop to the top of a small hill, placing himself in plain view of the Indian camp.

"He's going to get his ass blowed away," one of the men blurted.

Benoit swung his attention to the camp, expecting to see the warriors leveling their rifles at Harney. Instead, he saw one tall warrior walking through the throng yelling at the top of his voice, apparently giving orders. The man was carrying something at his side but it didn't look like a weapon. In one swift motion, he lifted it over his head and made a quick movement with his hands.

"It's an umbrella!" Benoit squealed. "A fucking umbrella."

Cooke laughed. "He didn't have a white flag, so he used the only non-weapon he could find. That must be the village chief."

As they watched, fascinated, the chief sprang on a pony and trotted up the hill toward Harney. Three other Indians fell into his wake.

On the hill, Harney waited patiently for the Indian entourage to arrive, turning every now and then to make a comment or issue an order to one of his aides.

"You think he's going to accept a surrender?" Benoit asked Cooke nervously.

"Not a chance in hell. After that speech last night Harney is going to try to kill every last one of these Indians and a chief hiding under an umbrella isn't going to stand in his way."

"My name is Roaring Thunder," the Indian said through an interpreter. "Perhaps you have heard of me?"

"And my name is General Harney," the soldier replied. "Perhaps you have heard of *me*? Among the Sauks, I am known as Mad Bear."

The Indians looked at each other in incomprehension. "What are the Sauks?" one of them asked.

Roaring Thunder shook his head. "Another crazy isan hanska name."

"I have not heard of you personally," Roaring Thunder said, turning to Harney. "But I imagine you are the chief who is here to avenge the soldiers killed in my camp last summer."

"That is correct," Harney said. "I am here to see that you are taught a lesson for your blatant disregard of the terms of the Treaty of Fort Laramie."

"It was not a fight we started," Roaring Thunder insisted. "The soldiers came into our camp carrying rifles and dragging two wagon-guns. They were the ones who started the shooting."

"That's what *you* say," Harney replied. "But today there are more than two dozen soldiers buried under the prairie not far from here who might take a different point of view."

"We aren't prepared to fight you," said Roaring Thunder. "As you can see," he said, turning slightly and sweeping his arm to encompass the camp below, "we have been peacefully hunting buffalo, not making war. See the racks of meat hanging up to dry? Why do you come here speaking of vengeance?"

"I come because you knew that would happen if you broke the terms of the treaty. You violated the pact and killed many soldiers. Therefore, today many Indians must die."

Roaring Thunder said nothing for several seconds. "What can I do to make you understand that we are peaceable? That we do not seek war?"

"Give up the men who killed the soldiers," Harney said sharply.

"You know I can't do that," Roaring Thunder said. "They are not in my camp. And even if they were, I could not force them to surrender."

"Give me the men who attacked the mail wagon last

autumn and killed the three men, then stole the box containing the gold."

"I cannot," Roaring Thunder said. "They are not here. I admit I have some men in the camp who took part in some of the raids against the trading post, but they are not subject to my command. I, myself, have done everything I could to keep the peace. If that were not so, we would be fighting now."

"You do not fight because you have the heart of a woman," Harney replied, leveling the supreme insult against an Indian warrior. "If you are truly warriors you will quit sniveling and come out and fight."

"There are many women and children in the camp," Roaring Thunder said, controlling his anger. "At least give me time to move them to safety."

"No," Harney said frostily. "That is just a ruse you savages use. The time for talk is over. You were warned that this day was coming and now it has arrived. The time for fighting is at hand, but I will give you time to return to your camp."

"They're sure taking a long time whatever they're talking about," Benoit said. "The chief has been up there for more than forty minutes," he added, looking at his pocket watch.

As he spoke, they could see the chief ride closer to Harney and stick out his hand.

"By God, Harney's refusing to take it," Cooke exclaimed. "I *knew* he wasn't going to even consider a surrender."

When it was obvious that Harney was not going to accept his proffered hand, the Indian threw his shoulders back and turned his horse, galloping back down the hillside much faster than he came up.

"By Jesus, they're in for it now," Warren muttered.

"I can hardly believe this is happening," Benoit mumbled.

"Hold your fire!" Cooke yelled to his men. "Don't fire until I give the order!"

For several minutes, a terrible silence hung over the valley. The only sound was the noise made by Roaring Thunder and his aides as they scrambled down the hill. But as soon as they splashed across the stream, the infantry let loose a fusillade that sounded to Benoit like a thunderclap from hell. "Jesus Christ!" he screamed. "The camp is full of women and children."

As he watched, a bullet from one of the new Sharps caught a boy of about six squarely between the shoulder blades and threw him five feet forward. "Holy Mother of God," Benoit yelped as he watched the boy slide forward on his stomach and come to a stop against a sage bush. A woman, apparently his mother, ran toward him but before she reached the unmoving boy, she herself was cut down in a hail of bullets.

"This isn't fighting," Benoit screamed at Cooke, tears streaming down his face. "This is slaughter."

"Get hold of yourself, lieutenant," Cooke told him coldly, slapping him across the face with a gloved hand.

Turning toward the camp he barked his order: "Fire at will, men! Targets of opportunity!"

Benoit sagged to the ground, not trusting his legs to keep him erect. Around him, rifles began to pop and the troops yelled to one another in exhilaration.

Benoit stared at the camp, focusing on a woman he guessed to be in her mid-twenties who was crawling along the streambed, dragging a wounded leg behind her. She almost reached the safety of a cottonwood tree when a bullet hit her in the back of the head, splitting it open and sending a cloud of red mist flying three feet in the air.

"Jesus God," Benoit muttered, leaning forward and expelling his breakfast of hardtack. Unable to control himself, he grabbed his stomach as his body was wrenched with a series of dry heaves.

"Here they come, sir," one of Cooke's sergeants yelled, pointing to a large group of Indians who had abandoned their attempts to combat the infantry's overwhelming firepower. They had mounted their horses and were racing upstream, moving parallel to Cook's troops, trying desperately to outdistance the powerful new rifles.

Cooke cupped his hands to his mouth. "Mount up, men!" he yelled. "Don't let them get away."

Benoit remained as if frozen to the spot as all around him Cooke's men swung aboard their horses and charged off after the Indians, firing as they went.

"Come on," Warren shouted, vaulting into his saddle.

"No," Benoit answered firmly. "I'm going to see what I can do for the wounded."

Red Horse and White Crane were halfway to the Miniconjou camp when they heard the gunfire.

"I *knew* it!" Red Horse said, reigning his pony to a halt. "The soldiers are attacking. I must go back and help."

"Wait!" White Crane said urgently, grabbing Red Horse's shoulder. "By the time you get back, it will be too late for you to offer any assistance."

"But what about Porcupine?" Red Horse said plaintively. "I can't just abandon her and her father."

"There's nothing you can do," White Crane said firmly. "You warned them to leave. Just hope they took your words seriously."

"They did not. I *know* they ignored me. I could see it written on Red Leaf's face."

"Then there's nothing you can do. We must follow our original plan; let's go find Blizzard."

"But he would have heard the firing, too. By now Blizzard probably is on his way to the mountains."

White Crane laughed grimly. "Not Blizzard! He won't pass up a fight. We must be watchful because I'll wager that right now he's heading our way, toward Roaring Thunder's camp."

"What a decision," Red Horse said ruefully. "Try to rescue Porcupine or search for Blizzard."

"Let's get off the trial," White Crane suggested. "We would make good targets."

Waiting impatiently in a grove of hardwoods, White Crane and Red Horse watched as a dozen members of Roaring Thunder's band galloped by, three warriors and the rest of them women with small children. They heard one of them call to the others: "There's some caves up ahead. We can take refuge there."

They had barely passed when a large group of soldiers came thundering behind them, firing their rifles as they rode. The dragoons were too intent on the chase to notice the two Indians watching from behind the trees.

"Blizzard won't be coming down the trail now," Red Horse said resolutely, convinced that nothing would be gained by riding back to the Brulé camp. "Let's go see if we can find him."

"Look at that!" Captain Howe yelled to his sergeant. "Those sons of bitches must be intent on committing suicide."

The NCO looked up to see where his officer was pointing. To their right, about three hundred yards away, two Brulé were racing their horses parallel to the troops, dashing to the south in an apparent attempt to get behind the soldiers and escape to Fire-in-the-Hill's encampment on the Laramie River. But to get away they would have to run a gauntlet of fire laid down by Howe's men, more than three dozen riflemen all trying to bring down the fleeing warriors.

"We must be crazy," Otter yelled over the thunder of his horse's hooves. "We should have stayed and fought."

"No," Jagged Blade yelled over his shoulder. "This way maybe we can escape to come back and fight the Whites another day."

They swooped down a small depression where a tiny stream cut through on its way to the larger creek, then clambered up the far bank. Just as they reached the top of the shallow rise, an Army bullet caught the Brulé named Otter high on his cheek, taking away most of his head.

"Hooray!" one of the troopers yelled happily, reloading his rifle. "I got me one of the treacherous redskins."

Jagged Blade's hair flew behind him in a long stream as he urged his pony forward, his eyes intent on the path in front of him. He tightened his arms around his horse's neck and buried his face in its mane, trying to become one with the animal and make himself a smaller target. He held his breath as his horse stumbled on a loose stone and staggered, threatening to fall. Then the animal found its footing and plunged ahead, seemingly as anxious to escape as its rider.

"If he gets over that crest, he's gone," Howe yelled in encouragement. "Get the bastard! That's an order!"

In response, a dozen rifles fired almost in unison, the bullets kicking up clods of dirt both behind and in front of Jagged Blade. But none hit the fleeing Indian. With a loud whoop, he disappeared over the hill, leaving the soldiers nothing to shoot at but his dust trail.

"I don't believe it!" Howe howled in frustration, uprooting a sage with a mighty kick. "That fucker got away."

* * *

"It looks as if the soldiers beat us here after all," Red Horse growled in disgust as they rode into the Miniconjou camp. All around them, tipis were smoldering after having been set afire by Cooke's dragoons. Bodies of Indians — men, women, and children — were scattered about the site, their contorted shapes forming the centerpiece for the otherworldly scene.

The silence was unnatural. Despite the evidence of recent frenzied activity, the only sound was the popping noise of the fire eating through the lodge poles.

"Every one of them is dead," White Crane said, moving swiftly from body to body. "The soldiers didn't leave a single one alive. Look at this!" he said suddenly, pausing over the cadaver of a large man. "This looks like Blizzard."

"Let me see," Red Horse said excitedly, hurrying as quickly as he could to his friend's side.

The dead man's face was in the dirt, his legs drawn up beneath him in obvious pain. "Let's see," Red Horse said, turning the body on its back. Pointed toward the sky was a faceless warrior, his face beaten to a red pulp by a soldier's rifle butt.

"Just our luck," he cursed. "How can we tell for sure?"

"Look for scars," White Crane urged. "He had a large one across his chest."

Red Horse looked down, but again he cursed in frustration. "His chest has been hacked to shreds, too. The soldiers must have been trying hard to make him suffer."

"His leg!" White Crane said. "Remember he was wounded in the attack on the wagon train."

Red Horse straightened out both of the dead Indian's legs and quickly examined the thighs. "Look!" he exclaimed. "Here on his right thigh. That's the scar from a bullet. I should know."

On the inside of the thigh, halfway between the hip and the knee, was a jagged round scar the size of a small boy's fist. "That's where he was shot," he said. "I remember it clearly."

"We need more evidence than that," said White Crane. "Let's look around and see what we can find."

"Here!" he called elatedly several minutes later. "Isn't this Blizzard's war club?"

Red Horse hurried over and stood staring at the weapon, a powerful-looking cudgel about two and a half feet long, painted red and black.

"Those are Blizzard's medicine colors," White Crane confirmed.

"It's his club," Red Horse nodded. "I remember it from the raid on the Crow camp." The head of the weapon was a carved ball about five inches in diameter, out of which protruded a five-inch-long metal spike. "Look," he said, turning it over, "here's the weasel that Blizzard carved into its back. It's his personal totem."

"It *must* be him," White Crane said earnestly. "The dead man has the right scar in the right place and Blizzard's war club is nearby. He wouldn't go off and leave his favorite weapon."

"Your reasoning is sound," Red Horse agreed. "I just wish we knew for certain."

"This is as certain as it will ever be," White Crane argued. "I think you can safely say your brother has been avenged. At least the soldiers didn't take his scalp," he added, reaching for his knife. "They conveniently left it for us."

"Hurry," Red Horse said agitatedly. "Now we need to go see if we can find out what happened to Red Leaf and Porcupine."

*   *   *

Benoit could hear the firing in the hills as the dragoons pursued the fleeing Brulé into the limestone bluffs that stretched along the creek. Fighting to control his aching stomach from rebelling further, he moved sadly among the Brulé tipis, searching for wounded. When he found a woman incapacitated by a bullet that passed through both her legs, Benoit scooped her up and carried her to the bank of the stream. Laying her gently on a clear patch of ground, he stared into her dark eyes.

"I'm not going to hurt you," he said, knowing she could not understand. "I'm going to leave you here for a while to see if I can find any others that are not fatally hurt."

Grabbing the remnant of a destroyed tipi, Benoit deftly affixed it to two of the lodge poles, making a crude lean-to so the wounded woman would be shaded from the sun.

Deciding that she was as comfortable as he could make her, he hurried back into the center of the camp.

Slowly, he wended his way from tipi to tipi, looking for more wounded. All those he found, though, were dead. The living had either tried to escape with the others or been killed by the soldiers on their quick passage through the camp. He was about ready to give up when he heard a noise behind a tipi a dozen yards to his right.

Hurrying to the spot, he was surprised to find only the body of a middle-aged man, who lay sprawled on his back with three gaping bullet wounds in his chest. He was about to return to the wounded woman when he heard what sounded like gasps coming from the underbrush behind the tipi. Moving cautiously forward, he saw a flash of blue. Parting the branches, he found himself staring at the back of a soldier so busily engaged in his activity that he had not heard Benoit approach.

Benoit's expression changed from puzzlement to fury. Reaching for his pistol, he drew it from its holster and leveled it at the trooper. "All right, corporal!" he said loudly, his voice dripping with outrage. "I have my sidearm pointed directly at the back of your head. I want you to stop what you're doing immediately and come out in the open."

Slowly the soldier turned around, his pasty white face screwed up in surprise.

"Take it easy, lieutenant," he whined, studying Benoit. "You can see I ain't armed."

"Pull up your trousers and get out here, corporal. Now!"

"I'm doing it, I'm doing it," he said hastily, fumbling with his buttons.

"What's your name, corporal? And what company are you with?"

"Connors, sir. H Company. Sixth Infantry. But," he added, looking shrewdly at Benoit, "I weren't doing nothing wrong. I was just following orders."

"There are never any orders to rape, corporal," Benoit said.

"It ain't exactly rape, sir. She's dead."

Benoit felt his stomach heave. "Corporal, I ought to kill you right here. Save the court martial board the trouble."

"I was jest going to get me a scalp, lieutenant. You know," he said with a leer, "one of them *special* female scalps. Then I reckon I jest got carried away."

Benoit heard a noise behind him, all the more audible because of the quiet that had descended over the camp. As he turned his head to see what had caught his attention, Connors made his move. On the back of his belt was a small knife he used for whittling. Drawing the knife, he leaped at Benoit, plunging the short blade into Benoit's left chest just below the nipple.

Benoit yelped in pain, loosening his hold on the pistol.

"Got you now, you sumbitch," Connors grinned easily, looming over Benoit who had fallen on his back, grasping at the knife handle.

"They'll think the injuns kilt you," Connors said, picking up Benoit's pistol and pointing it between his eyes. "I'll swear I seen 'em do it."

His finger was tightening on the trigger when his eyes suddenly flew open wide in shock. Dropping the weapon, he staggered backward, gurgling. Protruding from his chest and exiting out his back were arrows fired by Red Horse and White Crane.

"I wish we hadn't been so hasty," White Crane said, rushing to the fallen corporal. "I was hoping we could keep him alive long enough to make sure he died slowly and painfully." As Connors stared, terror-stricken but unable to move, White Crane drew his own knife and leaned forward, slashing Connors's throat in one quick, vicious swipe delivered so forcefully it all but decapitated him.

"The other soldier's still alive," Red Horse said, examining Benoit, who lay on his back, gasping for breath. "The knife was small so the wound isn't too deep."

"Good," White Crane said, wiping his bloody blade on Connors's shirt. "We may be able to extract some revenge yet."

"No," Red Horse replied. "Come and look. It is the soldier who saved us in the fight with the Crow."

"But that's Red Leaf over there," White Crane argued. "And I know without looking that's Porcupine in the bushes."

"I know you're right," Red Horse said. "But killing this soldier isn't going to bring them back. We owe him our lives. Besides, he was trying to capture that mongrel when we arrived. He took no part in the slaughter."

"Well," White Crane said, squatting and staring into Benoit's eyes. "Just what do you suggest we do?"

Fort Laramie

When the summons arrived, Dobbs was leaning over a soldier who had braced himself in the physician's sturdiest chair, his pliers buried in the private's open mouth.

"Come in!" he yelled without looking up. "Hold on, private," he said soothingly to the trooper. "It won't be but another second, then your toothache will be gone."

"Mmuuupppphhh," the soldier mumbled, gripping the legs of his trousers and crushing them into a ball.

"Here it is . . . here it is . . . " Dobbs crooned. "Come to poppa . . . come to poppa." Bunching his shoulders, he heaved as hard as he could. With a crack that could be heard across the room, the soldier's molar popped from his mouth.

"Bite on this," Dobbs commanded, handing the trooper a piece of linen he had folded into a tight square. "Keep rinsing your mouth with cold water until the bleeding stops and don't try to chew any jerky on that side of your mouth for a few days. Other than that, I think you'll live," he added, handing him the bloody tooth. "Here's a souvenir. Put it on your watch chain. It might bring you good luck."

"The colonel wants to see you," said the soldier who had been knocking at the door.

"Me?" Dobbs asked in surprise. "What's it about?"

"He didn't say, sir. Just told me to get you and Miss Inge. She's already in his office."

* * *

"At ease, Dobbs," Kemp said, returning the physician's salute. "You want to have a seat?"

Dobbs turned to look at Inge, who was sitting staring straight ahead, her face as colorless as a streambed boulder.

"Thank you, sir. I'll stand. I take it the news isn't good."

Kemp did not answer but handed Dobbs a thin sheaf of papers that had been sitting in the center of his otherwise clean desk.

"What's this?" Dobbs asked, accepting the document.

"A preliminary report from General Harney. It arrived by messenger thirty minutes ago. He wants me to forward it on to Washington since its going to be a few days before he gets here. He's building a small fortification on the Platte southeast of here," he explained, his voice heavy with sarcasm. "Going to call it Fort Grattan."

Dobbs frowned, scanning the papers. In five succinct paragraphs, Harney told of the fight with the Teton Sioux at their camp on the creek called Blue Water.

> The hostiles sought an escape by the only avenue open to them. But, although they availed themselves of this outlet for escape, they did not do so without serious molestation, for the infantry not only took them in flank with their long-range rifles, but the dragoons made a most spirited charge, which was supported by the whole body of the infantry, all of them being eager from the first for a fray with the butchers of their comrades of Lieutenant Grattan's party.

Dobbs felt his anger rising. "Sounds like a massacre to me," he said.

"Read on," Kemp said noncommittally.

Dobbs turned back to the document.

*The results of this affair were eighty-six killed, five
wounded, about seventy women and children captured,
fifty mules and ponies taken, besides an indefinite number wounded and disabled."*

"Sweet Jesus," Dobbs said. "What about our casualties?"

"The next paragraph," said Kemp.

Dobbs continued reading.

*The casualties of the command amount to four killed,
four severely wounded, three slightly wounded, and one
missing, supposed to be killed or captured by the
enemy."*

"Benoit!" Dobbs exclaimed, recognition dawning.
"He's one of the dead!"

Kemp shook his head. "He's the one listed as missing."

"God," said Dobbs, reaching for a chair. "Given the
way Indians usually treat adult captives, that doesn't
sound too optimistic."

"It isn't," Kemp said grimly. "But it's too early to say
anything for certain. I've already sent Ashby and young
Schmidt down to Harney's camp to see if they can find
any trail that might lead them to Benoit. I'll send
Legendre out, too, as soon as he gets back."

"And me?" Dobbs asked.

"I want you to go to Harney's camp, too. Help with the
wounded. Talk to everyone you can. See if you can find
out anything that might help us find out what happened
to Benoit. What really bothers me," he said, glancing
uneasily at Inge, "is that he's missing. If they killed him, I
would assume they would have just left his body there."

"Sir," Dobbs said hesitantly, "Maybe we shouldn't
discuss this in front of Miss Schmidt."

"It's all right," Inge said, throwing back her head.

"I've considered the possibility that they may have taken him off so they could torture him to death."

"We don't know that, Miss Schmidt," Kemp said.

"That's right, Inge. We don't know that."

"Then why else haven't you found his body?" Inge said, her eyes flashing.

Kemp shrugged. "The messenger, while he didn't want to tell tales out of his commander's hearing, said that Benoit didn't remain with his unit once the fighting started. He told another lieutenant, a man named Warren, that he was sickened by the slaughter and he was going to help the wounded. That was the last anyone saw of him."

"That sounds like Jean," Inge said.

"He may have wandered off and been detained by his fervor to help the disabled," Dobbs said weakly.

"Or he may have tried to take some of the wounded back to the Brulé at their camp south of here," Kemp added. "The point is, we just don't know. Although I don't want you to get your hopes up too high, I think it's a good sign that we haven't found his body."

"Good for who?" Inge asked. "Maybe he was so disturbed by what he saw that he planned to file a formal complaint against General Harney."

Kemp bobbed his head. "That's a possibility, too."

"Give me fifteen minutes to pack a kit," Dobbs said, "then I'll be on my way."

"I'm going with you," Inge said, springing to her feet.

"I don't know if that will do any good," Kemp said.

"If nothing else," Inge said, "I can help with the wounded. God knows, Jace is going to need all the help he can get."

"I don't understand it," Dobbs said. "It's been almost a week and we still have no idea what happened to Jean."

"Well, we know he's not dead on the battlefield," Inge said. "Troopers have been over every foot of the area."

"Ashby found more than a dozen trails heading out from the valley toward the Brulé camp that was on the Laramie."

"'Was' is the important word there," Inge said bitterly. "They packed up and headed for the mountains. Not that I blame them after what that son of a bitch Harney did."

"I agree with you to a certain extent," said Dobbs. "It was a slaughter. On the other hand, he was doing exactly what Washington wanted him to do. He was ordered to take revenge, and by God he did that. And then some."

"When is he leaving?" Inge asked. "I don't feel comfortable as long as he's near Fort Laramie."

"Not long. Kemp says he has orders to take his troops and go to Fort Pierre, daring the Sioux to attack him on the way. I guess the blood lust still isn't satiated."

"The sooner he leaves, the better I'll like it. What the hell has happened to Legendre? He should have returned by now."

"Who knows?" Dobbs shrugged. "He's not exactly the type to follow a timetable. But as soon as he gets back, Kemp is sending him right back out again. He's going to try to find the Brulé and see if he can learn what happened to Jean."

"I wish I could go with him," Inge said.

Dobbs looked at her sharply. "Don't even *think* that. You know Kemp would never go for it."

Inge smiled. "You mean you still haven't learned how persuasive I can be?"

"Inge . . ." Dobbs began. "What the hell is that?"

Inge shrugged. "You know how tone deaf I am. All those bugle calls sound alike."

"That's 'assembly,' but we've already had assembly and the next one won't be until eight o'clock. Let's go see."

Hurrying outside, the two of them found Kemp already there, seated on his horse and gazing into the distance, beyond the parade ground. As the troops scurried into formation, Dobbs saw several figures approaching slowly from the southeast.

"Who's that, colonel?" Dobbs asked, squinting.

"It's the Brulé, Roaring Thunder," Kemp replied. "He sent word he wants to surrender."

As the figure got closer, Dobbs could see a tall, middle-aged Indian riding in the lead, dressed in his finest regalia. Following a dozen paces behind him were two women, also dressed in their best. As they got closer, Dobbs could hear them chanting.

"Are they singing?" the physician asked in surprise.

"That's right," Kemp replied. "That's his death song. The poor bastard thinks he's going to be executed on the spot because of the fight with Harney."

"I'll be damned," Dobbs mumbled, his eyes wide. "And I thought I'd seen everything."

Kemp turned to him and smiled. "Just goes to show you, lieutenant. Never let anything the Indians do surprise you. And I mean absolutely nothing. They've got to be the most unpredictable people God ever created."

16

Pahukstatu Village
May, 1855

"It is time," Red Calf said.

"How do you know?" Knifewielder asked, sitting once more around the priest's fire. "How can you be so certain?"

"Morning Star has given me the signal. Today when He appeared in the east He was ringed in red. That means He is ready to accept the girl."

Knifewielder was silent, not sure whether to rejoice or be sad. In the seven months since Beaver Woman was abducted from her Cheyenne tipi he had seen her change from a sullen, frightened girl into a self-assured young woman on the edge of maturity. She had come to accept he and Bright Calico, in fact the entire lodge, including Angry Buffalo and his two wives, two mothers-in-law, and two young children, as her foster family. Even Bright Calico, who was normally very hard to please, had taken pride in Beaver Woman's metamorphosis.

"It is difficult," Red Calf admitted.

"Is that a statement or a question?" Knifewielder asked, agitated by the thought of Beaver Woman's fate.

"It is a statement," Red Calf replied. "I have seen the same reaction in other visionaries. Once they become attached to the girl captives, it is hard for them to accept the fact that they must die."

"Then why do we continue the ceremony?"

"Because Morning Star demands it," Red Calf said. "You yourself saw him; you know his existence is not a figment of an old man's imagination."

"That is true," Knifewielder conceded. "But a vision in the autumn is quite different from reality in the spring."

"Take consolation in this thought: If Beaver Woman has been pleasing to you, if she has proved herself to be a delightful companion and a person of pure heart, then she will be even more pleasing to Morning Star, who can appreciate her good qualities in ways you are unable to imagine."

"What you say is true, but that doesn't make it any easier."

Red Calf sighed. "You are learning the true meaning of the word sacrifice. You are having to give up something you love because in the end it will benefit all your people."

"Now I know how her parents must have felt."

"Exactly my point!" said Red Calf. "They loved her, too, but they adjusted to her loss. Now you and Bright Calico must learn to do the same. There is one caution, however. From now on the girl must not be left alone. Although we have been careful to hide from her role in the ceremony, in the next few days it will become apparent that she is the central character in a drama of vast proportions. The temptation for her to flee might be great. Either you or Old Dog must be constantly at her side."

*   *   *

Knifewielder's shoulders sagged and he had to look down so Red Calf would not see the tears building in his eyes. "What do I have to do?" he asked dejectedly.

The ceremony began with a series of intricate rituals, most of which only served to remind Knifewielder of his impending loss. Although the opening rites involved primarily the village spiritualists — Red Calf, the Morning Star priest; White Elk, the Keeper of the Evening Star bundle, and Old Dog, the Keeper of the Wolf Bundle — the number of participants gradually increased. Eventually, the entire village would be involved.

Essentially, Knifewielder explained to Bright Calico, the ceremony was designed to replicate the obstacles Morning Star faced in His struggle to mate with Evening Star. There was much singing, dancing, and feasting with heavy emphasis on symbolism.

Finally, on the fourth day, events began working toward a climax with a rite whose main theme was the destruction of the figures that represented Morning Star's struggle to fight his way to Evening Star.

Red Calf, dressed resplendently in leggings decorated with scalps that symbolized not only war and death but the renewal of life, played the major role in the service, representing Morning Star. First he sang and danced around the north side of the ceremonial lodge, then the south side, eventually working his way back to the altar. When he was finished, Beaver Woman was taken from the lodge and costumed for the first time as the Morning Star sacrifice.

"I know what is happening to me," she told Bright Calico when she produced the pots of red and black paint.

"And what is that?" Bright Calico said brightly, trying to be cheerful.

"I am going to be sacrificed to Morning Star. I heard talk of this ceremony when I lived with my father, Short Hair, and my mother, Red Berry Woman, but I never suspected it would be happening to me."

"And what did you hear?" asked Bright Calico, still trying to remain nonchalant.

"I heard," Beaver Woman said, her voice trembling slightly, "that the girl chosen as the sacrifice was put on an altar and killed in order to make a Pawnee deity happy."

"And you think that is what is going to happen to you?"

"I am sure of it," Beaver Woman said, biting her lip.

Bright Calico put down the paintbrush and grabbed Beaver Woman by both shoulders. "Are you afraid?"

Beaver Woman nodded. "Of course I'm afraid. I don't want to die. But I know that is the way things are and I am fortunate to be chosen to be an important figure. Many times I heard my father, Short Hair, and Knifewielder, too, say how much better it was to die in battle as a young man than to grow old and infirm. But when they go into battle they do not know they will die. As you apply this paint and make ready the special costume, I *know* I am to be killed. Yet it doesn't frighten me as much as I imagined it would."

Bright Calico was pondering how to reply when Red Calf stuck his head in the lodge door. "Are you ready yet?" he asked gruffly.

"Almost," Bright Calico replied, blinking back her tears. "Now," she said to Beaver Woman, "we have to paint you pretty so Morning Star will find you attractive."

Taking the pot of red paint, she covered the entire right side of Beaver Woman's body. "Red," she explained as she brushed on the mixture, "symbolizes day, the time of Morning Star. And black," she said as she painted the left side of Beaver Woman, "symbolizes night, the time of Evening Star."

When she finished the painting, Bright Calico handed Beaver Woman a ceremonial skirt and robe, both of which came from Red Calf's Morning Star Bundle. On Beaver Woman's head, Bright Calico placed a band of feathers arranged so they stood erect and ran precisely down the middle of her head, from front to back.

After the costuming was complete, they returned to the ceremonial lodge where they sang about Morning Star and his origin as a meteor. Finally, well after midnight, they paused and sat silent, waiting for the time to take Beaver Woman to the platform that had been constructed several days before.

Well before the time Red Calf had reckoned Morning Star would rise, they led Beaver Woman to the altar. By then, the entire village was awake since they all had been told earlier by a crier that the ceremony would climax at dawn.

As they walked solemnly from the ceremonial lodge to the platform, the major priests clad in their special garb sang four songs specific to the ceremony, songs honoring the bear, the mountain lion, the wildcat, and the wolf. Other animal-oriented songs were sung as Beaver Woman slowly mounted the platform and was tied to the scaffold, facing toward the east, toward Morning Star.

During the procession from the ceremonial lodge to the platform, four minor priests hid themselves in strategic locations surrounding the altar. When Morning Star's rise was imminent, one of the priests ran forward, barely brushing a torch he was carrying across Beaver Woman's arms and loins. As he disappeared back into the underbrush, another priest appeared. Timing his emergence precisely with the rising of Morning Star, he shot an arrow into Beaver Woman's heart, killing her instantly. A third priest then mounted the platform. Taking his ceremonial knife that had been chipped from flint, he made a small cut over Beaver Woman's heart, then smeared her blood on his face. The fourth priest danced by carrying a war club that he shook at the dead girl pretending to strike her.

At Red Calf's signal, White Elk, the Keeper of the Evening Star Bundle, approached with a portion of the meat from the special buffalo Knifewielder had killed the previous autumn and sprinkled it with Beaver Woman's blood. He then tossed the meat into the fire.

"This is the part I can't watch," Bright Calico whispered to Knifewielder, turning her back on the platform.

At Red Calf's signal every male in the village old enough to use a bow shot an arrow into Beaver Woman's body.

"The public ceremony is finished," Red Calf announced, urging the villagers to return to their lodges and prepare for the general feasting that would follow later in the day.

As soon as the crowd dispersed, the priests untied Beaver Woman's body and carried it onto the prairie well away from the village. Gently placing it face down on the ground they sang the song formally culminating the ceremony, a complicated chant listing the nine things that Beaver Woman's blood would nourish, beginning with the grass and ending with the eagle that would dine on her flesh. When the song was finished, they left her body unburied — as was often done with warriors killed in battle — and returned to the ceremonial lodge.

"I know you're sad," Angry Buffalo told Knifewielder as they dined on consecrated meat from the buffalo slain in the November hunt, "but you must put it behind you now."

"I feel very unfulfilled," Knifewielder said. "If my

daughter had died naturally there would be a period of mourning and I could find release for my grief. But with Beaver Woman's sacrifice, there is nothing I can do. I'm expected to be happy that she was killed."

"But this is much better than if she had died from disease or been killed by our enemies," Angry Buffalo insisted. "Both you and she were chosen for special roles in a ceremony that is vital to our people's existence. That should make you feel exultant, not sorrowful. While we sit here eating, she is celebrating with Morning Star, bringing him much happiness. He will show his appreciation by blessing us with good crops and plentiful game. Her death will enrich us all. Besides," he added, "I know what will help change your mood."

"Oh," Knifewielder replied, eyeing his friend. "And what is that?"

"I would like to lead a raid on the Cheyenne, to avenge the nine warriors killed in their attack. Will you participate?"

"Of course I will participate," Knifewielder smiled. "Perhaps I can extract special revenge against Short Hair and that she-devil, Red Berry Woman. But are you fit for war? How is your arm?"

"Much better," said Angry Buffalo, flexing his fingers in front of Knifewielder's face. "There is still some tingling in the fingers, but I can grip a war club and notch an arrow. I will be ready when it is time to go."

"I am glad . . ." Knifewielder was saying when Dark Eagle's son, Beaver, came running into the lodge.

"Hurry! Hurry!" he cried. "Warriors, you must get your weapons and run to the pasture."

"What is it?" his father asked. "Calm down and tell us what is happening."

"It's the Arapaho," the boy said excitedly. "They are trying to steal our horses."

* * *

"It's typical of those cowards," Angry Buffalo cursed as he and Knifewielder ran for their lodge seeking their bows and war clubs. "Trying to take advantage of us when our defenses are down."

"Hurry," Knifewielder urged, putting on a burst of speed. "I hear horses. They are driving them toward the village."

As they rounded Eagle Spirit's lodge and made for their own, thirty yards distant, the herd came thundering down the village path.

Beaver, Dark Eagle's son, had been running with Angry Buffalo and Knifewielder but was too small to keep up with the long-legged men. Seeing the horses, the two warriors jumped nimbly aside, but Beaver was caught in the open space. "Help me!" he cried in panic as he disappeared beneath the horses's pounding hooves.

"They're in the village," Angry Buffalo hollered to his wives as he dashed into his lodge.

"Hand me my bow," Knifewielder yelled to Bright Calico.

Taking the weapon, he ran back outside just as the herd, which was being driven by a half-dozen Arapaho warriors, was about to pass out of sight.

"Sons of dogs," he cried, notching an arrow. Hurriedly, he lifted his weapon without taking time to aim adequately. Instead of striking the invading warrior in the center of the back as intended, the arrow thunked into his shoulder.

With a yelp, Frozen Eye pitched off his pony and rolled over twice.

"Your scalp will decorate my lance," Knifewielder screamed, drawing his knife and running toward the fallen warrior.

He was so intent on his prize that he did not notice that the Arapaho named Cut Neck had turned to help his comrade.

Screaming his war cry, Knifewielder rushed toward Frozen Eye, who had pulled himself into a sitting position and was staring groggily around him.

Knifewielder's triumphant yell ended in a gurgle when Cut Neck's arrow slammed into his chest.

Angry Buffalo, who had discovered that his injured arm was not healed as thoroughly as he had thought, shifted his war club to his left hand and ran to assist Knifewielder. But before he could get there, Cut Neck had closed the distance.

Aiming directly at Angry Buffalo, he used the horse as a battering ram. Unable to change his direction, Angry Buffalo was caught in mid-stride and went tumbling under the force of the collision.

Cut Neck, rather than continuing his attack on Angry Buffalo, guided his horse to Frozen Eye, who had unsteadily gained his feet. Taking his comrade's offered arm, Frozen Eye swung onto the back of the pony.

As Angry Buffalo cursed wildly, the two of them disappeared after the stolen horses.

Staggering over to Knifewielder, Angry Buffalo saw that his friend was dead. Raising his left hand, he screamed a vow of vengeance into the darkening sky.

KEN ENGLADE is a bestselling author of fiction and nonfiction whose books include *Hoffa*, *To Hatred Turned*, and *Beyond Reason*, which was nominated for an Edgar Award in 1991. He lives in Corrales, New Mexico.

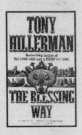

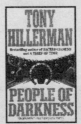

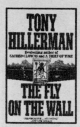

The bestselling author of
<u>Coyote Waits</u> and <u>Sacred Clowns</u>
takes you on a journey to
a distant place in the novel he has
wanted to write for decades....

In the chaotic Vietnam of 1975, American journalist Moon Mathias searches for the missing child of his deceased brother. But when he discovers that his brother was involved in dangerous work in league with the South Vietnamese army, Mathias must uncover a deeply hidden trail of evidence to find out the truth about his brother's death and his young niece's disappearance.

"Hillerman's novels inject fresh urgency to the age-old questions about good and evil that lie at the heart of all detective fiction."
—*Baltimore Sun*

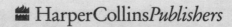 HarperCollins*Publishers*

Bestselling author Tony Hillerman's West comes alive in
Ken Englade's exciting new series about the tribes, the
settlers, and the soldiers who attempted to carve a life ou
of the golden West and made history along the way.

There was dissent among the leaders of the Brul
Sioux. The warrior Blizzard demanded violent actio
against an increasing white presence that threatened t
end forever his people's way of life. Badger, his riva
urged calm. But the peace between them could not las
and a violent confrontation set the rivals against eac
other in a fight to the death.

Stationed in Fort Laramie, Second Lieutenant Beno
was sickened at the government's heartless treatment c
the Indians, but he served his duty in a cruel attack o
the tribe—until he was critically wounded far from hi
command. Rescued from death by the Brulé Whit
Crane, Benoit was brought back to camp and nurse
back to life. As the attacks and counterattack
continued, both sides sensed that a showdown was nc
far off. But how it would start, and who would be le
alive were questions that nobody could answer.

00946

0 99455 00599 9

ISBN 0-06-100946-6

U.S. $5.
CAN. $7.